MOZART'S BLOOD

MOZART'S BLOOD

LOUISE MARLEY

KENSINGTON BOOKS
www.kensingtonbooks.com

KENSINGTON BOOKS are published by

Kensington Publishing Corp.
119 West 40th Street
New York, NY 10018

All Kensington titles, imprints, and distributed lines are available at special quantity discounts for bulk purchases for sales promotion, premiums, fund-raising, educational, or institutional use.

Special book excerpts or customized printings can also be created to fit specific needs. For details, write or phone the office of the Kensington Special Sales Manager: Kensington Publishing Corp., 119 West 40th Street, New York, NY 10018. Attn. Special Sales Department. Phone: 1-800-221-2647.

Kensington and the K logo Reg. U.S. Pat. & TM Off.

ISBN-13: 978-0-7582-4212-9
ISBN-10: 0-7582-4212-3

First Printing: July 2010
10 9 8 7 6 5 4 3 2 1

Printed in the United States of America

For Zack, *sempre*

ACKNOWLEDGMENTS

This novel took me on a wonderful journey that began during my days with Seattle Opera, went on through a tour of the Metropolitan Opera House, and culminated in a delightful afternoon spent exploring the historic La Scala Theater in Milan. I am deeply indebted to Stephanie Cowell, the author of *Marrying Mozart;* Nancy Crosgrove, R.N.; Dean Crosgrove, P.A.C.; Giovanna and Alessandro Forin, for Italian help; Francine Garino of La Scala; Zack Marley; Domenico Minotti, M.D.; my long-suffering and hardworking agent, Peter Rubie; Dick and Mary Tietjen of Seaview House in Port Townsend, for a place to escape and work, and to vent when it all got too weird; my first reader, Catherine Whitehead; the magnificent soprano and frequent colleague, Sally Wolf, for advice and answers; the docents of the Metropolitan Opera House; the Metropolitan Museum of Art Costume Exhibit; the Sisters of Mercy, for kindly answering my e-mail; and the incomparable Renée Fleming, both for her book and for her example. My sincere thanks to all.

1

Quel sangue . . . quella piaga . . .

The blood . . . that wound . . .

—Donna Anna, Act One, Scene One, *Don Giovanni*

The old woman hummed to herself as she crumbled bits of black paste into a little clay pot and added wine and water. "Good Roman wine," she said as she stirred it with a wooden spoon. "And honey," she added, smiling, showing blackened teeth. "To cover the taste."

She had told Ughetto and the other boys to call her Nonna. But she was nothing like Ughetto's *nonna*. Ughetto's *nonna* was plump and easy, with soft arms and warm fingers. This crone, this *vecchia*, was scrawny and dry and twisted, like a dead olive tree.

Ughetto knew what the black paste was. He had seen it often in his mother's tavern in Trapani. The sailors carried it in their pockets, wrapped in bits of Chinese silk or Indian cotton. Their eyes gleamed with anticipation as they unwrapped their little bundles, opening them carefully on the wooden tables. They shaved the paste into clay pipes with small, sharp knives, and when they smoked it, the tavern filled with the pungent scent of poppies.

Ughetto's mother always drove him out then, him and all six of his sisters. She shooed them down to the beach to search for mussels, or over to the docks to drum up trade for the tavern. They went running down the twisting streets, laughing, shouting, a horde of ragged girls with Ughetto, the baby, the only boy, struggling to keep up.

He wished his real *nonna* were here now, or his *mamma*. He wished his sisters were here, or he with them, though they ordered him about like a small slave. Home had been noisy and warm. Home had felt safe, most of the time. He didn't like being alone, didn't like this place, this Nonna, or Luigi, her slack-lipped son.

They had taken him in Trapani. Mamma had sent him to the docks, telling him to wait beside the pile of empty crab pots for a woman with a package. This Nonna had appeared, with her big-shouldered, big-bellied son. Nonna asked Ughetto's name, and when he gave it, Luigi picked him up and carried him onto a waiting boat.

Ughetto was the package, it turned out, and though he wailed for his sisters, there was no one to save him.

Now, in this fearsome little *casetta*, Ughetto wrapped his arms around himself and shivered with fear. Luigi had already carried two other boys, eyes glazed from the opium, legs flopping limply over his big arms, into the tiled room where the tub was, where the knives waited. Ughetto crouched in the atrium under Nonna's watchful eye, listening to the whimpers and moans as the deed was done. Luigi brought the boys back, swaddled in bloody linen, and carried them through the atrium and on into the tiny house.

Ughetto tried to turn his head away when Nonna held the cup to his lips, but she seized his hair with her brown claw and twisted his head to face her. *"Cretino,"* she hissed. "Don't be an idiot. Drink, or you'll be screaming."

He cried, "No! Mamma, Mamma." Hot baby tears burned his eyes.

Nonna showed her jumbled teeth. "No more *mamma*, little one. *Musica.*"

She pressed the cup against his mouth, forcing his lips open with its metal rim. The sweet strong wine flooded his tongue, and he had to swallow, or drown. He closed his eyes, and gulped pungent sweetness. The room began to dissolve around him. He spun, stomach and brain and feet all mixed up, like diving too deep from the rocks into the warm Mediterranean waters of Trapani and not knowing which way to swim to the surface.

Nonna tipped up the cup again, and he drank, drank until it was dry.

She spoke. Ughetto heard her voice, but her words made no sense. He tried to open his eyes, but the lids would not obey him.

Perhaps he would die. Boys did, hundreds of them. Everyone knew that. They died under the knife, or they died afterward, bleeding and swollen, burning with fever. Would his *mamma* know if he died? Would they tell her?

Would she care?

It was possible she would not. She had regarded him so strangely, ever since that night when the family—all six girls, Ughetto, his *nonna*, and Mamma—had gone down to the docks in the darkness to wait for the squid boats to come in. Far out on the water, the fishermen shone their torches over the water to entice the squid to the jigs. The lights danced on the waves, shifting as the water tossed the boats to and fro.

When the moon rose over the sea, Ughetto's sisters exclaimed at its brilliance. They turned, all of them, and lifted their faces into its silver glow. It was full and round, and its crystalline light turned the low roofs and rough-cobbled streets of Trapani into a scene of magic, a fantasy village, its dirt and poverty transformed by the moon.

Ughetto was seven years old, already wriggling with energy and pleasure at the novelty of the night. When an unfamiliar sensation came over him, standing there in the moonlight, it seemed part of the strangeness. He felt as if he were becoming someone else, someone new and powerful instead of small and insignificant. His skin itched, and his jaw ached. When he began to scratch at himself, his *mamma* slapped at his hands. He tried to hold still, but he felt as if he were burning, as if he had rolled in too-hot sand. He scrubbed at his belly with both hands, grunting at the fierceness of the sensation.

It was his *nonna* who seized him up then, lifting him in her arms as if he were still a baby. She hissed something at his *mamma*, who drew a sharp, shocked breath. His *nonna* carried him away, up through the moonlit streets to the tavern, leaving his *mamma* and his sisters on the docks. He remembered kicking at her, whining, but she only held him tighter, and made no answer. She bundled him into the tavern and into his bed, folding him into his blankets, ignoring his protests. She lit no candles, nor did she stoke up the fire, but held him there in the darkness. In time, the burning of his skin subsided. By the time his *mamma* and sisters came home with their buckets of squid, he felt himself again. But Mamma looked at him as if he were a stranger.

And now she was lost to him. It was Luigi's strong arms beneath him, Luigi's rough hand seizing his head as it lolled backward. There was movement, the air changing against his face as Luigi carried him. The smell of the bath filled his nostrils with the essence of vinegar. Water rose around his legs, warm as blood. His buttocks settled onto a wooden bench that was wet and hard and splintery. Hands took hold of his feet and pulled his legs apart.

Someone held his head, murmuring something, laughing.

Someone else wielded the knife.

There was pain, sharp and surprising, and he gasped, breathing water, choking. He struggled, and someone cursed. There was a splash, and more swearing, and then someone . . . Ughetto fought his eyelids, trying to see.

Someone was growling.

His eyelids lifted, and his mind cleared all at once, as if a fog had burned away under a quickly rising sun. He peered around him through slitted eyes.

Faces looked back at him, horrified faces. Nonna shrieked something, and an open-mouthed stranger, the surgeon, backed away, knife held out before him, dripping blood onto the tiled floor.

Luigi gave a guttural cry and dropped Ughetto's head into the water.

Ughetto blew water from his mouth as he grasped the edge of the tub with both hands. He pulled himself to his feet, dripping, hot, and angry.

There was blood on his thighs, warmer than the water. His head hummed with sounds and smells he had not noticed before: the wheeze of Nonna's breath in her aging lungs; the fetid odor of Luigi's sweat; the scent of blood on the surgeon's knife, on his clothes, his hands. The surgeon whimpered and backed away.

Ughetto splashed out of the tub. Nonna tried to seize him, and he struck at her with his nails, slicing her dark skin, drawing blood. She dropped him with a cry, and he whirled to slash at Luigi next. Luigi scrambled out of reach. The smell of his fear filled the room and made Ughetto's mouth fill with saliva. Ughetto rounded on the surgeon next, but he saw only his heels as the man fled.

Ughetto fell to all fours in a movement that felt perfectly natural. He spun in a circle and saw that Luigi and Nonna dared not come close to him. His mouth opened, and his tongue lolled, saliva dripping as he galloped from the room. He slid on the wet tiles, finding his footing once he reached the dirt floor of the atrium. The sun warmed his back as he dashed away from the house. He ran swiftly, strongly, too fast for them to follow. They had no will to chase him, in any case. The pungence of their fear assured him of that.

He raced toward the orange grove, eager for the sanctuary of its drooping branches.

2

Anima mia, consolati, fa' core . . .

My love, console yourself, take heart . . .

—Don Ottavio, Act One, Scene One, *Don Giovanni*

Octavia waited between the chaise longue and the mock fireplace as the rest of her colleagues, one by one, stepped through the Met's curtain. Heavy gold damask muffled the roar of applause. When the stage manager parted the panels for the singers to pass through, the noise swelled, waves of sound breaking over the stage, then ebbed again as the immense curtain closed. Perspiration soaked Octavia's ribs beneath the layers of Violetta's third-act peignoir. She leaned against the scrolled back of the chaise, one hand pressed to her heart. It still thudded with the emotion of the last scene.

The stage manager gestured to her, and she moved forward. The clapping beyond the curtain diminished as the audience waited, saving itself, gathering its energy.

Octavia drew a deep breath of preparation. This was the telling moment, after every performance. This was what mattered, not the fee, not the notices, not the dozens of small things that had gone wrong, the multitude of things that had gone well. Her conductors might love her, her stage directors respect her. Her colleagues might criticize behind her back, or ply her with compliments to her face, but in the end, that didn't matter, either.

The unfathomable, unpredictable creature that signified was the audience. It was to them, her public, that she offered herself. With every performance she delivered over the sum of her years of study and practice and discipline. And it was from them, and only them, that her reward could come.

She arranged the folds of the peignoir, straightened her back, and stepped out into the hot light of the spot.

She was met by thunder, a storm she never wearied of. Buffeted by the torrent of sound, she dropped into her curtsy, layers of lace and silk pooling around her. She lifted her face to accept her ovation. She didn't smile—Violetta's grief was too recent—but she opened her arms, gracefully, gratefully. The cries of *Brava, brava!* were her manna. They fed her in a way matched by only one other.

She bowed, and retreated behind the gold curtain. They called her back again, then again, and released her with reluctance only when the curtain rose and Octavia took her colleagues' hands to join in the company bow. Her heart soared as she savored her triumph. She knew well how transitory such glory was. These moments were ephemeral, fragile as bubbles of foam floating at the crest of a wave, and she knew better than to take them for granted. Such successes had not always been hers.

Octavia found her dressing room empty. Ugo usually waited for her there, relaxed on the little settee. He was in the habit of laying out a towel for her to use after her shower, of brewing a fresh cup of tea for her to sip as she took off her makeup.

The dresser also looked around the cramped space in surprise. "Your assistant isn't here tonight?"

"He was," Octavia said. "I expected him." She looked about for a note, for some reassurance, but she found nothing.

"Do you want me to go look for him?"

"Oh, no," Octavia said. "That's nice, Lucy, but it's not necessary." She went in and began to slip the peignoir off her shoulders. "He'll meet me at the reception, I imagine."

Lucy held out her hands for the peignoir. She opened the glass doors of the closet, extracted a padded hanger, and arranged the long folds over it.

Octavia unpinned her wig and fitted it over its Styrofoam stand. She pulled off the wig liner and ran her fingers through her hair to rub circulation back into her scalp as Lucy undid the hooks and eyes on Violetta's voluminous nightgown. Octavia stepped out of the hot costume, shivering as sudden goose bumps prickled across her arms and shoulders. She wriggled out of the nylon corset and pulled on a silk kimono.

The costumes from the first and second acts had already gone down to the costume shop to be dry-cleaned and stored for the next Violetta. The closet was empty now, a sign of the last night of the run. Lucy maneuvered herself toward the door with her arms full of fabric. Octavia took up a small wrapped gift waiting on the dressing table, and she perched this on top of the mound of ivory silk. "Thank you so much for everything, Lucy," she said. "I look forward to seeing you next year for *Rusalka*."

"That will be great," Lucy said. "I hear it was a wonderful show tonight."

"It went well, I think." Octavia held the door for her, and the dresser sidled out into the corridor, joining a little stream of other dressers, assistants, well-wishers. Octavia peered out, hoping that Ugo might make his appearance now, but he wasn't there. She closed the door and went to the dressing table. She began to rub cold cream on her face with tense fingers, her ebullient mood evaporating.

He should have told her he was going to be delayed. He knew how she worried.

Octavia, in silver-beaded black silk, stood with the other principals to shake hands with opera patrons who strolled through the Upper West Side apartment. Tuxedos and designer gowns studded the crowd. The air was redolent with the scents of money and privilege, a cultural incense that swirled over trays of champagne glasses, among white linen tables with platters of caviar and canapés, and over the heads of the gay bejeweled company.

The room warmed as more people pressed in through the French doors from the foyer. Octavia held her smile, accepted compliments, made polite conversation. The little line of singers dominated the room as if they were still performing. Admirers came and went, looking pleased to have touched the hands of these unique personages. When one person stepped away, another took the empty place, beginning afresh with comments and questions. The air grew close, and Octavia felt sweat begin to bead anew beneath the silk sheath, to trickle down the small of her back.

When the flow of well-wishers began to lag at last, she slipped away to the coolness of a large, elegant bay window facing the park. Someone pressed a glass of champagne in her hand, and she drank half of it down straight away. Not a good sign. Thirsty already.

She leaned close to the glass so she could see past the shimmering silver of her own reflection. A couple, walking hand in hand, was just crossing the avenue to go into the park. As she watched, they stopped to kiss. When they moved on, they slipped their arms around each other, melding them into one person in the glow of the streetlights. Octavia sighed and finished the champagne. Someone refilled her glass, and she drank that, too, though she knew she probably shouldn't.

Damn Ugo. She hated being alone at these things.

She tried not to think about where he might be, what unsavory character he might be meeting. She hardly knew enough to be able to imagine these things, in any case. He refused, ever, to tell her.

She turned away from the window, thinking perhaps it was not too early for her to make her escape. She found the shy young mezzo who had sung Annina standing just behind her.

"Oh!" Octavia said. "Hi, Linda."

"I just wanted to say good-bye," Linda said. She was a plump, freckled American with a sweet smile. "It was so nice working with you, Octavia."

"It was lovely," Octavia agreed. "You were a perfect Annina."

The girl shrugged. "Oh, well. *Comprimario* rôles. Where I'm stuck, probably."

Octavia said what she always said in such situations. "You must keep trying. I know what it's like." And she did. She had struggled herself, in ways this nice young singer could never understand. "You have to persevere."

"Oh, I'll hang in there." Linda gave a self-deprecatory laugh. "But you know what they say about opera—voice, voice, and voice."

"Yours is very pretty."

"That's nice of you to say." Linda put out her hand. "Yours is magnificent, Octavia. And I hope to see you next year for *Rusalka*. I'm hoping they'll cast me as one of the Wood Nymphs."

Octavia pressed her hand. "I'm so glad. If someone asks me, I'll tell them they should give you a contract right now."

Linda blushed and admitted, "I hope they ask you, then! A Met contract makes my whole year."

"Mine, too." Octavia set her empty glass on the windowsill. "I think I'm going to say good night to everyone. I'm tired, and I still have to pack."

Linda walked her to the door. Octavia thanked her hostess while someone from the opera's administration went to call for the limousine. Someone else retrieved her coat and escorted her down in the discreetly luxurious elevator.

It was a relief to be alone in the limousine, to stop smiling, stop being gracious. She leaned back against the leather seat, pulling pins out of her chignon to let her hair fall on her shoulders, strands nearly as pale as the silver beads on her dress. It wasn't a long drive to her East Side apartment, but she found herself drumming her fingers on her thighs. Restlessness. Another bad sign.

The doorman met her. She said, "Good evening, Thomas," as he held the door for her.

"Good evening," he said. "You look lovely tonight, Miss Voss."

She smiled. Ninety more seconds to be on, to be charming. "Thank you, Thomas. It's nice of you to say so."

He crossed the parquet floor to call the elevator. "Good show tonight?"

"It was, actually. Everything went well. And a lovely party afterward." As the elevator's doors slid closed, she said, "Good night."

With relief, she let her smile fade again as she felt in her bag for the apartment key. She could have asked Thomas if he'd seen Ugo, but they had learned long ago not to call attention to his comings and goings. She realized, halfway up to her floor, that her left foot was tapping a restive rhythm against the carpeted floor. She forced herself to stop, but she fidgeted until the elevator stopped and the doors opened.

She unlocked the apartment and stepped inside, hoping to find the lights on, perhaps smell something cooking in the kitchen.

Nothing. The empty apartment felt cold, though she knew that was an illusion.

She hung her coat in the foyer closet and kicked off her pumps, leaving them on the polished wood of the entryway. She went through the living room to her bedroom and flicked on the light over the dressing table. She was reaching for the zipper of her dress when she heard the door open.

She hurried back into the living room in her stocking feet.

He was just shrugging out of his cashmere overcoat and unwinding his white silk opera scarf. Anger glittered in his eyes. Whitened lines ran from his nose to his mouth, marring the smooth duskiness of his cheeks.

"What is it?"

"Don't even ask," he said, with the flat vowels of an American television actor. He didn't look at her.

"Ugo—are you all right?"

"Yes." He unbuttoned his tuxedo jacket and threw it across a chair. It missed, and he said, "Goddammit," under his breath as he bent to pick it up.

Octavia put her hands on her hips, tilted her head, and regarded him as she might a naughty child. As he straightened, he caught her look, and his mouth relaxed a bit. "Don't glare at me like that," he said in a lighter tone. "I'm here. I have it."

"I'm glad of both." Even knowing he had it made her feel better. She moved toward a stuffed leather chair and pulled its matching ottoman close.

He retrieved his case from where he had left it by the door. He nearly tripped over her pumps as he came back to the living room, but he didn't scold. "How was the opera?"

"You were supposed to be there, Ugo."

His eyes flashed again. He shook his head and began to undo the pearl buttons of his shirt. "I wanted to be. There were complications."

She went to the bedroom to slip out of her dress and into a short belted robe. She hurried back, impatient now, and dropped into the leather chair.

Ugo, seeing her haste, said, "*Poverina*. Feeling bad?"

"No, not really—but thirsty."

"Not really thirsty, Octavia. Not yet. You just get anxious."

"I didn't know where you were." She tried not to sound plaintive.

He turned his dark eyes up to her. "You have your own ways if you need them."

"It's not that," she said. "I just didn't know where you might have gone—if it was safe."

He pulled his shirt off and folded it neatly across a chair back. His arms and chest were dark against the clear white of his undershirt. "I'm always safe," he said. "And you can take care of yourself if you have to."

"No, Ugo. Never again."

"Don't say that. If it got bad enough—"

"Ugo, let's not talk about it."

He shrugged, more relaxed now. The lines in his face had disappeared, and his accent was his own. *"Va bene."* He sat on the ottoman and laid his case beside him. He snapped it open and withdrew his tools as she rolled up the sleeve of her robe and propped her elbow on the arm of the chair.

"So," he said. He wound the tourniquet around her upper arm, then flicked the syringe with his fingernail, popping the bubbles to the top. "Tell me. Did the duet with Germont *fils* go better tonight?"

"Yes, it did. It was fine. Beautiful, actually."

"Good. The best part of the whole opera."

"What, not my 'Addio del passato'?"

Ugo only grinned. He slipped the superfine needle into the vein of her wrist, then loosened the tourniquet. As he depressed the plunger, the cold liquid trickled into her flesh, and the flow of sweet energy began to pour up her arm, across her chest, through her abdomen. She sighed, letting her muscles dissolve, relishing the burst of warmth in her body that felt like the rising of the sun. She sensed it creeping through her veins and capillaries, tingling in her temples and her toes. She felt its silken texture in her throat, tasted it in her mouth.

Not that she wanted to taste it, ever again. Ugo's way was infinitely better.

Ugo withdrew the needle, touched her wrist with a bit of cotton, then looked at it critically. *"Niente,"* he said with boyish pride. "I'm awfully good, don't you think?"

She laughed. She felt wonderful, energized, utterly alive. "I do think!" She watched as the little mark of the needle closed and vanished, then rose from her chair to scoop up Ugo's jacket and scarf. "I'll help you pack, Ugo."

He rearranged the items in his case, checked the refrigeration sensor, and snapped the lid shut. He tucked the case under his arm and took his things away from her with his free hand. "I'll pack my own clothes, thanks. You get started on yours."

She smiled at him and pirouetted toward her bedroom. "You spoil me, Ugo."

"Don't I just."

"I meant it, you know." She stopped in the doorway, tightening the belt on her robe, looking back at him. "I could never go back."

"I don't want to hear that." He started toward his own bedroom, then made a detour to the foyer for her shoes. He carried them to her and pressed them into her hands. "Spoiling is one thing, Octavia. Ruining is another."

She laughed, took the shoes, and went into her bedroom, closing the door behind her.

"You still have sources in Milan?" Octavia asked.

"Carissima," Ugo purred. He had been out of the apartment all day, only returning just before the car arrived to take them to the airport. "Do I have sources in Milano? I have sources everywhere."

"It's been such a long time."

"Sì, sì. A long time. It will be good to be in Italy again."

He lay back on his pillow. Around them the first-class cabin of the British Airways jet was quiet. The flight attendant had drawn the window shades, blocking the moon that shone like a lamp above the cloud cover. Only one or two passengers were using their personal screens, but most drowsed in the reclined leather seats, accordion curtains drawn for privacy. Octavia, despite two glasses of excellent cabernet, felt wide awake.

"It will be dear in Milano, you know," Ugo warned from his pillow.

Octavia glanced across at him. His eyes were closed, their long lashes curving against his cheeks. He looked deceptively like a sleeping child. She leaned across the curtain and whispered, "How much for your supplier, dear Ugo, and how much for you?"

He opened one eye. "Don't be bitchy, *bella*. It doesn't become you."

She chuckled and poked him with a manicured finger. She pulled her oversize shoulder bag from beneath her seat and extracted her *Giovanni* score. She switched on her reading light and scanned the first pages. "Ugo, this is my favorite opera."

He didn't open his eyes. "You say that about every opera."

"I do not."

"Yes, *cara,* you do. Whatever opera you're working on is always your favorite."

"Can't sleep, Miss Voss?"

Octavia looked up to find the flight attendant, a slender man with a receding hairline, bending over her. His shirt collar was open, and she could see the pulse beating in his thin neck, just above his collarbone. She gave him her close-lipped smile. "No," she said. "It's curtain time in New York."

"I heard you at the Met last week," he said. "You were marvelous. *Bravissima!*"

"How kind of you to say so."

"Can I get you something, as long as you're awake? Tea, or sparkling water?"

"Tea would be lovely."

"Very good," he said, and walked away toward the galley.

Octavia opened her Bärenreiter score to the first ensemble. She ran her fingers over the staves, smiling to herself. She knew it perfectly, of course. This would be Octavia Voss's first performance of Donna Anna, but Teresa Saporiti had sung the opera's premiere in Prague, and many performances after that. Hélène Singher had sung the rôle in San Francisco and New York. The dark color of her voice had not been popular with audiences in those cities. Vivian Anderson had fared better. In Australia they had loved the richness of her timbre.

No, no one in the world could know the score of *Don Giovanni* better than Octavia did.

But performance practice was a fluid thing. Each new editor fancied that he knew more than the previous one, and she had learned long ago to bend with the winds of such changes. She had been tempted, more than once, to tell an arrogant conductor what Mozart had intended, but she had never done it. Restraint was another trait she had learned, over time, and with difficulty, but she had learned it.

The flight attendant returned with her tea and glanced down at the score. "Ah," he said. "Will it be Donna Anna?"

"It will. My first," she said, with just a hint of anxiety, a droop of the lashes.

"The perfect rôle for you! I wish I could hear it."

Octavia took the teacup in her hands. "If you're in Milan," she said, "send me a note at La Scala. I'll arrange a ticket."

He put his hand to his breast. "That would be wonderful! I may just do that."

"Please do," she said with a smile, then pointedly turned her page. He took the hint, backing away, turning to another passenger. Octavia sipped the tea, turned the page back, and began to study.

Ugo's closed eyelids trembled with mirth. "You know, darling, you're wasting your time with that one."

"I think he's sweet."

"Very. But he doesn't play for your team."

She chuckled. "You underestimate me."

"Oh, God. Such a diva. I can hardly stand it."

She blew him a tiny raspberry. He laughed and pulled his blanket up to his chin.

The moon was just setting when they landed at Malpensa. A limousine was waiting, with someone to speed them through customs and direct a porter with their bags. They were out of the airport within fifteen minutes, and riding through morning traffic toward Il Principe di Savoia. Ugo was quiet, his head resting against the seat as he watched their approach to the city. His complexion seemed a bit ashen to Octavia.

She touched his knee. "Are you all right? Didn't you sleep?"

"I did," he said. "But I need my valise."

"Just a little longer," Octavia said. She leaned forward to open the glass partition, and said, *"Più veloce, per favore!"*

"God, Octavia." Ugo turned his head to roll his eyes at her. "Any faster and we'll be roadkill. This is Italy, remember?"

"But you don't look well."

"I will look terrible smeared all over the highway," he said. He closed his eyes. "Just make sure he drives between the lines, *d'accordo?*"

She patted him. *"D'accordo."*

Ugo swayed a little on his feet as they walked into the colonnaded entry of Il Principe. Octavia took his arm, and his body felt hot through the sleeve of his coat. The assistant from La Scala guided them through the marble lobby, expedited their registration, oversaw their luggage. In the elevator's gold-flecked mirrors, Octavia saw Ugo scratching at his jaw and wriggling inside his shirt as if it had grown too tight for him. His nostrils flared, scenting something beyond the range of her own senses.

In their suite, they had to wait politely as the bellman pointed out the amenities, the flowers and fruit sent by La Scala, the Pellegrino and chocolates provided by the management of the hotel. He assured them the hotel limousine was at their disposal at any time.

Ugo leaned against a blue velvet armchair throughout the bellman's recitation. The moment they were left alone, he disappeared into the connecting bedroom, where his bags had been left, and closed the door behind him.

Octavia wandered through the curtained doors into her own bedroom. She pulled off her shoes and lay down on the big bed, tucking a cushion under her neck.

It troubled her sometimes that she and Ugo were not of a kind. She could not do for him what he did for her. What he needed was quite different from that which sustained her, and he would not allow her to help him acquire it. Too dangerous, he always said. And unnecessary.

Octavia tossed aside the cushion and got up again. She padded to the window and pushed aside the heavy draperies to look past the hotel's circular drive into the Piazza della Repubblica. The morning rush hour was almost over, the flood of taxis and scooters settling down to a trickle. The Duomo's forest of spires shone in the distance, and beyond it, the Galleria with its airy dome. It was good to be back. And surely, here, where there were people who understood him, Ugo could find what he needed.

She rubbed her arms and glanced across the suite at his closed bedroom door, irritated, worried, wistful.

She stripped off her traveling suit and shrugged into one of Il Principe's thick robes. She undid the clasp of her hair and took up her hairbrush just as Ugo's door opened. He lounged through the suite into her bedroom and flopped down across her bed, giving her a wide white grin. "That's better," he said, touching his temples. "Whole again."

She laid her brush on the bureau. "Ugo. You must let me—"

"Don't speak of it."

"But—with all you do for me—"

He lifted his brows. "Not for you," he said. He lifted a mocking finger. "For the music."

She made an exasperated sound. "Ugo, I know an herbalist—"

His face darkened, and he put up a narrow hand. "*Basta*, Octavia. I know Milano better than you do. I can handle it."

Octavia sighed. "When you get stern, you sound just like an American, Ugo."

"*O Dio, no!*" His grin returned, and he pressed his palm to his chest. "Not an American!"

She chuckled and picked up her brush again, but the flicker of anxiety persisted. She hoped his sources in Milan were more reliable than those in New York. She hated to think of him roaming the alleys of the old city, searching. She knew all too well how dark and dangerous the backstreets could be, and had always been. The architecture of the city had changed, but its nature had not.

When she had brushed out her hair, she crossed to the desk, where she had left her bag with the Mozart score. "Dinner tonight with the *maestro*," she reminded him. "Read-through tomorrow at ten, but you don't need to be there. Do please come to dinner, though, and help me talk to Russell."

"Mm," he said. "Delicious Russell."

She faced him, the score in her hands. "And you will behave," she said. "I want to sing Donna Anna without distractions."

"*Carissima.* I wouldn't dream of distracting you."

"Ha." She laid the score ready beside her bed and began to untie her robe. "I always feel filthy after I fly. I'm going to take a bath."

"Shall I wash your back?"

"Thank you, no." As she passed him on her way to the bathroom, she trailed her fingers across his head and gave his curls a tug. "You're a brat," she murmured.

He grinned up at her. "So true. So true."

Ugo propped his chin on his hand, gazing at Russell until the conductor's face reddened and he broke off what he was saying.

"Maestro," Ugo purred. "Please. Do go on with your story."

Octavia tried to kick him under the table with her sharp-toed Ferragamo, but she couldn't quite reach. They were dining in Il Principe's Acanto restaurant. It was a peaceful place, with neutral walls and rich wood trim. Murano chandeliers cast a gentle glow on the nondescript beige of Russell Simondsen's hair. The *risotto alla Milanese* had been rich with saffron, and the grilled salmon flavored with basil and bell peppers. Octavia felt relaxed and refreshed. She was eager to begin the three weeks of rehearsals.

Though Russell's features were painfully thin, there was something appealing about his fragile physique that housed such a gifted musical instinct. Octavia could hardly wait to sing Donna Anna under his baton. When Russell took the podium, his hesitant manner disappeared. He became a figure of power, a pale, steady flame.

She knew it was this that intrigued Ugo. She kicked again, and this time her shoe glanced off his shin. His lips twitched, but his eyes never left Russell's face.

Russell cleared his throat, glanced at Octavia, and stammered on about the performance of *Aïda* he had just conducted in Edinburgh. Ugo gave him a brilliant smile.

Russell said, a little plaintively, "Yes, it may seem amusing. But she simply wouldn't follow me, no matter what I did."

"Russell, dearest, I'm not laughing," Ugo protested. "I'm simply thinking what an absolute *bitch* she is!"

Octavia rolled her eyes, and Ugo smirked at her. She touched Russell's arm. "Ugo's right, if a bit crude, Russell. And I promise I will follow every one of your *tempi*." She gave him her close-lipped smile.

He smiled back at her. "We'll work them out together, of course."

She pushed her hair back from her face. She had worn it down, to trail on the shoulders of her white wool suit. She wore a discreet pair of diamonds in her ears and a matching pendant on a thin gold chain that accentuated her long neck. She had taken pains to present herself in the rôle of a young soprano on the verge of a great career.

She felt certain Russell believed it. He would not be the first.

Russell was still blushing, but his face was intent as he leaned toward her. "You know, Octavia, Nick Barrett-Jones was our Amonasro. I hope you'll like working with him."

"Ah," she said. "They say his voice is magnificent."

"Well . . ." Russell pursed his narrow lips. "Yes, the voice is good. But his singing—"

She tilted her head thoughtfully. "A little stiff?"

"Just not musical," he answered. When it came to music, all his diffidence fell away. His manner sharpened, and his voice steadied. "He looks well on the stage, and he learns his cues, but he just—" He waved one hand. His fingers were long and spatulate, the fingers of a pianist. "He doesn't make music."

Octavia listened, nodding as if it were all new to her, although she had heard a good bit of it in New York, and before that in Seattle. Nick Barrett-Jones, of course, had not had her advantages—specifically, her one great advantage. His was a career, by all accounts, that would never be more than mediocre.

She kept all of this to herself, only asking, "How is the alternate cast, do you think? I've heard wonderful things about Simone."

Simone would be the other Donna Anna. Russell said he had worked with her before and that she was pleasant and reliable. Animated now, he began to speak of the challenges of La Scala's orchestra.

Octavia, listening, looked across at Ugo. He had put his head back against his chair and closed his eyes. Russell noticed, too. He interrupted himself, leaning forward with a concerned expression. "Are you all right, Ugo?"

"*Sì, sì, Maestro,*" Ugo said. He straightened. "*Sto bene!* I'm just a little sleepy."

"Yes, it's late. And you had a long flight." Russell signaled to the waiter. "And Octavia needs her rest before the read-through."

"It was a lovely dinner, Russell. Thank you," Octavia said. As they walked together to the small bank of elevators, she said, "I'm looking forward to the read-through. And to working with you."

His ready blush suffused his thin cheeks again. Even his sharp-pointed nose turned red, and she thought, irrelevantly, how much he must hate that. "I am, too," he said. "It's about time you sang Donna Anna."

Octavia pressed her cheek to his, one and then the other, then she and Ugo stepped into the elevator. As it carried them up, Ugo propped himself against the parquet wall. "He's adorable," he murmured.

"Ugo, leave him alone. He's so high-strung."

"Would I hurt such a fine musician?"

"You mean," Octavia said dryly, as the door opened on their floor, "another fine musician. I don't want you adding poor Russell to your list of conquests. Let him concentrate."

"Concentrate on you, you mean, *bella!*"

"That would be nice." She unlocked the door, and they went in. As Ugo turned toward his room, she said, "Are you sure you're all right?"

He flashed his smile, very white in his dusky face. "I'm fine, just as I told Russell. I'm just dandy."

3

Che giuramento, O dei! Che barbaro momento!

What an oath, O gods! What a terrible moment!

—Donna Anna and Don Ottavio,
Act One, Scene One, *Don Giovanni*

When Ugo emerged from the elevator, he could see the glisten of
a cold rain on the pavement of the Piazza della Repubblica. The
night doorman started toward him, but he shook his head and
walked out through the glass doors to the street, buttoning his
overcoat as he went. He stood for a moment, scowling at the
cityscape through the haze of rain. Too many landmarks had
drowned under waves of modernization. From where he stood,
the square, dull towers of contemporary hotels blocked the view
of the Duomo. Small churches and open markets and ancient
palazzi had given way to office buildings. Even the old La Scala
was not the same. The new theater was larger, enormous really,
but its amenities and additions hardly replaced, in Ugo's mind,
the charm of the old one.

Ugo's sigh puffed into the cold air and vanished beneath the
raindrops. Though his jaw itched unbearably, he resisted scratching it. A crow perched on the façade above his head, and he heard
the patter of its heartbeat as it ruffled its feathers against the rain.

A mouse scurried through the drain beneath the street, claws scraping on rocks and dirt. Ugo sniffed, tasting its sharp small smell.

The doorman's pulse was thunder.

Ugo glanced at him, assessing his possibilities, then dismissing him. What the man had to offer was hardly worth the risk, and the need wasn't pressing.

He turned right, toward the city center. As he began the long walk, heat was already building in his spine, a radiant column that flamed through his nerves and flashed along his arms and his legs. The itch of his jaw spread to his chest, and he walked faster, striding along the tangle of wet Milanese streets, splashing through the occasional puddle.

Octavia sometimes went to an herbalist, a crone who kept her shop in one of the dilapidated buildings beyond the Basilica di Sant'Ambrogio. He had gone to her before, though he never told Octavia. He never mentioned Octavia to the herbalist, either. He didn't want her associating the two of them.

Ugo's mouth filled with saliva, and he spat in the gutter. Curse that man in New York! He knew little about him, except that his name was Domenico. He had never seen him. One of La Società's hopefuls had been the go-between, had made the delivery, taken the payment. But the source was this Domenico. It was probably not his real name, and he would not be easy to find. But Ugo intended to find him, and when he did, the deceiver would pay for his offense. He would harvest Domenico without the slightest pang.

Stupid, stupid man. Ugo dashed across the nearly empty lanes of Fatebenefratelli and walked into the Brera district, where he turned south, striding swiftly along the familiar streets.

His revenge—Domenico's reward—would have to wait until he returned to New York. For now, he trusted that the old signora had a supply of *aconitum lycoctonum*, or *aconitum vulparia* in a pinch. This was Italy, after all. She was a true *strega*, and she understood the *lupo mannaro*. She would be prepared.

Ugo hurried down Via Terraggio and cut through the Piazza

Sant'Ambrogio to the cramped street of Via Dolorosa, where the herbalist's shop huddled, windows barred, between a lawyer's office and a dry cleaner's building. The signora would be asleep in her tiny apartment above the shop, but when he knocked—well, she knew what he was. She would answer the door for the *lupo mannaro*.

The *strega* peered at him closely from her darkened shop before she undid the locks and opened the door.

Ugo smiled at her, and bowed. "It's all right, signora," he said. "I have a little time yet. You're safe."

"It's been years," she said. Her voice was as dry as pebbles in a jar, and her hair had gone white as sea foam. She opened the door just enough to admit him, then closed and locked it. She wore a chenille housecoat of a style Ugo had not seen in fifty years. She said, "I thought perhaps you were dead."

"Ah," he said. "But as you see . . ." He kept the smile on his face, but impatience quickened his heartbeat. He breathed deeply, trying to slow it.

The *strega* saw this, and shrank back from him. Her heartbeat increased. Ugo heard it as a rattle of snare drums, scratching at his nerves.

"A little time?" the *strega* quavered. "Not much, I think."

He let his smile fade. "*È vero*. We should hurry."

She turned and made her way through her crowded shop toward a back room. He followed her through the fragrant dark. The air was evanescent of forest floors and cave walls and ancient, musty storerooms. She pulled back a heavy curtain and led him past it into a tiny storeroom. She closed the curtain again before she moved behind a small counter and lighted a lamp. It had a shade of dingy yellow parchment that blocked more light than it admitted, but Ugo saw her perfectly in the dimness. Her hands trembled, and the smell of her fear warred with the scents of dried herbs and powdered spices. The counter was littered with boxes and jars. She bent beneath it to bring out a footstool, which she moved to a wall where more containers of various types and sizes lined a half dozen wooden shelves.

"You have it, then?" he asked, a little roughly.

"*Sì, sì,*" she said. She climbed up on the stool, bracing herself against the shelves. She stretched her arm to the very top shelf, and her housecoat hiked up in back to reveal thin legs marked by ropy blue veins. She grunted as she groped through the jumble of things, finally bringing down a brown glass jar with a cork stopper. She climbed off the stool and set the jar on the counter, panting a little from her efforts. "*Eccola,*" she said. She pulled the cork out, releasing a puff of dust. Carefully, she extracted something from the darkened interior.

"Is this all you have?" he asked.

"No. But use it." She held it out to him, a single twisted stem with dried follicles clinging to it. "*Subito,* before we make our arrangements."

He stripped the follicles from the stem and put three in his mouth, under his tongue. He closed his eyes. It tasted foul, but he was glad of it. The taste spoke of the power of the poison, bane to any other man, palliative to him. He tried to breathe deeply as he waited for his saliva to decoct the first essence of the plant, for the mucosa of his mouth to absorb it. His skin began to cool almost at once, the itching to subside. He could no longer hear the whisper of tires on the street outside, or the chitter of mice in the rafters. When the follicles were soft, he swallowed them and took three more into his mouth. He spread his hands and smiled at the *strega*. "You see, signora? Nothing to worry about."

She grinned suddenly, showing surprisingly good teeth. Her face creased with a thousand wrinkles. "My friend, there is always something to worry about with the *lupo mannaro*."

He took a long, sweet breath, relishing the steadiness of his heartbeat. "And now," he said. "How much do you have? And how much do you want for it?"

* * *

A quarter of an hour later, Ugo left the shop with a package, wrapped in newsprint, tucked under his arm. The locks snapped shut behind him as he stood in the street, sniffing the air, listening to the monotone hum of constant traffic. Even in the small hours, Milano vibrated with life and movement. He struck out again toward the Piazza Sant'Ambrogio, where he could hail a taxi. He would be safely in his bed at Il Principe before Octavia knew he had been gone.

It was a point of pride to him that Octavia slept well. In exchange for her company, and the glory of her music, he smoothed her path in any way he could.

Sometimes, though she would never know it, he watched her sleep. Her head lay in a fan of that glorious hair that reminded Ugo of the halo on a Botticelli angel. Her strong mouth relaxed, the lips going soft as a child's. Her eyes flickered behind their closed lids, and he supposed she was remembering, dreaming the dreams of centuries.

He sometimes thought that she might be the reason he had survived so long. Preserving and protecting such an artist—such a woman—was worth it, worth all of it. Any family either of them had was long gone. Loneliness might have overwhelmed them, its weight greater even than the weight of memories Octavia carried. But they had found each other, a strange grace no religion could explain. And whether he deserved such grace or not, Ugo was grateful.

Lost in his thoughts, Ugo didn't notice the rusted green Fiat that careened around the corner into Piazza Sant'Ambrogio until its tires hissed against the curb, throwing a fine muddy spray over the sidewalk. It spattered his slacks, and Ugo whirled, clamping his elbow tighter over the *strega*'s package.

The back doors of the little car opened, and two men jumped out. Ugo grinned. No doubt they had spotted his Armani overcoat. But these two had underestimated their quarry. He turned and began to run.

Sant'Ambrogio had already been a thousand years old when Ugo first walked through its Romanesque portico. Now he dashed across the atrium and ducked behind one of the twelfth-century columns with their carved Renaissance capitals. He paused to look back, and swore under his breath.

They had come after him. They looked young and strong, and they charged into the atrium from the *piazza*, raincoats belling around them. As he looked, one slipped on the wet mosaic, and the other grabbed his partner's arm to stop him from falling. The one that had slipped, a bald, heavily built man, looked familiar. A second later the two were running again.

Ugo didn't feel any particular alarm. He couldn't transform because he had taken the *strega*'s herb, but it wouldn't matter. These two couldn't know Sant'Ambrogio as he did.

He supposed he could drop the coat, let them take it and go, but he was disinclined to give them the satisfaction. They had mistaken their victim.

He grinned to himself as he slipped from column to column, hiding in the shadows, aiming for the narrow stair that led to the upper *loggia*. From there he could make his way around to the far side, descend again, and hide himself behind the bell tower that loomed beyond the church, a rectangle of stone against the rain-dimmed stars.

Ugo slipped down the gallery and in through the side door. The staircase was to his left. The door was closed, but it wasn't locked. He opened it silently and was about to put his foot on the first wooden stair when he heard the voice.

The accent was unmistakably English, though neither public school nor particularly common. London, Ugo guessed. Educated, but not aristocratic. Resonant, a nice rich baritone. The speaker was in front of him.

The voice said, "We have you now, I believe. Ugo, isn't it? My friends are in the nave, and I'm blocking the stairs."

Ugo stopped and glanced behind him. It was true, the two

men were standing just inside the door to the church. He looked forward again, peering up at the speaker, but he could see nothing in the gloom.

Ugo gave a sigh. He put his hands in his pockets and adopted a negligent slouch. "You have the advantage of me, signore," he said. "Who are you? What is it you want?"

"What we want, Ugo, is information. And my name I think you will recognize."

Ugo slouched further, letting his chin drop into his collar. "Will I?" he said, in a very American accent. "Am I supposed to guess?"

"Oh, no," the voice said. The man stepped down so that a dim shaft of light, slicing through the half-open stairwell door, fell on his face. He didn't look familiar at all. Ugo eyed him narrowly as he came forward and put out his hand. "I'm Domenico," he said. "I'm going to be your host for a bit."

4

Siam soli.

We are alone.

—Leporello, Act One, Scene Two, *Don Giovanni*

Octavia moved about the suite at Il Principe as quietly as she could, hoping not to wake Ugo. She had her breakfast carried into her bedroom, putting her finger to her lips to keep the server quiet. When she had eaten, and drunk the little pot of *espresso*, she showered, humming scales beneath the noise of the spray. She stepped out of the shower and toweled herself dry, and set about the task of choosing her clothes.

Octavia always felt a slight disorientation with each new rôle she undertook. At one time this had caused her problems, as the brittle gaiety of Violetta would spill over into the Countess, or the Countess's gentility would shade the youth and naïveté of Rusalka. She had learned to make a conscious effort to put aside one character as she took up the next. Today she would shake off the last shreds of Violetta, the desperately vivacious courtesan. She would put on, like putting on a suit of clothes, the outraged virtue and extravagant filial devotion of Donna Anna.

And for this Donna Anna, she would be the *prima donna*.

It had not always been the case. In the early productions, Zerlina, the flirtatious peasant girl, had been considered the *prima donna.* Even now, Zerlina was always a threat to steal the show. The rôle of Donna Elvira was also substantial, but Donna Anna had become, over the years, the principal female singer. And Octavia needed to present herself to Russell, to the director, and to the rest of the cast, just that way. Sympathetic, she hoped, and collegial. It was always nicer, and the music was better, if she and her colleagues were on friendly terms. But she wanted no doubt about what her position was. She knew from experience how quickly the balance of power could change in an opera production, how swiftly rumors and insults and treachery could spread, and how damaging they could be. She had paid the price too many times, in the early years, for misplacing her trust. It was an error she had no intention of repeating.

She pulled a black pantsuit out of the closet, and after a moment's hesitation, her favorite cream silk blouse. She wore modest earrings and tied her hair back in a long, elegant ponytail. The pale hair looked dramatic against the black jacket, but the understated style gave her the casual look she wanted.

She applied makeup with a judicious hand—a subtle eyeshadow, a pale matte lipstick. She blotted the lipstick, then lifted her upper lip to show her small, sharp incisors. They had retracted, slowly, from lack of use. She drew her lip down again to smile at herself in the mirror. It was well practiced, that smile: the lips closed, the corners of her mouth turned up to hollow her cheeks and exaggerate her cheekbones. No need, now, to hide her teeth, but the smile had become a habit.

She appraised herself with a critical eye. The style of her looks was not so fashionable in this century: the high-bridged nose, the wide mouth and strong jaw. Still, she managed to create an illusion of something like beauty. She looked about thirty, perhaps a bit older. Old enough to know what she was about, but not too old to be an *ingénue.* Her figure was trim without being thin, and her low heels would keep her from towering over the Don. She had checked, and learned that Nick Barrett-Jones stood no more than five-ten in boots.

She wound her trademark long scarf around her neck and opened the door of her bedroom to go out into the quiet suite, thinking about this man who would sing the amorous, and amoral, Don Giovanni.

Nick Barrett-Jones was an English bass-baritone who had been singing in European opera houses for several years. She had heard from one of the *comprimario* singers in New York that he fancied himself a ladies' man. In fact, the soprano had said, tossing her head, he fancied himself, period. He had told *Opera News* that he was perfectly suited for the rôle of Don Giovanni, vocally and temperamentally. Octavia's lip curled at the hubris. One of the lessons she had learned was to let her performances speak for themselves. Talking proved nothing.

Well, it wouldn't matter. Nick Barrett-Jones would have to learn his own lessons, soon or late, or not at all. Octavia picked up her score from the table beside the little couch. Yes. She would give this Nick Barrett-Jones his chance. His was, after all, the title rôle. He was the *primo uomo* of the production, and he would no doubt have his own worries about Leporello stealing his scenes.

But if he gave her any trouble—any at all—she would return to wearing high heels.

Usually Ugo woke before she left for her call, but this morning there was no sound from the other bedroom. She put on her long cashmere coat against the chill January wind that whipped the bare trees outside her window. She let herself out of the suite as quietly as possible. Her heels made no sound in the carpeted hallway. She bypassed the bank of elevators and ran nimbly down the brass-railed staircase, glad for the bit of exercise. It promised to be a long morning of standing about.

Russell had apologized to her about this first rehearsal. "The chorus has been called," he said, "and the stage director will be there. The concertmaster is coming to hear the *tempi*, to think about bow markings. We'll have to start at the top and work through."

"Russell," Octavia had said. "Of course you must conduct your rehearsal in whatever you way you think best." She had contrived to smile up at him, rather than down, a little trick of the bent knees and the tilted head, and he glowed with pleasure.

He squeezed her hand upon his arm. "Thank you, Octavia," he said fervently. "I do appreciate it, and I promise, once we've had a full read-through, we'll focus on your scenes."

She hadn't been able to resist murmuring, "Our Nick may not like that," but she regretted it when she saw Russell pale a little.

"Well," he said hastily. "But he's in most of your scenes, in any case."

"Oh, of course," she said. "Most."

The limousine driver turned right out of the Piazza della Repubblica, sweeping past the public gardens and on toward the city center. Octavia hoped she and Ugo could take a turn in the gardens this evening, a little exercise in the cold fresh air, a good gossip about the cast she would meet that morning.

Il Principe's driver chattered as he turned down Via Manzoni, lamenting the hideous rectangles of the modern hotels, and pointing with pride to the street where Versace and Valentino had their establishments. He offered to take Octavia there at any time she wished.

She smiled and thanked him, but she preferred browsing through the boutiques of the Brera district. Octavia had appeared in Milan once before, to sing the Countess in *Figaro*. She had strolled through the Brera then. Vendors sometimes called out her name, sang a snatch of music from the opera, even pressed some trinket upon her. Octavia's career was still new, and it was gratifying to be recognized. It pleased her, too, to think that these shopkeepers and waiters might be descendants of her very first admirers. It eased the sting of finding that Teresa's portrait was not among those displayed in La Scala's museum of great singers of the early days: Pasta was there, and Grisi, and Nancy Storace, a soprano Mozart had loved. But no Teresa Saporiti.

The staff of La Scala welcomed her at the artists' entrance, and a pleasant woman escorted her to the elevator to ride up to the Ansaldo rehearsal room. Octavia heard the first strains of the music of act one trickling from the Steinway, and the chatter and shuffle of the chorus arranging themselves behind the principals. A thrill of excitement quickened her breath.

Opera was work, and there were a hundred pitfalls. Singers would catch colds, costumes wouldn't fit, staging would change. Colleagues would have differences. But at the end, there would be the glory of an opera fully realized. There would be Mozart's transcendent music; there would be choristers who had been rehearsing for weeks; there would be the achingly beautiful dancers twirling about the stage; there would be costumes, flamboyant creations of color and fabric and imagination; and there would be some of the great voices of the world, trained in New York or in Indiana or in Bologna, voices for which everything had been sacrificed and to which every ear was drawn. The scenery was being built and painted; the lighting was being designed; the programs laid out, held against some last-minute casting change. The director and the conductor would be arguing, liaisons would be forming between performers of every sexual preference, and in the streets of Milan the melodies would be on the lips of cab drivers and clerks and cooks.

Octavia never tired of it. There had been failures, disappointments and betrayals and difficulties, but through it all, she sang. In those magical moments when everything came together, the breath, the voice, the music, and the theater, nothing else mattered.

"Octavia!" The director, a plump man with a sharp mind and a vast knowledge of opera, came to greet her as she stepped out of the elevator. *"Che piacere rivederti, carissima!"*

"E tu, Giorgio," she said. This was a significantly warmer reception than she had received the last time she came to La Scala. It meant Octavia's star was rising. She knew, of course, that it could fall just as quickly, but this was not the time to dwell upon that. She allowed him to press his cheek to hers, left and right, and then, smiling, she followed him into the rehearsal room.

It gave her a frisson of delight to see the chorus rise and applaud when they saw her. It was very nice indeed to see the lower members of the cast hang back, wait to be introduced, and then shake her hand and greet her in whatever their common language might be, German, English, Italian. Marie Charles, the soubrette who would sing Zerlina, struggled to say "I am zo glad, madame," when she met her, and Octavia pressed the girl's hand in both of hers, saying, *"Bien sur, chérie, moi aussi."*

When the introductions were complete, Octavia glanced at her watch. "Oh, look at the time," she said. "We're to start at ten, and here it is! Let's not keep Russell waiting."

They began at the top of the show, omitting only the overture. Octavia marked her first passages, not feeling completely warmed up yet, and then began to open up when they reached "Ma qual mai s'offre." Nick Barrett-Jones displayed the richness of voice, especially at the top, that caused world-class companies to hire him. He would make a handsome Don, with his blue eyes and wisps of brown hair curling at his neck. At times his voice was glorious. His musicianship, though, was disappointing, shallow and derivative.

Luigi Bassi, the first Don Giovanni, had also been a handsome man, but an impressively stupid one. He had possessed a great voice, and Mozart liked his acting, but he never grew in the part. It was as if, once he learned it, it had been carved into the marble columns of the Nostitz Theater in Prague, never a nuance or shading to be changed.

Ugo claimed someone in New York told him Nick Barrett-Jones learned his rôles from recordings. This first read-through seemed to support the rumor.

Brenda McIntyre, the Australian woman singing Donna Elvira, was past her youth and heavy with middle age, but she had the perfect dark, edgy soprano for a woman half-mad with frustrated passion. The Commendatore, Lukas Weiss, was a weathered man of sixty. His dry bass fit the role of the ghostly father to perfection: noble, furious, unrelenting. He confided to the cast, before they began, that he had sung the Commendatore a hundred times.

"Then, Lukas," Octavia said, "we are all honored to be part of your one hundred first performance!" Everyone smiled at that, agreeing, and she felt they were off to a good start.

The rôle of Ottavio was to be sung by a pudgy tenor with a clear, high voice, the perfect Mozart instrument. Octavia had sung with Peter Wellington before, and always liked his work. His short stature was a little awkward for love scenes, but they were both professionals. They would manage. At the first break, she touched his arm. "Peter," she said. "You sound marvelous, as you always do. And is David here?"

"Oh, yes." He pointed to the table where Russell sat with the stage director and the concertmaster. "And we're both just dying to hear all about your *Traviata* in New York! Is it true that twit of a conductor was after one of the chorus boys again?"

Octavia smiled. "Peter, you know I never gossip except with Ugo." He laughed, and she turned to wave at his partner. David kissed his fingers in her direction.

The nicest surprise of the cast was Zerlina's young lover, Masetto. He was tall and broad-shouldered, thin, surely no more than twenty-six or twenty-seven. His dark hair set off his eyes, which were a surprising light brown that made Octavia think of caramels. He sang with a natural musicianship and an instinctive characterization. She turned to watch him from his very first notes. Massimo Luca, she thought, had a bright future. She couldn't wait to tell Ugo all about him.

When the lunch break was called, the director approached the principals. "Someone will show you your dressing rooms," he said.

The singers tripped along after a cheerful woman with a clip-board. They rode down to the stage floor and crossed through the ellipse to the narrow corridor leading to the artists' dressing rooms. La Scala was new to Marie Charles, and she exclaimed over everything they passed.

Octavia's dressing room was the closest to the stage. Brenda McIntyre raised her eyebrows at this, pressed her lips together, and went into her own dressing room, closing the door firmly behind her.

Octavia pretended not to notice, though she found the show of ego tiresome. She wished this cast could be a friendly one, especially because Russell was so sensitive.

She thanked the assistant and said, "Marie, I'll see you after the break," before she went into her own dressing room.

Ugo had proclaimed the dressing rooms at La Scala to be shoeboxes with showers, but Octavia didn't mind them at all. They were certainly cramped, and although lavish effort had been spent making all of the public areas of the new La Scala as elegant and inviting as possible, none had been wasted on these little spaces. No adornment brightened the walls, but a small bouquet of roses in a glass vase, sent by Russell, rested on the makeup table. A little Schulze Pollmann upright piano stood ready against one wall. Octavia lifted the lid and struck a chord, nodding to herself. It was in good tune.

The shower was as compact as it could be, but someone had kindly equipped it with shampoo and French soap. Tiny bottles of creams and lotions waited before the lighted mirror, with a welcoming note from a Milanese *profumeria*. There was an electric kettle, with packets of Nescafé and tea in a basket. The assistant returned to knock on her door and to ask, in halting English, if she would like to go to the canteen for lunch or have something brought in.

Octavia answered her in Italian. "Giuditta, I'd love to stay in. I'm a little tired from the time change. Do you think perhaps you could bring me something?"

Giuditta smiled with relief at being able to respond in her own language. She went out and came back bearing a tray with a tomato and fennel salad and a *panino* of *prosciutto* and *mozzarella* and basil, with a bottle of mineral water and two chocolates on a doily. She laid it on the makeup table and then withdrew. Octavia ate, idly leafing through an Italian copy of *Opera News*. She saved half the *panino* for Ugo. She heated water in the electric kettle and poured it into the teapot. With a cup of tea in her hand, she lay back in the velvet chaise longue and wondered where Ugo was. Usually, if he had slept in, he would join her at the rehearsal hall by lunchtime. Perhaps, she thought, he was too tired. It had been a long flight, and she had told him he didn't need to be there this morning.

She let her head fall back against the cushions. Faintly, through the layers of the opera house, she heard the strains of violins and flutes. The cranking of machinery and the scraping of plywood sounded from the tower as set pieces were moved about. The distant fragments of music began to coalesce into the first bars of the overture, and Octavia closed her eyes, remembering.

Such a feeling of haste there had been, in those early days. Teresa Saporiti had only recently joined the Bondini theater troupe, and they struggled to master Mozart's new opera.

No one knew if *Don Giovanni* was meant to be a tragedy or a comedy. The opera opened with the attempted rape of Donna Anna and the murder of her father, the Commendatore, by Don Giovanni. The rejected lover Donna Elvira spent her time alternately screaming her rage or avowing love for her seducer. But the other characters played comic rôles, Leporello as the hapless servant keeping a catalog of the Don's conquests, Masetto and Zerlina as the peasant bridal couple whose wedding the Don tried to ruin. The first act ended with a festive party scene, dancing choristers, a band onstage, and sly jokes. But the opera's climactic scene was one of pure tragedy, with the Commendatore's cemetery statue coming to life to drag an unrepentant Don Giovanni into the flames of hell.

The singers stood by, helpless and confused, as Bondini and the librettist, da Ponte, had screaming arguments at rehearsals. Mozart was little help, procrastinating the overture until the night before the opening, keeping copyists working frantically to have parts ready in time.

All the singers suffered under accusations of incompetence and laziness. Teresa, the youngest of the Bondini company, agonized over all of this, fearful of losing her opportunity to create a Mozart rôle.

But at last, the premiere of *Don Giovanni* was to begin. The composer was on the podium. The Countess Zdenka Milosch, so they said, was in the audience. The instrumentalists' parts were on their music stands. The singers were ready.

Teresa had rouged and powdered her cheeks. Her hair was dressed in a towering coiffure. Her paniered skirts draped over a ruffled petticoat beneath a boned and embroidered stomacher. She carried a painted fan in one gloved hand and a lace handkerchief in the other, and she stood in the wings with the other cast members to hear the overture for the very first time.

The music began. Teresa leaned against a plaster pillar, pressing the handkerchief to her lips. Liquid notes cascaded from the strings and the winds, the oversize orchestra making a sound that penetrated her very bones. She felt it in her fingertips, in her eyelids, in her beating heart. She heard Donna Anna's music weave into the whole, as closely as the weft of a tapestry. There was the Commendatore's theme, presaging the fiery end of Giovanni to come. There was the persuasive, sensual melody of "Là ci darem la mano," when the Don would seduce the country bride, Zerlina.

Teresa's eyes opened. She didn't want to be seduced by Luigi Bassi, the Don Giovanni of this first production. Teresa Saporiti wanted to be seduced by—or to seduce—Mozart.

She peered out past the proscenium, where he stood at the harpsichord, sweat dripping down his cheeks to mark his black tailcoat with powder from his wig. He was a small man, and he had a profane way of speaking, but his mouth was tender and sweet. His hands were finely made. He coaxed magic from the orchestra with those hands, and worked miracles upon the harpsichord. His eyes, brown as chocolate and sparkling with humor, enchanted her. His laugh was irresistible, making even sour old Pasquale Bondini laugh with him.

And his music—his music was utterly, stunningly sensual. It made her thighs tremble and her belly dissolve.

Teresa Saporiti was nineteen, and she had never been in love.

Giuditta knocked gently on the dressing room door, startling Octavia. She blinked and sat up to look around the dressing room. Ugo still had not come. Her tea had grown cold in its cup, and the *panino* looked tired and limp on its plate.

"Signorina," Giuditta called softly. "*Maestro* is ready for the second act."

Octavia shook herself and stood up. "*Grazie,*" she called back. "I'll be there in a moment. I fell asleep."

The door opened, and Giuditta bustled in to take the tray. "Your tea has gone cold! Shall I make another pot?"

"That would be so nice," Octavia admitted. "I'm still tired from the flight."

"*Ma certo,*" Giuditta said in maternal fashion. "I'll make it now. You can carry a cup up to the rehearsal hall."

Octavia took a moment to reapply her lipstick and brush her hair. She accepted the cup of tea from Giuditta and carried it in her hand as she climbed the stairs to the rehearsal hall.

The cast and chorus were already assembled when she went in, and all eyes turned to her. She nodded to everyone, an apologetic hand at her throat. "I am so sorry, Russell, everyone. It was such a long flight yesterday, and I fell asleep in my dressing room."

Russell hurried to take her hands, to assure her she had not delayed him in the least. The chorus smiled at her. Lukas said something understanding, and Marie Charles dimpled. Massimo Luca gave her a limpid look from his caramel eyes, and she began to feel fully awake.

Only Brenda McIntyre, the Donna Elvira, frowned and looked

away, tapping at her score with thick fingers. Octavia took a chair near her, setting her teacup on the floor beneath her chair. "Brenda, I don't know if anyone told you, but I finished a run of *Traviata* in New York just the night before last. I feel like it's the middle of the night still."

The woman's face softened a bit, and she pointed at the teacup. "You should try some chamomile right after the performance," she advised, with a sanguine nod. "It soothes the body and the throat, and helps you to sleep."

"Oh, thank you," Octavia said. "I'll try that. I never thought of chamomile."

She picked up her score, hiding her irritation beneath an expression of contrition. Chamomile, indeed. Ugo would love it.

Russell tapped his music stand with his baton, and the pianist opened his score. He played the opening bars of the second act, and the read-through was under way again.

Octavia sat back in her chair, listening as the characters of Leporello and Giovanni and Elvira teased and flirted and raged at each other. When Masetto began to sing, she sighed with pleasure. Massimo Luca's voice was even more flexible now, fully warmed up, his tall figure already taking on his bucolic character. He stood with his lean legs apart, his head up, none of the usual chin-tucking basses too often employed. His eyes gleamed with pleasure in the music, in the responsiveness of his own voice, in the give-and-take with Marie Charles. Octavia lowered her eyelids, thinking that her own eyes must gleam as well. Perhaps it was just as well Ugo had not yet arrived. If he caught her staring hungrily at a toothsome young bass, she would never hear the end of it.

It's your own fault, Ugo, she thought. *He distracts me from my worry about you.*

When it was time for her "Non mi dir," she turned her body slightly, so that Massimo would have her profile to watch. She sang with all the tenderness she could muster, feeling those caramel eyes on her face. The long B-flat of the recitative floated in the big room, and she saw Russell nod and smile. She barely glanced at her Ottavio, but Peter wouldn't mind. Time enough when they began staging.

Russell kept the rehearsal moving, stopping only to deal with a few problems that cropped up here and there in the ensembles. By four-thirty, they had made it all the way through the show. The concertmaster, with a huge orchestral score under his arm, came to congratulate the principals and take his leave. The stage director shook Octavia's hand and assured her she would be a marvelous Donna Anna. She gave him a deferential smile. "Oh, I hope so," she said.

"*Sì, sì,*" Giorgio said, patting her arm in paternal fashion. "I have no doubts about you at all. You will be superb, and I will help you to develop your character."

"Thank you," she said. How Ugo would laugh!

Ugo's continued absence nagged at her. The sky beyond the tall windows of the rehearsal room had turned dark, and a fitful rain spattered the glass. He should have been there long before. He could at least have called the theater if he wasn't going to come, could have asked someone to bring her a note.

She gathered her coat and gloves, feeling piqued. She would scold him for making her worry. It wasn't fair, when she had her rehearsals to worry about, when she had Russell to make happy and this self-important Nick Barrett-Jones to deal with. Even now, Nick was making his purposeful way toward her, and she supposed there would be some invitation, some social thing she would have to beg off.

She was surprised, and pleased, when Massimo Luca reached her first.

He smiled down at her. He had a distinct cachet about him that reminded her of the smell of freshly turned earth, or new-mown grass. "Madame Voss," he said in his rumbling bass.

"Octavia, please," she said, laughing.

He made a slight, almost invisible bow. "Octavia, then, thank you. Several of us are going to dinner, and we would be delighted to have you join us."

Reluctantly, Octavia shook her head. "I am so sorry," she said in Italian. "I would love to come with you, Massimo—truly—but my assistant is not yet here, and I need to see what has become of him."

"*Che peccato,*" he said. "Shall I leave you the address of the restaurant, in case?"

She accepted a note from him, with the name of a well-known restaurant not far from Il Principe. "How nice of you," she said. "If I can, I'll come, but please don't wait for me. I have no idea what—" She broke off, looking up at the windows. The storm had begun in earnest, a noisy rain rattling against the panes.

"Could we at least drop you at your hotel?"

It was hard to resist the prospect of being in a car with Massimo Luca, but she shook her head a second time. "Russell will be taking me," she said. "We have some things to discuss."

Massimo gave her a regretful smile and turned to go. Octavia put a hand on his sleeve, finding his arm hard and lean beneath black leather. "Ask me another time, will you?" she said. It was delightful to look up at a man, to have to tip up her chin to find his eyes. Why were so many male singers short? Only the Wagnerians seemed to reach a decent height.

The young bass bowed to her. "*Ma certo,*" he said softly. "Octavia. I promise."

In the limousine on the way back to Il Principe, Russell pulled out his score and pointed out several details to Octavia. She listened and nodded, but by the time the doorman was opening her door and extending his arm for her, she had almost forgotten. She bade Russell a distracted farewell and hurried through the cold rain to the glass doors of the hotel. She barely nodded at the concierge's formal greeting as she hastened through the pillared lobby to the stairs.

She unlocked the suite and threw the door open. "Ugo? Are you here?"

She checked the bathroom, but only her own face looked back at her from the tall mirrors. She pushed open the connecting door to Ugo's bedroom. Nothing had been touched. She went back into the suite and looked at the telephone. No message light flashed on it.

She scanned her own bedroom, in case he had somehow fallen asleep on her bed or on one of the brocaded chairs. There was no sign that anyone except the maids had been in the room. The water in the flowers had been changed, and the fruit and chocolates neatly arranged on the coffee table. The bedcovers were turned back.

Pulling off her long scarf, winding it nervously around her hands, Octavia went to the window. She shouldered past the heavy drapes to look out over the rain-haloed lights of the city. The headlights of evening traffic blurred to streams of yellow light.

"Ugo," she whispered into the night. *"Dove sei?"*

Despite the richness of the room behind her, the heavy brocades and damask and silks, she felt cold and alone. She had not felt this way in a very, very long time.

She stepped back from the window, letting the drapes fall together again. She would order room service, have a long bath in the enormous marble bathroom. Perhaps she would drink a glass of wine and go straight to bed. The real work of staging and interpretation would begin tomorrow morning. She must try to remember Russell's notes, and she must try not to worry about Ugo. There was, in any case, not a damned thing she could do about it.

For the hundredth time, she cursed him for not telling her where he went, or who he met. She could not go to the police, nor to friends. There was no one to turn to except the elders, and she dreaded seeing them.

And in any case, what would she ask? Had they seen Ugo? Or had they seen the wolf?

5

Via.

Go on.

—Zerlina, Act One, Scene Two, *Don Giovanni*

Seventeen-year-old Teresa Saporiti flung open the door of her father's tiny stone house and ran out to the cobbled balustrade to lean against it, pressing her hands to her mouth to keep her father from hearing her sobs. Beneath her the blue waters of Lake Garda sparkled joyously in the August sunshine, mocking her torment. Behind her the voice of her father had gone still. The soft call of a black-necked grebe from the shore carried through the quiet. F and B. A distant part of her mind noted the tritone without knowing, at that moment, that the tritone would forever be connected in her mind with the day she left home.

Teresa pressed her hands to her eyes and tried to stem her tears. She couldn't let Babbo see her cry. He would think she had weakened, that if he kept trying, he could persuade her to stay. But she couldn't! She couldn't stay here in Limone, cooking and cleaning for her *babbo*. She didn't want to marry one of the boys who plied the fishing boats on the lake or tilled the vines in the hills, and cook and clean for him. She wanted to sing. She *needed* to sing.

She dropped her hands to her chest, pressing them against her breastbone. Her desire flamed there, in the very center of her. Her longing drew her away from Limone to the city, where there were theaters and orchestras and audiences. She loved her father, and she loved her home, but she loved music more. It wasn't enough to sing in the *chiesa* on Sunday mornings. It wasn't enough to sing for her father, accompanying herself on the little clavier that had been her mother's. It wasn't enough to sing for weddings and funerals and first communions and birthday celebrations. She needed the stage. She needed a larger audience, and she needed a higher level of music-making. She craved it with a physical passion that burned away even her guilt at the prospect of leaving her father alone.

When she had composed herself, she straightened and turned. She would go back inside, let Babbo say it all again, let him talk until he was empty. He would tell her she could never come back if she left, that he would disown her. She would beg him for understanding, but Babbo, bitter and resigned, would shake his head.

And then, because her nature and her need left her no choice, she would pack what little she had that was her own—an extra pair of shoes, two simple dresses, the books of music her mother had left her—and go.

The distance from Limone sul Garda to Milano was too far to walk. Teresa began *a piedi*, just the same, to save the small amount of money hoarded from her little singing engagements. She carried an ancient valise that had once been red brocade and now was a sort of faded rose beige. She hung a little string bag over her wrist, and into this she tucked the letter that would introduce her to the aunt of one of her friends. She was a seamstress who lived in Milano and who, the friend thought, might allow her to stay for a time.

All the first day Teresa walked, with the sun on her neck and the stones of the road grinding beneath her feet. She reached the village of Cecina at sunset. Footsore and feeling utterly alone, she found a *trattoria* where she carefully measured out enough *lire* to pay for a bowl of soup and half a loaf of bread. Men eyed her as she ate, and she pulled her hat down over her head to hide her bright hair. She stayed on, reluctant to leave the shelter of the *trattoria*. She was nodding over her empty bowl when the old *nonna* who ran the kitchen came to stand before her, arms akimbo.

Teresa startled and said, "Oh, signora! I'm sorry. I'll go."

The old lady clicked her tongue. She shook a shaming finger at a man who was leering from a corner, and then she put out a hand to help Teresa up. Teresa stood and was gathering her things to leave when the *nonna* said, "No, no. It's dark outside now. I have a place."

She led the exhausted girl up a set of narrow, bare wood stairs to a storage room. There was a pallet there, resting amid sacks of flour and bottles of olive oil. "My son uses that sometimes," she said. "When he works late. You can sleep there tonight, and no one will bother you."

"*Grazie,*" Teresa said. "Thank you so much, signora."

"*Prego.*"

Teresa fell onto the cot and was asleep before her benefactress had reached the bottom of the stairs. She didn't wake until morning sunshine found its way into the storeroom through a dusty window. She rose, used the privy, and went downstairs to find the old woman waiting for her with a packet of bread and sausage.

Teresa, her eyes stinging at the kindness, kissed both her wrinkled cheeks before she took her leave. She was already on the road before she realized she had never learned her name.

When she reached Gardone Riviera she found a man with an oxcart carrying a load of fish to Brescia. He was a grizzled man in his fifties who looked a bit like her father. He raised his brows when she approached him. After she asked him for a ride, he thought for a long time, scratching his thatch of gray hair. By some logic she could not guess at, he decided to grant her request, giving her a nod and a grudging, "*Sì, va bene.*"

Before he could change his mind, she pushed her old valise under the bench seat and climbed up to sit alongside him. He

snapped the reins over his ox's back. The ox, a placid brown creature nearly as grizzled as his owner, ambled off toward Brescia.

Teresa learned that the man's name was Giulio. He was brusque,
given to short answers when she spoke to him and aiming blunt
questions back at her. As they rattled and rumbled down the
road, he asked what a young girl like herself could be thinking of,
traveling with no escort. With flushing cheeks, she told him her
ambition.

Giulio gave her a narrow-eyed look. "A singer," he said with
disdain. "Everyone in Milano is a singer. What makes you think
they will want you at La Scala? Are you any good?"

Teresa's breath caught in her throat, overwhelmed for a moment by her own audacity. She had taken a terrible risk, surely,
made an awful mistake. And what if Babbo truly would not let
her come home?

But still she felt that need in her breast, that drive that could
not be suppressed. She blew out her lips in defiance and sat
straighter. She was a head taller than Giulio. She lifted the brim
of her battered hat and said, "I will sing for you, signore. Then
you may judge for yourself."

He snorted. "What will you sing, *ragazza?* A folk song? A lul-
laby?"

"No," she said firmly. "I will sing opera."

And so, as the oxcart clattered along beside the glistening waters
of Lake Garda, Teresa Saporiti gave her first performance away
from home. She sang Gluck, "O del mio dolce ardor," then Per-
golesi, "Se tu m'ami." Her voice rang against the rocks of the
shore and carried out over the water, blown by the summer
breeze. The ox flicked his ears back and forth, and Giulio flicked
his black gaze over her from time to time.

When she finished the second aria, she lifted her chin and
gave him a challenging look.

He surprised her by breaking into wheezy chuckles. His
cheeks cracked into a web of wrinkles above his beard. "*Sì,*" he
said. "*Sì, sì, sì.* You will be a singer, I think."

Teresa gave him a brilliant smile. She had passed her first audition in this unlikely place! "Thank you, signore. I must be a singer. I couldn't possibly do anything else."

"*Dimmi, ragazza.*" He settled against the slatted back of the seat, and let the ox's reins hang slack from his hands. "Tell me why you *must.*"

It was a long day's ride to Brescia. The aroma of fish wafting up from the cart bed grew more intense as the day grew hotter. The ox's tail swished back and forth, fighting flies. The waves broke gently against the shore as Teresa told Giulio of her mother's beautiful voice, her thwarted ambition, her illness. She spoke of life in Limone sul Garda, and how constrained she felt there, as if the small houses crowded together by the lake were a prison of sorts, a prison created by traditions and customs that had not changed in hundreds of years, that no one would allow to change.

Giulio said, "They say the people of Limone live a long time. Is that true?"

"There are several people in our village who have lived more than a century."

"But not your *mamma.*"

"No. But my mother wasn't born in Limone. She came from the Casentino."

"And your father?"

"He will live a long time, I suppose," she said, her voice soft and sad. "And he will be angry with me forever."

"He will get over it," Giulio said sagely. "And then he will be proud of you."

The hope that this was so stole Teresa's voice for several minutes.

When they reached Brescia, she tried to give Giulio a few of her precious *lire*, but he shook his head. "No, no, little Teresa," he said. "You paid me in song."

She thanked him and climbed down from the cart. Her legs

had gone stiff from bracing against the roughness of the road, and she stood for a moment stretching them.

"Teresa," Giulio said, scowling down at her. "Be very careful. There are men who would take advantage of a young girl on her own."

"I can take care of myself," she said as she tugged her valise from under the seat.

He growled, as if he were angry. "You think, *ragazza*, because you're tall and strong, you can deal with them. But I warn you—city men have their ways."

She smiled up at him, and pulled her shawl over her shoulders. "Thank you, Giulio. *Grazie mille.* I promise I will remember."

He picked up the ox's reins and clucked his tongue, whether at the ox or at her, she couldn't tell. The cart rattled away. She waved to Giulio one more time before she turned to survey the cobbled, twisting streets of Brescia. With her string bag on her arm and her valise in her hand, she began knocking on doors where signs informed travelers of rooms to let. After inquiring at various establishments, she found she could not afford to pay for even the most modest accommodations. Darkness was falling over the city, and her anxiety rose to meet it.

She bought fruit and cheese, and sat on a bench in the central *piazza* to eat it. She begged the use of the vendor's outhouse, and when she emerged, she saw that the nightly *passeggiata* had begun. Couples wandered arm in arm around the *piazza*. Families with children in tow called to each other. One or two single men eyed Teresa. She escaped their curious gazes by turning down a dark street lined with fine houses.

On an impulse, she began testing the doors of outbuildings and shacks. People were coming and going on the street, but darkness hid her. Her old boots made no noise on the packed dirt, and she stayed in the shadows, out of the occasional lamp-light that filtered through drawn curtains.

When she found an unlocked door into a carriage house, she

slipped through it and pulled the door closed behind her. The carriage house was dim, but she could see that a conveyance of some kind, a curricle or other light cart, rested with its shafts propped on blocks. Bits of tack and neatly coiled rope hung in orderly fashion on the walls. There were burlap sacks filled with something that smelled like oats or wheat, and empty sacks stacked beneath a small window. The whole place had the air of being ready to use at any moment. It was hot from the summer sun, but she supposed it would be chilly by morning.

Teresa was too tired to worry about being discovered or to do anything about getting cold. She felt her way to the pile of burlap sacks. Hoping there were no vermin hiding beneath it, she lay down and pulled her shawl and her cloak over her. She slept nearly as soundly as she had above the *trattoria* the night before. She awoke to voices in the street outside her little haven. She rose hastily. She tidied the pile of burlap, then, cautiously, opened the door to scan the street. Two workmen carrying shovels were just passing. She shrank back and waited until they were out of sight. Then, trying to look as if she belonged there, she marched out into the road with her valise in her hand. She turned toward the *piazza* and went in search of the stop for the Milano coach.

Once she found it, she spent a few precious *lire* for the privilege of sitting inside, away from the dirt thrown up by the horses' heels. She stowed her valise in the carrier behind the coach and went around to the passenger door. The driver was helping a frock-coated gentleman and a lady in a wide-brimmed, many-veiled hat up the high step into the interior. When he stepped back down, he eyed Teresa's dusty skirts and country hat, grinned, and turned away.

Teresa pushed the string of her bag up her elbow, gripped the sides of the door, and clambered up, kicking her skirts free of the step with some difficulty. She stumbled slightly as she achieved the passenger compartment.

The lady in the hat peered at her through her veils. She wore a traveling ensemble of muslin, with an exquisite quilted jacket topped with a ruffle of lace at the throat. Her feet, resting on a corduroy pillow, looked like those of a child. They were encased in soft pale leather with delicately pointed toes and a little sculpted heel. The scent of lavender surrounded her.

Teresa said tentatively, *"Buon giorno, signora."*

For answer, the woman emitted a deliberate, audible sniff. Teresa flared her own nostrils and realized with a flood of embarrassment that her own perfume was that of Giulio's load of fish. Her boots were spattered with the soil of the streets, and her cotton dress was hopelessly wrinkled. The lady's eyes assessed Teresa, taking in her drooping dress, her worn boots, her cheap hat. The gentleman also stared at Teresa, as unabashedly as if she were a piece of goods for sale, until the lady elbowed him and hissed something, and he looked away.

Teresa's cheeks burned as she settled herself on the opposite seat and tucked her bag beneath her feet. She took off her hat and laid it on the seat beside her with a pang of shame. It did indeed look forlorn when contrasted with the lady's confection of lace and satin. She did the best she could to smooth the long pale coils of her hair, her only wealth, then rested her head against the plush of the coach seat.

Her eyelids grew heavy the moment the coach rumbled out into the road. She had had no breakfast. The coach was poorly sprung, and the seats smelled of mildew. Still, compared to the fishmonger's cart and the bed of burlap, it felt like luxury. She folded her arms and let her chin drop to her chest. It had been a hard two days, full of uncertainty and discomfort. Teresa missed her father, and she missed the comforting splash of the waters of Lake Garda. Yet, despite her rumbling stomach and her loneliness, she fell asleep, and she dreamed.

Teresa's dreams had always, since her earliest childhood, been intense. Often she had difficulty knowing which was dream and which was real. The night her mother died, Teresa had been in the middle of a dream of being lost in a crowd of people when her father's wails woke her. She struggled up from sleep to realize that her little house was full of people—her uncles, their wives, the physician, and the priest. When she staggered through the dark into the light of the kitchen, she felt as if she were still in a nightmare.

For days afterward she couldn't shake the feeling that if she could only wake up, all of these people would go away and her mother would be alive again. She was eleven, and though she knew her mother had been ill, she had not expected this. She wandered through the house, expecting her mother's voice, her mother's willowy form, a glimpse of her unbound blond hair falling to her apron strings.

When she had been younger, dreaming strange and sometimes wonderful things, she tried to convince her mother they were real. Nuncia Saporiti laughed and tweaked her little daughter's braids. "Dreams!" she would say. "Trust your *mamma*, I learned the hard way. Dreams are never real. They have no meaning!"

The young Teresa frowned and wandered away. Surely Mamma could never be wrong—but perhaps Mamma didn't have the same dreams Teresa did. Perhaps because Mamma came from the Casentino, and not from Limone, and she didn't have the waters of Lake Garda in her blood. . . .

And now, drowsing in the coach from Brescia to Milano, with an unfriendly lady and a hungry-eyed man for companions, with the shocks of ruts and rocks jarring her spine, Teresa dreamed. She saw again her father's stricken face as she left, and in her dream she reached for him, but he turned away. She found herself on a wide stage, in a strange gown, a garment even more elegant than that of the veiled lady sitting across from her. Her hair felt heavy, piled on her head in loops and curls. There were other people, singers, wearing gowns and frock coats. Lights glared on their rouged cheeks and reddened lips.

The dream changed, and she heard her mother singing as she swept the stone floor of the house beside Lake Garda. Teresa, outside the house, leaned across the balustrade to take a peach from laden branches that hung low over the water. The fruit was soft and ripe, fragrant with sugar and sunshine. She parted her lips and sank her teeth into its flesh.

But it was not a peach she tasted. It was hot, and salty, with a bitter iron tint. She put her fingers to her lips, and they came away red with blood.

With a shudder, she woke. The lady opposite her snored gently, her veils lifting and falling with her breath. Her companion, however, was wide awake. He had lifted Teresa's skirts with the toe of his smooth leather boot and was gazing at her exposed leg. His parted lips gleamed with saliva.

Teresa jerked her leg away. *"Basta!"* she exclaimed. She bent to smooth her skirt back down over her ankles.

The lady awoke with a start and glared at both of them. "What's happening?" she demanded.

Her husband, for such he must be, Teresa thought, soothed her with quiet words, avoiding Teresa's eyes. But the lady sat stiffly, wakeful now, staring at Teresa through her swathes of silk.

Teresa turned her head away and gazed out the carriage window at passing fields of wheat. The ripe seed heads nodded in the hot sun as if bowing to the girl watching them. She put her fingers to her lips, remembering her dream. It was always good when Mamma came to visit her in her sleep. It was good to dream of singing, of what might be. But a peach full of blood . . . what did that mean? What was real?

Teresa Saporiti's first sight of Milano was of the lacework spires of the Duomo rising above the city center. The coach stopped in Via Mengoni, short of the Duomo's wide stone plaza. The driver opened the door. Teresa could hardly wait to be out, to drink in the sights and sounds of the fabled city, but she waited politely for the older couple to alight first.

The man stepped down. The lady stood up to adjust her ample skirts before leaving the carriage. While her husband was turned away, speaking with the driver, she faced Teresa.

"A word of advice, signorina," she said in a hoarse whisper.

Teresa got up from her seat, but she couldn't straighten in the cramped coach. She stood awkwardly, her shoulders hunched, her head against the roof. "Yes, signora?"

"Stay away from married men," the woman said. "People will think you're a tart."

Teresa, hot and hungry and tired, lost her temper. "A word of advice for you, then, signora," she said. She didn't whisper. She let her clear, strong voice carry outside the carriage.

The woman already had her gloved hand out the door for assistance down the step. "I hardly think I need advice from someone like you," she began.

Teresa interrupted. "Your husband wants watching, signora. He has a wandering foot."

The lady froze, and her veils rippled as her head swiveled back toward Teresa. Teresa said icily, "Could you step down? I'm weary of standing here, bent over like an old woman."

With a hiss of fury, the woman whirled, nearly stumbling over the high step. Her feet landed heavily on the ground, and she grunted at the shock of it.

Teresa gathered her things and followed. The last she saw of the couple was the lady marching into a nearby hotel with her husband scurrying after her. The driver followed with their bags, leaving Teresa to retrieve her own. She pulled it down from the luggage carrier and stood with her hat in one hand, her valise in the other, looking about at the bustle of the great city.

The Duomo's majestic spires pierced the blue sky, huge beyond anything she could have imagined. Workmen, looking no larger than birds, crawled over the cathedral's enormous roof. After three centuries, the huge church dedicated to Maria Nascente was still not finished, but still its glories were more than the girl from Limone could take in. She couldn't count the buttresses, the spires, the statues that adorned every surface. The structure dwarfed every other building she could see.

She turned in a circle, tasting the city's shape and flavor. *Palazzi* stood with churches at either shoulder. Most streets were wide enough for carriages to pass, with room on either side for pedestrians. Here and there were shops, fruit stands, a *trattoria* or two.

In the distance, the two stone towers of the old fortress, the Castello Sforzesco, loomed over the surrounding countryside. And much closer, just a brief walk north in Via Mengoni, she could see the square roof of the new theater, La Scala, completed just two years before. The old theater had burned to nothing, but the wealthy patrons of Milano had seen to it that the new one went up as quickly as possible.

She stood gazing at it, trying to absorb the fact that she was actually here. She had reached Milano, and La Scala was only a few steps away. Her goal was within her grasp.

6

. . . m'innamori, o crudele . . .

. . . you make me love you, cruel one . . .

—Donna Elvira, Act One, Scene Two, *Don Giovanni*

When Octavia's dinner arrived she ate everything. Sometimes during the rehearsal period she had little appetite, but she knew she would need her strength. She drank a half-bottle of Tuscan wine, finishing her second glass as she soaked in the tub, bubbles frothing beneath her chin. She welcomed the wave of fatigue that swept over her as she climbed out, and she tumbled into bed with a sigh of complete exhaustion. Surely Ugo would be waiting for her when she woke.

Tired as she was, sleep still did not come quickly. The melodies of the opera ran through her head, maddeningly. As usual they were not her own, but those of the other rôles, Zerlina's and Donna Elvira's and even Leporello's "Catalogo." When her eyes closed at last, the music was still playing in her brain, like a radio with no off button. She dreamed, and it was, again, of Teresa Saporiti.

Teresa and Mozart, panting, tumbled together onto a pile of cushions in the salon of the Countess Milosch. Teresa's head spun as much with giddiness over the success of the opera as with the wine she had drunk. She had laughed until she could hardly stand, had danced while Mozart played the Countess's excellent harpsichord, had dined on roast pigeon with new potatoes and sweet dumplings. She had stayed close to Mozart, longing to be near him, to possess this plump little genius of a man. She would not have dared to go further. But the Countess, with her burnished black hair and hard, knowing eyes, had managed to seduce them both together.

Zdenka was on Mozart's other side, pressing her lips to his throat. Teresa would not be outdone, but slid forward until her body covered Mozart's. Emboldened, she found his mouth with hers, tasting wine and tobacco and an oddly pungent flavor that was all his. She reveled in the kiss, in the movement of his lips against hers, in the thrill that ran from her toes to her throat. She was thoroughly drunk on success and excitement, and she felt at that moment she could have anything she desired.

Distantly, she suspected that it was the Countess's hand, not Mozart's, that crept beneath her skirts, that tore away her small-clothes to find her hot, yearning center. In a remote way, she understood this was a shared moment, that it was not only she, but Countess Milosch, joined with Mozart, possessing him, taking him in this moment of passion.

She didn't care. Her body flared, melted against Mozart, against the Countess's hand. When she cried out, she didn't know whose laugh it was that throbbed in her ear. She didn't know whose breath warmed her cheek, whose groan vibrated against her breastbone. But she knew, a moment later, that it was the Countess's teeth she felt breaking her skin.

The bite flooded her with feeling, a second orgasm of heat and pain and surrender. She felt faint, and at the same time exquisitely aware of every smallest part of her flesh, lips swollen with lust, eyes blind with it, skin tingling with shock even as her bones ached for more.

The Countess's teeth released her, and Teresa fell back against the pile of cushions, spent and shuddering. She turned her head to Mozart. His eyes were closed, his mouth open in a sated smile.

His neck was bleeding, but there was so little blood that it hardly seemed significant. Teresa put a shaking hand to her own throat. Her fingers came away smeared with red, but there wasn't enough even to trickle down into the fall of lace over her low-cut bodice.

The Countess chuckled. Teresa realized it was her voice she had heard. "Lucky little signorina," Countess Milosch murmured, her hand caressing Teresa's hip. Her voice throbbed with spent passion. "Lucky to have shared the tooth with Mozart."

Teresa sighed, and her eyes, like Mozart's, fluttered closed. She fumbled to find his hand, and clutched it. The Countess rose, shook her skirts back into place, and left them. Teresa pillowed her cheek on Mozart's shoulder.

It was Constanze's voice that woke her. Teresa struggled to open her eyes. The lids were gluey and resistant. Pale dawn light through damask curtains striped the rugs and polished floors of the salon. Constanze was shaking Mozart's shoulder, saying, "Wolfgang! Wake up! You're due at the theater!"

Teresa rubbed her eyes with her fingers, and Constanze glared at her, her small face rigid with anger. Teresa shrank back against the pillows.

"How could you let him fall asleep here?" Constanze demanded. She shook Mozart again. "He's supposed to conduct a rehearsal! And there's another commission that came in last night, the moment the opera was over, and he doesn't even know yet. . . ."

Mozart stirred at last, groaning, and Constanze tugged at him until he sat up, one leg still propped on a silk cushion, the other stretched out, toes caught beneath the legs of a French love seat. He pried his eyelids open with his fingers, and when he saw his wife, his infectious laugh bubbled out into the quiet salon. "Stanzie!" he cried. "Oh, Stanzie, wasn't it marvelous? The best yet. I could compose a dozen more *Giovannis!*"

"Oh, Wolfgang, I could just kill you!" his little wife shrieked.

Octavia Voss startled awake with the remembered sound of Constanze Mozart's furious voice in her ears.

She sat up, confused for an instant. No. She was not in Prague, but in Milan. Milan of the twenty-first century, with the wintry sun spilling through the drapes. Il Principe. *Don Giovanni.* She was Octavia, not Teresa.

Ugo!

She threw back the covers and snatched up the thick robe from the foot of the bed. She hurried out into the suite and across to Ugo's door.

It stood open, as she had left it the night before. He had not returned.

7

. . . m'abbandoni, mi fuggi,
e lasci in preda al rimorso ed al pianto . . .

. . . you abandon me, you flee from me,
and leave me prey to remorse and to grief . . .

—Donna Elvira, Act One, Scene Two, *Don Giovanni*

Ughetto woke naked and shivering, curled beneath an orange tree's drooping branches. He didn't know how he had gotten there. He remembered only Nonna's sour wine, and Luigi's strong arms carrying him toward the tub. Now the smell of oranges filled his nostrils, and the ground scratched his bare buttocks as he struggled to sit up. His thighs felt sticky, and when he looked down, there was something dark drying on his skin. It flaked off when he rubbed at it. Dark crescents had appeared beneath his fingernails. The perfume of orange blossoms mixed with some earthier scent he could not identify, though it seemed to come from his own body. He hugged himself against the chill. He didn't know what to do. He didn't know where he was.

He grasped one of the branches to pull himself to his feet. When he pushed out of his shelter, a little drift of white flowers showered his bare shoulders.

The rising sun had not yet burned away the morning mist. His feet brushed dew from the patchy grass. He looked about for some sort of habitation. The grove stretched into the fog, the ghostly shapes of the trees fading into the gray. Birds he couldn't see twittered among the trees.

His head ached ferociously, and the sour aftertaste of wine, bitter with opium, clung to his tongue. Not knowing what else to do, Ughetto turned toward the morning sun and crept forward.

When he heard the footsteps crashing toward him, his shaking legs collapsed, and he huddled, whimpering, on the wet grass.

It was Luigi's hard hand that plucked him from the ground, yanking on his thin arm and shaking him as a dog shakes a rat. *"Ecco!"* he grunted. "Found you at last."

Ughetto squealed and struggled against Luigi's grasp, but Luigi hauled him up and threw him over his shoulder as if he were no more than a sack of flour.

"Paid good money for you, lad, and you're going whether you like it or not," Luigi said.

Ughetto kicked his feet, once, but Luigi slapped the back of his thigh, a hard blow on his cold flesh. With a sob, Ughetto went limp.

Fifteen minutes' walk brought them back to the *villa*. Nonna had been waiting in the atrium, watching for them. She wore bandages on both her scrawny forearms, and she had a folded blanket in her hands. When Luigi set Ughetto on his feet, Nonna held the blanket out at arm's length. The boy stood, swaying, as Luigi draped the rough wool around his shoulders. Nonna, keeping her distance, shooed Ughetto into an inner room of the *villa*.

The room was small and bare, with a shutterless window that gave a view of the bay. One of the other boys was there, too, dressed and clean. His eyes seemed a little hollow, but his cheeks were pink and his short black hair neatly combed.

When Nonna shut the door, he came close to Ughetto's chair and bent to look into his face. *"Che successa?"* he asked softly. "Where did you go?"

Ughetto shook his head. "I don't know." He sniffled. "I woke up in an orange grove." He scrubbed at his tears with the heel of one hand and looked about him at the simple blackened wood furniture and whitewashed walls. A little fire burned in a grate. There were three cots, but only one had been slept in. "Where's the other one? The other boy?"

The boy straightened. "They won't tell me. He didn't come back, after." He backed away and sat on one of the black chairs. "I thought you were gone, too. I thought you died."

Ughetto's heart thudded suddenly as it all came back to him. He recalled the tub, the warm water, the surgeon's knife. He remembered screams, but he was sure they weren't his. His nose twitched at the memory of the scents of blood and poppies and fear.

He shivered and pulled the blanket tighter around his shoulders. He didn't want to look down at his body, to see what had been done to him. No one had told him whether he would look different, or simply be different. Forever.

"Do you hurt?" the other boy asked. He was older, perhaps nine or ten.

"N-no," Ughetto said, a little shakily. "I'm cold, and—" His tears threatened again, and he swallowed a sob. "I wish my *mamma* were here."

There was a little pause, and then the older boy asked quietly, "Do you sing?"

Ughetto stared at him, not understanding.

"Sing," the boy repeated. "Do you have a good voice? Is that why they chose you?"

Ughetto said miserably, "I don't know."

The other boy sighed and leaned back in his chair. "I don't know, either."

The other boy's name was Maurizio, but he said everyone called him Mauro. He and Ughetto stayed in the *villa* for three more days, sleeping on the cots in the small room. Mauro said Luigi and Nonna would keep them until they were certain they weren't going to sicken and die. Ughetto asked how Mauro knew so much, and he answered that there had been a *castrato* in his town, one who had suffered the knife, but never developed a voice. Mauro said the other men laughed at him, and the women sniffed when he passed them, and made jokes behind his back. He spent his life doing tasks no one else wanted to do, cleaning privies and hauling garbage, simply for the privilege of being allowed to stay in the town.

"That's what will happen," Mauro said glumly, "if we can't sing. There's nothing else for us to do."

"Why did your family sell you, then, Mauro?" Ughetto asked in a small voice.

"Same reason as yours. Money."

Ughetto wanted to protest this, to say that his *mamma* would never have sold him, but even as he opened his mouth to say the words, he understood that it wasn't true. The tavern brought in very little money, especially since his *babbo* had died. His *mamma* might have known no other way to support her family but to sell her little son. And for months now, his mother and his grandmother had behaved differently toward him. It seemed to him it had begun the night they had waited on the docks for the squid fishermen, but maybe it began when they knew they were going to send him away.

How could they do that, he wondered? Surely his *nonna*, at least, loved him. It had seemed so, before. But perhaps she had stopped. And if a grandmother's love could stop, Ughetto thought bleakly, then anything could happen.

The thought pierced his heart like the twist of a knife beneath his breastbone, a pain much worse than that between his legs. That hurt had already dulled to a distant aching. Mauro seemed to suffer much more from it. He winced when he sat down, and he moved carefully when he was on his feet.

Luigi and Nonna left them alone for the most part. They never examined them, never checked to see if their wounds were healing. They fed them well, bringing trays to the room, giving them clean clothes and warm bedding. On their last day at the *villa,* Luigi carried their dinner into the room and set it down, then went back to stand in the doorway. "Pack your things," he said. "We're leaving in the morning." He was gone, the door closed and locked, before they could ask him where they were going.

Mauro took his plate from the tray. "They're afraid of you," he said to Ughetto.

"What? Who's afraid?"

"Luigi and Nonna. They watch you as if they expect something strange to happen. As if they don't know what you might do."

Ughetto stared, dry-mouthed, at Mauro.

Mauro persisted. "Why do they do that? What happened?"

"I don't know," Ughetto said.

"You did something, didn't you? Before you ran out into the orange grove?"

Ughetto's voice rose and thinned, a child's plaintive tone. "I don't know," he said again.

"You must know!" Mauro said. "What do you remember?"

Ughetto gave a sigh from deep in his own small soul. "I remember the knife, and the water . . . and then nothing." He didn't want to talk about slashing at Luigi, and at Nonna. He didn't want to tell Mauro how the surgeon had fled, in case Mauro, too, would be afraid of him. He turned his head to hide his omissions. Mauro, though he barely knew him, was all he had.

Ughetto was glad, when morning came, to leave the *villa* behind. He and Mauro settled on a pile of straw in the back of an oxcart. Luigi and Nonna saw them off with smiles and waves, but Ughetto caught the weighted looks that passed between them as the cart driver whipped up his oxen.

As the cart pulled away, heading north on the road that wound from Napoli to Roma, Nonna picked at her bandages with her fingers and blew out her lips. She turned back to the *villa* before the cart had rounded the first bend in the road.

* * *

Ughetto, at eight, was the youngest of the twelve boys at the *scuola*. The oldest was seventeen, tall and slender, smooth of cheek and sweet of voice. He was called Leonino, the young lion, and he would soon be off to San Marco to sing in its choir. He strode proudly about the music rooms and the *salotto* with his nose tilted up to remind everyone of his importance.

The *scuola* sat on a pine-topped hill east of the city. It was an airy structure of stucco and stone, with a lavish view of the immense dome of St. Peter's below its sun-washed courtyard. For months Ughetto felt reasonably happy there. His longing for his home and his family subsided to a dull if persistent ache, felt mostly in the lonely hours of darkness. He slept on a cot next to Mauro's in the dormitory. There was plenty of fish and bread and olives to eat at long tables beneath the arbor of grapevines in the courtyard. He had no chores except his music lessons, which surprised him.

He was the smallest of all the students. There were boys already coming into their height, of course, the older ones, but even the younger ones were bigger, stouter, taller than Ughetto. He fell into the habit of hiding himself when the rest of the boys bathed. They all washed their hair and scrubbed their bodies in an enormous sink of marble, laughing, teasing, splashing each other. Ughetto waited so that he could bathe alone, even though the water was not so clean when everyone else was done. He didn't even bathe with Mauro.

Once Leonino, leaving the bath, caught Ughetto just coming for his turn. "What's this, little one?" he cried. "Afraid to take off your clothes with the rest of us?"

Ughetto shrank away from him, gripping the bath sheet around his middle. "I just—I don't like—" he stammered.

Mauro appeared as if from nowhere, stepping between Leonino and Ughetto. He wore a bath sheet as well. His chest was dark and smooth, and his arms already showed curves of muscle. "Leave him alone," he said to Leonino. "He's shy."

The older boy laughed. "Better get over that, little baby. None of us has much left to be shy about!" He stripped off his own towel and danced naked in a circle around Ughetto, cupping what was left of his genitalia in one hand and waving the towel in the other like a flag.

Ughetto averted his eyes from the sight of Leonino's mutilated testicles.

Each of the boys looked different. Some had little empty sacks hanging between their legs. Others had irregular flaps of flaccid skin that stopped at the very top of their thighs. Some, like Mauro, had nothing left at all, their surgery as smooth and effective as if the entire apparatus had been snipped off. Ughetto's fingers had told him that his own testicles were small and flat. He found them shameful.

Mauro said, "Go away, Leonino. Ughetto can bathe when he wants to."

Leonino danced away, wearing his bath sheet like a cape, snorting with laughter. Mauro folded his arms. His hair was still wet, dripping down his neck. "Ughetto. Do you want me to stay with you?"

Ughetto shook his head. "No, thank you, Mauro."

Mauro gave him a curious look.

"I'm sorry," Ughetto mumbled. "We just never—even in the sea, we were never naked."

Mauro grinned at him. "That's it, then," he said cheerfully. "It's because you were raised by women. We were all boys, and we swam naked in the river all the time. It was the only bath I ever had at home."

"But would you do it now, Mauro?" Ughetto asked, staring at his bare toes. "Now that—I mean, now that they—"

The smile left Mauro's voice. "Maybe not," he said sadly. "It was different when we all looked the same."

"I don't want people looking at me," Ughetto said.

"I know." Mauro turned to the door, saying over his shoulder,

"I'll bet you get used to it, in time. I'll watch the door for you till then."

Grateful and relieved, Ughetto waited until the door shut behind his friend before he laid the towel aside and went down the steps into the water.

An old castrato called Brescha taught the boys scales and intervals. He would often point to the dome of the Basilica and say, "There! See that, *ragazzi?* Work hard, and one day perhaps you can sing in the Cappella Sistina, as I did. You can follow in the footsteps of the great Brescha." He stroked his enormous belly, and his eyes grew distant. "They say they still speak of me at St. Peter's. They talk of my voice and my art."

When they were alone in the dormitory, some of the boys jeered at Brescha. They laughed at his spidery legs, the swell of his stomach, his quavering soprano.

Mauro never joined in the jesting. His eyes were shadowed when he listened to the old man, and his lips paled with anxiety. One day when they were alone, Ughetto touched his arm, and said, "Mauro. Are you so sure you won't be able to sing?"

Mauro gave him a bleak look. "I can't hear the scales," he said.

"Yes, you can," Ughetto asked, tightening his fingers. "I'll help you. They're easy."

"Easy for you," the older boy said. He shook off Ughetto's hand. "I hear you sing them, and your voice is true."

He was right. Ughetto's voice, a sweet, clear soprano, surprised everyone with its reach and its flexibility. The masters were pleased with him, and he was already beginning to learn turns and roulades, to study the patterns of recitatives and the simplest of arias. The more he learned, the more confident he felt. But Mauro . . .

"It might be all right for you," Mauro said then. "But for me—" He turned to stare down the hill at the city of Rome sprawling at their feet. "I can't hear the scales, and my voice is sour. No one will hire me. They will put me to work in the brothels," he said bitterly. "A eunuch."

"No!" Ughetto said. "No! You don't have to do that! I will take you with me, wherever that is. You can be my serv—I mean, you will be my assistant!"

Mauro turned his back. "I will be no one's slave," he said, and he stalked away, his shoulders stiff. Ughetto wanted to run after him, but Brescha called his name, and he had to go and take his lesson. The next time he saw his friend, they spoke only of casual things. Mauro never mentioned the brothels again.

It was only a few weeks later that Mauro disappeared from the *scuola*. Ughetto rose one morning as usual and found his friend's cot empty, its blankets stripped. Mauro's small possessions had vanished from the dressing table they shared.

Ughetto went to breakfast, hoping to find Mauro at the table, but he wasn't there. He asked Brescha what had become of him, but Brescha wouldn't tell him. He begged the other masters to tell him where Mauro had gone, but no one would speak of it. Their faces closed, and they turned their backs. They reminded him of Nonna at the *villa*, turning her back before the oxcart was even out of her sight.

When he was free from his lessons, Ughetto wandered to the courtyard to stare down the road toward the city. He had lost his home, his mamma, and his sisters. Now his only friend had left without a word. Or had been sent away.

He imagined Mauro would have said he had his music, that he should be content. But Ughetto felt freshly bereft. He wondered what else there could be for life to take from him.

8

Ma il giusto cielo volle ch'io ti trovassi . . .

But a just heaven willed that I should find you . . .

—Donna Elvira, Act One, Scene Two, *Don Giovanni*

Octavia showered, and vocalized, and ate the breakfast brought up for her, though it might have been straw for all that she could taste it. She dressed casually because today would be the first staging rehearsal. She wore a black cashmere sweater with a scarlet silk scarf around her neck. She pulled on a pair of lined wool slacks that gave her room to move, and she chose her most comfortable shoes. The rain still pattered against the windows. As she reached into her closet for her Burberry, she caught sight of herself in the mirrored door. She heard Ugo's voice in her mind. "Oh, *bella,* not that scarf!" She grimaced and went to the bureau to take out one in a neutral silver-gray.

Ugo had become the arbiter of her taste a very long time ago. She supposed she had come to rely on him more than was good for either of them. But after such a long time alone, she had welcomed someone who cared about what she did and what she wore.

As she ran her scales, he often would say, "Not so high this early!" She wished he were here to remonstrate with her now.

She moderated her vocalize as he would have wanted, saving the top notes for when they mattered.

She would mark the rehearsal, of course. It was silly—amateurish—to use full voice for staging rehearsals. When someone boasted that Callas never marked rehearsals, Octavia had to restrain herself from snapping, "Oh, yes? And how long did her voice last?" The sophistry irritated her. And it was a terrible example to extol to young singers.

She felt a faint stirring of thirst as she went down the stairs to the lobby, and a thrill of unease made goose bumps rise on her arms. She thrust the feeling aside, telling herself it was only anxiety over Ugo. She should be all right for days yet. Surely, sometime today, he would show up at the theater, grinning ruefully, telling some tale of getting lost, or meeting someone, or having forgotten to warn her he might be away.

Octavia leaned back in the limousine seat and watched the rain-drenched buildings of Milan spin by. Ugo had every right to disappear if he wanted to. Theirs was a relationship forged by unique bonds, and it was utterly voluntary.

But she had come to depend on him. She had abandoned the old ways and settled, with grateful relief, into the way of life Ugo made possible. She had begun to feel protected, in a way she had not done since her father's death, which was a very long time ago indeed.

Teresa had had no choice in the way she led her life. Zdenka Milosch, Countess of Bohemia, had seen to that.

Octavia closed her eyes, remembering the sharp features of her seductress. She had seen Zdenka Milosch only a few times since those early days in Prague. Except for Ugo, the Countess was the only person who knew Octavia's secret. Teresa's secret.

After that evening with Mozart, the night of the premiere, Teresa Saporiti had avoided Countess Milosch when she could, but it wasn't easy. At Signor Bondini's invitation, the Countess attended rehearsals and performances whenever she wished. The theater company depended upon her seemingly limitless funds and endless lists of highborn acquaintances. And Countess Zdenka Milosch liked keeping a close eye on her investment.

The Countess had an armchair set for her in the wings, from which she watched the entire second performance of *Giovanni*. As Teresa made her exit after the first scene, she rose from her seat and seized the young singer's arm. "Lovely, my dear," she murmured into her ear. "Passionate."

Teresa, still trembling from the drama of berating Don Giovanni and kneeling at the Commendatore's side after Giovanni ran him through, averted her eyes. She tugged her arm free with a muttered excuse and hurried to the cramped, dark dressing room she shared with Caterina Bondini. She had to walk sideways to fit her panniered skirts through the doorway. She pushed past the rack of costumes that filled most of the space, and sat down on the stool before her dressing mirror to stare at herself in dismay. Her face flamed with embarrassment, and her hair was falling out of its arrangement. She patted fresh powder onto her scarlet cheeks and repinned her hair. As she rose to return to the stage for her scene with Ottavio and Donna Elvira, she swore to herself that what had happened the night before would never be repeated.

As she stood in the wings, awaiting her cue, she looked past the proscenium and saw Herr Mozart beside the harpsichord. He played the chords for Masetto's recitative, smiling up at the singer. His cheeks were pink, his eyes bright as buttons in the flicker of the oil lamps. Teresa's heart fluttered, watching him, listening to the magic his small hands brought from the keys.

Teresa had not yet felt the thirst. That would come later. What she felt now was only hunger. She hungered for Mozart.

The limousine slowed, and Octavia Voss blinked, bringing herself back to the present. Even after all these years, these rushes of memory, detailed and vivid, undimmed by the passage of years, had the power to unnerve her. It was both the curse and the gift of Zdenka Milosch's bite. The sword of genius cut two ways.

The car turned into Via Filodrammatici and pulled up near the artists' entrance. Octavia stepped out of the limousine, remembering to smile at the driver and thank him. She glanced over her shoulder at the looming statue of Leonardo scowling at her across the Piazza della Scala. She frowned in return, drew a deep breath, tightened the belt on her coat. She must put aside her anxiety—and her memories—and concentrate. When the rehearsal was over, at the end of the day, both would still be there.

She nodded a salute to Leonardo, whose expression did not relent. She smiled and shrugged, and turned to go in through the glass door.

They spent the entire morning on the first scene, giving Octavia cause to be glad she had worn comfortable shoes. Nick Barrett-Jones could not, it seemed, learn his blocking. Again and again Octavia lightly sang her lines as she chased him out of Donna Anna's house into the imagined garden. She sang them at least half a dozen times before he could remember where he was supposed to go, which way to turn, when to stop and face her.

The rehearsal space was enormous, to match the stage, and it echoed with their voices and footsteps. There were as yet no real sets to work with, only a wood framework against one wall to simulate the noble house of Seville. Strips of masking tape marked the floor where the shrubs and columns and garden gate would be. It was to be a completely new production, from the costumes to the lighting to the set design. If only their Giovanni could manage to learn his staging.

Nick sang everything full voice, as well, which made Octavia's nerves flare. After the fifth run-through of the opening of their scene, she seized his arm and pushed him into position.

"There's your mark, Nick, dear," she hissed into his ear. "Stand still, for pity's sake, and let's get past this."

He grinned at her as if she had made an excuse to get close to him, and bellowed the first phrase of the trio. Octavia put a hand over her left ear to block out his volume and sang her own part *sotto voce*. Russell colored and winked at her from his perch on a tall stool beside the Steinway. No one else sang out. Even Richard Strickland, the Leporello, marked his aria, but this seemed to make no impression on Nick Barrett-Jones.

He should have been a tenor, Octavia thought wearily. *He has the ego for it.* Whereas Peter, her Don Ottavio, was as mild and unselfish as she could possibly wish, one of the nicest tenors she had ever worked with.

Only in the duel between the Commendatore and Don Giovanni did Nick Barrett-Jones show flair for the rôle. He was surprisingly good with the épée, wielding the sword with the ease of long practice. The staging of the duel went swiftly, and soon Richard lay on the floor, the Don standing over him.

"A fencer," Peter said. He and Octavia were standing to one side, watching.

Octavia nodded. "Too bad that scene goes by so quickly."

She could not escape to her dressing room at the break this time. One of the patrons of La Scala had arranged a luncheon for the principals, to be served in the airy foyer behind the *loggione*, the upper gallery. Russell took her arm as they all trooped out to the elevator and wound through the carpeted corridors.

"It's going to be beautiful, Octavia," he said.

"Thank you, Russell," she said. She felt the trembling of his fingers under her elbow. He was so highly strung, like a piano wire stressed to the breaking point. "I do hope so."

"I was sure your voice would be perfect for the rôle. Your high notes are glorious, of course, but your low voice is so clear. None of this muddy, choking stuff some sopranos have."

"I've been lucky," she said modestly. "I had a great teacher."

"Who was it? Did you study in New York?"

"Oh, no, I grew up in a tiny place no one ever heard of. You wouldn't recognize my teacher's name, I'm afraid."

"It's hard to believe this is your first Donna Anna," he said.

"Oh, well," she said lightly. "So many times in the studio, you know, and then I must have sung the arias dozens of times in auditions."

"It's not really the same, though, is it? I mean, with the staging, and the ensembles . . ."

"I was terribly nervous, of course, Russell. I still am, really. This is Milan, after all." She laughed a little. "Thank goodness they don't still throw things at the stage!"

"Only flowers," he said. He released her elbow and patted her arm with still-unsteady fingers. "For you it will be flowers."

They reached the door of the foyer, and Russell stood back to let her go ahead of him. The patron, a Signor Ammadio, hurried past the faux marble columns to bow to Octavia, lavish her with compliments on her Rusalka, which he had heard in Paris. She smiled, nodded, shook his hand and that of his wife and two of his friends. Nick came behind her, and the admirers shifted their attention to him, and then to Peter and Marie, Richard and Brenda. The alternate cast had also been invited, and the room was crowded. Octavia found Russell waiting for her at the buffet table, an empty plate in his hand.

The table was set with dishes of *antipasto*, the traditional *salsicce* and olives, freshly made *bruschetta*, a salad of tomatoes and *mozzarella* and basil drizzled generously with a vividly green olive oil. At the far end, a caterer in a white apron was dishing out *risotto alla Milanese*. "Signor Ammadio has been generous," Octavia murmured. Something in her stomach turned, and she bit her lip, wishing the nausea away. It was another sign of the coming thirst.

"Please, go ahead," Russell said, ushering her ahead of him.

Octavia picked up a pair of silver tongs and transferred two olives, a slice of cheese, and the smallest piece of *bruschetta* she could find to her plate. She took a little salad and allowed the chef to give her a small spoonful of *risotto*, hoping the rice might settle her stomach.

There were mirrors at the end of the room, and bouquets of

flowers in standing vases. A spinet piano was tucked into a sitting area. Octavia found a chair at one of the tables scattered around the room, set with flatware and white linen. A bottle of sparkling water was open in the table's center, and Octavia filled her glass and drank it down immediately. Russell joined her, and to her dismay, Nick Barrett-Jones, his plate heaped with salami and cheese and tomatoes.

Octavia let the men talk while she refilled her glass and sipped it more slowly this time. The bubbles felt good in her throat and in her stomach. Nick took a huge bite of bread and salami. "The food in London is never this good!" he chortled through a full mouth. "I love singing in Italy."

Russell ate more slowly, but with obvious pleasure. Octavia took a forkful of tomato and *mozzarella,* and put it in her mouth. The nausea didn't return. She managed several mouthfuls of salad, and some *risotto,* before her throat closed and she laid down her fork.

The chef was at her side in a moment. In Italian, he said, "Signorina, do you not like the *risotto?* Would you like me to bring you something else?"

She took a deep breath, putting one hand on her breast. *"No, no, grazie mille,"* she said, in the same language. *"Il risotto è perfetto.* It's just that I haven't been feeling very well."

He murmured another offer, and at her refusal, whisked away her plate, frowning over his uneaten creation.

Nick waved a piece of *bruschetta* in Octavia's direction. "You speak beautiful Italian."

She shrugged. "My first teacher was Italian," she said. "He insisted."

Russell nodded. "It's why your inflection is so good in the recitatives," he said. "And probably why it doesn't seem like your first Donna Anna."

"I coached the rôle thoroughly in New York, of course. I didn't want to disappoint you."

His thin cheeks colored again, and the tip of his nose reddened. "You would never do that," he murmured.

Nick got up to replenish his plate, and Octavia drank more sparkling water. She looked around her at the roomful of singers and admirers. Marie sat with Massimo, her head close to his as she chattered in French, gesturing with a salad fork. Brenda's table companions were Lukas and Peter, and Peter's partner David. They were speaking German. When Nick came back from the buffet, he grinned down at Octavia. "Good thing you speak English," he said. He laid down his full plate and pulled out his chair to sit down. "I sing them all, but I speak only one."

"That's brave of you," Octavia said mildly. "You've sung in Paris and Vienna and Rome, as I recall. Don't you speak a little French or German, at least?"

He made a dismissive gesture. "No. That's why theaters have managers!"

Octavia heard Russell's slight sigh of irritation. She avoided looking at him. She picked up her water glass and drained it.

Octavia was not in the next scene, and she had been scheduled for a costume fitting. Giuditta came to guide her to the costume shop, where the gown for Donna Anna hung on its dress form, an elaborate creation in the *robe à la française* style. Octavia smiled over its silver floral brocade and emerald green silk taffeta. The stomacher was an embroidered panel of silver satin, and as the seamstress fitted it around her, she murmured approval. The whalebone stays and busks of the past were long gone and unlamented. This costume, though it would be hot under the lights, was easy to slip into and would be light to wear.

The seamstress and the designer walked around her, pinching seams here, lifting hems there, chattering about alterations.

"You are so slender, Signorina," the designer said. "You will look like a dream. Over there is your mourning dress, but it's not yet ready to try on. It's been cut, but not sewn."

Octavia glanced over at the costume. It hung in disjointed layers of black velvet, black silk, and a rich plum brocade.

"Everything's beautiful," Octavia told him. "I love the colors."

He held up a hooded cloak of green velvet so dark it was almost black. "A domino," he said. "For the second act."

Octavia smoothed the material with her hand. She looked around at the dress forms holding other gowns, at the men's suits, the racks of choristers' costumes, all in jewel tones. The fabrics simulated the costumes of the late eighteenth century to perfection. "The whole production looks marvelous," she said. "I loved the sketches."

He smiled and bowed his thanks. The seamstress helped her out of the gown and back into her sweater and slacks, whispering admiration of the labels. By the time Octavia had brushed her hair and tied it back, and followed Giuditta back to the rehearsal room, Brenda and Nick and Richard had finished the second scene and were taking a break.

Brenda sat in a chair that barely accommodated her wide hips, fanning herself with her hand. Her round face was red, and her mascara had run, flecking her cheeks with black. Richard was at the Steinway, leaning over the pianist for a closer look at the score. Nick, with a white towel slung around his neck, lounged against one wall, while Massimo Luca and Marie Charles conferred with the director about their first entrance.

Russell laid his baton on his stand and beckoned to Octavia. When she came close, he said, "You can go home if you like. We won't get past the next scene, and you look a bit tired. Are you all right?"

"I'm fine," she said. "Although if you don't need me, I will go and rest. The costumes are gorgeous, by the way."

"Oh, good." He looked up at Massimo and Marie, and said, "Excuse me. I think they're ready." He lifted his baton, and the pianist struck the chords of Zerlina's and Masetto's entrance. Octavia stepped back, out of the sight line. Nick walked past her to join Richard for his entrance, but as he passed, he touched her shoulder with his palm.

She shuddered and pulled away. He gave a slightly embarrassed laugh. "My, my," he said in an undertone. "A little jumpy, aren't you?"

"Sorry," she whispered back. "I didn't know you were there."

He had no chance to respond. The director beckoned to him and to Richard and began walking about the set, pointing to their marks, posing to show them what he wanted.

Octavia turned away, resisting an urge to rub away the touch on her shoulder. It had been a silly reaction. Nick wasn't attractive, but he was hardly disgusting. There was no reason she should shiver at his touch. No reason at all.

Octavia stood once more in the window of her suite, gazing out into the heavy darkness. The rain had stopped, but beyond the tall windows of Il Principe the city streets still gleamed with it. Despite the warmth of the suite, Octavia felt she had never known Milan to be so cold. She tried to convince herself to eat something. She had eaten very little all day, and she would lose weight she couldn't spare.

Ugo, Ugo, dove sei? She rubbed her temples with icy fingers and stared down at the boulevards leading away from the Piazza della Repubblica. A chilling truth washed over her, insistent as the rain. If Ugo didn't come back soon, she would have to go into the streets, or . . . She shook her head and turned away from the window. She couldn't bring herself to consider the consequences.

She had first met Ugo on a dark, foggy night in San Francisco when her thirst had driven her into the streets.

She left the Palace Hotel very late at night, avoiding chance meetings with Caruso and Fremstad and her other colleagues who were staying in the same hotel. She prowled down Market Street toward the Embarcadero, hunting. It was late, and the streets were empty, but she knew there would be a few people in the Ferry Building, or in the plaza. She pressed on toward the docks.

Her very first sight of him had been on the footbridge span-
ning the Embarcadero between Market Street and the Ferry
Building plaza. He was a slight, dark figure appearing out of the
mist. His shoulders were narrow, and he was no taller than she.
He looked vulnerable.

She wore a heavy scarf tied under her chin that night, hiding
her bright hair from anyone who might recognize her from the
Carmen rehearsals. She was singing the rôle of Micaëla, and her
name was Hélène Singher, a young soprano from a French village so small no one could find it on a map. After endless auditions and multiple disappointments, Hélène had won a post with
the Metropolitan Opera's touring company, and she had been so
relieved that she hadn't considered how she would manage in
the western territories of America.

It was to be a fabulous production. Caruso was the Don José,
and the great contralto Olive Fremstad would sing the vixen,
Carmen.

But rehearsals were going badly. Caruso resented being sent to
a place he considered primitive and dangerous, and had complained incessantly on the long train journey from New York. In
San Francisco, he and Fremstad had screaming arguments. She
was a two-hundred-pound Wagnerian, and Caruso stood no more
than five foot eight. Their backstage clashes were as dramatic as
any staged before their audiences. The contralto's great bosom
thrust at Caruso's livid face as if she could crush the fire of his
temper with her flesh. The barnlike Grand Opera House rever-
berated with their big, angry voices.

Hélène had left the train in Chicago, driven by a desperate
thirst. By the time she returned to the station, her train had departed for the West without her. She caught another train, but
she was a day late arriving in San Francisco, and she missed the
first rehearsal.

She found the entire company on edge. Their first production,
The Queen of Sheba, had been excoriated by the press. Caruso, already upset by the recent eruption of Vesuvius and the rumored

destruction of his native Naples, swore he would abandon the cast if the quality of its performances did not improve. The company argued and fought its way through every rehearsal.

In the midst of this turmoil, neither conductor nor colleagues had any forgiveness for a young, unknown soprano. Everyone treated Hélène as if she were still a *comprimario*, as if she had been handed the plum of Micaëla by default. She felt thwarted at every turn.

Hélène had heard Bizet play the tunes of his opera in a *salon* in Paris. She knew what he intended in Micaëla's aria, but though she argued every point with all her energy, the conductor wouldn't listen to her.

Her costume, too, was a disaster, a concoction of gathered, printed cotton that turned her slim body into that of a dumpy Spanish peasant. The costume designer, like everyone else in the production, paid no attention to Hélène's pleas, and Hélène had no doubt that the diva had her thick-fingered hand in the matter. Fremstad's broad figure was impossible to disguise as the seductress Carmen. The contrast between her ample outlines and Hélène's slenderness would be anything but flattering.

A heavy silver fog had rolled in from the sea to obscure the waters of the bay. The stars disappeared behind it. The fog bell tolled every few minutes from Alcatraz Island, its deep gong slicing through the mist to reverberate off the bricks and cobblestones of the city streets. Hélène crept along the footbridge, hardly able to see where she put her feet. A gaslight at the end, where the stairs led down to the Ferry Building plaza, gave her a goal. There were always people in the plaza, even on a foggy midnight. She would find someone there who could slake her thirst, and then dash back to the Palace, hoping against hope that no one would see the young singer returning unescorted at an unsuitable hour.

The slender young man was leaning against the railing, looking out into the curling fog. His black hair, half hidden by a flat cap of gray twill, gleamed beneath the gaslight. He wore a well-cut jacket and slim trousers, with heeled boots. He seemed out of place in the midnight darkness of the Embarcadero. He looked like a schoolboy who had escaped his chaperone in search of some deviltry.

She stepped softly as she approached, thinking to surprise him.

When she was within five steps of him, he lifted his head and smiled at her. Even in the dim light, she could see that his eyes were as black as coal, and his features narrow and delicate. She pulled her cloak more tightly around her and allowed her lips to curl at the corners. Inevitably, such men surmised that an unescorted woman, late at night, was a streetwalker. For her, it was a useful assumption.

"Buona sera, signorina," the young man said softly.

Startled, she almost responded in the same language. She blinked and caught herself. *"Bon soir,"* she breathed, with her close-lipped smile.

"Ah," the young man exclaimed. "French, not Italian. Forgive me."

"De rien," she said. She came closer. This one, so slight and young, should be easy. The bandanna of silk he wore around his neck was loosely tied, and his collar fell open beneath it, baring his throat as if in invitation.

"You're out late, mademoiselle," he said. His wide smile showed very white teeth.

"Indeed," she murmured, moving closer to him. "The hour is far gone, isn't it? Perhaps you would like to escort me to the Ferry Building."

"Ah. Headed for Oakland, are you?" The fog bell tolled again, a deep, resonant tone that seemed magnified by the fog. The young man put out his arm for Hélène to take, and when she put her fingers on it, she felt thin, corded muscle through the gray worsted of his coat. A man in a tall hat and a long fur-collared overcoat came up the wooden stairs from the plaza just as they were going down. He eyed them disapprovingly, and pulled the hem of his coat away so Hélène's cloak would not touch it.

"You see," the young man said to Hélène, snugging her hand tighter beneath his arm. "That gentleman is convinced you're a soiled dove."

She tucked her chin so she could look up at him. "And what do you think, sir?" she asked demurely.

They had reached the plaza. Drifts of fog swirled beneath the gaslights, and the damp air carried the tang of salt and fish. Subtly, Hélène guided her companion to the left, into the shadows beneath the footbridge.

He followed her lead, but he chuckled as they stepped into the darkness. "What I think," he said lightly, "is that you look too clean and healthy to be a whore."

"*Vraiment,*" she answered, her tone as light as his. "Are whores always dirty?"

"In my experience they are."

"Perhaps you need to widen your experience, sir." She released his arm and turned to face him, standing very close so that her breasts touched his chest. The thirst was on her, driving her. Her lips felt hot, and her belly clenched with need. She lifted her hands to his shoulders and put her face close to his.

He said, "You're wasting your time, mademoiselle."

"Why?" Her voice was throaty, throbbing.

"I have no money."

"Ah." She let her fingers trail across his open collar, linger on his throat, just where the jugular vein throbbed its little endless dance beneath the fragile skin. He smelled deliciously of verbena and soap and tender, unspoiled flesh.

"Ah, but it's not money I need, young sir." Her voice was throaty, and her breath came quickly. Her upper lip swelled and began to retract. She couldn't stop it. She opened her cloak and moved in, pressing her body against his, putting her hand on the back of his head to bring his throat to her lips. She dared not wait any longer. She would lose control, drink too much. . . . And she had sworn to herself she would never do that again.

Her breath hissed in her throat as she bared her teeth.

The sound that came from him was no longer a laugh, but a growl, deep in his throat. His hand came up, slender but devastatingly strong. His fingers were hard as iron as he caught her throat just beneath her jaw. He thrust her back and held her at arm's length.

She felt the cold air on her teeth and knew that he must see them, the long, gleaming canines ivory pale in the darkness, their tips razor sharp.

His hand squeezed her throat, shutting off her air. That didn't matter. She could manage without air for quite a long time. But his other hand was drawing up her skirts, scratching at her cotton stocking, searching for that place . . . that one vulnerable place . . . digging in with sharp nails, tearing the fabric, probing for the artery's pulse.

She realized, with a shock, that he knew.

Desperate now, she gripped the back of his head with her hand and pulled at his hair, forcing his neck back, loosening his grip on her throat. The growling deepened. She pulled harder and felt that lethal claw against her skin.

With a strangled cry, using every bit of her considerable strength, she tore herself free. She stumbled back a step, and another one, one hand held out before her as if that would stop him. With her other hand she palmed her upper lip, forcing it down over her teeth. Her skirts, of their own weight, fell back over her torn stocking. She stared at him in horror.

Tendrils of mist swirled between the two of them, obscuring his face. For a moment Hélène thought she saw the red eyes of an animal through the fog. "What—what are you?" she said. "*Mon dieu!* What are you?" Her hand went to her aching throat, and she remembered, with dismal foreboding, that she had a *sitzprobe*, an orchestra rehearsal, in the morning.

His look of youth and innocence returned as the mist cleared, and he smiled, touching his perfect teeth. "Why, mademoiselle," he said. "It is not what I am, but what you are that is so very interesting."

"You tried to kill me," she said, her voice going flat.

"Were you not going to kill me?"

There was a step behind them, and two men, drunken, leaning on each other, staggered past. Hélène seized the moment to arrange her skirts, to wrap her cloak around her, to pull the hood well forward. When the men had passed, she stood very straight and looked into the black eyes of the strange young man. "I was not going to kill you," she said. "But I could have."

He raised one slender eyebrow. "Indeed?"

She turned on her heel and started across the plaza. The thirst raged dangerously in her, but now she would have to get away from this . . . this creature. He understood what she was, but perhaps it was not too late to escape exposure.

His footsteps pattered behind her. "Mademoiselle, wait," he said. "Tell me what you meant."

She stopped, staring at her feet, folding her arms. He was not going to let her go, it seemed. "Perhaps I should kill you after all," she said in an undertone.

He put out his fingers and tipped up her chin. His eyes were as cold as the waters of San Francisco Bay. "I doubt you could," he said.

She stared at him. "Stand aside," she said. "I have to go."

"To do what?"

"I think you know."

"But I can't let you do that," he said.

"Why not?" she asked. "If you let me go now, no one will have to die."

He gave her a boyish grin and said softly, "If you killed someone, I would not care. It's this other thing you do . . . I can't allow it."

A rage born of frustrated need surged in Hélène's bosom, and she shoved past him, forcing him to stumble back. A trio of people came out of the Ferry Building. She hurried toward them, past them, into the bright lights of the waiting area. A ferry had just docked, and a few people were disembarking. A yawning ferryman in a blue uniform stood at the open door, his wispy hair lifting in the breeze from the water.

Hélène glanced back over her shoulder, but she didn't see her tormentor. She dug into her pocket for boat fare, bought a ticket from the ferryman, and hurried onto the boat.

"Be a bit late," he called after her. "Because of the fog."

She didn't answer, but strode swiftly toward the prow of the ferry, where one or two other passengers lounged in the seats. She would find someone, anyone. And if she had to kill, it would be on his head. Whoever, and whatever, he was.

Octavia Voss sighed as the memory left her. She let her hot forehead touch the cold thick glass of Il Principe's window. It had seemed so awful, that San Francisco night in 1906. But it had been the best possible thing that could have happened.

The next day's rehearsals began at the top of the second act for most of the cast, while Octavia and Peter went off with the director's assistant to work on the Donna Anna–Don Ottavio duet from act one. As they left, Massimo Luca whispered to Octavia, "*Peccato!* I was hoping to see you this morning."

She smiled, murmuring, "Work, work, work."

"Perhaps we could lunch together," he said.

Now she chuckled. "You're flattering me, Massimo."

He gave her a boyish grin. "Not at all."

She and Peter followed the director's assistant and a pianist down one floor to a small rehearsal room, where their marks had been taped on the floor, and chairs and a couple of music stands had been arranged to indicate the set.

The pianist opened his score. "Would you like to sing it through once first?" he asked.

Peter smiled at Octavia, his round cheeks creasing pleasantly.

"I'd love that," he said. "I haven't sung 'Dalla sua pace' in weeks." He patted his chest. "I warmed up this morning, just in case. God forbid I should crack the G in Milan, even in rehearsal!"

The pianist laughed, and Octavia chuckled. She touched Peter's arm, warmed by his easy collegiality. "I feel just the same," she said, and nodded to the assistant director. "Let's sing it."

Fortunately, she, too, had warmed up before coming this morning. The intervals of "Or sai chi l'onore" were devilish, shifting swiftly from high to low, every word of text laden with emotion. Octavia had experimented, over the years, with different techniques, different interpretations, each production a little more nuanced, each performance shading this way and that, from the most dramatic to the most heartbreakingly lyrical. Her interpretation had changed substantially since Teresa, half trained and inexperienced, first undertook the part.

This morning Octavia poured her anxiety and loneliness into the music. She sang full voice for the first time since she had come to Milan, and the release of the soaring melodic leaps was a relief after controlling herself so carefully. She held back only on the sustained As, knowing there was a long way to go in this opera. If she gave too much too early, her second-act music would suffer. She had learned that lesson from unhappy experience.

And as always, when she sang Donna Anna, she remembered her own father's death. He had died long, long ago, but his loss was as fresh in her recall as if it had happened last week. The memory brought the throb of real feeling into her voice, the weight of true grief that never dimmed. It was a sorrow, she knew all too well, that few could bear. She turned to Peter, her Don Ottavio, Donna Anna's betrothed, and she sang Mozart's sublime music from her heart.

When the final A major chord sounded, Peter put a hand to his plump cheek, cupping it as if to comfort himself. His eyes were red, and his lips quivered. The pianist struck the D major chord for his recitative, but Peter choked, "Wait—wait a moment."

Octavia touched his arm. "Peter, what is it? What's wrong?"

He dashed at his eyes, and then he laughed. "Damn you, Octavia!" he said. "How am I supposed to sing after that?" He took her other hand and pulled her close to him to buss her on the cheek. "Divine," he murmured. "Absolutely divine. *Brava!*"

The sincerity of the compliment made Octavia's own eyes sting, and she blinked furiously. This would never do. Only with Ugo could she let her guard down in such a way.

She drew away from Peter, smiling. "You are too kind, my friend. Thank you so much. I'm encouraged! Now come, carry me away with your 'Dalla sua pace.'"

He returned her smile a little ruefully. He rubbed his pink hands together, cleared his throat, and nodded to the pianist. The D major chord sounded again.

Octavia closed her eyes to listen to Peter's clear, sweet tenor as he began the recitative.

There had been no "Dalla sua pace" in that first production. Antonio Baglioni, the first Ottavio, had had to make do with "Il mio tesoro," in the second act. Teresa had listened from her dressing room, that first performance after the bite.

Teresa stared at herself in the dim glass as she listened to the aria. A small oil lamp flickered among the jars of powders and creams. The petals of drying flowers dropped here and there on her makeup table. Antonio's slightly nasal tenor drifted from the stage as she brushed a little fresh powder on her nose and trailed her fingers over the skin of her throat.

It was the oddest thing, the swiftly fading marks there. She had been intoxicated with wine, with triumph, and especially with the closeness of Mozart that night. She knew the Countess had closed her mouth on her neck, but she could not remember feeling pain. It had not been frightening, but sensuous; not disturbing, but deliciously wanton. She had felt, that night, that she could do anything she wanted to do, have anything she craved, and no one would criticize.

She was weary of criticism. She knew Signor Bondini was

pleased with her appearance—everyone teased her about her figure, and even Mozart called her *il piatto saporito*, a tasty dish—but Bondini was never satisfied with her singing.

The marks of the Countess's bite were half a thumb's length apart, more deep than wide. They were scars of the tooth, and they shook her composure and troubled her dreams. When she touched them, a wave of heat swept up from her belly to her cheeks. Her upper lip pulsed, as if bruised.

What was this? she wondered. Lust, yes. Her yearning for Mozart had not abated. Rather, it was as if their brief night together had stoked the flames of her desire, so that its heat flared through her body. Even now she could hardly wait to be back onstage, looking down at his compact figure, his fine hands on the harpsichord, his merry dark gaze turned up to the singers.

But it was more than that. Something primal had happened to her, something that burned in her blood as well as her mind.

The tenor's aria was coming to an end, and she rose to take her place for her final entrance. At the last moment, she seized the ewer waiting on a side table and poured herself a cup of water. She drank it greedily, nearly choking in her haste.

Thirst, she thought. That was what had changed. It was as if Zdenka Milosch's bite had parched her, stolen every bit of moisture from her body. She had drunk water, wine, even beer in an effort to soothe her burning throat, but it seemed to Teresa Saporiti that there was not enough liquid in the entire world to satiate her thirst.

9

Il scellerato m'ingannò, mi tradì!

The villain deceived me, betrayed me!

—Donna Elvira, Act One, Scene Two, *Don Giovanni*

The Fiat raced through the center of Milan, turning again and again down the short streets, moving too quickly for Ugo to read the street names mounted on the sides of the buildings. He caught sight of a restaurant he recognized, Iris, which he knew was in the center of the city. He turned his head just in time to see the ancient wall fragment that marked the center of Piazza Missori. Floodlights shone on its blind arches and illuminated the silhouettes of a few late-night passersby. In the distance the Duomo rose, its thicket of spires glittering with fairy lights. The car rounded a corner and shot past the circular wall of San Satiro on its way north. It slowed as it nosed its way into one of the dark neighborhoods, where apartments and shuttered shops clustered together as if to protect themselves from the intrusions of progress.

Domenico saw Ugo peering out at the streets, and laughed. "It will do you no good to look," he said complacently. "Where we're going no one will find you."

Ugo leaned back against the seat. *"Che peccato,"* he said lightly. "I would have liked to share your charming company with one or two friends."

Domenico grinned. He was not a bad-looking man, Ugo thought, though a bit sallow. He had crooked teeth, and he wore his brown hair a bit long, making him look foppish. But it was nice that his voice was good. Ugo was sensitive to voices.

"I suspect," Domenico said, "that being a friend to Ugo is a dangerous thing."

"You will learn that for yourself very soon, signore," Ugo said. He favored Domenico with his most winning smile.

"Oh, I think I'll be all right." Domenico held up Ugo's package, which he had ripped from his hand as his two thugs—Società hopefuls, Ugo had no doubt—forced him into the backseat of the Fiat. "I'll just take care of this for you, shall I?"

Ugo raised his eyebrows. He purred, "Do you think that's wise, my friend? You're playing about in something you don't understand."

Domenico thrust the package inside his coat and narrowed his eyes. "I understand more than you think, Ugo," he said, putting an unpleasant inflection on the name. "Stories of your little— What shall we call them?—Mutations, perhaps—have reached me." He buttoned his coat and patted the slight bulge made by the *strega*'s carefully wrapped bundle. "We'll have no trouble with that, though, will we?"

An utter fool. But it was not the first time someone had miscalculated the *lupo mannaro*.

The man in the front passenger seat turned sideways to look over his shoulder at Ugo. He was pitifully young, Ugo thought. His burnt-ginger hair was clipped to his scalp. He had the burly shoulders and thick neck of a bodybuilder, a type of narcissism Ugo particularly detested. There was no intelligence in his pale-lashed eyes, only that old, familiar hunger. Seeing it filled Ugo with ennui.

He put his head back against the cracked vinyl of the seat and sighed theatrically. "Tell me, my new and unexpected friends," he said in a silky tone. "What is it you want of me? It can't be my little purchase there. There must be some service you think I can perform for you."

He rolled his head to face Domenico and let his eyelashes drop suggestively. He let his Italian accent thicken. "Perhaps you have a taste for *la bestia*."

Domenico shook his head. "I prefer not to speak Italian."

"Truly? And yet your name . . ."

Domenico laughed, and his strong voice echoed in the cramped confines of the little car. "I'm not stupid, Ugo. My real name is a private matter."

Ugo chuckled. "I will not argue the question of your intelligence, signore. *La bestia*—the beast—I thought perhaps your appetites inclined in that direction."

Domenico ignored this. The driver of the Fiat was nearly as youthful as the ginger-haired man, but bald as an egg. He wore a tasteless array of earrings that made him look, Ugo thought, like an advertisement for an American cleaning product. Ugo remembered, now, where he had first seen this man, and the memory filled him with fury.

The driver swung the little car into a shadowed entryway and braked abruptly just in time to avoid crashing into a scrolled-iron gate. Beyond the gate was a small courtyard, one of the surprising hidden spaces one found sometimes in Milan, with shrubs and a lovely old cedar growing in the center.

Domenico glanced ahead, through the windshield, and said, "We're here. Marks, you get out and lock the gate behind us. Benson, park over there, behind the tree."

"Benson," Ugo murmured. "We've met before, haven't we? New York, I believe. Battery Park, wasn't it? How nice to see you again."

Benson grinned. "The pleasure's all mine," he said.

"I was a little disappointed, though," Ugo said as Domenico opened the door and waited for him to climb out. "Your product turned out to be inferior. I intended to let you know. I had no doubt you would make good on my loss."

"Gonna make real good," Benson said. Ugo shuddered at the grammar but kept a smile on his face.

Domenico put his hand under Ugo's arm and directed him toward a basement entrance. "We're going to have a little fun, Ugo."

"Veramente," Ugo murmured. "I am sure we will."

He shook off Domenico's restraining hand as they went through a narrow door. He thrust his hands in his pockets and affected a casual air as they waited for the elevator, a grim affair of steel and linoleum. Domenico punched a button, and the elevator descended, depositing them in a subterranean corridor that was even grimmer, with a cement floor and walls that might once have been white but were now a sort of hopeless dun shade. At the end of the corridor was a locked door, which Domenico opened with a skeleton key. He locked it again when they were inside, evidently shutting the redoubtable Marks and Benson out.

"Such charming accommodations," Ugo said.

The room was little more than a shoebox, with a steel-spring cot in one corner that held the thinnest of ticking mattresses, a toilet and sink that looked as if they might fall off their fixtures at any moment, and a fly-specked light fixture depending from the cracked ceiling. The room smelled of moldy cement, with a whiff of something that might have been urine, or might have been the wine that had apparently been spilled in one corner and left to desiccate.

Domenico laughed. "You don't need to stay long, Ugo. Simply tell me what I want to know, and you can be off to whatever odd little activity you had planned tonight."

Ugo stepped into the middle of the narrow room and turned to face his captor. He shrugged and held his hands out, palms up. "Since you brought me to this cozy *camerino* to ask your questions, rather than simply inviting me out for a *cappuccino*, I assume that what you want to know will be something I won't want to tell you."

Domenico nodded. "It's true, I'm afraid." He reached into his pocket and brought out a small coil of gray nylon cord. "I prefer not to hurt you, if I can avoid it." He held up the cord, and though his face was solemn, his eyes glittered with something like anticipation.

Ugo allowed himself a visible shiver. "I simply loathe pain, *mio amico*. Like you, I would prefer you not to hurt me."

Domenico began to pay out the cord, nodding toward the cot. "Just move over there, if you would, please," he said.

"Oh," Ugo said lightly. "I don't think so, thanks."

"Have it your way. I'll get Marks and Benson in here to help, if I need to."

"Well, yes," Ugo said. "I think you do need to, actually. I hate being tied down nearly as much as I hate pain."

Domenico took a step toward the door, but before he could reach it, Ugo had leaped to block his path. "Truly, my friend," he said, "I hate being tied down." He put out his hand and gripped Domenico's wrist. His accent flattened, and the focus of his voice fell back in his throat, the voice of an American born and bred. "And I hate being toyed with. What do you want, man? Tell me what it is, and maybe neither one of us will have to get hurt."

Domenico pulled back. Ugo held on, his fingers biting into the other man's skin. He knew it must hurt, but Domenico gave no sign.

Ugo smiled up at him. "Very good. You tolerate pain. How much, I wonder?"

Domenico's eyes narrowed. "Tell me how to find them," he said in a low tone.

Ugo widened his eyes in his most innocent manner. "Find who?"

His adversary was having none of it. "You know who. The elders. La Società."

Ugo released Domenico's wrist with a flare of his fingers. He pressed his hand to his chest. "*Gran Dio*, Domenico! You can't be serious. They would destroy you in a heartbeat! I can't have that happen to my new friend."

Domenico leaned toward him, his lip curling. "I'm completely serious, of course. You must know that by now." His breath was sour, and Ugo knew he was hiding nerves. "I've risked everything to get this information," Domenico said. "And I mean to have it."

Ugo closed his eyes for a moment, shaking his head. "My friend, my friend," he said. "You have no idea what you're asking. I wouldn't want you to—"

Domenico kept his eyes fixed on Ugo's face as he shouted, "Benson! Now!" His voice was deafening in the tiny room with its cement walls and uncarpeted floor.

Ugo heard the rattle of the lock, and the door swung open. Marks stood outside, a witless grin on his face. Benson, bald head shining with sweat, sidled in, a small, flat case under his arm. Ugo gritted his teeth. He could guess the wicked instruments it would hold: pliers, possibly syringes, if this Domenico was truly inventive. Certainly it would hold knives.

He was haunted by things that cut, he thought. He had been bedeviled from the start by fools who thought they could bend his will to theirs by applying a sharpened blade.

He would much have preferred not to spend another moment in this room, with these particular tormentors. But until the *strega*'s herb wore off—or until the pain was intense enough to defeat it—he was stuck with them.

He sighed, shrugged, and sauntered across the room to the cot.

Benson, evidently disappointed at the ease of his submission, followed, and struck him between his shoulder blades with a hamlike fist. Ugo sprawled in ignominious fashion to the floor, catching his cheekbone on the edge of the metal frame. Benson laughed, and Domenico snapped at him, "Just get the answers, Benson. And be quick about it."

10

. . . un altra sorte vi procuran . . .

. . . another fate awaits you . . .

—Don Giovanni, Act One, Scene Two, *Don Giovanni*

He found it a relief to leave Benson with his victim in the basement room. He had no problem with violence, of course. It was the indignity of having to stoop to such tactics that offended him. It was distasteful. And messy. He hated getting his hands dirty.

In a perfect world, it would all be done for him, out of respect.

Ugo was right, of course, about Benson and Marks. They were cretins. Idiots. They were unsuitable in every way. They would never be allowed into the society.

But he—surely he, when the elders understood what it was he really wanted—he would win their acceptance. His special gifts should be considered an asset. And when he had found the one—the one who had shared the tooth with Mozart—his gifts would be prodigious.

He disdained riding in the Fiat again. He walked a couple of blocks on the narrow, uneven sidewalk until he reached one of the boulevards, where traffic moved no matter what the hour. He flagged a taxi and gave the address of his hotel, then sat back, watching the early morning lights of Milan flicker on as the taxi rocketed up the Corso Venezia, swung left, and ground to a stop in front of the Westin Palace Hotel. The night doorman hurried out, yawning, to open the door for him. *"Buona sera, signore."*

"Indeed," he answered. He stripped off his jacket as he walked through the lobby, thinking he might just throw it away. It seemed to have soaked up the smell of that basement room, and he didn't want to think about what was happening there right now.

In his room, he stripped and stepped into the shower to stand under a stinging stream of hot water for several minutes. He needed to sleep, of course. There were still a few hours left for him to rest. But the book called him, even now.

He wrapped himself in the thick white hotel bathrobe and went to the desk drawer where he had hidden it. He made sure his hands were completely dry before he pulled it out and began to fold back the moleskin wrappings.

The old witch had written it in Latin, and he had retained no more than a few words of that language from his public school classes, despite the relentless drilling by his Latin master. But it hadn't been hard to find people who could not only read Latin, but decipher her spidery handwriting.

He congratulated himself on the care he had taken in asking for translations. He had photocopied the fragile old pages and presented them in unrelated segments to his scholarly contacts, so that none of them could put the greater picture together. When they asked about the context, about the source material, he had had vague answers ready, mentions of research, of a possible book deal, even of a long-forgotten family connection.

But the book itself, even though it was illegible to him, had mystical power. It represented his deepest desire. It had ignited a longing in him that overwhelmed all his conditioning. He had learned of the society inadvertently, a secret whispered in underground circles where deviants gathered to intoxicate themselves, to medicate themselves with drugs and sex. He had followed the rumors, found the group of hopefuls, men of the likes of Benson and Marks, who thought they could win immortality. The book itself had been a surprise, a serendipitous discovery.

The ancient was furious, of course. One of his contacts, a limp little man with thinning hair and round, anxious eyes, had died of her rage. But it had been too late. He had the book in his possession, and he would have died himself rather than give it up.

He let it fall open, taking care with its brittle parchment. He had pored over the translations until he had committed them to memory. It was a journal of sorts. A diary of atrocities. And when Mozart appeared in its pages, he knew what he had to do.

He forced himself to close the book, stroking its cover with fingers reluctant to leave it. He wrapped it again in the moleskin and bound it with ribbon. He put it back in the drawer, hiding it under a stack of shirts. He shrugged out of the bathrobe and made sure the drapes were closed against the rising sun and the alarm set before he lay down. He pulled the blankets up to his chin and closed his eyes.

Sleep didn't come at once, but as he had for years now, he recited the words of the book silently to himself. He resolutely refused to think of the basement room, of the hapless Ugo in the hands of that brainless Benson. Thinking about it only inflamed him with impatience.

Instead, he repeated the mantra of the Countess's journal until, at length, he slept.

11

Vorrei, e non vorrei; mi trema un poco il cor.

I want to, and yet I don't; my heart trembles a little within me.

—Zerlina, Act One, Scene Two, *Don Giovanni*

Ughetto mourned for Mauro, but he carried on with his daily lessons with Brescha, with the harpsichord master, with the dancing master and the language tutor. Praise was hard to come by at the *scuola*, but Ughetto knew, by the knowing nods his teachers gave each other, that he was doing well. They began to allow him to go with them and the older boys into the city for private concerts in the *villas* and *palazzi* of Roman noblemen. Ughetto heard the music of Jacopo Peri, and of Monteverdi. He marveled at the daring new form, *dramma per musica*. A performance of *L'Orfeo* brought him to tears, and left him speechless with admiration when he was presented to the composer after the concert.

Ughetto excelled in his diction classes. His turns in the galliard pleased the dancing master. The scales and harmonizations on the harpsichord came easily to him. And he sang with increasing joy, this boy who had known no music but Sicilian folk songs. He waited through three solid years of vocalizes before Brescha allowed him real music. Then, with the other students, he sang madrigals and motets, and before long he was given three short *da capo* arias to sing by himself.

The experience was a revelation. The thrill of hearing his own voice carrying the melody, imparting the emotion of the text through his own artistry, finding the affect and the phrasing and the intent of the music with his own skill, was like nothing he had ever experienced.

When the *scuola* held a private recital for a few invited guests at the end of the summer, he was allowed to sing one of his arias, "Se tu m'ami," with Brescha accompanying him on the harpsichord. He had arranged a little surprise for his teacher, a cadenza at the end which he had worked out all on his own. Brescha's heavy cheeks reddened with pleasure when he heard it, and Ughetto felt a surge of pride.

He found himself wishing his *mamma* and his *nonna* could hear him, but he repressed the thought the moment he recognized it. Every boy at the *scuola* had been similarly sacrificed. They were the lucky ones, because they could sing. Poor Mauro had lost everything.

The day of Ughetto's twelfth birthday arrived and passed unremarked. He didn't mention it to anyone, but he was fairly certain he knew the day. Between lessons he wandered out behind the *villa* and scrambled up the slope beyond it, ducking under the low-hanging branches of the pine trees that grew there. A medieval ruin of tumbled stone and brick crowned the hill. Ughetto climbed to the highest point, a bit of broken wall that had no doubt once been a tower, with a commanding view of the city below and the harbor to the west.

Ughetto sniffed, trying to detect the salt air of the sea beneath the pungent scent of pine forest but having no success. Closing his eyes, he attempted to recall the smells that had colored his childhood: the seaweed-strewn beaches; the sour wine smell of the tavern when he and his sisters went to clean it in the mornings; the rich scent of his *mamma*'s fava bean soup, thick with wild fennel and spiced with red pepper. For one moment only he had the memory, and held it. When it dissipated he sighed and opened his eyes.

For a long time the pain of Mauro's absence had been sharp, nearly unbearable. After a year or so the pain had begun to dull, though it left a bruise on Ughetto's youthful soul. The ache of missing his home and his family was almost gone, buried under layers of experience, of music, of new acquaintances, new knowledge about clothes and comportment and the intricacies of society.

And now, he was twelve. His loneliness was a hard, constant knot, deep in his belly, that never loosened. Music was his consolation. It was ubiquitous, a constant element in his daily life. Harmonies filled the modest courtyard of the *villa*, runs and roulades twined through the drooping grapevines, and the old olive tree in the courtyard seemed as redolent with melodies as it was with the firm black olives that dropped into the boys' hands at harvest time.

On a September day, when the Mediterranean sun blazed on the white stucco of the *scuola*, making the courtyard too hot to sit in, Brescha called for Ughetto to come into the little *salotto* where he taught his voice lessons.

Brescha drew himself up, stroking his great belly with a veined hand, posing beside the harpsichord. "Ughetto," he said. "I have had a letter from the Capella." He paused, letting his eyes stray to the window and the distant silhouette of the dome of St. Peter's.

Ughetto suppressed a groan. Brescha had a weakness for dramatic pauses.

He waited, giving Brescha his moment, before he prompted, "Yes, Maestro?"

Still staring down at the symbol of his lost career, the old *castrato* said, "How old are you now, Ughetto? Twelve, I believe."

"Yes."

Brescha turned slowly to face him, looking down the slope of his great nose as if he were Pope Gregory himself peering from his ambo. "You're a very lucky boy," Brescha said.

Ughetto blinked. "Am I, Maestro?"

Brescha breathed through his nose, swelling his chest and his belly. "You are," he said. "My old friend, who is now the choir-master at St. Peter's, came to our little recital last week. And now, you—you, Ughetto, at only twelve—have been invited to sing with the Capella Sistina. A piece by a new composer named Alle-gri. A great honor."

Ughetto tipped his head to one side and peered up at the singing master. "A solo?"

Brescha tossed his head. He put his hands on his hips and snapped, "Already such ego, and you have not even sung in pub-lic! Does it matter whether you sing a solo or simply as part of the *coro?*"

Ughetto let his long black lashes drop modestly to his cheeks. "Of course it matters, Maestro. I am *your* student. I take your reputation with me wherever I go. Should a student of the great Brescha sing in the chorus?"

Brescha snorted and turned again to look down the hill at the dome of St. Peter's, linking his hands behind him. "You're a scamp, Ughetto," he said. "But as it happens, you are correct. It's a *Miserere*, written for nine voices, one group of five and one of four. You will sing the high part in the smaller group, because you have the notes. The piece isn't finished yet, but it's to be ready for All Souls in the autumn. You'll have enough time to learn it. I will coach you in every note."

"Of course, Maestro," Ughetto said. His heart fluttered with pride and pleasure. He walked up to stand beside his teacher and follow his gaze down toward the city. "Every note."

Ughetto was slower to grow into his height than any of his classmates. The boys near his age were already tall, sprouting the spidery limbs that were typical for *castrati*. They stumbled as they walked through the *salotto*, tripping over furniture that had stood in the same place for years. It was as if they had not yet learned what to do with their overlarge feet, how to manage their arms. They compared heights and measured their chests to see whose was the deepest, the longest. They towered over Ughetto, whose arms and legs and feet remained stubbornly proportioned to his height. They called him *topolino*, little mouse, and *nano*, dwarf. They cooed baby talk at him and ruffled his hair when he passed.

He had begun to grow embarrassing hair under his arms, and between his legs. He hid his body beneath the long-tailed shirts they all wore, and dressed in private, where no one could see him.

He was ashamed of his thin, bare chest. When a few black whiskers appeared on his chin, he plucked them with his fingernails. The men of Trapani sported proud black beards, brushing them till they gleamed, trimming them weekly to keep them thick and full. But none of the other boys at the *scuola* had facial hair. Every day Ughetto checked the mirror anxiously to be certain no more whiskers had appeared. He didn't need anything else to draw his schoolmates' attention to him.

Their teasing turned to abuse when Brescha made it known to everyone that his prize pupil had been engaged to sing with the Capella Sistina. Envy sharpened their jibes and put muscle in the blows they aimed at him when the masters weren't looking. It didn't help that Anselmo, the *direttore*, hired a dressmaker to fit him for a new gown and breeches. When one of the other masters objected to the cost, Anselmo said scornfully, "A student of our *scuola* does not make his debut in rags!"

Anselmo, also a *castrato*, had had a short and not very successful career singing choral parts in Venezia and Firenze. As he often proclaimed, with rigid pride, he had found his true calling in running the *scuola*.

"Ughetto needs to do something about that mop of curls, too," he snapped. "He looks like a poodle." He arranged for a *parrucchiere* to come up from the city to style Ughetto's hair. The other students stared at Ughetto as he sat in the courtyard under the scissors and combs and oils of this worthy. They snickered at him afterward, flipping their own unwashed locks to mock him.

Had Mauro still been there, Ughetto could have downplayed the fuss and laughed at it. But he had no one to buffer his sudden rise to prominence. He slept alone, as he had always done, though other boys shared beds, snuggling together like overgrown puppies, sometimes grunting with passion in the darkness. He had no money, so when the others went down to the market to shop for trinkets or sweets, he stayed at the *scuola*, practicing, studying, reading from its collection of books. He let them believe he was too conceited to join in their recreation. He concentrated on learning the roulades and the *glissandi* that would be required of the *Miserere*, and tried hard not to care that his colleagues hoped he would fail.

Each week a few more manuscript sheets would arrive at the *scuola*, and Brescha would seize them to study himself. When he was satisfied he knew them thoroughly, he would call Ughetto to come and begin work. And though Ughetto's skill on the keyboard was growing, Brescha insisted on teaching him every line by rote, asserting that there could be no mistakes. "You will be singing under the composer's own direction, Ughetto. This can lead to a great career, following in my footsteps at St. Peter's, or perhaps at San Marco, or Santa Maria dei Fiori!"

"What about my name, Maestro?" Ughetto asked after one long voice lesson. He and Brescha were both exhausted. The summer was fading, and the breeze in the waning afternoon was cool and refreshing. They sat in the courtyard under the olive tree, and Brescha allowed Ughetto to share in his snack of watered wine, olives in brine, and slices of *pecorino romano* on fresh bread.

"Your name?" Brescha said absently.

"Yes," Ughetto said. He ran his hand through his hair, cut in the fashion so that it just brushed his shoulders. "Ughetto is a little boy's name. Shouldn't we change it?"

Brescha considered this, pulling at his lower lip. "You were christened Ugo, I suppose."

"I don't know my baptismal name. My sisters and my mother always called me Ughetto."

Brescha put down his cup and regarded Ughetto. "You had sisters? You never mentioned them."

Ughetto nodded. "Six sisters," he said. "All older."

Brescha raised his eyebrows, and it seemed to Ugo that he paled a little. "Six! And you're the seventh child?"

"Yes." Ughetto was surprised to see Brescha cross himself. "What is it?"

But the old *castrato* only pressed his lips together, shaking his head. Ughetto opened his mouth to ask him again, but Brescha threw up his thick hand. "Never mind, never mind. You're right about the name. You need a name worthy of your voice, something dramatic. Memorable, but simple."

"Ugo is simple."

"Too simple, too ordinary. It should be something beautiful, like—like Floria, because you're a young flower of a singer. Or Angelino, Brescha's little angel!"

Ughetto was about to protest the excess of this suggestion, but a burst of hoots erupted from the other side of the olive tree, forestalling him. Brescha cursed and shook his fist at the lanky forms in the shadows, who raced away amid shrieks of laughter.

Ughetto's cheeks flamed, and he slumped in his chair in an agony of embarrassment.

Brescha had risen, as if to go after the other boys, but then he sighed and sat down heavily, arranging his great belly over his thighs. He shrugged and picked up his cup again, patting Ughetto's shoulder with his free hand. "Don't worry," he said. "They're jealous of your early success. It was the same for me in my day." He sipped delicately at the wine. "They hated me because I never had to audition. Everyone came to me, you see, begging me to sing in their churches." He reached for the olive dish and pulled it closer. "We'll come up with a name you like. I know how it is to have to live with a name for a long time. I knew my career would be a long one, and so I chose my name with care. We'll do exactly the same for you."

The amber warmth of September melted into the cool, gilded days of October. The hazelnut leaves turned and fell, and the beekeepers collected their harvest and pressed it into clay bottles. The breezes carried the sweet tang of honey into the courtyard of the *scuola*.

By the time the last of the manuscript pages arrived from Signore Allegri, Ughetto had sung the part so many times that it ran incessantly round and round in his head, even in his sleep. When he woke, the text was on his lips. When he laid his head on his pillow, the notes danced before his eyes. One day he protested to Brescha that he couldn't sing it anymore, that he was sick to death of every page of it.

"Aha!" the *maestro* cried, slapping his thick hand against his chest. "Then now—now you are ready!"

Ughetto protested, "I've *been* ready!" His voice rose in complaint, and at the top of the rise, it broke, the pitch collapsing. It dropped an entire octave, ending in a toneless scrape, like the croak of a frog.

Ughetto and Brescha stared at each other. For a long moment, neither spoke. Then Brescha, jowls trembling, said, "What was that?"

Ughetto shook his head. "I don't know." His voice rasped in his throat with unsteady vibrations. He didn't recognize either the feeling or the sound. He was afraid to speak again. He put a hand to his neck, as if he could fix it that way, and stared round-eyed at his teacher.

"What have you been doing today?" Brescha demanded.

Ughetto only shook his head. He didn't dare open his lips.

"Were you running? Screaming in the cold?"

"No," Ughetto whispered.

"Don't whisper. Speak!"

Ughetto stared at his teacher in horror as an idea began to take form in his mind, a terrible idea. He shook his head, wordlessly. Cold fear began in his loins and spread upward through his belly and his chest.

But it couldn't be. It wasn't possible.

He remembered the flakes of opium dissolving in dark Roman

wine. He remembered the strong arms of Luigi lifting him, lowering him into the warm water. He recalled the splintered bench in the tub, and the hands on his ankles, opening his legs. He would never forget the flash of pain from the knife.

And he remembered the screeches of Nonna and her son, the surgeon's wide, frightened eyes before he scuttled away like a cockroach before a broom.

Ughetto felt an urge to touch himself beneath his trousers, to explore what the surgeon's knife had left to him.

He remembered blood. But whose blood had it been?

Brescha came close, bending his great height above him. "Ughetto," he said. Anxiety made his voice scrape, too, but it stayed in its high register. "Speak to me, dear boy. Let me hear your voice."

The endearment made Ughetto's lips tremble. With difficulty, squeezing his hands tight together, he said, "Maestro. I don't know what's wrong."

And he heard, with horrified ears, the froglike sound of his voice. Its pitch wavered as it searched for a register to settle in.

Brescha clutched his robe with one hand, as if he could steady himself that way. With the other he rubbed his brow, and then his eyes. He looked away, as if he couldn't bring himself to look into his protégé's eyes as he spoke the awful news.

"Ughetto," he said. His voice throbbed with sadness. "Your voice is changing."

They met, several hours later, in the *direttore*'s private office. It was a lovely room, with an enormous Venetian vase in one corner and a broad writing desk of polished pine in the other. A clavier stood against one wall, its inlaid wood cover closed.

Ughetto stood before the desk, his head hanging. Anselmo sat behind it and glowered up at him, his face suffused with fury. Brescha stood behind Ughetto. The old *castrato*'s eyes were red, his lips swollen from having wept for a solid hour.

Ughetto had shed no tears. Shock had made him cold, then

fevered, then icy cold again. He stood very still, facing Anselmo across the desk but avoiding his eyes.

"How could you not have known?" Anselmo shrilled.

A distant part of Ughetto noticed that when the *castrati* were upset, their voices went up. Not down. He didn't dare answer the *direttore*, because he knew already that his voice would go lower. He already understood that his voice, his only real asset, was seeking a new register, probing the depths for where it would settle.

He stared at the terra-cotta tile beneath his feet. The clean wool and linen of his new gown and breeches mocked him, reminders of the glory that had just this day slipped from his grasp. He wondered if it had left anything in its place.

Brescha cleared his throat and said in a shaking voice, "Ughetto has always been shy. He bathes alone. And who would—" He choked on a sob. "Who would have suspected?"

Ughetto lifted his head and turned to look at Brescha. He was amazed, even now, at how wounded the old singer was, how grieved. Brescha wasn't angry. Brescha behaved as if his heart was broken. There had been no word of anger until they faced Anselmo.

Anselmo frowned at Brescha, whose lip began to tremble. "I blame you," Anselmo said sourly. "You should have examined him."

Fresh tears coursed down Brescha's heavy cheeks, and he quavered, "You're the *direttore!* Why didn't you examine him?"

Anselmo was thinner than Brescha, but just as tall and ungainly in his proportions. He stood now, and Ughetto felt smaller than ever. His head reached no higher than Anselmo's chest. "Who brought Ughetto to us?"

Brescha said, "Those people from Napoli, Luigi someone and his crone of a mother. Ughetto comes from . . . Where is it, Ughetto?"

Ughetto cleared his throat and tried to steady his voice, but it was no use. He scratched out, "Trapani," and fell silent again.

"Sicilia," Anselmo said darkly, as if that explained everything. He toyed with a paper knife on his desk, making it catch the sunlight. "If we'd known . . . perhaps it would not have been too late. Ughetto, you should have told us."

Brescha stepped forward, and for the first time since he had known him, Ughetto felt his long, fleshy arm surround his shoulders. Brescha cleared his throat, and his reedy voice was steadier when he said, "Anselmo. This is not Ughetto's fault. He didn't know. No one knew. And now we must take care of him."

"Take care of him! Can he get our money back?"

"He was eight years old when he came here," Brescha said. "Exactly my own age when I started my training. What do we know, when we're that age, Anselmo? Can you remember?" His voice trembled again. "Did you know what your body would look like?"

The *direttore* scowled and looked away. "We are disgraced," he said bitterly. "Thanks to your ambition, Brescha!"

Ughetto could not stand in silence anymore. He said, in that new voice he didn't recognize, "Don't blame Maestro Brescha, signore, I beg you. He is hurt enough."

Brescha's arm tightened around his shoulders, and Ughetto felt his ungainly body shake with suppressed sobs.

Anselmo stood up abruptly, dropping the paper knife. "Out," he said, fixing Ughetto with his angry gaze. "Today. We will tell the Cappella Sistina you ran away."

"No!" Brescha exclaimed.

"Yes," was the answer. "It's the only way to save our reputation."

Ughetto stared at him. "But where will I go?"

Anselmo spread his hands. "How should I know? Go back to your family!"

"I have no money," Ughetto said. His voice sounded unfamiliar to his own ears, the voice of a stranger. "How do I get there?"

Brescha turned him toward the door. "I will give you money, Ughetto. The money you would have earned from the Cappella."

"You will not!" Anselmo snapped.

Brescha paused and looked over his shoulder. His jowls trembled now with anger. "Anselmo, tell me. Did you choose the knife? No. Did I? No. And no more did Ughetto." He looked down at Ughetto, his eyes glistening. "He has been my greatest pupil. If I am to lose him, I will at least give him a chance in life."

12

Io so, crudele, come tu diverti!

I know, cruel one, how you amuse yourself!

—Donna Elvira, Act One, Scene Two, *Don Giovanni*

Teresa stood in the road while her friend's aunt read her letter of introduction. The house was a narrow, dark building with stone walls and no garden at all. The door opened directly into the road, with no step or stoop to separate it. The aunt, named Gilda, was a stout, mustachioed woman with black hair and a glint in her dark eyes that did not bode well for Teresa's petition.

"Signora," Teresa pled. "Only a few weeks, until I—until I find work."

Gilda raised one thick eyebrow and looked Teresa up and down. Teresa fidgeted. In the last three days she had felt more like a capon at market, assessed for how much meat she might provide, than a seventeen-year-old girl away from home for the first time.

"Not married," Gilda said in a flat tone.

Teresa dropped her eyes in what she hoped was a modest manner. "Not yet, signora."

"You can pay?"

Teresa fumbled in her little string bag and brought out the tiny cotton pouch where she had stowed her meager savings. She opened it, and showed the interior to Gilda. "This is what I have, signora," she said. "It's not much."

"Hardly anything," Gilda grumbled. She looked over her shoulder. "But I can use it. My husband isn't working just now."

Hopeful, Teresa bent to pick up her valise, but when she straightened, Gilda had put out a forestalling hand. *"Aspetta, aspetta,"* she said.

Teresa put down the valise again. Gilda glanced over her shoulder one more time, then stepped out into the road, pulling the door closed behind her. "I have a room you can have, for a while," she said in a low tone. Her face was grim. "But you stay away from my husband."

As gravely as she could, Teresa said, "Of course, signora."

Gilda said, "I mean it. One improper glance, and you're out. *Capisci?"*

Teresa sighed, suddenly overwhelmed by the weight of impending years. Would she, one day, look like Gilda? Would she have a growth on her upper lip, a thickened waist, a sour expression?

"Capisco, signora," she answered tiredly. "I will promise whatever you like. I only need a place to lay my head, a place to wash, perhaps a bit of food if you can spare it. As soon as I can afford a rooming house, I'll go."

Gilda nodded. "How many *lire* are there in that little purse?"

Teresa had no need to count them. She knew precisely how many were left after her coach trip, after her meager meal of soup and bread, and her only other meal on the road, oranges and cheese. She told Gilda the number.

Gilda nodded again, and held out her hand. Reluctantly, not knowing what else to do, Teresa turned over the pouch and let the *lire* fall into the older woman's palm.

"Bene," Gilda said, and unexpectedly, she smiled. Her teeth were surprisingly good, and for a moment Teresa saw the resemblance to her niece in Limone. "Come in, *ragazza,"* she said, as

pleasantly as if Teresa were an expected guest. "Come in and let me show you your room."

The room Gilda gave her was barely as wide as her outstretched arms, but it was enough. The bed was clean, if a bit hard, and there were a ewer and basin on a rickety marble-topped stand. There was no wardrobe, but Teresa had so few clothes it hardly mattered.

Gilda's cooking showed her Limone roots. She made *pasta* with braised onion sauce, fish from the Lambro fried in butter, salads of arugula and fennel, and *carpaccio* of veal with sliced beets and grilled tomatoes. At first Teresa found the traditional Milanese green olive bread too salty for her taste, but she soon learned to savor it, dipping thick slices into olive oil.

Ippolito, the man Gilda so jealously guarded, was a stubby creature with the veined nose and reddened cheeks of a drinker. He said little, but he ate a great deal, and washed everything down with sour red wine. Teresa sat at table with the two of them for lunch and dinner, sitting as far as she could from Ippolito, studiously keeping her eyes on Gilda. She offered to help in the kitchen, but Gilda, it developed, was as jealous of her recipes as she was of her husband.

The couple had had a daughter who died in infancy. There had been no other children. When he worked, Ippolito was a stonemason. Gilda informed Teresa that Ippolito was between jobs because there was little construction in Milano at the moment. She spoke without a hint of irony, giving no indication that she heard the constant hammering and shouts of builders on nearly every street of the city.

Ladies came daily to the little house, carrying bolts of cloth. They stood on a wooden stool in Gilda's *salotto*, gossiping cheerfully while she measured and pinned and cut.

Teresa borrowed Gilda's soapstone iron. She heated it on the wood stove, then pressed her best dress. She washed her hair in cold water in the basin in her room and scrubbed her cheeks until they were pink. She put on the dress and wound her hair up as neatly as she knew how. She took her mother's music book in her arms for luck and started out of the house, intending to go straight to the theater.

Gilda stopped her in the hall. "Where are you going?"

Teresa bit her lip. "I'm—going to look for work."

"What work, in that dress? Do you plan to be a charwoman?"

"No, signora. A—a singer."

Gilda's eyes widened, and she stared at the girl for a long moment. Her mustachioed lip pursed. "Well," she said. "I suppose singers have to come from somewhere."

Teresa started again for the door.

"No, no, no!" Gilda cried. "You can't go like that!"

Teresa stopped in the little hallway, her hand on the latch. "*Cosa?* What is it?"

"Your dress!" Gilda said.

Teresa looked down at herself. Her gown, if such it could be called, was of brown muslin. She had sewed it herself with inexpert fingers. The petticoat was also brown, but there had not been enough muslin, and so the sides and back, where the overskirt hid them, were of pieces of leftover beige cotton. The bodice had no boning, but Teresa was slender and not overlarge in her bosom, and she had hoped it would not matter. Still, the whole effect was rather cheap looking, and she knew it.

She sighed, remembering the elegant gown of the lady who had shared her coach. "This is all I have."

Gilda clucked her tongue and crooked a thick finger, drawing Teresa into the living room. Before Teresa knew what was happening, she was standing in her shift and Gilda was dropping a different dress over her head, muttering to herself as she pulled the laces tight on the bodice, as she bent to check the length of the hem and to tweak the overdress into place over the petticoat. The whole ensemble was in shades of blue, the bodice the blue of a midnight sky, the skirt that of a robin's egg. The petticoat was even paler, an ice blue for which Teresa had no name. The skirt was not nearly so wide as that of the lady from the coach, but it draped beautifully over the petticoat, and the bodice was stiff with whalebone and topped with a fall of creamy lace. Teresa stood very still, hardly daring to move in the lovely creation.

"Gilda!" she breathed, not realizing she had used the aunt's given name. "What fabric is this? Whose dress?"

"It's mostly silk damask," Gilda said shortly. "The petticoat is satin. And it was to be for the wife of the doctor in the next street."

"Why did she not—"

Gilda snorted. "She died. Not much of a doctor, do you think?"

Teresa shivered. It was not a good omen. But it was a lovely dress, and only a bit too big in the waist. Even as she thought about it, she felt Gilda's strong fingers tugging at the laces, adjusting the skirt. "Did she pay you?" Teresa asked after a moment.

"Half in advance," Gilda said. "She still owes me the other half."

"I will pay you for it," Teresa said. "I promise."

Gilda gave a rough laugh. "You do that, *ragazza*," she said. She stepped back, nodding appreciatively. "You're much prettier than the doctor's wife was, anyway," she said, and her unexpected smile broke out. It softened her dark face and made her look years younger. "Just tell everyone who made your gown."

For three days straight Teresa presented herself at La Scala. The first day she could not even get in the door. The second day she managed to get in through the delivery entrance, but was promptly ejected by an officious man in a frock coat who flourished a cane at her as if she were a bothersome dog. By the third day, after standing beside the stage entrance and approaching every single person who passed her, she knew there would be no straightforward way to win an audition. The singers laughed, and the orchestra members averted their faces, out of embarrassment for her, she suspected. The director, it seemed, did not use the stage entrance.

As she trudged back toward Gilda's home, lifting the skirts of the blue gown to keep them from being muddied, she felt something close to despair. She couldn't afford a voice teacher who might have a contact at the opera. She didn't have an accompanist. She had not attended any of the conservatories, which might at least lend her petition credibility.

She walked slowly, her head down, her music clamped under her arm, hardly knowing where she turned or which street she was taking. When she heard the strains of an organ, she stopped. She lifted her head and looked around, hoping she wasn't completely lost.

She found herself on Via Falcone, opposite a small, rather odd little church with a circular wall and a soaring bell tower to her right. The music was unfamiliar, but she thought it might be Bach, or perhaps Handel. She had just started across the street, thinking she would go into the church, sit down for a time, and listen to the organ, when she heard a sweet and rather eerie voice rise to join the organ.

Teresa caught her breath. What was this? It was certainly a soprano voice, but it was like nothing she had ever heard in Limone. She hurried, afraid it would stop before she could find its source. She had to circle all the way around the little church before she found the entrance on Via Torino. There was a niche with a figure of the Virgin set into it, and a plaque beneath that said *Santa Maria presso San Satiro*. Teresa scarcely glanced at these as she hurried in through the wooden doors. She crossed herself automatically as she entered the nave.

It was a lovely place. She glanced around, surprised at how large it seemed once she was inside. It took her several moments to realize that the church's spaciousness was an illusion. Whoever had designed it had created a trompe-l'oeil effect by painting vaulted arches on the walls. A Mass was in progress, with worshippers standing in the pews and the priest chanting the ordinary from the altar. The music—that glorious voice, with the reedy tones of the organ underlying it—wound through the resonant space, slender and full at the same time.

The singer began a long *melisma*, figures of eighth- and sixteenth-notes, winding up the staff and then down again. Did the singer never breathe? The passage seemed to go on an impossibly long time.

Teresa sidled into a pew, crowding next to an old woman in a black scarf. She peered over her shoulder into the organ loft to try to find the singer.

Around her, as the *Sanctus* came to an end, the worshippers knelt, but Teresa had lost track of the liturgy. She could see the singer now, and she still stood, distracted by his voice and form. She had heard about such creatures, of course. There were singers of this ilk in Roma, and in Napoli and Venezia. She had not thought to hear such a voice in a Milanese church.

Someone tugged at her skirt, and she realized she was the only person standing in the nave except the priest. Abruptly, she sank to her knees, hoping the floor wasn't too dirty. Still she kept her head turned toward the organ loft.

When the *Amen* began, she bent her head and closed her eyes, listening with the purest admiration. The Mass went by in a blur, Teresa simply waiting for each part the *musico* would sing. His artistry stunned her. Some objected to the knife, claiming it was unnatural and cruel. Teresa, at that moment, was not so sure. If it was mutilation that created such singers, would it not be worth it? Would even she, given the chance to sing those long *melismas*, those piercing high notes, accept it? She just might, if it would do her any good.

As the congregants filed out of San Satiro, Teresa went in search of the stairs leading down from the organ loft. She stood in the shadows, waiting. When he came down, he had doffed the dark robe and was dressed in a modest suit, only his height and his long arms and neck assuring her that it was, in fact, the *castrato*.

She stepped forward. "Sir," she said softly. "Your singing is magnificent."

He had a fleshy face, with a shock of black hair springing up from a high forehead. He started to smile at her, his round, beardless cheeks creasing, when someone behind her hissed, "Capon!" and thrust past with a sharp elbow that sent Teresa staggering into the wall.

The *musico*'s smile faded. He stood very still, his cheeks flaming, his eyes downcast. The man who had insulted him swept through the doors and out into the gathering evening.

Teresa regained her balance and tucked her book of music securely under her arm again. She repeated in a clear voice, "Magnificent, sir. The most beautiful thing I've ever heard."

The tall *castrato* smoothed his lapels. "Thank you, signorina," he said. His voice was high and fluting, rather like an adolescent boy's, but richer and more resonant. "It's strange that men such as that one gather in the opera house to hear my kind sing, yet hate to come face-to-face with us when we're not in costume."

Teresa took a step toward him. A seed of hope began to germinate in her breast, nearly stealing her breath. "Sir," she said. "Did you say—do you indeed sing at La Scala?"

Now the *musico*'s grin reappeared. "When they need someone with long breath and fast notes, I do," he said. "And they don't mind my other—hmm—let us say, shortcomings."

His smile encouraged Teresa. She began to smile, too, and she put out her gloved hand. "I am Teresa Saporiti," she said. "Your newest and most ardent admirer."

He took her hand and bowed over it. "Signorina. Vincenzo dal Prato, *al suo servizio*. And I never have enough admirers."

13

⌒

Mi par ch'oggi il demonio si diverta . . .

It seems to me that today the devil is enjoying himself . . .

—Don Giovanni, Act One, Scene Two, *Don Giovanni*

Ugo was no stranger to pain. Beginning with that first, slashing pain that fully revealed his other nature for the first time, pain had pursued him.

It wasn't always his own. More often it belonged to others, and he was responsible for a fair amount of it. He took no pleasure in making people suffer. Even though his victims were invariably fools, of little use to themselves or anyone else, hurting them gave him no sense of satisfaction. What he mostly felt was resignation.

Ugo had always found there was something musical about pain. It had rhythm and tempo and color. Different kinds of pain had different timbres, different sonorities. And like hearing a piece of music again and again, until it was as familiar as an old friend, there was yet something new in each experience.

In the basement room, Domenico asked him one more time before the symphony of pain commenced. "Where are they?" he demanded. "Where do they hide their compound?"

Ugo shook his head. "You don't want to know this, my friend."

Benson, eager to begin Ugo's torment, hauled him off the floor by one arm and shoved him onto the bare mattress. He pulled a nasty-looking pair of pliers from his case, and he brandished it, grinning, showing an expanse of gum and crooked brown teeth.

Ugo managed a shrug, though his gut quivered with a nauseous expectation. "I did warn you, my poor Benson," he said. "I hope you'll remember that."

For answer, Benson snarled something wordless and seized Ugo's foot.

Domenico headed for the door. He didn't look back as he knocked and waited for Marks to let him out.

Benson wielded the pliers, probing at Ugo's toes, eyeing his victim for a response.

"Such a cliché," Ugo had said. "Nails? Surely you can think of something—" He broke off, grunting.

This was a focused sort of pain, like the skree of an untuned violin. His stomach clenched as the nail gave way, and a burst of perspiration ran down his forehead and into his hair. The straps bit into his wrists as his body heaved. When the spasm released, he drew a noisy breath. "Something more original," he finished, panting. Blood dribbled hotly over his foot. "Use your imagination."

For answer, Benson slapped him, making his teeth rattle.

"Oh, yes," Ugo crooned. "Subtle. Like your hairdo."

Benson slammed a fist against his cheekbone, a blow of sheer brute violence like the crash of cymbals, or the blare of a whole row of trombones.

Benson twirled the pliers in his fingers and glared at Ugo. Blood spattered his muscle shirt, and his bald skull was slick with sweat. "All this can stop any time."

"And spoil your fun?"

Benson leaned forward, pressing the nose of the pliers into the sole of Ugo's foot. "Look, you little fag," he snarled. "We get what we want, or you die. Simple as that."

"You think you want it, my dear Benson," Ugo said wearily. "You would regret it."

"Regret living forever? Who could regret that?"

Ugo managed a breathless laugh. "Who promised you that? You won't live forever, Benson. Not you."

The pliers pressed harder, until Ugo felt the skin break and a fresh trickle of blood begin. "Why not me?" Benson snapped. "Not good enough for you?"

"*Esatto*," Ugo murmured. "Not good enough."

Benson swore and reached for a fresh tool.

He proceeded through his case, trying this instrument and that, growing more and more desperate as the air in the room grew rank with the smell of blood and sweat and desperation. When he brought out the nipple clamps Ugo said, with a choking laugh, "Oh, my God, Benson. You've been visiting those sex shops again."

The barb elicited a kick that sent waves of pain through his ribs. Ugo writhed and swore in Italian, thinking of the *forte* passages of the big symphonies of Khachaturian or Mahler. Perspiration poured from him, soaking his shirt and his hair. When the spasm passed, he lay back and regarded Benson from beneath lowered eyelids. He said hoarsely, "Almost there, *mio amico*. Almost. But not quite."

Benson tried a cigarette lighter. The smell of branded skin filled the little room and drove Benson out. Marks came in his place and stood staring down at Ugo, shirtless now, bleeding from his chest and his toes and from a particularly nasty laceration of his navel.

"Stinks in here," Marks said.

"*Veramente?*" Ugo answered. "I hadn't noticed. It's awfully hot, though."

In truth, he was burning with thirst, but he saw no point in saying so. At least being thirsty meant he wasn't going to wet himself. Not that it would bother him, but the smell was already oppressive.

His nostrils twitched hopefully. If his sense of smell was growing sharper, maybe . . .

Before he completed the thought, Benson returned, and Domenico came with him.

Ugo said through gritted teeth, "Domenico. My new friend. Where have you been? You've missed all the fun." With difficulty, the straps making him awkward, he pushed himself upright, grunting at the agony in his ribs.

Domenico, his face drawn and his eyes bloodshot, stood as far from the fouled cot as he could in the confined space. He looked as if he hadn't slept any more than Ugo had.

Ugo regarded the three of them, standing in a row like boys in a bad Gilbert and Sullivan. He wished, for a moment, that he could just tell them. It would be such a pleasure to watch the elders destroy them.

But La Società would not like that. They wouldn't like it at all.

He licked his lips and swallowed, striving for some moisture to wet his tongue. "Come now," he said. "If you can't stand to watch this little display, dear Domenico, how will you ever have the guts to deal with the elders?"

"I can stand it," Domenico said. He grinned. "I'd do it myself if Benson didn't enjoy it so much."

Ugo closed his eyes, assessing himself. His chest felt as if it were on fire. Benson had burned his hands, then his chin. His navel bled. His toes ached, and his ribs. He hurt, and he hurt a lot. But it was not yet enough.

Closer, though, he thought. *We're getting closer.*

Benson's eyes were hollow, and sweat streamed down his naked skull. "Anybody else would have given in by now," he said.

"Are you whining, Benson?" Ugo said. "But I'm the one on this cot. Domenico, my dear friend, surely you realize the elders would tear your heart out before they let a cretin like this into the society!"

"Shut up," Domenico said. He took a step closer. "Come on,

Ugo, put an end to this. I'm tired, so you must be. And I'm not bleeding."

"You have all your toenails, too," Ugo said. "Something happened to mine."

Benson dropped the pliers and reached into his case for something else. His lips pulled back in a forced grin, showing his expanse of pale gums as he held it up to show Ugo. It was an electroshock baton. The price tag still hung from the handle.

"Oh, a brand new toy," Ugo breathed. "Lucky boy."

Benson's grin wavered. Domenico came closer. "You idiot, ignore him!" he snapped. "Use the damn thing!"

An hour passed, and the crescendo of pain swelled. Ugo tried to give himself up to it, to hurry things along. He made no effort to hold back his moans or the gasps that burst from him. But he was still himself when Benson, with a curse, flung the shock baton on the floor.

"It's no good!" he spat. "The guy's not human!"

Ugo saw Domenico's fist clench. Benson saw it, too, and took a swift step backward, out of reach. "Of course he's not human," Domenico hissed. "That's the whole fucking point."

Benson's lips opened, but it seemed he had no answer.

Domenico leaned over the bloody cot, his hair dark with sweat. His breath was sour with fury and urgency. "I want to know how to find them," he said. "And you're going to tell me. I won't stop until then."

He reached into the pocket of his leather jacket and pulled out a small, flat object wrapped in white paper. He kept an eye on Ugo as he tore off the paper, revealing a small, gleaming knife.

Ugo felt the itching begin on his chest, and he kept his face still to hide his rush of satisfaction. Through dry lips, he croaked, "Oh, *bravo*, my friend. A scalpel. I hope you didn't harm the doctor."

"Surgical supply," Domenico grated. He held the blade out as he approached the cot. "Get his pants off, Benson," he said.

Benson said stupidly, "His pants?"

"His pants!" Domenico shouted. "Damn it, what do you think the scalpel is for? We'll see what he thinks about losing a testicle!"

Ugo began to laugh.

14

Ah! ch'ora, idolo mio, son vani i pianti . . .

Ah! Now, my love, tears are in vain . . .

—Don Ottavio, Act One, Scene Two, *Don Giovanni*

During a break in the staging rehearsal, Octavia slipped away from the little group sipping *cappuccino* in the canteen under the ellipse. She paced the corridor, twisting her scarf between her hands, and counted back the days since her infusion in New York. It was only five. She should be all right. She should be able to make it ten days with ease, though it had been a long time since that had been necessary.

Before Ugo's coming, thirst was always her greatest worry. It was not only in San Francisco that Hélène had gotten in trouble. She had been dismissed from a cast in Chicago for missing a performance. There had been other near things, and not only for Hélène. Teresa, sailing on a private yacht from Naples to Venice, had not dared to use the tooth on board. By the time she disembarked, she was desperate. When she fed at last, in the shadows of the Ponte di Rialto, she took too much. She never forgot her victim's woebegone face as his breath faltered and his heart ceased to beat.

Indeed, she remembered the face of every person who had not

survived the tooth. Those faces haunted her sleep. Her perfect memory resisted all attempts to edit them out.

But now, with fond nostalgia, she was remembering Vincenzo del Prato. The *castrato*'s plump, sweet features were as fresh in her mind as the day she met him.

She wandered out of the ellipse, through the stage door, and into the empty theater. She stood for a moment in the orchestra, looking up at the *loggione* far above. Just so she had stood that very first day she had been allowed at last to enter La Scala, vouchsafed by Vincenzo. The restoration of the old theater was so faithful that it hardly seemed possible her old friend was not still here. She thought if she turned, just so, she would see him standing center stage, winking at her during his bows as he had done the last time she saw him alive.

She sighed and tipped her head up to gaze past the soaring façade of four balconies to the sculpted trompe l'oeil ceiling with its splendid chandelier. There was a hidden passageway there, in the rafters of the theater, where compassionate Milanese had stowed Jews to save them from being sent to the internment camps. In 1943, the Allies had inadvertently bombed La Scala, smashing its roof and the upper levels to dust. Yet now it was restored to its glory, its history retained. The theater's memory was even longer than Octavia's.

Impulsively, she strode up the aisle toward the lobby, winding her scarf around her neck as she walked. She ran lightly up the stairs to where the *palchi* ringed the first balcony. She wanted to step into one of the boxes. She thought if she could simply sink into a plush chair and gaze out into the theater, she would feel calmer. She tried several doors to the boxes, but they were all locked.

She wandered along the marble corridor, glancing into the reception room, trailing her fingers along the wall. She had been in Australia in 1943. Vivian Anderson was at the Theatre Royal in Sydney, and she and the rest of the cast had heard the account of the destruction of La Scala on the wireless. Vivian bought a *Times* and pored over the newspaper, trying to find out how bad the damage was.

"Vivian," someone asked her, glancing over her shoulder. "Have you sung in Milan?"

She bit her lip and folded the newspaper hastily. There had been nothing in it. It was hard to get news out of Italy during the war. "No," she said. "I've never been there. It's just so sad. That beautiful old theater!"

"Oh, I know," the other singer had said. "We all feel connected to La Scala."

"Miss Voss?"

Octavia whirled, startled out of her recollection by the approach of one of the opera house tour guides. "Yes?" she said, more sharply than she intended.

The guide, a pretty young Frenchwoman, blushed. "I'm sorry, I just—it looked as if you wanted to go into one of the boxes."

Octavia took a breath and managed a smile. "Actually, I did. You probably have keys, don't you?"

The girl's blush subsided, and she stepped forward, pulling a ring of keys from the pocket of her blazer. "I do. Which one would you like? The double box is lovely."

"That would be so nice," Octavia said. "Thank you, Miss—"

"I'm Francine," the girl said, her blush rising again. "Just let me know when you leave—I'll be over there." She pointed to the pillared reception room on the other side of the corridor.

"Thank you, Francine," Octavia murmured. "I only have a few minutes before the rehearsal starts again. But this will be so restful." Francine nodded, as if this were perfectly natural. She unlocked the door and held it wide for Octavia to pass through.

Octavia closed her eyes as the door clicked gently shut behind her. She waited in the silence for the space of a breath or two. When she opened her eyes again, the sensation that swept over her was one of stepping into a different century. Of coming home.

The perfection of the recreation of the double box stunned her. Its blue and white ceiling appeared unchanged since it had been painted in 1813. The fireplace looked as if at any moment a maid might come in to lay a warming blaze. The floor was the original marble, the brass fittings and velvet draperies a perfect revival of the early days.

Octavia leaned forward to look out into the theater. It was bigger now, of course. The stage was twice the size it had been, and the seating had been expanded. But the silk damask curtain, the towering proscenium, and the tiers of seats basked undisturbed now in the afterglow of two hundred years of music. They seemed to be waiting, secure in their elegance, for the magic to begin again.

Teresa had stood in the center of the stage of La Scala, with Vincenzo watching from the wings after murmuring instructions to the accompanist. The director and his assistant sat in the middle of the house, their heads bent together, talking. As the accompanist played the opening bars to Amore's aria from *Orfeo*, their voices rose, as if having to sit through an audition was an inconvenience.

Her voice faltered on her first phrase. They didn't notice. They were not even listening.

> *"Gli sguardi trattieni*
> *Affrena gli accenti . . ."*

The accompanist, a plump man with a powdered queue and a reddened nose, scowled at her over the harpsichord. Teresa took a deeper breath and lifted her chin. She took a long step forward, to the very edge of the stage, and fixed the director with an icy stare. She began to sing again, and her voice rose into the theater, finding the resonance of the curving walls, the wooden seats, the high dome of the ceiling.

> *"Rammenta se peni,*
> *Che pochi momenti*
> *Hai più da penar!"*

And now, at last, they stopped talking. The director and the assistant turned to her, straightened, and listened. The assistant's mouth opened, and stayed that way. The director put a hand to his powdered wig, and then to his cravat.

Teresa let her gaze rise to the *loggione* as she finished the aria. She sang the final cadenza to her imagined public, the listeners who would come, who would hear her and remember.

Octavia remembered that day with a clear poignance that made her heart ache. She knew, now, that she had not sung with technical perfection, or even showed her voice to best effect. The aria was too limited in its range for that, with none of the dramatic, sustained notes that would later become her hallmark. She had been only seventeen years old, after all. But she had made music, and the walls of La Scala had rung their response.

Octavia put her chin on her hand and closed her eyes again. They were all gone, of course. Long gone. The director, and his silly, foppish assistant. Vincenzo. Mozart.

Only she, of all that time, was still here. And Zdenka Milosch. And, of course, Ugo.

Oh, Ugo, she thought, with a fresh pain in her breast. *Che successa, mio amico?*

She heard a door open and close far below, and she startled, opening her eyes, coming abruptly to her feet. She shook herself. She knew better than to dwell in the past like this! And Ugo must surely come back soon.

But as she left the box, the unease that had been building in her for the past days made her legs tremble. Something was wrong, or he would have sent word. Ugo was as tough as they came, and smarter than most. He must be in terrible trouble, and there was nothing she could do to help him.

Giorgio ran Octavia and Peter through their blocking for the first scene of act one, and then gave them a break while he started on act two with Nick Barrett-Jones and Richard Strickland, the Leporello. Octavia and Peter sat in chairs at one side of the rehearsal room, sipping bottles of water and watching Nick and Richard work.

Richard was as jolly as he was plump, the sort of singer who kept everyone laughing with his asides and antics. He was the perfect Leporello, Giovanni's servant and sidekick. He had performed the rôle dozens of times, and he slipped into the blocking easily.

But Nick Barrett-Jones was even slower now than he had been earlier in the week. Peter groaned as Giorgio repositioned him a third time beneath the window for his "Deh, vieni."

Octavia leaned close to Peter and whispered, "Our Nick doesn't look too well today."

Nick's hair was still damp from the shower he had evidently taken during the lunch break, and his eyes were reddened. His voice sounded rough, as if he hadn't slept.

"Must have been out on the tiles last night." Peter snickered.

The singers tried again, and Octavia felt sorry for Brenda, who kept coming forward, ready for her entrance, and then having to step back as Giorgio struggled with Nick. Richard slapped his round stomach and rolled his eyes at his colleagues, who covered their mouths to hide their laughter.

Massimo Luca stood to one side, waiting for his part of the scene. Octavia felt his eyes on her, and she turned. He looked a little tired, too. He lifted one hand in greeting and smiled. She smiled back and wished Nick could get on with it so she could hear Massimo sing again.

At last Brenda had her moment, beginning her duet with Nick in which the lovestruck Donna Elvira gives in once again to Giovanni's wiles. Octavia nodded approval at the easy flow of Brenda's dark soprano. She didn't sing full voice, but not quite *mezza voce*, either. Nick began to force his own voice, covering Brenda's tone.

"Too bad," Peter murmured when this happened. "Brenda sounds so lovely." Octavia nodded agreement.

The scene went forward, with Giovanni putting the hapless Leporello into his clothes to pretend to make up to Donna Elvira.

When they reached Massimo's entrance, Giorgio called a halt. He turned to Peter and Octavia. "You two might as well go," he said with a little sigh. "We won't get past this scene this afternoon."

Peter immediately excused himself, saying he and David were going to the Galleria to do some shopping. Octavia tucked her score into her bag and busied herself winding her scarf around her neck, lifting her hair out of her collar. She didn't look forward to going back to Il Principe alone, to face the empty suite, to spend the evening trying to assess how thirsty she really was.

But there seemed to be nothing else to do. She belted her coat and slung the bag over her shoulder. She had just reached the door of the rehearsal room when she found Massimo at her elbow.

He held the door for her and followed her out into the corridor. "Doesn't Giorgio need you?" Octavia asked.

He grinned down at her. His forelock, black and glossy, flopped charmingly over his forehead. "In a moment," he said. "They went back to the duet again."

"Good grief," Octavia said. "Again? You'll be here forever."

"I know. It's wearing, all this standing about."

"It certainly is."

They glanced back through the small window. Giorgio was putting Nick in position once again, and Brenda was mopping her brow with a lace-edged handkerchief.

"But I thought—" Massimo went on, turning back to Octavia. "You're at Il Principe, right? Not far. I have my car, and I thought we could have dinner."

Octavia hesitated. It would be so nice to have company, so long as this charming young man didn't think . . .

He grinned and pushed back the lock of hair. "Just dinner," he said. "A little *trattoria* I know in the Brera. They make a wonderful *cioppino*, and they'll be thrilled to meet you. Say yes, Octavia. Dinner, some wine . . . Nothing else. I promise."

Disarmed, she burst into laughter. After all, if Ugo showed up, he could join them. And she wasn't yet so thirsty that there was any risk. "Yes, of course, Massimo. Thank you. I'd love to have dinner."

She went back to Il Principe and took a long bath. She put on a pair of American jeans, with a white cashmere sweater and heeled boots, and she twisted her hair back with a silver clip. When Massimo called from the lobby, she took up a lambskin blazer and a long silver scarf and ran down the stairs to meet him.

His car, a beautifully maintained vintage Mercedes, had a deep, dark charm that suited Massimo Luca. The doorman opened the door for her, and she climbed in, settling back against the deep, well-worn leather seats. It was good to be going out. She had left a note for Ugo, in case, and she had her cell phone with her. She glanced over at Massimo as he took the wheel. Passing headlights illuminated his profile, the cut of his lean chin, the curved blade of his nose. He gave her his slow smile.

"I like the jeans. You look about twenty years old," he said.

"Flatterer. I'm older than you are."

"You don't know how old I am."

She tilted her head, watching him as he negotiated the twists and turns of the streets leading into the Brera district. He wore a leather jacket and a white shirt, open to show his strong, smooth neck. "I'll guess," she said. "Twenty-eight?"

His brows rose. "How did you know that?"

She laughed. "Call it experience."

"Shall I guess how old you are?"

"You can guess, but I'll never tell you."

"I've read your bio, though."

"You know perfectly well singers' bios are all lies." He laughed, his rich baritone filling the car's interior. She touched the carefully preserved leather of the dashboard with her hand. "This is a marvelous auto," she said. "And you're probably proud of its age."

"Yes. It was my father's. He gave it to me after I graduated from the university. We've kept it in the family a long time."

"Tell me about your family."

"I will, at dinner. Here we are."

The *trattoria* was tiny, with white lace curtains at the windows and no more than a dozen tables. They went down two steps from the street, through the door that opened directly into the dining room. The *padrone*, a compact man with a brush of white hair, came bustling out to meet them. His wife came behind him, smoothing her apron. There was a little fuss of introductions, of choosing the best table, of settling them with an *aperitivo*. No one produced a menu, but Massimo had evidently arranged everything. An *antipasto* of olives and *bruschetta* and grilled eggplant arrived, with a glass of pinot grigio, and was followed by a salad of tomatoes and basil and *mozzarella* liberally drizzled with green, fragrant olive oil. By the time the *padrone* brought them a decanter of red wine and bowls of *cioppino* bristling with shrimp and clams in their shells, Octavia had heard all about Massimo's father, a physician, and his mother, a designer for one of the minor Milanese fashion houses; she knew about his married sister and her twin daughters; she knew his brother was a great worry to the family, skipping from job to job; and she knew that Massimo had studied in La Scala's own school, and had tested himself in regional opera houses before accepting rôles at the big theater.

"And now," he said. They were wiping their fingers on warm, damp towels. Their bowls were replaced with tiny glasses of *limoncello* and a plate of crisp *biscotti*. "Tell me about you."

Octavia shrugged and sat back in her chair, cradling her glass in her fingers. She had perhaps drunk more than she should already, but she loved *limoncello*, and it always made her think fondly of Sorrento. "There's nothing much to tell, really. You've already read my bio." He laughed, and she smiled up at him from beneath her lashes. He was remarkable, really. Such poise, at such a young age. She had not been nearly so sophisticated at twenty-eight, even though, at that age, she had been the slave of the tooth for nine years.

"Tell me what's not in your bio, Octavia," he said. He leaned closer to her, so she could just catch the scent of him. It was not strong, but distinctly male, tinged slightly with citrus, and, some-how, very Italian. "Tell me what your family's like," he said, grin-ning, showing white, straight teeth. "Tell me who your lovers are."

She chuckled. "I have no lovers, Massimo."

"Not possible." He put an elbow on the table, propped his chin on his fist, and fixed her with that light brown gaze. "I'm sure you have a hundred. A thousand, like Don Giovanni."

"Hardly. I've been too busy for any of that." She set down her glass, forcing herself to leave a little in the bottom. She looked pointedly at her watch. "Massimo, this has been the most divine dinner. Fetch your friends so I can thank them, and then we'd both better get our rest."

He nodded, and signaled to the waiter. Soon they were being bowed out of the restaurant by all the staff, with good wishes for the success of the opera. Massimo held her arm as they walked to the car and took her hand to help her into her seat. His skin was warm, his fingers strong, deliberate in their touch.

As he walked around to the driver's side, she scolded herself. She had enjoyed it too much. She couldn't afford to get close to anyone, least of all this sweet young man. It didn't help that the wines and the liqueur had made her head buzz and her inhibi-tions recede nearly beyond her reach.

He smiled at her as he turned the key and the engine purred. "This was nice," he said.

Octavia wanted to say something sharp, something that would stem the rising feeling between them. But the appeal of his smile stopped her. "It was indeed," she said weakly.

He had his hand on the gearshift, but he didn't move it. He leaned across it and pressed his lips to hers. His mouth was cool, his lips firm. He tasted slightly of lemons.

Octavia meant to pull back. She told herself to pull back. But it was, after all, only a kiss. She closed her eyes and enjoyed the sweet taste of Massimo's mouth, the gentle insistence of his hand on her chin.

When he broke the kiss, he didn't pull away immediately. His hand stayed where it was, stroking her cheek, cupping her jaw. "Invite me to your room, Octavia."

Gently, she removed his hand and placed it on the steering wheel. "It's not a good idea," she said.

He put the car in gear, still watching her. "I think it is," he said. "But I promised."

"Good memory," she answered. She tore her gaze away to look out at the lights of the city. The shops were closed now. Even some of the restaurants were closing their shutters. As the Mercedes carried her toward the hotel, she felt a pang of regret. She supposed the room would still be empty. And her mouth tingled with remembered pleasure, making her body tingle, too. It had been a long time.

When they reached the hotel, the doorman started out to meet the car. Octavia reached for the door handle, but Massimo reached across to stop her. Before she could speak, he kissed her again, lingeringly this time, his lips moving against hers, his hand running up her arm to touch her breast, down to caress her waist.

He seemed so guileless, touching her as a boy might, tentatively, but with the promise of delights to come. Her breath came faster, and she considered changing her mind.

Then, abruptly, she thrust his hands away from her and drew her head back, breathing hard.

In the light that came from the hotel entrance, she saw that his lean cheeks flamed.

"Massimo—I'm sorry, but I have to—I have to go." She reached for the door handle, but the doorman, seeing her movement, was there before her.

"What happened, for God's sake?" Massimo asked.

"Thank you for dinner," Octavia said hurriedly. She picked up her bag from the floor and swung her legs out. "I'll see you tomorrow."

The doorman kept his eyes averted as he closed the door. The tires hissed as Massimo swung the Mercedes sharply around the drive and sped out into the street.

Octavia covered her mouth with her hand as she hurried into the lobby, which mercifully was empty except for the night clerk. She kept her head turned away as she waited for the elevator, and when it came, she went in without looking back into the lobby.

That old feeling was in her belly, the throbbing in her throat, the bee-stung swelling of her lips. When she reached her floor, she already had her key in her hand. She let herself into the suite and didn't stop even to take off her coat, but hurried into the bathroom, her hand still over her mouth.

She flicked on the light. Gingerly, almost afraid to look, she lowered her hand. She used her forefinger to lift her upper lip.

Relief made her sag against the counter. Her teeth looked no different from the way they had that morning, at least in no way she could detect. Her incisors were straight and blunt. Her canines were sharp, but no longer than anyone would expect. She turned away from the mirror and went through the suite and into her bedroom with dragging steps, pulling off her jacket and scarf. She stripped off the rest of her clothes, leaving them where they fell on the carpet. With trembling hands, she found a nightgown, and then the thick bathrobe. She unclipped her hair and collapsed across the bed.

Poor Massimo. She should never have gone out with him. Loneliness was no excuse.

She closed her eyes. The room was too warm, and her head spun with wine and with shame. The faces danced through her mind, so many faces, some of them beautiful, some plain, all of them shocked and fearful. Even the most recent of them had been gone a hundred years, yet remained painfully fresh in her perfect memory.

How would she ever forgive herself if she added Massimo Luca to their number?

15

Me già tradì quel barbaro; te vuol tradir ancor!

The wretch has already betrayed me; you could be next!

—Donna Elvira, Act One, Scene Two, *Don Giovanni*

The days after the premiere of *Don Giovanni* brimmed with celebrations at the Nostitz Theater. Mozart was elated, and Bondini strutted with pride as if he had written the opera himself. The dressing rooms were flooded with flowers, and the singers found themselves acclaimed in the cafés and shops, applauded when they walked through the Old Town Square. The Countess Milosch sent notes to each singer, and Count Nostitz himself came backstage to commend them all for their triumph.

Teresa knew there were musical things she should work on, improvements she could make in her reading of the rôle, but her heart and her body burned with a different obsession. She could think of nothing but Mozart. She haunted the artists' entrance when he was expected at the theater. She came early, hoping to see him, and she stayed late, trying to catch him alone. She fabricated questions about the music to have excuses to talk to him, but if he had any memory of what had happened between them and Zdenka Milosch, he gave no sign. He no longer referred to her as the *piatto saporito*. And Constanze seemed to be at his side whenever he wasn't conducting.

Teresa stood in the doorway of her dressing room, watching them leave together after a performance. She had removed her costume and she was in her dressing gown, brushing the powder from her hair. As the Mozarts passed her in the corridor, she reflexively touched her neck. The marks had healed quickly, though they were so deep. She knew Wolfgang must have the same marks. As the Mozarts passed, Constanze looked up at her, and there was a spark in her eye, something fierce and protective that made Teresa step backward into her dressing room, bending her head in acknowledgment of Constanze's right.

She went to her dressing table and reached for the pitcher of water she now kept there all the time. She poured a tumbler of water and drank it down. She touched her forehead and her wrists, but she felt no fever. Why was she so thirsty?

As she pinned her hair up again and put on her street dress and shoes, she told herself she must accept that she was nothing more to Mozart than the creator of his Donna Anna. She was simply another singer, one of dozens he worked with. The moment they had shared had meant nothing to him. There was nothing left of it but the bite marks, and even those were disappearing faster than she would have thought possible.

She stood staring blindly at the rack of costumes against the wall. Everyone else had left the dressing room, and the racket of sets being moved had subsided. The theater would be empty now, everyone gone home or to various receptions. Teresa didn't feel like going to a party, nor did she feel much like going back to her empty room. Absently, her fingers probed her neck, touching the last traces of her encounter with Mozart. Her throat felt parched again, though she had just drunk a full glass of water. She supposed it could mean she was ill. She felt a nearly unbearable restiveness. Her hands twitched at this and that: her hair, her skirts, the flowers on her dressing table. Her feet would not be still, tapping toe and heel, toe and heel, a nervous rhythm.

She pinched the wick of the candle on her dressing table and left the dressing room with a restless step, shutting the door behind her with an irritable bang. The sound resonated down the corridor and into the empty theater. She walked back to the darkened stage and stood just beneath the proscenium arch. The hundreds of candles that had lighted the performance had recently been extinguished, and the fragrance of melting wax filled the darkness. The gold leaf on the walls glimmered faintly through the gloom.

Teresa longed for Vincenzo. She wished there had been a *castrato* rôle in *Don Giovanni,* so he could have been there. Vincenzo had sung for Mozart before, and the composer liked his voice. But styles were changing. The days of the *castrati* were fading, and Vincenzo's opportunities were fading with them.

Teresa wished she could flee back to Milano. Vincenzo would chaff her for being in love with Mozart, a married man. He would tease her, and he would comfort her.

But she couldn't go yet. There were performances yet to give, and other productions after this one. She sighed and turned to go to the artists' entrance.

There was no light left in the corridor except a single oil lamp flickering beside the outer door. Teresa put out her hand to feel her way down the narrow passage, working her way toward the faint glow.

When the light disappeared, she thought at first that the lamp had guttered out. She stretched out her other hand to feel the opposite wall, and her groping fingers encountered something warm and solid.

She drew back, but not before a strong hand gripped her wrist. A man's voice said, "Ah, I've caught my own *piatto saporito!*"

Teresa tried to pull away, but his fingers were iron hard. He pulled her close to him, and she felt the heat of his body burn through her dress. "Let me go!" she demanded.

"Why should I do that, my tasty dish? This is just what I've been hungry for."

She leaned away from his sour breath, but his other hand caught her neck and pulled her close. She felt his lips, thick and moist, mash against her neck. "Leave me alone!" she said. "How dare you!"

Both his arms went around her waist, and he yanked her off her feet. She squirmed, and her struggle made him turn so the light from the gas lamp fell on his face. It was one of the stage-hands, a thick-bodied man hired for his strength alone.

"I'll see you're fired!" she hissed, and tried to rake his cheek with her fingernails.

He laughed and pressed her hard against the wall. She was helpless against his weight and muscle. She tried to kick at him. He threw her to the floor, where she landed with a grunt of pain. Before she could move, he was upon her, pinning her arms, mouthing her cheek. He thrust his hips against hers, leaving no doubt about his intent. He began scrabbling at her skirts to lift them, and when he succeeded in that, he reached a hand be-tween their bodies to unbutton his trousers. One of his heavy boots bruised her ankle as he shoved her legs apart, and she gave a long, sobbing scream of protest.

"Just enjoy it!" he panted in her ear.

She drew breath to scream again, then paused with her lungs full of air. She released the breath in silence, letting her cry die unvoiced. Something had changed. She felt a new sensation in her throat, in her lips, in her teeth. It was like lust, and yet un-like. It was a desire all its own, an instinctive appetite, predatory, cunning, and irresistible.

She let her body relax, softening beneath her assailant. He gave a coarse laugh at her evident submission. "Now, now!" he said. "That's better!" He lifted his head over hers, no doubt in-tending to kiss her.

The strange thirst that had plagued Teresa for days was now in complete command of her. Her lips, hot and swollen, pulled back. Her teeth throbbed, and she opened her mouth wide.

As the man bent his head, she angled her own so that it would not be his mouth she met with hers, but that soft place where the heart's blood pulsed just under the skin. There was no reason in it. There was only her need, and it was more urgent than anything she had ever felt.

She sank her teeth deeply into the left side of his throat. The small sound the skin made as it broke sent a shudder of pleasure through her. It shocked her, but it didn't stop her.

He gave a hoarse cry, which died away in a whimper. He tried, too late, to pull away, but her teeth were locked into his flesh. When he fell onto his back, she followed, covering him with her body. She braced her hands on the floor, on either side of his head, and she drank.

Deep draughts of fresh, hot blood sparkled in her mouth. They soothed her burning throat, calmed her mind, flooded her muscles with vitality until she brimmed with it, a vessel no longer dry.

His body quivered helplessly beneath her. His whimpers turned to moans, then silence. He convulsed once, from head to foot, then lay still as stone.

Teresa didn't know how much time had passed. She came to herself with a sort of slow horror. She struggled awkwardly up from the floor, adjusting her skirts and her smallclothes. The man's arms were flung out, blocking the passage, and she stumbled over one of them as she went to her dressing room for a candle. When she lit it and carried it back, she looked down at the stagehand lying inert in the corridor. She crouched beside him to place a reluctant hand on his chest. He neither breathed nor moved.

She lifted the candle to look more closely at him. She seemed to remember that he was slow of mind, that the stage manager had shouted at him for mistakes and misunderstandings.

She moved the candle so that its flickering light fell over his throat. She saw the two puncture wounds there, dark, with small rivulets of blood trickling away, disappearing into the collar of his shirt. She recognized those marks, and the realization shook her. She tried to make the sign of the cross, but her fingers would not obey.

She ran back to her dressing room with the guttering candle to look in the mirror over her dressing table. There was blood on her lips, and blood on her dress. She rubbed her mouth clean with a towel, then dipped the towel into the ewer of water and scrubbed at the spots on her bodice. They thinned and spread, soaking permanently into the fabric.

She gave it up just as the candle guttered out, leaving her in darkness. She fumbled for her wrap. As she felt her way back out into the corridor, her toe struck the heavy body stretched across her path, and her stomach quivered. No life remained in that body. No spark ran through those muscles, no thoughts—even slow ones—fired in that brain.

But she, as she stepped over him and ran lightly out into the cobbled street, felt more alive than she would have thought possible. Her heart fluttered between remorse and relief like a night moth between two flames. Her body thrummed with energy. And for the first time in days, she was no longer thirsty.

But Mozart? Did he still thirst?

Teresa didn't sleep that night. She paced her room, a tiny hotel in the shadow of St. Nicholas Church, and wished the sun would rise so she could go out and roam the streets of Prague. She wanted to see Mozart, and ask him. She wanted to ask Countess Milosch what had happened. Zdenka Milosch had bitten her, and bitten Mozart. But neither of them had died. Teresa had not even felt weak.

As the long night wore on toward dawn, Teresa wrestled with her guilt. A man had died. He was a bad man, and he had meant to hurt her, but he had been a human being. It didn't matter that she hadn't meant him to die, that she had been driven by an instinct she couldn't resist. She had bitten him, and then she had drunk his blood until there was no longer enough left in him to sustain his life.

And what would happen in the morning? His empty body still lay in the backstage corridor. Frantically, she tried to remember what she had done with the bloody towel. Had she dropped it in her dressing room? In the corridor, or the street? She couldn't recall.

Her room was on the top floor of the hotel, where she could just see the Gothic spires of St. Vitus rising from the far side of the river. When they began to glimmer with early morning light, she tore off her ruined gown and put on a clean one. She pinned up her hair, washed her face, and put on a warm coat. With the bloodied dress bundled into a sack, she left her room and hurried down the stairs, and walked quickly through the dim square toward the Nostitz Theater. At a corner just off the square, she stuffed the sack with its damning evidence into a rubbish bin.

The light was growing with alarming speed. Vendors were loading their handcarts, and shopkeepers were opening their shutters. Teresa began to run. The Nostitz was dark tonight. Teresa didn't expect to meet anyone from the Bondini company, but she feared the cleaning staff might come early, while no one was about.

She rounded the corner into the alley behind the theater, and froze.

Countess Milosch was standing in the artists' entrance, holding the door ajar. A man in a long, dark coat with caped shoulders stepped out. He had what looked like a rolled-up carpet over his shoulder. Teresa flattened herself against the brick wall of the corner building just as the man, with a nod to the Countess, started down the street toward her. He wore a dark hat with a deep brim that dipped forward over his eyes.

Teresa was unable to move as the man walked toward her with a purposeful step. He moved lightly on his booted feet as if the roll of carpet, with its gruesome burden, weighed nothing. He came closer, and then closer. Teresa could hardly breathe.

As he reached her, his eyes peered out from beneath the brim of his hat.

Teresa had just begun to breathe again, thinking she was out of danger, when the man's lips parted and he smiled.

It was the briefest of smiles, a slight curling of the corners of the mouth, pleasant lines carved into lean cheeks. But he showed her—with evident deliberation—his canines. They were brilliantly white in the shadow of the hat brim, and extraordinarily long and pointed. Teresa's heart faltered, and she fell back against the wall so that the rough bricks caught at her hair.

As he strode past her, his lips folded over those fearsome teeth, hiding them from view. He nodded, and was gone, leaving her panting in horror.

"Why, it's our little *piatto saporito!*"

Teresa whirled and found Zdenka Milosch at her shoulder.

The older woman's lips curled, rather as the man's had, but the Countess kept her mouth closed as she smiled, and her cheeks barely moved. Her dark eyes had a flat look, as if no light reflected in them. "So, my dear," she said. "I expect you're feeling better today."

Teresa didn't realize she had been holding her breath until it suddenly hissed in her throat. She put her hands on her hips and glared at the Countess Milosch. "What have you done to me?"

The Countess's slim shoulders lifted. "Two great gifts," she said. Her tone and her expression were careless, as if Teresa's feelings didn't matter in the least.

"Gifts," Teresa snapped. "A thirst so terrible someone had to die?"

Zdenka smiled again, and this time, for just a moment, she allowed her teeth to show. They were even longer than the man's had been, with wicked tips. Teresa's blood ran cold at the sight of them. She resisted a sudden urge to feel her own teeth with her fingers, to see if they had changed. To stop herself, she crossed her arms, pressing her fingers into her ribs.

"My, my," Zdenka said. "So fierce." Her upper lip pulled down again. "But I suppose you must be, to succeed as you have at such a young age. To impress Mozart, and da Ponte."

"My voice impresses Mozart," Teresa said.

Again, the negligent shrug. "Perhaps," the Countess said. "But it may be your figure, after all." Her eyes shifted to the vista of the sun, as if she were growing bored with the conversation. "I think your voice is a little thin, myself. A *voce bianca*, they call it, don't they? A white voice."

Teresa's cheeks burned with sudden resentment. It was just what the director at La Scala sometimes complained of, that her range was marvelous, but her voice was white. Again, Teresa demanded, "What have you done to me, Countess Milosch?"

The Countess's eyes came to back to hers. A sort of cool amusement lifted the corners of her mouth, though her eyes were still opaque. "Signorina." She dipped thin white fingers into the small string purse that hung at her waist and brought out an exquisite little mirror with initials chased on its silver case. "Look." She held the mirror up to Teresa's face.

Despite herself, Teresa looked into the mirror. She saw her own familiar features, her cheeks flushed with anger, but her eyes sparkling with energy and life.

"You are lovely," the Countess said, as casually as if she were commenting on the weather. "There is good reason for them to call you the tasty little dish. And imagine, my dear." She smiled again, that close-lipped, protective smile. "You will look just like this for a very, very long time."

Teresa looked away from her reflection and into the Countess's cold eyes. "What do you mean?" she whispered, suddenly as chilled as she had been hot a moment before. "A long time?"

Zdenka chuckled, a sound as devoid of mirth as a sob might have been. "Unlike most people, you now have control over life—and death."

"You—you know what happened last night."

"I've been expecting it."

"How? How could you know?"

Zdenka gave an impatient sigh, closed the mirror with a click, and tucked it into her bag. "It's been ten days since the premiere," she said shortly. "Since you were so fortunate as to share the bite with Mozart. It was time."

"And why did you—you sent this man to—"

"You'll learn all of this," Zdenka said, gathering her skirts up and turning toward the street. "But next time, please don't leave your rubbish for someone else to pick up."

She stepped off the sidewalk, but Teresa followed her. "He was a man," she said weakly.

Zdenka started across the street, but she spoke over her shoulder. "Precisely. Merely a human. He was insignificant in life, and we certainly don't want him acquiring significance in death."

She was gone a moment later, striding away with a strong step, her skirts swirling with the speed of her passage. Teresa stood in the middle of the street, staring after her. Zdenka had spoken of two gifts, but had neglected to tell her about the second.

Teresa wandered through the Old Town Square, bemused and shaken. The lovely buildings of Prague were dim behind the images that still filled her vision: the man lying so still in the corridor of the theater, the bloodstains on her mouth, the ruined dress—and Zdenka Milosch's long, sharp teeth. Around her traffic increased, with carriages and handcarts rattling over the cobbled streets, vendors crying their wares, and the bells from the cathedral ringing out across the river.

Those bells sent a chill through Teresa's body. She stopped, hardly knowing where her feet had carried her, and looked up.

She found herself standing before the soaring white façade of St. Nicholas Church. The morning sun gleamed on its sculpted towers, and the bells were ringing, calling the faithful to morning Mass. People passed Teresa, smiling, nodding to her as they made their way into the church.

With a pang, Teresa realized she had not been to Mass in weeks. She suddenly longed for the anonymity of the confessional screen, and the reward afterward of Holy Communion. She would savor the taste of the dry, sweet wafer on her tongue. Surely a sip of sacramental wine would wash away the taint of blood in her mouth. And in the familiar rituals before the altar, she could find herself again, think this through, find the reason for what had happened.

She picked up her skirts and hurried up the stone steps.

Delicate stucco carvings graced the interior of St. Nicholas. Its walls bore deeply colored frescoes, and sunlight slanted through a great *oculus Dei* to gleam on the marble floors and statues. Teresa looked about for the font and hurried toward it, reaching out to dip her fingers, to bless herself.

When her fingertips touched the holy water, she gasped so loudly that people nearby turned to see what was wrong.

Teresa pulled back her hand and thrust it under her opposite arm. She wanted to suck on her burned fingers, but she didn't dare. She backed away a step and watched with growing dismay as an elderly woman in a black scarf dipped her fingers and crossed herself, followed by a middle-aged woman wrapped in a knitted shawl, and then a man in a frock coat. A youth with un-powdered hair curling over his high collar touched the water with his fingers, crossed himself, and genuflected.

None of them cried out or winced away from the touch of the blessed water. But it had scalded Teresa's fingertips.

She took another backward step and bumped into someone. She couldn't pull herself together enough to apologize, but whirled to blunder back toward the square, heedless of the little crowd of people trying to come in through the doors. She stumbled over the lintel, and then stood outside on the steps in the bright sun-shine. Now she did put her fingers in her mouth to soothe them, while tears coursed down her cheeks. Her tears were warm against her cold skin, but they were not so hot as the water in the font had been. It had neither steamed nor bubbled, but it had burned her as surely as if she had put her hand into a boiling pot.

On the next night of *Don Giovanni*, Teresa arrived early at the Nostitz Theater. She checked that her costumes were in order, that her props were in their proper place, before she went down the cramped corridor to the conductor's dressing room. She knocked, and when there was no answer, she opened the door and slipped into the darkened space.

It was hardly more than a closet. A powdered wig hung on the high back of a wooden chair, glowing faintly in the darkness. Her ghostly reflection shone in a dim mirror. She bent toward it and lifted her upper lip to inspect her teeth. There was something bothering her about her teeth, although she felt certain they looked no different. She ran her finger across them, measuring them, wondering. Was the tip of her right canine perhaps a little sharper than it had been yesterday? She took her finger away and turned from the mirror.

A frock coat hung from a hook beside the door. Teresa put out her hand and stroked it, imagining it invested with Mozart's warmth.

An image suddenly rose before her eyes, as clear as if she were looking at a painting. She snatched her hand back, but the image did not fade. She saw Constanze, plump and petite, brushing the frock coat, scolding gently as she worked the brush over the sleeves and skirts, turning to shake her forefinger at . . . at Mozart.

Teresa blinked, and shook her head. What nonsense was this? Why should she have Constanze in her mind's eye, as if she had in reality seen Mozart's wife brushing his coat, upbraiding him for some offense? It was as if she had been there, when of course she had not.

Her heart thumped in her ears, and she leaned against the wall, wondering what was happening to her. It was not the first time she had imagined a memory that was not her own. In the past days, she had remembered a letter from Leopold Mozart, though she had never met him. She had imagined that she remembered a concert, an organist playing some composition of Bach, a concert and a piece she had never heard. And now Mozart's wife . . .

She heard voices rise in the corridor, the singers arriving, the stagehands cursing and laughing together, the dressers chattering among themselves. Teresa stood very still, twining her fingers tightly together. She heard him coming, his voice calling out to someone about a violin part, and then a complaint about a cadence in the overture. He didn't sound like himself, she thought, but perhaps she imagined that because she no longer felt like herself.

They had shared the bite, Zdenka said. Two great gifts.

The door opened, and he came in with a little rush of cold air. He closed it behind him and bent to put a match to the candle. When it flared, he straightened, pulled off his overcoat, and turned to the hook beside the door.

He saw her and froze.

Swiftly, she breathed, "Maestro. I have to speak with you!"

They were so close she could feel the heat of his body and smell the scent of bay rum on his cheeks. For a moment she thought he might order her out of the dressing room. His dark eyes looked fierce and hard. But as he put up a hand to run it through his already tousled hair, she saw that they were neither. They were brilliant, as if with fever. Or with fear.

"What do you want?" he said hoarsely. "I have to think of the performance."

"So do I," she said, with a spark of resentment. "But I need to know what has happened to us!"

He dropped his hand, and stared at her. "Us?" he said, so softly that if she had not been watching his face, she could not have been certain he spoke the word.

She stared back at him. "We can't avoid it, sir," she said. "Something has happened, and we need to understand it."

He turned abruptly away from her and picked up the wig. "I have to change."

"Herr Mozart," she said, in a sharp tone. She saw his back stiffen, but he didn't turn back to face her. "Wolfgang," she said more gently. "Have you been thirsty?"

A silence stretched in the cramped room. She heard him breathe, in, out, in, out. When he swung round at last, his features were etched with misery. His full lips, those lips she longed to kiss again, trembled. "I went across the river in the middle of the night," he said. "To an inn just by St. Vitus. My throat burned so, and I thought—I thought a glass of beer might—" He dropped his eyes.

Teresa said, "Who was it, Wolfgang?"

His eyes fixed on the floor. "I don't know. A woman. A whore."

"Did she die?"

He managed a hollow chuckle, a pale specter of his usual merry laughter. "Oh, yes. Oh, yes. Yes, I do think she died."

"And did you—did you leave her there?"

"I didn't know what else to do. I didn't—I *don't*—understand anything! She came up to me in an alley behind the cathedral, and I just—I didn't mean to—"

"I know," Teresa said quietly. She put her hand on his arm and felt him trembling.

He blurted, suddenly speaking quickly, "It was—it was like the Commendatore in scene one, lying on the stage as still and empty as an old sack. It always gives me chills, the Commendatore lying there dead while everyone sings over his head. And now I think, I fear, that I will end up like Giovanni, sucked down into hell to live with the devil!"

Teresa gripped his arm with her fingers. "Stop," she said firmly. "Stop it, Wolfgang. It wasn't your fault, and it wasn't mine. The Countess made this happen."

A knock at the door made them both jump. "Fifteen minutes, Maestro," someone called.

Mozart's eyes flew to the door, and then up to Teresa's face, pleading, helpless.

"Answer," she whispered.

"*Ja*," Mozart croaked. "*Danke.*"

"I spoke to her," Teresa said in an undertone. "To Countess Milosch. She said there were two great gifts."

"Gifts!" Mozart spat. "Curses."

"She said I wouldn't age," Teresa said hastily. "At least not for a long time." She had to hurry, she knew. She could barely dress and get into makeup in fifteen minutes. "Do you know what the second one is?"

Mozart began to shrug out of his street coat. "Tell me," he said. His voice was bitter. "Did you live beside the water? Was your mother a singer?"

It was Teresa's turn to stare. Shocked, she managed to say, "Yes. I'm from Limone, a village on Lake Garda."

"*Ja,*" Mozart snapped. He pulled on the powdered wig and adjusted it with his fingers, tucking the long curls of his own hair under its net base. "*Ja,* I remember that."

"You can't remember. I never told you."

Mozart pulled the frock coat off its hook and put it on. "*Nein,* you never told me. But since that night, I remember it just the same." He pulled at his lapels and fluffed the dangling locks of the wig over his shoulders. His eyes had gone bleak. "I know your father cried when you left home. I know your house was full of people the night your mother died."

Teresa sagged back against the wall, one hand to her throat. "*Gran Dio,*" she breathed.

"Or *diavolo.*" He put his hand on the latch of the door. "I don't want your memories, Teresa. My own are more than I can bear."

"It isn't my fault, Wolfgang."

"No. But it is no gift to me."

He didn't look at her again. He opened the door and stalked out, leaving the door ajar behind him. Teresa followed, turning toward her own dressing room, heart-bruised and shocked.

And still, despite everything, her mind turned toward the opera ahead.

Caterina Bondini and Caterina Micelli, the Elvira and Zerlina, were already fully made up. They paced the end of the dressing room, vocalizing, and both eyed Teresa suspiciously. She hurried to strip off her street dress and begin powdering her cheeks and her throat. She hummed as she did her eyes and her lips, and began to run her scales as she tugged on the towering edifice of her wig. When the five-minute call came, she jumped up and began tying on her petticoat. Signora Bondini, with a reproachful twist of her lips, went to the door to call a dresser to help her with her stays and panniers. When the first strains of the overture sounded, Teresa pulled away from the dresser, though the top buttons of her bodice were not yet fastened, and hurried toward the stage.

She had not had enough time to warm up. Usually she vocalized for twenty minutes before even coming to the theater, and sang for another twenty after her makeup was finished and her costume secure. And this rôle, with its fearsome intervals and rapid *coloratura*, had always meant extra time to prepare her voice.

A flutter of nerves quivered under her breastbone as she took her place for the opening scene. She had not felt so nervous since that first day on the stage in Milano. She wondered if there was any voice in her throat at all.

The opening bars sounded, and Leporello began his complaint about the hardships of serving his master Don Giovanni. Teresa stood beside Luigi Bassi, ready to make the entrance for the opening trio. As she came into the lights of the stage, she began to sing:

> *"Non sperar, se non m'uccidi,*
> *Ch'io ti lasci fuggir mai . . ."*

Her voice had never felt so flexible, so strong. She dragged at the Don while he tried to hide his face. She swore he would have to kill her to get away without being exposed, while he sang his avowal that she would never discover his name, and Leporello laughed at the commotion.

When the trio came to its end and Teresa ran offstage, she felt a wave of relief. She knew she had sung well. She had felt no stiffness in her voice, no dryness in her tone. She waited eagerly by the set machinery for her next entrance.

Antonio Baglioni, the Don Ottavio, appeared at her side just as the music for their entrance sounded. Teresa ran ahead of him to the stage to lament over the body of her fallen father, the poor Commendatore. She began her song of blood and death:

"Quel sangue . . . quella piaga . . ."

As she gripped Baglioni's arm, she saw him wince under the fierce strength of her fingers. At that moment the memory of Mozart writing the music appeared in her mind. She had a jarring feeling of recognition, of puzzle pieces falling into place, so that she couldn't understand how she had not seen it before. She saw the notes on the page, as she always had, but she also felt, in her being, the shape of the music as he had intended it. The curve of the phrases crystallized. The meaning of the swells and diminuendi deepened. She sang on.

". . . tinto e coperto del color di morte . . ."

She felt Mozart's surprise from where he stood at the harpsichord. His eyes lifted to hers, and a moment of understanding flashed between them. She turned back to Don Ottavio and went on with the scene, but it was different now. The music was something unified, not a succession of notes and rhythms but a living creation of sound in which every *forte*, every *piano*, every accidental had meaning. Her voice became more than a solo instrument. It became a part of the whole, connected to the strings and the winds and the harpsichord. She could see beyond the current scene, sense the whole of the opera, the progression of harmonies, the relationships of keys and *tempi*.

She knew in her soul that music had changed forevermore. Mozart's genius, something rarified, far above her own small talent, was now part of her own memories. This was the second gift Zdenka Milosch had spoken of.

She might still be the *voce bianca*. But no singer on the stage made music the way she did that night.

The burden of such a gift would make itself clear in the months to come. But for that moment, that particular evening, Teresa sang as she had never sung before, and it all seemed worthwhile.

16

Ohimè, respiro!

Ah, I breathe again!

—Don Ottavio, Act One, Scene Two, *Don Giovanni*

Benson, predictably, elected to cut Ugo's trousers off, despite a polite request to unzip and remove them properly.

"Roberto Cavalli," Ugo sighed as Benson began to saw at the fabric with a knife. "What a waste."

Benson leered at him. "Too small for me."

Ugo was tempted to make a remark about the repugnance of Benson wearing his clothes, but at that moment Domenico leaned over him, holding the scalpel an inch from his eyes.

"Where do I find them, Ugo?" Domenico grated. "I'm tired, and I want to know now." He brandished the scalpel, just a little, and Ugo felt it brush his eyelashes.

"It's clear you have no stomach for this, my friend," Ugo said. "Why don't you simply let me out of here and take my word for it? You don't want to know this. You really don't."

Domenico exhaled noisily and straightened. "Strip him, Benson."

Benson, his bald scalp gone pink with heat, ripped Ugo's shorts from his body, holding them up like a tattered flag. He grinned at Domenico and said, "Hey, you want me to do it?"

Ugo could see that Domenico considered this for a bare second. He had it right, evidently. Domenico had no personal taste for violence.

But his captor visibly steeled himself. "No." He reversed the scalpel, holding it in his fist like an icepick. "See this, Ugo? Do you want to be a eunuch?"

"*Castrato*," Ugo said softly. "The word you want is *castrato*." The centuries-old scar in his groin tingled. It was time.

He twisted his head to look at Benson. "Farewell, my brutal friend."

"What does that mean?" Benson blustered.

Ugo said, "Your boss had it backward. About my medicine."

"What?"

Domenico snapped, "Shut up. Just get Marks in here."

Benson went to the door. A moment later, they gathered around the noisome bed, Benson's eyes greedy for more agony, Marks looking confused and a little fearful, Domenico weary and a bit nauseous.

Rather fussily, his lips pulled back in distaste, he placed the edge of the knife against Ugo's right testicle and pressed it into his skin.

This new, exquisite pain flashed through Ugo's groin and up through his abdominal wall to pierce his solar plexus. There was no music in this sensation, but there was a fierce potency in it, the *slancio* of transformation.

Blood began to roar in Ugo's head. His teeth ached, and the follicles in his skin erupted all at once, like a hundred thousand tiny volcanoes. His brain began to burn, synapses afire with change. His bones swelled. His spine curved and lengthened. The shackles that held him to the cot were no more than threads, and he burst them effortlessly. He growled, then roared, and leapt up to claw at Benson's stunned face.

Canis lupus sicilianus.

Ugo ceased. The wolf began.

17

Rammenta la piaga del misero seno,
rimira di sangue coperto il terreno . . .

Remember the wound in the unhappy breast,
recall the ground running red with blood . . .

—Donna Anna, Act One, Scene Two, *Don Giovanni*

Octavia arrived early in the rehearsal room. Massimo had not yet arrived, but Richard was there, and Giorgio. They had their heads together over a score, conferring. Giorgio looked up as she came in.

"We'll start with your entrance, Octavia, I promise. As soon as everyone's here."

She slipped out of her coat and draped it over a chair. "If we have a few minutes, then, I'll run down and get a coffee." Giorgio nodded and spoke to Richard again.

Octavia shouldered her bag and went back out into the hallway. In the elevator down to the canteen, she caught herself running her finger over her teeth, and she forced herself to put her hand in the pocket of her slacks. When the elevator doors opened, she found herself looking up into the caramel eyes of Massimo Luca. He had a cup and saucer in his hand, with a small *cornetto* in a napkin. His eyelids were heavy, as if he hadn't slept. He bore a purple bruise in the hollow of his jaw, with abraded skin around it, as if someone had struck him with a fist. She could see someone had treated the mark with ointment of some kind, but a trickle of blood oozed from beneath it.

"*Buongiorno,*" Octavia said. "Massimo, what happened to you?"

He said abruptly, "*Buongiorno.*" He looked away, as if she might not notice if he turned his head.

"Are you all right?" She touched her own jaw. "You should ice that—"

"No." He said it in the Italian way, sharp and short. She let her sentence go unfinished. He made an exasperated noise, and then gestured with his coffee cup. "I don't want to talk about it, if you don't mind. Let me buy you a *cappuccino.*"

"That's sweet of you, Massimo. I can get it. I just—"

The elevator doors began to close. He had no hand free, but he stuck his booted foot out to stop them. He gave her a rueful smile. "I want to apologize to you, Octavia."

"Apologize!"

She stepped out of the elevator. He moved his foot to allow the doors to close, then turned back toward the canteen. She walked beside him, waiting for his explanation. When they reached the canteen, he pushed the door open with his hip. "*Ma certo,* Octavia," he said in a low tone. Two people brushed past them in the doorway. He waited until they were gone before he said, "I broke my promise to you."

She looked at him blankly. "Promise?"

He set his burdens on a nearby table and took her elbow to escort her to the counter. It was hard not to notice the warmth of his hand, nor to appreciate anew the comfort of a tall man at her shoulder. When they had obtained her *cappuccino* and were headed back to the elevator, Massimo said, "I promised dinner only, nothing more, and then I—well. I'm sorry."

As the elevator bore them up, she sighed. "Massimo, I'm the one who should apologize. It was a lovely evening. I enjoyed it all—the dinner, the conversation, everything."

The elevator stopped, and the door slid open. "Let's begin again, Octavia," he said quietly. "Next time I'll keep my promise."

She looked up at the chiseled line of his jaw, the line of his neck outlined by the open collar of his white shirt. "Massimo. I think it's better not to have a next time." As he shot her a look, she said hastily, "My assistant will be back soon, and . . ."

"But your assistant—he's not your—" Massimo didn't finish his thought, but Octavia knew what he was asking.

She laughed a little. "No, no, he's not. He's my assistant, and my friend. But he will certainly want me to concentrate on the opera."

They reached the rehearsal room and went in to find Giorgio and Russell with their heads bent together. Angelo Marti, the Don Giovanni from the alternate cast, was seated in one of the folding chairs, chatting with Peter and Richard. He lifted a hand in greeting when he saw Octavia and Massimo. They crossed to him.

"*Che successa?*" Massimo asked. "I didn't expect to see you here."

Angelo shrugged. "I receive a call this morning," he said, in heavily accented English. "Barrett-Jones, he is . . ." He seemed to be searching for a word.

Massimo said, "Octavia speaks excellent Italian, Angelo."

The bass-baritone smiled at her. "*Bene!* That's so much easier." He went on in Italian, "Your Giovanni is ill, it seems. Flu or something. They asked me to sing your rehearsal."

Octavia frowned. "He was fine yesterday. I hope we're not all going to get it."

Angelo stood up and pointed at Massimo's face. "You've been boxing in your free time?"

Massimo shook his head. His eyes darkened with what Octavia took to be anger. He didn't answer Angelo but turned abruptly away, a muscle flexing along his jaw. Octavia watched him, surprised by this side of him, then remembered the angry hiss of the Mercedes's tires as he had spun away from Il Principe.

There was no time to press him further. Giorgio called places to finish scene two, beginning with "Or sai chi l'onore." Peter and Octavia knew their blocking thoroughly, and Angelo knew his as well, so Giovanni's scene with Leporello went swiftly forward. Marie arrived, and Giorgio, with a satisfied nod, pressed on into scene three, for Zerlina's and Masetto's argument.

Massimo and Marie began, with Giorgio coaxing the most amusement he could out of Zerlina's charming "Batti, batti." Everything went well, with Russell conducting from his stool beside the piano.

The couple turned in the direction the audience would be. Massimo, according to Giorgio's direction, swept Marie into his arms and sang his lines with his cheek pressed to her hair.

"Guarda un po' come seppe questra strega sedurmi!"

When he lifted his head, Octavia bit her lip with concern. Blood trickled freely now down his jaw.

He felt it and pulled a handkerchief from his pocket to press against it. Marie turned to see what was happening and exclaimed in sympathy.

But Russell, with a gasp, turned away and leaned on the piano, blood draining from his face. Octavia, watching from a few steps away, rushed to him and put her arm around his shoulders.

"Russell! Are you all right, dear?"

His body trembled beneath her hand, and he choked, "Sorry! So sorry, everyone . . . I just . . ."

Giorgio trotted over, his face pink with concern. "Russell, do you need a doctor? Someone, call down to the infirmary—"

"No, no," Russell protested, weakly, but with energy. "No, I'll be fine. Oh, my God, it's so embarrassing. . . ."

Octavia took a firmer hold on his shoulders and guided him to a chair. "There, now, Russell. Put your head down. You're feeling faint?"

He did as she bade, bending to put his head on his knees. In a muffled voice, he said, "Yes. It's . . . I'm so sorry. . . ."

"Is it the blood?" Octavia asked, in a tone meant only for Russell's ears.

He nodded without lifting his head. "I can't stand the sight of it. So childish, I know."

"It's all right, Russell. No one likes the sight of blood. But we don't have to tell them. I'll just say you're feeling faint, shall I?"

"Thank you," he said, with obvious misery. "So kind."

Octavia patted him and straightened to face the others. "I think Russell might need a little break for some food," she said. "He's been working too hard, and he's feeling a little faint."

Giorgio nodded vigorously. "Of course, of course. We'll all take a break. Shall I send someone—"

"No, thank you, Giorgio," Octavia said firmly. "Why don't you all go down to the canteen, and when Russell's feeling better, I'll walk down with him."

"*Sì, sì, va bene,*" Giorgio said, and the others agreed. Angelo and Richard turned to walk away with Giorgio, and Marie, with a glance up at Massimo, followed.

Massimo hesitated, looking down at Russell, still bent over his knees, and at Octavia. He lowered the handkerchief, leaving a smear of blood on his cheek.

"You might want to visit the *pronto soccorso* for that," she said.

"No. It will stop bleeding in a minute." He swiped at it again. "See you downstairs?"

"Yes. We'll be along in a minute."

He nodded, turned, and strode toward the door. She watched his retreating back, wondering what could have happened between their dinner last night and this morning, what it was that he wouldn't explain.

She patted Russell's back, waiting for him to feel better, and contemplating a disturbing urge to lick the blood being wasted on Massimo's cheek.

Octavia hardly knew how she got through the long hours of rehearsal. She left before Massimo, and even before Russell, who seemed fully recovered from his faintness of the morning and looked as if he might be waiting for her when they were released for the evening. She hurried out, shrugging into her coat as she went, wrapping her scarf several times around her throat against the chill evening breeze. She thought someone spoke her name, but she didn't turn. She flagged a taxi, though she knew the doorman at Il Principe would scold her for not calling for the limousine. All she wanted was to be in her suite, the door closed and locked. Her throat had begun to burn.

The smell of blood that had clung to Massimo all day had nearly driven her mad.

When she shut the door of the suite behind her, she stood in the center of the lush carpet, shivering. Her teeth throbbed, and she was afraid to look at them. She hugged herself tightly, as if she could hold in this drive, this awful desire. It had been more than a century since she had resorted to the tooth. Was Ugo right? If she was thirsty enough, would she lose control?

18

Dalla sua pace la mia dipende;
quel che a lei piace vita mi rende.

On her peace of mind my own depends;
her wishes are the breath of life to me.

—Don Ottavio, Act One, Scene Two, *Don Giovanni*

Hélène found a willing enough victim on the ferry, but the delay had made her ravenously thirsty, and out of control. She didn't know, when it was over, quite what she had done, but she feared the worst.

The next morning, at breakfast in the Palace dining room, she saw the *Chronicle* headline. A body had been found on the ferry, dead of mysterious causes. A bad photograph showed the very face she remembered, whiskered, thick-nosed, middle-aged. Lifeless.

Hélène abandoned the poached eggs and fresh biscuits set before her and blundered out of the hotel, her empty stomach roiling. She turned north, toward the bay, walking as fast as she could in her heeled boots. She paid no attention to where she was going, only following the soothing lure of the waves and the clanging of the warning bell from Alcatraz.

After a walk of thirty minutes or so, she found herself on Battery Street, skirting the foot of Telegraph Hill on her way to the shore. Thick gray fog roiled above the bay, hiding the roofs of

Sausalito on the opposite shore. The tang of fish from the wharf reminded her of the salt taste of fresh blood. As she paced the grass above the beach, the hem of her skirt grew heavy with the damp.

She had meant not to kill him! She had tried to hold back, to stop before she went too far. It was the great danger in getting too thirsty, in letting too much time lapse between feedings. Her own reluctance made her inefficient, even after all these years. She resisted the thirst, and she resisted its satisfaction.

Somewhere above her, hidden by the fog, a seagull gave its tritone call, F–B, F–B. For a painful moment, she was Teresa Saporiti again, leaving her home in Limone sul Garda to begin her life as a singer. Sorrow filled her breast for lost innocence, and for the heartache of a life lived alone.

She turned to walk back toward the docks, where the fishing boats bobbed as they waited for the fog to lift. She wrapped her coat more tightly about her and pulled her scarf down over her forehead, retracing her steps along the shore. The fog swept up over the beach, and she walked into it, glad to be isolated with her misery and her guilt.

He seemed to coalesce out of the drifts of fog, first his flat cap, then the sweep of his gray worsted topcoat, the jut of white that was his stiff collar. His face was a blur of shadows against the gray, but Hélène recognized him instantly.

She swerved abruptly to her left to avoid him, but he moved easily, wolflike, and blocked her path. "I need to talk to you."

"Leave me alone," she said. "You've caused enough damage."

His smile was as cool as the fog itself. "You have no idea," he said lightly. "But I'm going to explain it."

"Explain what? Why you made me kill some poor innocent man?"

He shrugged. His black eyes were as cold as the fog. "He wasn't innocent. I've seen him before. He haunts Jackson Street for whores. He doesn't always pay for what he takes."

"I don't care. I didn't intend to kill him."

He put out his hand and gripped her elbow. She tried to pull away, but his fingers were like steel. "Hélène. I've come to you as a friend."

"A friend!" she spat. Her lip curled and she knew her teeth were showing, but she didn't care about that, either. "Are you going to expose me?"

He pressed a hand to his chest, and laughed. "Expose you! *Mon Dieu, ma chérie!* We are both creatures of secrecy. To expose you would be to expose myself. And besides, who would believe me?" He turned her toward the beach. "Come now, mademoiselle. Let's go down to the water's edge and make ourselves comfortable. I have a great deal to tell you."

"I have a performance tonight."

"Yes, I know." He gave her a cool smile and urged her forward with a steady pressure under her arm. "*Carmen.* With the great Caruso. And Fremstad. I hear she's a bitch to work with."

"How do you know that?"

"We've been watching you, Hélène."

She missed a step, stumbling on the grass. "Watching me?"

He guided her to a long piece of driftwood, an ancient log with a single disintegrating branch pointing its silver-gray arm at the sky. It lay a few feet from where the water foamed over the sand, washing bits of sea wrack up onto the beach. He made an elegant gesture with his free hand, inviting her to sit.

Hélène, with a wary glance at him, sat down. The top of Nob Hill was just beginning to show through the mist. Everything else hid behind its shifting veils. The bay itself was invisible, present only in the faint slap of water against the shore. She felt as if she and this man, this stranger, were alone in the world. He frightened her, with his black eyes and dusky skin, his knowing, pitiless smile.

He sat down beside her, leaning negligently against the splintered branch.

"Who are you?" she asked.

"I'm someone who cares what happens to you."

"You've been watching me."

"Yes."

"For how long?"

The turn of his wrist, the opening of his fingers as he gestured were as graceful as any dancer's. "We first began to wonder about you in New York."

"We? Who else?" She stiffened. Her scarf had fallen back, and wisps of her hair, dampened by the mist, began to curl around her chin. She wanted to flee. She had been so careful and had convinced herself she was safe, but now a sense of hopelessness swept over her, more chilling than the fog from the San Francisco Bay. She had escaped detection for so long. Only Zdenka Milosch, she believed, knew of her existence, and she had not seen the Countess since Teresa Saporiti's last performance.

"The elders," he said quietly. She brought her gaze back to his face and saw a flash of something there, a crinkle of the eyelids, a slight softening of the lips. It looked for a moment like sympathy, and it frightened her even more. She could trust no one. It was too dangerous. She had learned that from Countess Milosch.

She started to rise. He caught her back, but this time his hand was gentle. "I've heard you sing," he said.

"What does that matter?" she demanded. The mist absorbed her voice, drank it as if she had no resonance at all.

"Yours is a great gift," he said. "I don't want to lose it."

She stared at him, confused. "Who are these elders? And what do you want?"

He took a breath, and released her arm. "I'm going to tell you." She settled back onto the cold driftwood, watching him.

"The elders," he began, "are like you, Hélène. Or may I say, Teresa?"

Her fingers flew to her mouth.

He smiled. "Please don't worry. The elders of La Società have known about you from the very beginning. About you and Mozart."

"*Gran Dio,*" she breathed.

At that he grinned, his teeth white against his dark face. "Indeed."

"And are you—are you like me?"

He shook his head. "No. I am something quite different."

"What?" she demanded. "What something?"

"That doesn't matter now. What is important is what the elders of La Società want you to do. Or more precisely, what they want you not to do."

"Where are these—these elders? Why don't they come to me themselves?"

"Oh, they rarely leave their compound. They prefer privacy."

"But if they're like me, they need . . . they need to . . ."

He nodded. "They do. But there are many who want to be what they are. What *you* are. An endless stream of them, really, who go in search of the bite. Who beg for it."

Hélène stared at him, all thoughts of flight gone. "Beg for it? But don't they know what can happen? More than half of them die of it."

"No one," he said softly, "thinks that will happen to them."

"And so . . . these elders . . . are they careful?"

"Absolutely not."

"They—you can't mean that they kill them. All of them?"

"All."

Her lips parted again, but she could find no words. She searched his face for some emotion, some regret or guilt or sadness, but she found only pragmatism.

He nodded, as if he understood what it was she was looking for, and as if he knew she had not found it. "They want me to talk to you about that. About being careful."

She blurted, "I don't like them to die."

"But they must. Otherwise, there are too many of them. La Società fears an epidemic, and the threat of exposure that would bring."

"Some die even when I'm careful. When I hold back."

"Not everyone can bear the weight of memory."

She sighed, remembering Mozart. "I know."

Then this strange man, this puzzling creature, stood up and put out his hand to lift her to her feet. "I'll walk you back to your hotel."

The hand that had felt so hard a few moments ago now had a friendly warmth. His fingers were gentle under her arm as he walked beside her up over the strand, onto the grass and the road beyond.

As they walked, Hélène said, "What will they do if I refuse?"

His voice was level and uninflected. "Some do refuse. I know how to deal with them."

"They die."

He shrugged. "It is regrettable, but necessary."

She stopped on a street corner and faced him. People walked by them, hardly glancing at the tall young woman and the slight man. She lifted her chin and gave him a challenging look. "You would kill me."

He looked into her eyes, and she read in his a reflection of her own long loneliness. "I don't want to," he said in a confiding tone. "This is a hard world. There are so few of my kind, and the ones I've met I don't care for. But when I heard you sing in New York, and again at rehearsals here in San Francisco—I felt more joy than I've known in half a century. It's not just your voice— which is spectacular—but your *music*. It touched even me. And I thought I was beyond touching."

"You don't want to kill me," she said flatly. "And I don't want to kill them."

He took her hand in his. "Let me find another way," he said.

Her laugh was short and bitter. "Another way? There is none."

"There may be."

She tore her hand from his and turned away. Her wet skirts swung heavily around her ankles. "I have to change and go to the Opera House."

"Please, Hélène." And more softly, "Teresa. Don't do anything until I—"

Over her shoulder, she said, "You can't help me. Leave me alone." She stalked away toward her hotel, her back stiff with anger and fear.

She sensed his presence, dark and very still behind her. Watching.

19

Perché mi chiedi, perfida?

Why do you ask me, unfaithful one?

—Masetto, Act One, Scene Three, *Don Giovanni*

Octavia came to herself, finding that her retreat into memory had kept her standing in the center of her suite, her scarf hanging limply from one hand, her coat half off her shoulders, trailing on the floor. The curtains were open and the city lights sparkled through the darkness.

She called, "Ugo?" There was only reproachful silence.

She started toward her bedroom, then paused. Ugo's case was in his room. He would be furious if she opened it, but—he had been gone so long. Surely he would understand if she—if she simply took the briefest look inside. There might be a vial there, something to tide her over, to sustain her until Ugo reappeared. He could hardly object to that. He didn't want her hunting in the streets.

She turned, stepping over her coat and scarf where she had dropped them. Seizing upon the slender chance, she hurried to Ugo's room and opened the door wide.

Something about the too-tidy bedroom made it seem cold. Though Ugo's clothes hung in the closet and his suitcases were stacked neatly beside the bureau, the room had an uninhabited feeling. Octavia turned on every lamp before she began opening drawers.

The case, a rather small rectangle of embossed brown leather, was in the bottom drawer of the bureau. She pulled it out and carried it to the bed. She dropped to her knees on the carpet and snapped open the locks.

The interior of the case was as orderly as Ugo himself. There were four syringes neatly Velcroed into place in the lid, with disposable needles in their sealed packages tucked into a pocket beside them. She lifted out the small square of absorbent toweling, bleached to a brilliant white, and found beneath it a package of alcohol wipes and one of tiny, clear bandages. There was a coil of tubing and a plastic box holding several clean, empty ampoules.

Feeling hopeless and helpless, Octavia lifted the packages out and searched the corners of the case. She sat back on her heels, holding the towel to her chest, and stared into its emptiness. Nothing. There was nothing in the case to help her.

Carefully, trying to put everything back exactly as she had found it, she repacked the case and replaced the folded towel. She snapped the case shut and stood.

She looked around Ugo's room, as neat and tidy as her own was perpetually messy. She didn't know, really, where he kept her supply, nor did she know how he stored the herb he used to stop his transformations. She sometimes imagined him running through the hills, breathing the wind, feeding in the wild. But she never asked if he missed it. He was adamant in refusing to speak of the other side of his nature.

It was possible, she supposed, that Ugo was weary at last of taking care of her. But surely, had that been the case, he would have given her some indication. He had simply vanished, without warning, without a trace.

She put the case back in its drawer and went to the closet. She pushed back the folding door and found that all of Ugo's things were there, his beautiful jackets and slacks, his two tuxedos, even his opera scarves hanging, smoothly folded, on a padded hanger. She touched them with her fingers and sniffed the faint scent of the sea that clung to his skin and hair.

He laughed at her when she told him she could smell it. "You have a dog's nose," he had said once, reaching out with his slender fingers to tweak that feature. She had slapped at his hand and made some silly remark, and they'd laughed together, secure in their affection, in having found companionship at last.

But that was long after San Francisco.

20

Batti, batti, o bel Masetto, la tua povera Zerlina!

Beat me, beat me, dear Masetto, beat your poor Zerlina!

—Zerlina, Act One, Scene Three, *Don Giovanni*

It seemed that all of San Francisco's high society attended the opening night of *Carmen* at the Grand Opera House on Mission Street. The theater glittered with jewels and furs and rich fabrics, and the air was close with cigar smoke and perfume.

Fremstad, though unconvincing as the gypsy dancer, sang magnificently, her rich voice winding with apparent effortlessness through Bizet's sensuous melodies. The lengthy and enthusiastic ovation for Caruso's Flower Aria brought the show to a halt. But Hélène, in her unflattering costume, struggling with the stubborn tempo of her conductor, had no more than a moderate success as Micaëla. She took her bows as always, curtsying, smiling out into the house despite the humiliating coolness of her applause. It was a relief to go back through the parted curtain.

When the curtain came down for the final time, Hélène forded a stream of people crowding the stage. She found her way down the cramped hallway to her dressing room, trying to keep her composure despite her disappointment and fatigue. She was alarmed to find the dark-haired, slender stranger waiting outside her door. She tried to push past him, but he slipped inside after her.

"Get out," she said. "The dresser will be here in a moment."

"Please," he said, in a gentle tone that belied his hard hand on her arm. "You must talk with me. It's for your own good."

She pulled away from him. "You think I'm a fool. I'm no biddable girl, remember?"

"Indeed you're not!" When he smiled, his face took on a boyish charm that made her mistrust him all the more. "Hélène," he said. "You sang gloriously tonight. And your interpretation was flawless."

"*Merci,*" she said bitterly. "Too bad the San Francisco audiences don't agree."

"They're barbarians. They don't understand your voice."

She gave a bitter laugh. "And so now you will stop me from ever singing again?"

"No!" He took her chin in his fingers and looked into her eyes. "I want just the opposite. Please. *Per favore,* Teresa." He dropped his hand.

"Don't speak Italian here," she snapped.

"Let me take you home."

"And if I don't?"

The dresser rapped on the door and called, "Miss Singher? Are you ready?"

"You have to get out," Hélène said, turning away from the stranger's dark gaze.

"Not until you agree."

She glared at him over her shoulder. "Why should I? All I know about you is that you tried to kill me."

"I did not." He gave her that deceptively sweet smile again. "I only showed you that I knew how."

The dresser repeated her knock.

"Promise me," he said. "I'll wait outside."

She gave a noncommittal shrug. He chuckled and moved to the door to hold it open for the dresser.

Hélène took her time after the dresser had carried Micaëla's costume away. She put on her new Eton suit of dove gray, with its circular skirt folded at the bottom in the latest style and jacket trimmed with silk braid and tiny ivory buttons. She brushed her hair up into a chignon and touched her cheeks and lips with rouge. When there was nothing else she could think of to do, she opened the door.

He was leaning against the wall, a slim, chic figure in a tailored overcoat and white opera scarf. He straightened as she came out, and offered her his arm.

"Ugo," he said.

"What?"

"My name. It's Ugo."

"Oh. Italian. Really?"

"*Ma certo, bella.* I was born in Sicily."

She narrowed her eyes as she looked at him. "How long ago, Ugo?"

He grinned, took her hand, and tucked it under his arm. "Trust me, *bella*. I'm older even than you are."

As they made their way up Market to New Montgomery Street, Hélène said, "You're not coming to my room."

"It's not necessary. Not now. We can talk in the courtyard lounge."

"You know my hotel." Her feet dragged on the wooden sidewalk. Her world looked as bleak as it ever had, her career in ruins, her life in the control of this Ugo. She longed, as she often did when she was sad, for the little stone house on the shores of Lake Garda. She didn't even know if it still stood there.

"*Bella,*" her companion said quietly, squeezing her hand against his side. "I know everything about you." His waist was as lean and hard as a boy's. "Anything I couldn't find out for myself I read in Zdenka Milosch's diary."

She caught a swift breath and lost her footing for a step. "Diary?"

He took her elbow to steady her. "Yes. Odd, isn't it, that some-one with such long and perfect recall should keep a diary? But our Zdenka is nothing if not arrogant. She imagines that the de-tails of her life are too fascinating to leave to one memory, no matter how remarkable. And a good thing it is for me. I'm not like you. My memory is long, but far from perfect. And she let me read her diary, at least the parts that relate to you."

"And so . . . Mozart."

He grinned at her. "Oh, yes, *carissima*. Mozart, and a rapacious stagehand, and a thousand other details of the early days, when I was not present but Zdenka was."

"And was it she who told you how to—how to kill one of my kind?"

His look was sympathetic. "Oh, yes. She, and the others of the society. Though I might have guessed. I've dealt with death a great deal, I'm afraid. And the femoral artery is so vital. It makes sense, doesn't it? Heart's blood."

They reached the Palace and made their way through the lobby to the Palm Court, where upholstered chairs were scat-tered here and there around an ebony grand piano. The lounge was full of celebrants, many of whom murmured as they walked by, recognizing one of the singers of the night's opera. One or two gentlemen rose and bowed as Hélène passed them. She inclined her head in thanks, and Ugo nodded acknowledgment as if it were he, and not she, who had performed.

A woman in pink satin with cascades of ivory beads gave her a sidelong glance and murmured something to her companion. They both laughed, and Hélène's cheeks burned.

Ugo led her to a corner where one of the courtyard's namesake palms provided a bit of privacy. Soon she had a glass of brandy in her hand, and Ugo, his own glass of port set aside on a low piecrust table, leaned toward her and spoke in Italian.

"La Società is very strict about their numbers. Many want what you have, and think they can acquire it. They are the foolish ones. But Zdenka and the other elders know you are not foolish. You are, in fact, most desirable, and a credit to your—let us say, to your kind. They have no regrets that you became one of them."

She touched the brandy to her lips and set the glass down. "I was hardly given a choice in the matter."

"I know." He patted her hand. "But you have managed it very well, haven't you?"

"Managed it?" she said bitterly. "Survived it, I think you might say."

"No, no, I wouldn't say that, Teresa."

"Call me Hélène. And speak English."

He shrugged, and switched languages. "Sorry. Hélène. But you did manage. Your previous persona lived a very long time, and yet somehow melted into obscurity, avoiding scrutiny and questions. And then you, dear Hélène, appeared as if out of nowhere, but quietly. You auditioned at the Paris Opéra, and then at the Metropolitan, a very proper rise. You keep to yourself and behave in a professional manner." He smiled. "Well—perhaps one or two lapses. Quite unavoidable, of course."

"Lapses," she repeated. She picked up her glass and took a deep swallow. "I thirst. Sometimes I thirst so that I cannot bear it."

"I know." He took her hand in his and held it.

It felt strange to her, oddly appropriate, as if he were a friend. But of course that couldn't be. She had not had a friend—not a true friend—since Vincenzo died. Not since Teresa had been forced to disappear more than fifty years before. She had dared to reemerge only when everyone who had known her was gone. She took a new name, and she started again.

His gaze was soft on hers, as if he understood what she was thinking. "La Società is offering you a choice."

"Kill or be killed? A poor choice, I think."

"No. Listen to me, Hélène Singher." He squeezed her fingers and then released them to pick up his glass. "I am part of the choice."

"Sex? You could find that anywhere!"

Now he laughed with real mirth. "No, no, not sex! The kind you can offer doesn't interest me."

"What, then?"

"I will supply you with what you need. With *sangue*."

She nearly spilled brandy over her Eton suit. "That's not possible!"

"Oh, but I assure you," he said, "it is."

"But how would you get it?"

His eyes narrowed a little, and the hard glint she remembered from the first night she had met him shone out of them. "As I said, there is an inexhaustible supply of fools."

She narrowed her own eyes, trying to see behind his urbane façade. "You're telling me," she said slowly, "that I would no longer need to . . . resort to the tooth."

"An interesting phrase. You can do that if you prefer. But when you do, it must be final."

"How would you give me what I need?"

He put his dark hand inside his coat and pulled out a small, flat packet tied with tabs of linen. Holding it low, so that no one else could see, he unfolded it to reveal several gleaming needles, a roll of black silk, and four empty vials of dark glass.

Hélène eyed the apparati. "What is all of that?"

"You can guess, surely."

"I need to think about this."

"You must think before you grow thirsty again, *bella*. They won't tolerate any more randomly chosen members of La Società."

She put a tentative finger on one of the vials. The glass was thick and brownish, cold to the touch. She felt like a trapped animal, her back to a corner, with no escape from her tormentor. And yet—

She looked up at his finely cut features, his full lips, his delicate, rather narrow nose. His black eyes could be frightening or appealing. She shouldn't trust him, but there was something in those eyes, and the touch of his hand, that tempted her. They spoke of comfort, beguiled her with the possibility of no longer being alone.

She opened her mouth to ask him more about La Società, but before she could speak, his nostrils flared suddenly. He threw his head up and froze, the way an animal does when it hears something. His eyes narrowed, and he said urgently, "Get up! We have to get out of here."

"What's wrong?"

"Don't say anything." He gathered the needles and vials into their cloth case and folded it. He tucked it into his inner coat pocket even as he stood, pulling her to her feet. "Hurry, please!"

She glanced around her at the crowd in the courtyard. The hour had grown late, well past midnight, but the crowd had hardly diminished. Whatever Ugo thought he had heard, evidently no one else had. They talked on, sipping their drinks, smoking.

Hélène lifted her long coat from the chair and slung it over her shoulders as she let him tug her past the palm tree and on toward the door. As she passed the woman in beaded satin, the lady gave a tipsy laugh and scattered droplets of champagne across her bosom.

As they reached the door, Hélène said, "Ugo, what is it?"

He cast her a glance that glittered like obsidian. "Something's coming." His grip on her hand hardened. "We're going to find shelter."

"Surely the hotel—"

"No. Bricks, and flimsy wood. Come. This way."

He pulled her out through the lobby and into the street. They set off at a near run toward Market Street. He turned left, drawing her with him up the slope toward Golden Gate Park. As they drew near it, Hélène heard a distant rumble, as of thunder. She glanced up into the April sky. It was almost perfectly clear, with stars glimmering through faint wisps of high fog. Dawn already brightened the eastern horizon. The moving waters of the bay shimmered silver and green under its rosy light.

The park was deserted, and oddly silent. Hélène peered up into the trees, wondering what had become of the birds. Surely they should have been singing their morning greetings by now. Ugo led her to the highest point in the center of the park, where a grassy field stretched on either side of them, and there he stopped. He stood still, his head lifted, his eyes fixed on something she couldn't see.

The rumble came again, and this time it didn't fade, but grew louder. Hélène whirled involuntarily to look behind her, thinking a train was bearing down on them or that a wagon full of logs was crashing through the park. There was nothing there.

Just as she turned back to Ugo, to beg him to explain, the first temblor hit.

It felt as if the log she had imagined began to roll beneath her feet, and a heartbeat later it was ten logs, or fifty. The earth groaned as if its bones were breaking, and the ground shifted so that if Ugo had not held her wrists with an iron grip, she would have fallen. Church bells began to ring in the city below them as the temblor shook their towers. The city itself seemed to moan, a long, painful sound that lasted for a minute or more. When it stopped, there was a moment of respite, a sort of suspension when even the breeze was stilled. Then, ten breathless seconds later, another great temblor shook the city.

Ugo pulled Hélène to her knees, and he knelt beside her, one arm around her back, the other hand pressing her head down. Trees began to fall, randomly, their impact intensifying the shaking of the ground. Tearing noises ripped the cool morning air as building fronts began to collapse, spilling bricks and glass into the streets. A great roar began in the area of Chinatown and rumbled across San Francisco as the earth bucked and rolled.

Hélène clung to Ugo and gritted her teeth. It felt as if the world was coming apart around her.

Fire bells began to clang, a different, shriller sound than the church bells, and in the distance, thin screams pierced the deeper noise of the temblor. The shaking went on and on, making seconds into hours, minutes into days. Whole buildings began to crash to the ground, timbers splintering on impact. It seemed to Hélène as if the city gave one great, unison death cry.

A branch from a falling tree sailed above her head, so close that the newly budded twigs caught at her hair and her cloak. Ugo pulled her down even farther, until the two of them were huddled on the grass, the dew soaking their clothes and dampening their faces. There they stayed for long, long minutes.

At length, as if reluctantly, the undulation of the earth beneath them subsided. Still they knelt, waiting, wary of what would come next. When they stood at last, Hélène gazed at Ugo in wonder.

"I would have died without you," she whispered.

"Ah," he said. "It's always nice to be appreciated."

21

Al ballo, se vi piace, v'invita il mio signor.

My master would like you to come, if you care to, to the ball.

—Leporello, Act One, Scene Three, *Don Giovanni*

Ughetto caught sight of himself in the uneven glass window of a tiny *trattoria* just off the Piazza San Ignazio, and shuddered. His tunic, new and spotless such a short time ago, and the envy of the other boys of the *scuola*, was now dark with dirt and dried sweat. His hair had grown out of its fashionable cut and hung limp and oily around his shoulders. His stylish coat, folded in the height of Roman style, had caught on a scrolled-iron gate when he was escaping an enraged shop owner and was rent almost in two. He still wore it because it was all he had. And in the slack purse that hung from his waist, there was nothing. The last of Brescha's pennies had been spent the day before, and he was hungry.

The emptiness of his purse and his belly mocked the emptiness of his heart. It was, he thought, the third blow. The final blow. He had lost his home, then his friend Mauro. And now even his consolation was shattered. The loss of his music—a gift he had never expected, one thrust upon him—was the worst of his losses. He could not see how he was to survive it.

A middle-aged couple, dressed in evening clothes, came across the plaza to the *trattoria*. The woman's hand was on her escort's arm as she stepped daintily in her soft-soled slippers. As they approached, the man eyed Ughetto and moved in front of his companion as if to shield her from something distasteful. Ughetto, chagrined, stepped away from the window, back into the alley alongside the restaurant. As he did, a door opened and a short, thickset man in a grease-stained apron came out, lugging a tin tub. Ughetto's nostrils twitched at the smell of decaying crab and oyster.

The man hissed something at him and waved a hand to shoo him away.

"Signore," Ughetto said softly. *"Ho fame."*

"Go find your food somewhere else," the man snapped. "You're bothering my customers."

"I'm not!" Ughetto protested. "I'm only standing here, sir." His voice rose and broke, a fractured melody he had become accustomed to in recent days.

The man's face softened a little. "Well," he said gruffly. "Stand someplace else."

Ughetto saw the easing of the scowl, the flicker of sympathy in the *padrone*'s eyes. "Sir," he began, with a little flicker of hope. "Do you have some work for me? I could—I could wash dishes or sweep floors, as I did in my *mamma*'s tavern." Ughetto took a step closer to the man, hoping his youth and obvious need might move him somehow.

The *padrone* eyed his dirty clothes, his unwashed hair. At his apparent hesitation, Ughetto took another step. "I can shuck oysters," he said. "Whatever you need."

"You speak well, young man, but I can't take you in like that. My wife wouldn't like it. You need a bath."

"I know. I have no place."

A woman's voice from the kitchen pierced the darkness of the alley. The man shook his head. "I'm sorry, really I am. I can't help you."

Ughetto drew breath to ask again, but then gave it up. Weariness settled over him. He settled for a shallow bow. "Thank you for considering it, sir."

The man withdrew into his kitchen and closed the door on its warmth and brightness. Ughetto leaned against the cold brick wall behind him. He closed his eyes. He longed to go home to Trapani. He yearned for the hot sun, the fresh salty tang of the sea, the clatter and bustle of his mother's tavern. But it was a long way to Sicily. He hadn't the strength to walk there. And even if he had boat fare, he could starve to death before he reached his village.

When he felt a touch on his hand, he barely flinched. Lassitude made his eyelids heavy. He lifted them halfway and found a man's fleshy face close to his. The man licked his narrow lips with a quick, darting tongue. His breath smelled of wine and garlic. When Ughetto didn't move away, he touched him again, more confidently this time, running his hand up Ughetto's arm and onto his shoulder. He held out his other hand so Ughetto could see the little pile of coins in his clean-scrubbed palm.

In a throaty whisper, the man said, *"Va bene, ragazzo?"*

Ughetto stared at the money, thinking about what it meant. A plate of *pasta*, perhaps. A room for the night. A bath.

He was no stranger to propositions, of course. At the *scuola*, some of the older boys made use of the younger ones. Becoming a *castrato* didn't put an end to sexual impulses. Ughetto's refusals had been a matter of reticence rather than repugnance.

But now—now, what did it matter? What did he care what this man thought, this fat little man with his bloodshot eyes, his blob of a nose, his eager palmful of money?

It would be nothing. He would use his hand, let the man spend himself against this very wall. He would flee into the darkness with his purse not quite so slack, and he would find a place to wash his hand—and himself. It would cost him no more than a few moments' disgust.

He put out his palm, and the man poured the money into it.

Ughetto forced a smile to his lips as he dropped the coins into his purse. He reached under the man's coat and groped for the buttons on his trousers. His customer—for such he was, and there was no denying it—pressed hungrily against him. He put a hand on the back of Ughetto's head and pulled it forward, trying to push his lips against Ughetto's. Ughetto turned his face away, and the narrow, wet lips found only his earlobe. The man snuffled against his jaw, groaning with pleasure as Ughetto's hand found its goal.

But when Ughetto began to rub him, the man drew back. "No!" he said hoarsely. "No, not for all that money!" He gripped Ughetto's shoulders with both hands. "Turn around, boy. Take off your britches."

Ughetto removed his hand. "No."

"Yes! I paid you, now do as I tell you." He shoved at Ughetto, pushing him against the wall, trying to turn him by force.

Ughetto pushed back against him, but weakly. Hunger and hopelessness had drained him. "No," he said in his cracked voice. "Not that."

"Yes! Or else give me back my money."

Ughetto stared at him. He didn't want to give up what he had already taken, and his hand was already fouled. The man shook him. "Turn around, you." He pulled with one hand and pushed with the other, until Ughetto found his face grinding against the bricks of the wall, his cloak thrust to one side, his trousers pulled down to his thighs. The night air was cold against his buttocks, and he shuddered as the man seized him with his hot, rubbery fingers.

A moment later, there was pain. It was different from that first, slashing pain in the tub at Nonna's villa. This pierced deep into his body, like the stroke of a sword, and he cried out. The man hissed at him, giving no quarter. The pain rose, filling Ughetto's belly and chest, and he tried to squirm away. The man gripped him tighter, thrust carelessly into him, without regard for his anguish.

A growling filled Ughetto's ears, and his fingers felt as if they burst into flame. That growling—had he heard that before? And the claws digging into the brick wall—were they his? He had seen them before. All at once, the agony of pain withdrew. He whirled.

The man behind him began to scream, a high, thin wail that grated on Ughetto's hypersensitive ears. His spine bent and stretched, causing him a deeper pain, dull and insistent, utterly different from that he had felt a few moments before. He fell to all fours on the cobbled alley and felt the scrape of claws against rough stones. He drew a breath scented with rotting fish, urine, the feces of rats and pigeons. His nostrils flexed, sorting the smells, prioritizing. The fear of the man behind him was the sharpest scent of all, the savory smell of prey. His lips pulled back in a hungry snarl. The man's scream grew wilder as he tried to back away, losing his footing on the cobblestones, falling hard on his backside. He fell against the rubbish bins, spilling oyster shells and crab carcasses. Ughetto gathered himself, ready to pounce.

As his muscles tightened—gloriously long muscles that hugged strong, flexible bones—he heard footsteps inside the *trattoria*, the running feet of men pounding through the kitchen toward the back door.

His mouth opened, long teeth laughing at the man lying prostrate and crying in the alley. Then he spun about to bound across the *piazza* in great fluid leaps.

He was gone before the door opened and men came pouring out.

The dome of the Basilica of St. Peter had been completed at last in 1626. Its great silhouette, seen from below, blotted out the night stars. It was said that Pope Gregory liked to stand at his window gazing out on this immense creation and listening to his choir sing beneath the fabulous murals of the Cappella Sistina. Their slender voices carried up to him on the night air, reassuring him of Christendom's renewed power.

In the shadow of the dome, where elaborate gardens wound around the basilica and the apartments of His Holiness, Ughetto's awareness returned. He found himself, as he had before, curled on his side beneath the branches of a tree, scratched and cold and bloody. This time it was not an orange tree, but a half-grown cedar newly set into the landscaping. And this time he knew, beyond any doubt, that it was not his own blood that flaked from his hands and stained his naked chest. He put his hands to his face and scrubbed away the dried blood that clung to his lips and chin. The taste of meat was in his mouth. He was no longer hungry.

There were only shreds of his clothing clinging to him, fragments of torn linen and ripped pieces of his cloak. The buttons at the neck were gone, burst from the fabric. The seams of the sleeves had also burst, and what was left of the garment flapped uselessly about his thin body.

As he blinked into full consciousness, he scrabbled on the ground around him, searching for his purse. When he found it, he fell upon it as if it could save him somehow, make sense of all that had happened. The few coins it held clinked as he struggled to his feet and emerged from the meager shelter of the cedar.

He tipped his head back to look up into the sky. Beyond the majestic curve of the dome, a few stars clung stubbornly to life. The spire of St. Peter's soared above everything, and caught the first light of dawn before it could reach the city below.

Someone, or something, had died last night. Ughetto knew it in his bones. He was still capable of feeling regret for a life lost, but he felt a fierce gratitude—even pride—that it was not *his* life. His body hurt with a deep ache, a reminder of the humiliation and pain he had suffered in the alley behind the *trattoria*. But that hurt would heal. And, he swore, he would never suffer that particular pain again.

In the shadow of the Basilica of St. Peter, Ughetto resolved that whatever happened to him from now on would be of his own choosing. He was no longer a boy, subject to the whims and orders of his elders. He was a man. His life was his own.

He gripped his purse in his hand and started back down into the city to find clothes and a meal. He could return to Trapani, he supposed. There might be enough money in this purse for boat fare. He imagined himself showing up in his mother's tavern, meeting his sisters again. He wondered if they would fall on his neck with glad cries or shrink away from him.

But he wouldn't go back to Trapani, not now. Despite everything, he could not expose his sisters and his *mamma* to the peril some other poor soul had experienced last night. He couldn't go home until he understood what it was he had become.

The trade of prostitution was a handy one for Ughetto. Those who felt cheated out of full service had little recourse. There was no authority they could complain to. Transactions took place in isolation and darkness. Ughetto gave reasonable service, refusing only that one ultimate humiliation. Then, money obtained, he scampered away down cramped lanes or cluttered alleys where his customers, older and heavier and usually intoxicated, could not follow.

Ughetto became adept at managing his clients. He lounged prettily near the Fountain of Four Rivers in Piazza Navona or leaned against the Column of Marcus Aurelius in Piazza Colonna. He wore modest clothes, inexpensive but clean. He acquired a good razor and a mug and brush, and kept his chin smooth as a boy's. He let his hair grow long, curling girlishly around his clean jawline. He found a back room where the *padrone* asked few questions and where Ughetto could sleep away most of the daylight hours. At night he worked, and when he earned enough money to cover his room and his meals, he spent any extra on concerts. When there was nothing left over for such indulgences, he sat in churches to listen to *castrati* sing.

One of his patrons invited him to a private concert in the *salotto* of a wealthy Roman who lived near the Palazzo del Quirinale. His patron, Cesare Ricci, was a successful wine merchant from Umbria. He was content with Ughetto's sort of service. He wanted nothing more than a body to hold, someone to caress him, to give him release without him having to make much effort.

He found Ughetto first at the Piazza dei Fiori. Their first encounter was as brief as Ughetto's other arrangements, but the second time Cesare sought him out, he treated him to a meal afterward.

Ughetto wondered at this, that Cesare would be willing to be seen with him in public, that he cared about what Ughetto liked to eat, what wine he preferred. None of his other customers showed the slightest interest in his personal tastes, sexual or otherwise. Ughetto, surprised and touched, repaid Cesare's generosity by listening to him talk, sometimes for hours. Soon he knew all about Cesare's wife and his four daughters, about his *villa* on the shores of Lake Trasimeno, about his vineyards and his vintners. Ughetto had little experience of kindness, but Cesare Ricci, with his plump body and smiling dark eyes, seemed to Ughetto the very embodiment of that virtue.

When they had known each other for a few months, Cesare began to express concern over Ughetto's circumstances. He would tuck a little extra money into his pocket, or leave him a bottle of wine from a recent shipment. He embraced him each time he bade him farewell, and told him the date of his return. Ughetto began to look forward to those dates. And Cesare, though he never knew it, was the only one of Ughetto's customers allowed to kiss him.

Cesare wanted company for the concert near the Palazzo del Quirinale, but he could not openly bring a lover. "You will be my nephew," he told Ughetto. "Those breeches are adequate, but I'll bring you a better shirt and cloak. Be sure your shoes are clean. And tie back your hair, or better yet, I'll give you money for a haircut."

Ughetto wasn't offended by these instructions. On the contrary, he found Cesare's concerns rather sweet, and faintly amusing. He had chosen his shirt and cloak precisely because they gave him an impoverished look, and he was perfectly happy to change them.

And he wanted, very much, to go to the concert. He had heard of Francesca Caccini, a Florentine woman well known in Rome for her singing and her compositions. Everyone at the *scuola* knew of her. She wasn't allowed to perform in the churches, of course, but the fashionable *salons* in Rome vied with each other for opportunities to present her.

Ughetto did everything Cesare asked of him. He brushed his secondhand leather slippers until they glowed. He found a barber in Via Lugari, not so fine or so fashionable as the *parrucchiere* Anselmo had hired for him, but one who could cut his black curls into a respectable style for a young man of middling means. When he met Cesare in Piazza dei Fiori, his patron's brows rose and his smile was admiring.

"Ughetto, my dear. You wear those clothes as if you had been born to them."

Ughetto struck a laughing pose, one hand held out, the other on his hip. "Perhaps I was, dearest Cesare. You must leave me a little mystery."

Cesare laughed, and caressed Ughetto's cheek. "We will enjoy this, my young friend," he said. "And then afterward . . . I know a little *ristorante* with a private room, where we can be comfortable. We will indulge ourselves, this one evening."

Ughetto only smiled. He would see to it that Cesare had plenty to drink during the concert. And then more at dinner. It would all be easy enough to manage.

When they reached the house of Cesare's associate, they walked in through an elegant marble courtyard studded with sculptures. Some were new, but many, Ughetto saw, were ancient, from the Greek and the Roman Empire periods. A servant bowed them in through the door, took their cloaks, and announced them. Cesare introduced Ughetto to one or two people in the manner they had planned, and the two of them found chairs near the harpsichord.

Cesare beamed, lifting a glass of good Roman wine, puffing his modest chest with pleasure in their surroundings, in the company, at the prospect of fine music.

Ughetto kept his eyes modestly down, bowing if necessary to other gentlemen, once or twice to passing ladies. He took care to drink sparingly, and he suppressed an urge to fidget with impatience as he waited for the musicians to appear. When at last they did, he gave up any pretense of conversation with Cesare and allowed himself to focus completely on the ensemble.

Caccini's only beauty was in her music. She was a woman of forty-three, with a long nose and an underslung jaw. Her hair was threaded with gray, and her eyebrows were thick. But her voice enchanted Ughetto. Her breath was naturally not so long as that of a *castrato*, and so her *fioritura* was not so dramatic. But her *legato*, and her phrasing, and the limpid way she passed from the chest voice into the upper register, was everything Brescha could have wanted. Ughetto found himself, after her first aria, staring at her with his mouth a little open, his heart beating fast with admiration.

He was so caught up in the moment that when Cesare's hand found his under cover of the applause, Ughetto startled and snatched it away. Coloring, he said in a rush, "Oh, I'm sorry, Cesare. I was . . . I was concentrating. She's a wonderful singer, don't you think?"

Cesare, frowning, said, "You're gazing at her like a man in love. Surely that's not the way your inclinations lie, Ughetto?"

Ughetto swallowed a rush of resentment that this should be anyone's business but his own. It was hardly fair. But then, little in his life had been fair. He leaned back in his chair, and manufactured a mischievous quirk of his lips at his patron. "Cesare, dearest," he said softly. "Is that what you think?"

Cesare's brow smoothed, and he looked around the *salotto* at the other guests. "Well," he said. "Perhaps it's best that you look that way. As you're my nephew, naturally you would be entranced by an accomplished young woman."

Ughetto let his eyelashes sweep down against his cheeks. *"Sì, sì, carissimo,"* he said. "Naturally."

Caccini went to the harpsichord, then, and settled herself on the bench. She announced that the ensemble would undertake one of her new compositions. The room quieted, and Ughetto closed his eyes to let the strains of the motet wash over him. The harpsichord had gone slightly out of tune from the heat of the room, but he didn't mind that so much. It was a very respectable piece. He was warm and had drunk a little wine. There was food to come, and a clean bed, with only a small amount of effort to be expended beforehand. Odd that such modest comforts had come to mean so much to him. Nothing limited a man's ambitions, he supposed, like a few hungry nights in the cold.

It was, until near the end of the concert, a perfect evening. When the ensemble left the floor for an interval, more wine was poured and trays of smoked oysters and garlic-stuffed olives were passed. Cesare chatted happily with his Roman acquaintances, and Ughetto nodded respectfully at everything he said, the picture of a devoted nephew. At one point a woman approached him, a tall, bony woman with narrow black eyes. "Do I know you?" she demanded.

Ughetto bowed to her. "I haven't had the pleasure, Signora. My name is Ughetto."

"Ughetto. Where are you from?" She regarded him with an obsidian gaze that made him wish for Cesare by his side.

He made a deprecating gesture. "Such a tiny town, Signora. You would never have heard of it."

She stared at him a moment longer, her features as set as one of the sculptures in the courtyard, before she then turned away in a swirl of black bombazine. Cesare appeared at Ughetto's elbow. "You've met the Contessa, I see," he said.

"Have I? It wasn't exactly a meeting," Ughetto said.

Cesare shook his head. "No, it wouldn't be. She's from the north somewhere, Prague, or Vienna. They say she's a great music lover."

"She's rude."

"Yes, they say that, too. Come now, Ughetto, the concert is going to resume."

When Caccini came in again, with the ensemble at her heels, everyone sat down with a scraping of chairs, laughing and chattering as they arranged themselves into new patterns. Ughetto found himself separated from Cesare, standing at the back of the room near an arched doorway. Cesare looked up to find him, and Ughetto waved as a patter of applause broke out.

Caccini curtsied, then held up one hand for silence. "My friends," she said. "I'm eager to present to you a new face, and a new voice, to sing a recitative and aria I composed last year. Please welcome one of the fine young singers of the Cappella Sistina. This is Leonino!"

A tall young man with the exaggerated limbs and long torso of a *castrato* swept into the room. He came to the harpsichord and bowed, then stood looking out over the audience, his head held high as if he were visiting royalty.

Ughetto stiffened.

Leonino's eyes drifted almost negligently over the faces before him, until they came to rest on Ughetto. There, they stopped. His lips curled and he inclined his head, ever so slightly.

Ughetto stared at his old tormentor from the *scuola*. Leonino stared back, a second longer than could be considered polite, before he turned to the composer and nodded. She struck a rolled chord, ending in a brief trill, and Leonino began to sing.

His dark soprano was rich in the middle register, and his *melismas* were long and flexible. His voice thinned, though, as it rose above the staff, and his sustained notes verged on stridency.

Ughetto disciplined his face into impassivity. Brescha would have had scathing criticisms of Leonino's technique, of the tension in his jaw and the offending arch of his tongue that choked his upper register. But Leonino was singing, which was more than Ughetto himself could say.

When Leonino finished, with a long trill and roulade, the applause was hearty. He bowed several times, then, with a gleam in his eye, started across the crowded room toward Ughetto. The ensemble began its closing piece just as he reached the doorway where Ughetto lounged, trying to look at ease.

"Why," Leonino cried softly in his high voice. "If it isn't little Ughetto! All grown up now, aren't you!"

Ughetto straightened and held out his hand. "Hello, Leonino."

Leonino shook hands, then ran his fingers through his hair, artfully tousling his coiffure. "So?" he said archly. "What did you think of my aria?"

"I thought it was fine."

Leonino's eyes narrowed. "Fine? Is that all you can say?"

Ughetto shrugged. "It's a lovely piece, competently sung. What do you want me to say?"

Leonino leaned closer to him, bracing himself against the arch of the doorway with one long arm. "I know what it is," he hissed. "You're jealous because you can't sing anymore."

"That's perfectly true," Ughetto said simply. "I am. But I still can say only that the aria was fine."

Leonino pulled back, folding his arms and looking down his nose at Ughetto. "You were always an egotist, as I recall," he said. "And now look at you! What are you, a servant? Someone's valet, perhaps?"

"No. I'm a guest here."

Leonino laughed. "Do they know about you? What was it you were going to be called—Angelino, wasn't it? Or Floria. And now you're just . . ." He flipped a negligent hand and began to turn away. "Just Ughetto from Sicily. The botched job."

Ughetto knew that he should let Leonino have the last word, let him turn away to his admiring public. But his barb had hit home, and it hurt. It hurt more than a mere physical pain that would pass in time. This hurt would grow deeper, planted in the soil of hope, nourished by disappointment and frustration. Ughetto couldn't help himself.

He said, in a clear, carrying tone, "As long as we're remembering the lessons of the *scuola*, Leonino, I should mention to you that you need to watch your upper register. It's growing shrill."

Leonino whirled, his face dark with anger. Several people standing nearby turned, too. Even under the cover of Caccini's music, Ughetto's words had reached their ears, and their avid interest was like the flicker of candles on every side. The Contessa materialized on Ughetto's left, her black gaze brilliant.

"How dare you," Leonino hissed. His elongated fingers seized Ughetto's arm, pinching his tricep between long fingernails. As Ughetto tried to pull away, Leonino's nails tore through the delicate fabric of the new shirt Cesare had bought for him.

Ughetto felt his lips pull away from his teeth, and a low growl escaped his throat before he could suppress it. The candles around him seemed to blaze up, as if the room had caught fire. His vision blurred, and a fierce itch crawled across his throat and his chest.

Leonino fell back, his eyes wide. The people around him caught noisy breaths, and some uttered wordless exclamations. The music died away in the sudden silence. Cesare, from across the room, lifted his head to see what was happening around Ughetto.

Before anyone else could move, the Contessa seized Ughetto's elbow with an iron grip. She steered him out through the arched doorway, into the lamplit marble courtyard, and beyond, into the blessed coolness of midnight.

"Now," the Contessa said in her dry voice. Her face, with its sharp nose and long chin, was as ageless as the sculpture of Diana Ughetto had so recently walked past. Her voice was uninflected, without accent, a voice that could belong to any age, any country. Her eyes burned into Ughetto's as if they would delve directly into his brain. "Tell me about your family."

Ughetto reclined on a long, low couch in the atrium of the Countess's villa. He stared at his fingertips, which still burned. The itching of his chest and neck had subsided, and his jaw, though it felt tight and swollen, had ceased throbbing. His fingers looked as they always did, the nails short and, on this night, clean. But the burning persisted, as if at any moment those claws would extrude, tear at the pale cloth of the couch, at the Countess's lean face.

"I don't understand," he said. His voice cracked like a piece of thin glass. "What do you care about my family?" He struggled to sit upright, but the Countess's hard hand pushed him back. "What do you care about *me?*"

She held out a tumbler of water. "Drink this. You're still hot."

"On fire," he groaned. He took the glass and drained it.

As she took it back and refilled it, she said in that noncommittal tone, "Just tell me. You have sisters?"

He turned his head so he could see her face clearly. It held no expression at all. "I think you already know I have sisters. Why is that?"

With a faint, dismissive gesture, she said, "I'm going to explain it, Ughetto. But tell me."

"Yes, I have sisters. Six of them."

"All older?"

"Yes."

"Brothers?"

"No."

"Ah." She handed him the refilled glass and then sat back in her own chair, pressing the fingertips of one hand against the palm of the other. "A seventh son, after six sisters. Naples, I imagine. Or was it Sicily?"

"Sicily." He drank from the glass, then set it on the floor beside the couch. He sat up, slowly, feeling as bruised as if he had been in a fight. But tonight, there had been no fight, and no blood. This Countess had seen to that.

She had brought him here, where no servant met them, where no carriages rolled or pedestrians walked. Her *villa* was tucked away in some corner of Rome, it seemed, where no one could find it. Where no one would find *him*. She had fed him some bitter herb, soaked in wine, and sat beside him like this, her black gaze unreadable, until he began to feel like himself again.

"I've told you about myself," he said. "Now you can explain to me. Who are you? Why have you brought me here, and what do you know about me?"

Her mouth curled at the corners, ever so slightly. "You may call me Countess," she said. "And I brought you here because you are a *lupo mannaro*. I have need of such as you. And you, I think, need me."

Ughetto felt as if every droplet of blood drained from his body at that moment. He wanted to rise from the couch, flee this awful woman and her pronouncement, but he was as helpless as an infant. *Lupo mannaro* . . .

"Yes," she said, as if he had spoken aloud. "Didn't you know?"

"*Sacrilegio,*" he breathed, his heart seizing with horror.

Again, the faint dismissive gesture, just a flick of her fingers. "Oh, yes, indeed. But it doesn't matter. The *lupo mannaro* can live nearly forever, unless he is very, very stupid." Again, the infinitesimal curl of the lips. "I don't think you're stupid, Ughetto. And I will teach you."

22

Grazie di tanto onore.

Thank him for his courtesy.

—Don Ottavio, Act One, Scene Three, *Don Giovanni*

Octavia smoothed Ugo's opera scarves again and straightened his jackets on their hangers. It wouldn't do for him to know she had gone through his things.

Despite all they meant to each other, there was a separation between them, a chasm no intimacy could bridge. Ugo had always had a deeply ingrained habit of secrecy. He never revealed anything he didn't have to. She supposed he was protecting himself, and her.

Surely, though, in the current circumstances, he would understand her invading his privacy. He had been gone six days. She burned with need, and he wouldn't want her to go out into the streets. Nevertheless, she took a last look at the closet before closing the door, to make certain everything appeared to be undisturbed.

She gave a final tweak to a pair of gray slacks, then paused.

There was a small safe tucked into one corner of the closet, the kind of safe most good hotels provided for their guests. Ugo never wore jewelry or carried much cash. But the door of the little safe was closed and locked. He must have had a reason for that.

Octavia backed away from the closet and sat down on the bed, wondering. She touched her teeth with a forefinger. A warning tingle ran through her jaw.

"Well," she said aloud to the room. "I have to try. Sorry, Ugo. You'll just have to give me a pass on this one."

She rose again, went to the closet, and pushed the door as wide as it would go. She knelt on the thick carpet before the safe and examined it. It was a combination safe, with directions for choosing a combination affixed to the top. Four sets of two digits. People used birthdays, she knew, or anniversaries. 00-00-00-00. Ugo could have used her birthday, 01-11-1763. She tried it, without success. He might, she thought, have used the day he first revealed himself to her. In the American style, it would be 04-17-1906. She tried it that way and then reversed it in the European way, 17-04-1906. Ugo wasn't entirely sure of his own birthday, but they had chosen a date to celebrate it. 31-10-1617, All Hallows' Eve, their own private joke. She tried that, but it didn't work either.

She sat back on her heels, shaking her head. "Ugo, Ugo. So secretive, and after all this time. What am I to do?"

She sat there for a long time, until her feet grew numb and she knew she would have to move. She stood and was halfway to the door when it struck her.

With a short laugh, she spun on her stockinged feet and went to kneel again before the safe. 27-01-1756.

Mozart.

Through the awful dawn of that day in San Francisco, Ugo and Hélène huddled beneath Ugo's topcoat on the fog-damp grass of Golden Gate Park, listening to the great city fall apart below them. Hélène flinched with each new temblor and started with alarm as the bells of the fire wagons began to clang along Market Street.

Ugo held her hands tightly in his and said, "Don't listen to it, Hélène. There's nothing we can do now. Talk to me."

"Talk?" she exclaimed. Her voice was tight with fear and shock. "Talk about what?"

He pulled his topcoat more securely about the two of them and answered her in as calm a manner as if they were still comfortably settled in the Palm Court at the Palace Hotel. "Tell me about Mozart."

Hélène swallowed and hugged herself, trying to stop her shivering. "Mozart," she repeated. "But . . . if you knew about me, you must have known about Mozart."

"I never met him," Ugo said lightly. "I watched him conduct several times. He was a nervous type, wasn't he?"

"He was highly strung," Hélène said, a little defensively. Mozart's hand had trembled in hers the last time she saw him. But then he had been so ill.

"Oh, yes? Sensitive, then."

She took a shaky breath, and then a steadier one. Ugo, this strange, dark man, was so calm beside her, no matter how much the earth shook or how terrible the sounds coming from below the hill. This odd scene would be added to her prodigious memory, this little haven of warmth and serenity in the midst of havoc. He had pulled his French-backed topcoat above their heads, a sort of makeshift tent, against the chill and against the sight of refugees streaming into the park. The growing light showed dimly through the fine black fabric.

"Yes," she said. "Mozart was sensitive to everything—light, cold, emotions." She sighed, remembering. "He loved chocolate."

A tremor shook the park, and a few voices reached them, crying out in panic. Hélène caught a sharp breath, but Ugo seemed to be indifferent to what was happening beyond the shelter of his topcoat. "What kind?"

"What?"

"What kind of chocolate did Mozart like?"

She gave a shaky laugh. "What a question! Viennese, of course. He loved truffles."

"Do you like them, too?"

Hélène shook her head. "No. I used to, before I . . . When I was young. Now I don't like the taste of sweets at all. And after Mozart and I—he lost his taste for them, too. When someone sent them to the theater, he gave them to the stagehands."

"What else?"

The noises around them intensified. Children wailed in their mothers' arms. A woman's high-pitched voice screamed grief, and many others soon joined her. A man barked commands in deep tones, trying to organize the crowd. Another tremor shook the park, and Hélène began to rise, but Ugo held her back.

"It's not safe," he said. "Just stay here. We'll hold our little bit of ground, and when the quake is over—"

As if to punctuate his words, a new temblor rolled beneath them, and shrieks in every vocal register filled the park.

"But shouldn't we do something?" She lifted the cover of his coat enough to look around her. Streams of people were still flooding into Golden Gate Park, away from the now-burning city. Off to her right, stretchers were being laid on the grass, and a makeshift hospital was being set up. Other people were taking cover as she and Ugo were, holding blankets over their heads or propping up bits of furniture they must have carried from their homes.

"You can't fight an earthquake," Ugo said as calmly as if huddling beneath a topcoat in an open field were an everyday occurrence.

Hélène sank down again and wrapped her arms around her knees. "This is awful."

"Yes. And it's going to get worse." He pulled the coat up again, until it covered their heads. "Just keep talking."

Hélène closed her eyes. Mozart's face rose in her memory, as clear as the first day she met him, or the last day she saw him. He was much changed by then, of course. Illness had made him puffy. His fine hands were swollen and useless. His eyes were shadowed, his ruddy cheeks gone gray.

But when she first met him, he was delightful, with sparkling eyes and a funny sort of staccato laugh that no one could resist.

"His hands," she began, "were soft as a woman's. They were small, even tiny, but his fingers were long—he could reach a ninth on the harpsichord without any effort. He spoke quickly, as if his mind were always several steps ahead of his tongue. It made him stammer sometimes."

The sounds and sensations of the disaster beyond their slender shelter dropped away from her as she let herself drift back to those strange days after Zdenka Milosch had revealed the truth, and she learned that she and Mozart shared the same fate.

Nothing in those succeeding weeks had diminished her longing for him. She wanted to touch him, to breathe in his scent, to possess him. She dreamed of their solitary encounter, their ménage à trois with the Countess. She suffered through memories of Mozart and Constanze, memories that weren't hers but that tortured her with sensuous details and made her long to experience them for herself.

Mozart avoided being alone with her, turning away if he was about to encounter her in the corridor, avoiding her at receptions or dinners. It was so painfully evident that the rest of the company assumed they had had a falling-out over some detail of music or interpretation.

Bondini even asked Teresa one night, at the penultimate performance, what she had done to offend Mozart. Teresa, growing edgy again with thirst, snapped, "Our *maestro* is impossible to please!"

Bondini sniffed. "Who are you in comparison to Mozart?" he said.

"I'm not comparing myself! I wouldn't dream—"

"We have to keep him happy," Bondini said. "Prague adores him, and so does Count Nostitz."

"And they don't adore me, isn't that what you mean?" Teresa said, her voice rising. "Because Mozart is angry with me, everyone must be?"

Bondini shrugged. "This is theater life, Teresa."

She put her hands on her hips and glared at him. "No more

the *piatto saporito!* One moment you all love me, the next you hate me."

He glared back. "I don't need two *prima donnas,* I can tell you that! My company can manage without you. You can go back to Milano when the run is over."

Teresa cried, *"Con piacere!"* and fled the theater.

That night, as Mozart had done, she went across the river. In the warren of lanes around St. Vitus, she found a young man, hardly more than a boy, reeling drunkenly out of a tavern. When he saw her he grinned and hung his arm around her neck, groping at her bosom with his other hand. He dug in his pocket for money and offered her what he had left after his night of drinking. She led him into an unlit alcove beneath one of the flying buttresses that supported the outer walls of the Cathedral, and he stumbled gleefully after her.

As he fumbled with her skirts and struggled to undo his breeches, she caught a glimpse of his face in the light of a passing torch. Her heart quailed. He had the round chin and full cheeks of youth. His lips were slack with beer and his eyelids drooped unevenly, but his neck was firm and smooth, and his body was hard with muscle. She pulled back, hating herself.

"Whassa matter?" he slurred. "Don't—don't change your mind now, miss, I'm just—" He giggled. "I'm just having a bit of trouble with these goddamned buttons."

It was the curse that persuaded her. It seemed she no longer had a god, at least none she could turn to. The boy grasped her around the neck and pulled her down on top of him, thrusting aimlessly at her with his hips.

She let her body go pliant, let him throw his arms around her and pull her tight against him. Even as his fingers still struggled with the fastening of his breeches, she found the hollow of his neck with her lips. He gasped with pleasure and then with pain as she struck, driving her canines through the skin to the sweet, generous vein beneath.

Just as the last button of his breeches broke free of its threads, she began to drink. The boy's body had its own will, it seemed, and it sought her even as she slaked her prodigious thirst on its life force. He lasted longer than the stagehand had, his youth and his strength resisting to the last. The grinding of his hips against hers ceased, little by little. His breath came in shallow gasps, at first ecstatic, then desperate. He never fought her. His embrace slackened and his body grew limp, but he never tried to push her away or to struggle against her.

She knew, when she drew away from him, that he was dead. She stood up, rearranging her disordered clothes, and looked down on him, a youth lying on the pebbly ground beneath a church window, his breeches undone, his eyes staring at nothing. She bent and pulled his breeches closed.

As she started back toward her rooms, she felt so full of life it seemed she could hardly contain it. She felt enormous, as if she could stretch her arms above her head and touch the stars. She felt powerful, as if her voice could fill the entire city without effort. She fairly danced across the bridge, only stopping herself from running because there were other people there, men giving her appraising glances, one or two couples raising their brows at the sight of a solitary young woman tripping through the streets in the middle of the night as if the darkness were nothing to her.

She paused in the center of the bridge, looking down into the dark, moving water. A memory came to her, but this one was dim, its colors and sounds and feelings faint, as if very far away—or very old. It was not vivid and immediate like the memories of Mozart she had been experiencing.

She remembered a boat floating on this very river. It was a plain wooden craft such as she had never seen in her life, with splintered oars and crude bench seats. There was a man rowing it, a tall, thin man. He turned to look at her, and as if through a dark mist, she saw his teeth as he smiled.

His teeth were long and white, reflecting moonlight on their elongated tips. Somehow, Teresa knew this was Zdenka Milosch's memory. She had not only shared the tooth with Mozart, but with the Countess. She had acquired Mozart's memories, but she had also absorbed those of Zdenka Milosch, dim and dark and ancient.

She left the bridge and walked on more slowly toward her lodgings. As she walked up the stairs to her room, the young man's memories began to invade her mind. He had a mother, and a father, and an older brother who teased him about being virginal. He was a bricklayer, hired to work on the very church under which he had lost his life. He was in love with a girl who wanted none of him, because she was pretty and had a good dowry, and he was only a poor, plain laborer.

Teresa went into her room and shut the door. As she lay down on her bed, still fully clothed, she thought that she must find a way to close off these memories as surely and firmly as she closed and locked the door to her room. She couldn't restore the young man to life, though she regretted being the cause of his death. It did her no good to carry his memories alongside her own.

She must even, she thought, block the memories of Zdenka Milosch. The only ones she wanted to keep were her own.

And, of course, Mozart's.

The final fête to celebrate the closing of the opera was held at Count Nostitz's palace. Carriages lined up in the street outside the theater to carry the singers to the celebration. Mozart lingered in his dressing room after the curtain calls, and Teresa loitered in the doorway of hers, hoping to catch him before he left. When he finally hurried down the corridor toward the waiting carriages, she followed on quiet feet and managed to be handed into the same carriage as he. They were very late, the last to leave the theater, and they had the carriage to themselves.

When Mozart saw her, he turned his head away, staring fixedly out into the dark streets of Prague.

"Sir," she said, the moment the door closed on them. "Can we not talk a bit?"

"There's nothing to talk about," he said. His voice had a dull sound to it, a lifelessness that chilled her.

"I beg your pardon, but there's everything to talk about!" she said urgently. "I've been discharged from the Bondini company. This may be our last chance."

"I'm going home to Vienna," Mozart said. "I need to be with my wife."

Teresa pressed her fingers to her lips to stop their sudden trembling. "You blame me, don't you, Wolfgang?"

He turned on her suddenly, his eyes dark with suffering. "If you had not brought her to me . . . that horrible woman . . ."

"I didn't!" Teresa protested, her voice catching on tears. "She was there, but it was you I wanted—"

"I'm a married man!" he thundered. The inside of the coach vibrated with his voice, and she stared at him, open-mouthed. "You knew that!"

"But you—" She stammered, and tried again. "But, Wolfgang, I've seen you with other women, and I thought you and Constanze . . . perhaps an understanding . . ."

The misery in his eyes grew, and they reddened. He hung his head. "Yes," he said. "You're right. I wanted to lie with you, too, though I would not perhaps have done it so publicly. But now God has punished my libertine ways."

Teresa put out her hand to touch his, but he snatched it away. She took hers back and cradled it against her chest as if it were injured by his scorn. "Wolfgang," she whispered. "We can bear it, surely? God has turned His back on us. But there are these . . . these gifts, as the Countess calls them."

"Gifts?" he said, and gave a despairing laugh. "You mean carrying around your memories, and hers? It's a curse!"

"My memories are not so terrible," Teresa said.

"Hers are."

"Yes. I know." She paused, and then said, tentatively, "But yours, sir, are magnificent."

His eyes came up to hers, startled. "They are?"

"The music. I hear it differently now. I hear things I never knew were there."

"And my other memories?"

She gave him a tremulous smile. "Good and bad, as everyone's are, I suppose."

His gaze fixed on her, and his face hardened as if he had suddenly aged. "And what are you going to do about your teeth, Teresa?"

Her face suddenly burned, and she involuntarily lifted her hand to cover her mouth.

"That does no good," he said. "When you sing, you have to open your mouth, don't you?" His voice rose again, making the windows of the carriage rattle. "Look at this!" He used one forefinger to lift his upper lip.

Teresa, hardly able to breathe, leaned forward to see better in the dim light.

The change was nearly imperceptible. Mozart's teeth were not so white as her own, but stained faintly with the coffee he drank so much of. His canines were marginally longer than she remembered them, although she doubted, if she weren't looking for the change, that she would notice it. They were sharper, though, surely, more pointed than they had been.

With a sudden thudding of her heart, she put her fingers against her own teeth.

"Yes," he said, with a grimace of a smile. "Yours, too, Teresa. Had you not noticed?"

"I—" She couldn't go on. She had tried not to notice. She had ignored the tingling of her jaw, resisted the compulsion to stroke her teeth with her fingertip.

"But I could hardly miss it," he said, with a sort of grim satisfaction. "I stood below you, at the harpsichord, as you sang 'Or sai chi l'onore' and 'Non mi dir.' What will you do about them?"

"They—they aren't so bad, really," she said weakly.

"They will be." He turned his head again, to stare at the countryside rolling by in the darkness. "You saw hers, didn't you? And in her memories . . ."

"Her memories are dim."

"Clear enough."

Teresa had no argument for this. Vague though the shapes in the Countess's old, old memories were, their substance could hardly be in doubt. There were many like her, and like that man Teresa had remembered in the ancient wooden boat, his long, sharp teeth gleaming through the darkness.

"How old, do you think?" Teresa breathed.

But Mozart didn't answer.

All of this she told Ugo as they huddled among the refugees in Golden Gate Park. She talked for an hour or more, until the shaking of the earth stopped. Ugo let his coat drop, and they looked about them.

Hundreds of people sat or squatted on the grass, and hundreds more were still crowding into the park. On the horizon, smoke obscured the view of the bay, and the red glow of flames flickered through the gray. Hélène stood up, peering through the trees to where the roof of the Grand Opera House should rise on Mission Street.

"It's gone," she said in an undertone. "The Opera House is gone."

Ugo was at her shoulder, looking down on the wreckage of the city. It appeared that the entire district south of Market Street, from the waterfront to the Mission, was ablaze. From their vantage point, it looked as if the Ferry Building, too, might succumb. "I wonder what happened to the Palace," he murmured. "And to Caruso, and Fremstad, and the others."

She looked at him over her shoulder. "There must be thousands dead down there!"

"Yes," he said calmly. "Thousands. But we're not dead, nor are all these people around us. There will be no more performances of *Carmen*, whether Caruso and Fremstad survived or not. We should think what to do next."

"I'm under contract. I have to get to New York."

"Yes, no doubt. The question is how."

"I have to get to Oakland, to the train."

"If the Ferry Building burns, there will be no ferry across the bay. But I'll think of something."

She turned so that her body faced him, and she gazed into his utterly composed face. "Do you think I will go with you, without knowing what you are?"

His black eyes gleamed briefly before he dropped his eyelids. "Show me your teeth."

Obediently, as if it were the most natural sort of request, he parted his lips and showed her. His teeth were white and even. His canines were only slightly longer than the teeth around them, and only slightly sharper.

"You are not like me," she said flatly.

"I told you I was not." He closed his lips, and the corners of them curled in a spare smile.

"I can't trust you. I can't trust anyone."

He took her arm, and this time his grip was gentle, dangerously comforting. "I know. It will take time." He shrugged into his topcoat again, and adjusted her shawl around her shoulders. "Come this way," he said, tucking her hand under his arm. "There's someone I know who can help us."

It was there, the small refrigerated carrier. Octavia couldn't see how it worked, or how it was powered, but when she touched the clasp, it popped open with a silky click.

The vial, a single, tiny cylinder of glass, made her mouth water. It was only half full. But, she told herself, it *was* half full. It would buy her a little time, at least.

She retrieved the rest of the equipment from Ugo's embossed case: the tubing, the foil-wrapped alcohol swabs, a pack of tiny bandages, and a little cellophane bag of cotton balls. She laid it all out on the smooth comforter of the bed. She remembered, of course, the order in which Ugo did things, as she remembered everything, with precision and clarity. The weight of memories, the onslaught of small and large details, had never troubled her.

She had learned to sort through them at will, picking the ones she wanted or needed, disregarding the rest. It was rather like performing a rôle on stage, thinking only of her character's wants and needs and intentions, putting aside her personal concerns.

No such blessing had fallen on Mozart.

Octavia set that memory aside, too, for the moment. Using the mirror as a guide, she wound the elastic around her arm and swabbed the inside of her elbow, where the vein was prominent and where she thought it would be easiest. As she found the needle and filled the plunger from the vial, she thought how odd it was, really, that in all these decades she had never done this for herself.

"Spoiled," Octavia muttered to herself as she poised the needle over her vein. "And now you pay." She tried to dart the needle through the skin and into the vein, the way Ugo did with such deftness, but succeeded only in skittering the steel across her skin, bringing a slender thread of red blood from the dermis.

"Cretina," she spat this time. "No fancy stuff." She placed the needle over the vein and pressed it in, feeling every millimeter as it slid through the venous wall. She pressed the plunger with her thumb and watched the precious *sangue* drip into her vein.

The burning in her throat began to subside immediately. Welcome warmth traveled up her arm to branch across her chest, where her lungs could take it up, spread it to her belly and her back and down her legs. Her toes tingled, and she sighed with relief.

Five days, she thought. Half a vial should get her through five days. Surely, by then Ugo would return. And if not . . .

When the syringe was empty, she pulled the needle from her skin. She watched the tiny wound bleed a tiny drop, and then close almost immediately. In an hour, the spot would be invisible, just as it had been that first time.

She began to put the things back in their places, being careful to leave everything just the way she had found it. She didn't want Ugo to complain that she had left things amiss.

As she coiled the length of tubing, she reflected that this could be only a stopgap. She felt better now, but it wouldn't last. If Ugo didn't come back, she would have to go for help. She would have to go to the elders' compound.

The thought made her shudder. She would be perfectly happy if she never laid eyes on Zdenka Milosch again.

23

Brutto, brutto si far quest' affar!

This affair is turning ugly!

—Zerlina, Act One, Scene Four, *Don Giovanni*

Ugo reawakened slowly, becoming aware of his body bit by bit. His toes were cold, and his back felt damp. The gluey tangle of his eyelashes resisted as he lifted his lids.

Gloom shrouded the dank space around him. Experimentally, he extended one hand, testing the surface he lay on. His fingertips encountered icy stone. He wriggled upright. Chills rippled across his back as cold air met wet skin. He felt across his belly and thighs. No shred of his Roberto Cavalli slacks remained. He was naked.

For a moment he sat still. Roberto Cavalli? Odd, that he should remember such a name. That he should remember any names at all.

He put his hand to his forehead, as if to rub sense into it, and he was startled. No claws scratched his skin or elongated his fingers. He traced the contours of his nose, his cheek, his beardless jaw. He ran his palm down his throat to his chest. It, too, was smooth and hairless.

Ugo. He was Ugo.

Octavia would be missing him.

Octavia! And that bastard Domenico. He shot to his feet as awareness returned to him in a flood.

How many days had the wolf been abroad? And where had its wild feet carried him?

Remnants of rough hair and claws, shed by the wolf, slid under his feet as he moved, but no scrap of clothing had been left to him. He was not hungry, which meant the wolf had fed. A wave of loathing filled him. There would, no doubt, be bloody bones somewhere in this cave of cold, wet rock. Ugo didn't want to see them.

A shaft of gray light marked the end of the cave, a few yards away. Ugo made his way toward it, shifting his shoulders as he walked. They still felt swollen, as if his own body had not yet reclaimed itself. Scars from Benson's attempts at torture marked his chest and belly. The burns on his chin stung, and his toes burned, both with cold and with pain. His groin smarted from the place where Domenico had, just barely, touched him with his silly little scalpel.

Ugo knew, from long experience, that he would recover from all these hurts in a matter of hours. His body would thrum with the vibrant health of youth, and his skin would glow. His scars would vanish as if they had never been. Such was the power of the *lupo mannaro*.

He wondered if Domenico or his two thugs had survived. It was possible, though he doubted it. It had been a very small room, and a very angry wolf. But whatever had happened in that basement room, it was not in his memory. He didn't know—he had never known—if the wolf had a memory.

Ugo moved out into the light, squinting against the glare of early morning sun on fields of snow. He found himself on a ledge of snow-powdered stone. The mouth of the cave yawned behind him. To the south of him, three great mountain peaks rose, white and forbidding. Three less impressive mountains rose above a town beneath the slope on which he stood. A thread of blue twisted through a valley dark with evergreens, and buildings ranged along it, their roofs sharply slanted. Church spires abounded. He couldn't guess, yet, what mountains these were, or what river meandered at their feet. He would find out, soon enough. But first, he needed clothes.

He lifted his face into the fresh breeze and sniffed. There was woodsmoke on the wind, and the scent of bleach. He stepped to the lip of the stone ledge, his bare toes scuffing the thin layer of white.

Now he could see a highway far below him, and a small city. Houses scattered between his perch and the town, each nestled among narrow pines and thickets of alpine broom. The wolf had not climbed too high, it seemed. Ugo, shivering now, squatted on the ledge and lowered himself, using his hands, onto the snowy slope below. The wolf, no doubt, had leaped effortlessly up, his prey in his teeth.

There were rocks under the snow, and the sharp tines of pine-cones. Ugo skidded downhill, ignoring the small stabs of pain in the soles of his feet. He fell twice and had to catch himself on his palms. He was aching with cold by the time he reached a two-lane macadam road at the bottom of the hill. He sniffed again and turned in the direction of the smoke, working his way through the trees and brush above the road. It would be awkward to be caught walking naked by one of the infrequent cars passing by.

It was awkward enough, once he reached the house, to figure out how to approach it without being seen. Tendrils of fragrant smoke rose invitingly above its alpine roof. Freshly washed laundry flapped on the clothesline, making Ugo's nose twitch with the sharp smell of laundry soap and bleach. He peered at the sheets and towels, disappointed that there were no clothes to steal. He would have to get inside. It was too cold to wait until dark.

Shaking now with cold, he hunkered behind a clump of broom and eyed the house. Even a half-frozen sheet was beginning to look inviting. He was debating the wisdom of bursting into the house when the laundress emerged from the back door, a basket on her hip. She was tall and stooped, with a shock of white hair that ruffled in the breeze as she began pulling the sheets from the line. The sheets were stiff, and she struggled to bend them into manageable shape with swollen arthritic fingers.

Ugo rubbed his chin and chest again, to be certain there were no remnants of rough fur on his body, and then stepped out of the shelter of the woods. He called, in a high, boyish tone, "Ma'am? Ma'am? Can you help me?"

The woman whirled to face him, clutching the frozen sheet to her chest. *"Comment?"*

Ah. French.

Ugo took another hesitant step, modestly covering his groin with his hands, but allowing the remnants of his wounds to show. *"Madame. Madame, pouvez-vous m'aider?"*

The white-haired woman lowered the sheet and eyed Ugo's naked, shivering body. She looked wary, but not afraid. At least she didn't drop her frozen laundry to rush back into the house. *"Qu'est qu'il y a?"*

Ugo came a little bit closer, letting his lips visibly tremble. Still in French, he said, "I'm in a bit of trouble, madame. And I'm freezing."

The laundress kept a careful eye on her naked visitor while her hands automatically worked at the sheet. With a crackle of stiff linen, she succeeded at last in folding it. She dropped it into the basket at her feet and straightened, holding her back with both hands. Her voice was clear, the voice of a much younger woman. "What happened to your clothes, monsieur?"

Ugo shrugged, careful not to move his hands, and dropped his eyes in shame. "They took them. They beat me up, but that wasn't enough, I guess."

"They left you in pretty bad shape, it looks like."

"Not so bad. I'm just awfully cold."

"Who were they?"

Ugo let himself shiver violently. "My girlfriend's brothers, madame. They—" He shivered again. "They caught us when we were—"

She was unrelenting, this woman. "Were what?" she snapped.

Ugo's voice trembled most convincingly. "I love her, madame, really I do. I wouldn't have—if I didn't—but they think I seduced her, just for—just for sex."

"Hmm." The woman pursed her lips. Her eyes were a pale blue, her glance shrewd. "You spoke to me in English first."

Ugo nodded. "I'm American. An exchange student."

"Where are you supposed to be in school?"

Ugo hunched his shoulders and inched closer. He made up a name, not having an idea where he was. "Lycée Ste. Marie."

"There are hundreds of those. Which one?"

From his memory, Ugo plucked the name of a village. It had been Hélène's village, and this woman could hardly deny there was a Lycée Ste. Marie there, since the place had never existed. "The one in Pontalie."

She tipped her head to one side, evidently trying to place the name. "I don't know it. What's it near?"

"Um . . . the closest city is Rennes."

He started at her sudden open-throated bark of laughter. "You're a long way from Rennes, my young friend! A very long way. And all for a tumble!"

"Am I? Where—what is this place?"

The laughter died. "If you look down the mountain toward the river, you'll see the rooftops of Lourdes. Do you know it?"

"Lourdes?" It was a strange place indeed for the wolf to have left him. "I can't imagine how I—"

"We're in the *commune* of Aspin-en-Lavedan. A short walk from Lourdes itself."

Ugo had gotten close enough to the woman that one of the sheets still fluttering on the clothesline brushed his elbow. He gave her a pitiful look. "Madame . . . I'm half frozen."

"Yes," the woman said. "I can see that." She bent and picked up her basket. "Well, you look as if you've done all the harm you're going to. Come into the house. I'll find something for you to put on."

Ugo followed her through the door and into a cheery kitchen, blessedly warm. A merry fire crackled in a woodstove and a large pot of some fragrant soup bubbled on a gas range. His hostess set the laundry basket near the woodstove and adjusted the damper. Over her shoulder, she said, "Do me a favor, and don't sit down until I get you some clothes. God knows what muck you have on you."

Obediently, Ugo stood beside the woodstove, glad of its wave of heat. Strains of Dvořák played softly from somewhere. He looked around and spotted a small CD player on a sideboard. As the woman returned from a back room, a pile of clothes in her hands, she followed Ugo's glance. She said, "Don't get any ideas, my friend. I'm old, but I'm not helpless."

Ugo took the clothes from her hands. "Madame," he said with complete sincerity, "I don't want to steal it. It's just that I recognize the music. It's the overture to *Rusalka*."

"So it is. Are you a music student? Do you play?"

"No, not really. But I love opera."

"This is a live recording from a performance in Paris."

Octavia had sung *Rusalka* in Paris last year. A sudden urgency made Ugo's heart race.

"What's your name, my young friend?" The ice-blue eyes regarded him with frank curiosity.

"I'm Zack. Zacharie, in French, but everyone calls me Zack."

"Hmm. Very American. I'm Laurette, but you can go on calling me madame. I think you've taken enough liberties."

Ugo said humbly, "I know. I appreciate your help."

Laurette gave another barking laugh. "What are you going to do about the girlfriend?"

"I don't know." He shook out a pair of worn corduroy trousers and a flannel shirt. Laurette had also provided a pair of boxer shorts and a well-darned, thick pair of wool socks. Feigning embarrassment, he moved behind the stove and turned his back as he began to dress. The clothes chafed against the raw places on his chest and belly. His toes looked ghastly, the nails gone, the cuticles torn and bruised.

"I'll get my cell phone. Do you want the police first, or the doctor?"

Ugo said hastily, "Oh, no. Please, no police. And I don't need a doctor!"

The pale eyes fixed on him again. "Why, Zacharie? If what you say is true, these—brothers, you say—they attacked you. That's a crime."

"But I'm hoping Annette's brothers won't tell her parents, now that they—they think they've settled things."

"Very chivalrous. But not very smart. What about when you go back to school?"

Ugo buttoned the flannel shirt and turned back the overlong sleeves. "I think I might just call my parents. Go home."

"Well, suit yourself." The music rose, filling the warm kitchen, the opening scene of the opera. Laurette said, "Sit down at the table there. The soup is ready. I was about to have lunch."

"This is so kind of you."

Laurette shrugged. "It's all right." As she ladled soup into wide pottery bowls, she said, "I've met other exchange students, but never one who speaks French as well as you do."

Ugo blinked innocently at her as she came to the table with a loaf of brown bread on a cutting board. "My mother is French," he said.

"She's not going to be happy with you." Laurette took a bread knife from a drawer and laid it beside the cutting board. "Getting in trouble like this."

Ugo picked up his spoon. "I know. I'll explain to them somehow." He turned his head toward the little CD player. It had very good speakers for a small device. When "The Song to the Moon" started, Ugo put down his spoon. "Octavia Voss," he said.

"Yes. You really are an opera lover, aren't you? She's rather new on the world scene."

Distracted, Ugo said, "I was there, actually. Last year."

"You were?"

He caught himself and managed a shaky response. "With my parents."

Laurette stared at him. "How old are you, Zack?"

"I'm . . . eighteen."

"Or sixteen," Laurette said dryly. "Or twenty-five."

Ugo dropped his head and picked up his spoon again.

"You should call the police."

Ugo shook his head. Laurette shrugged, and sighed. "*Eh, bien.* I'll go see if I can find you some shoes."

As she rose from the table, Ugo said, "I'll send you money for the clothes when I get home."

She waved a hand. "No need for that. I was going to give them away anyway. They were my son's, and he doesn't need them now."

She was gone several minutes. When she returned, she had a pair of worn sneakers in one hand and a dilapidated jacket in the other. "These should get you through."

"Thank you. I really mean it. Thanks."

Laurette laid the shoes on the floor beside Ugo's chair.

The soup was delicious, and once Ugo tasted it, he couldn't stop until his bowl was empty. "More?" Laurette asked.

Ugo said, "I've imposed enough, I think."

"True," his host said. "But my son was always hungry, and it's only soup."

Ugo accepted another bowl and ate three slices of fresh bread. He tried not to think about what his last meal might have been. "Did you make this? You're a wonderful cook."

Laurette didn't answer. She began clearing the table, glancing out the window from time to time. Ugo bent to pull the sneakers on. Like all the other clothes, they were too big, but they would do. The thick socks helped, and the space in the toes was welcome. His toes were particularly sensitive. He tied the laces loosely.

He stood and pulled the jacket over the shirt. "Thanks again, madame," he said. "You've been really nice."

"What do you intend to do? Walk down to town?"

"I think so."

Laurette set the soup bowls in the sink and turned, leaning her hip against the counter. "Look, young man," she said. "With that innocent face of yours, I can't tell what you're up to. But whatever it is, you can't wander around with no money and no identification. No passport! How are you even going to call your family?"

Ugo thrust his hands into the pockets of the comfortable old jacket. "I'll work it out," he said. "I'll find a way."

"Steal something, you mean."

"No, no. I can hitch a ride back to Pontalie. Get my things."

"I'm sure your mother would never forgive me if I didn't see you were taken care of. I've called my son. He'll run you to the train station." She opened a drawer under the counter and pulled out a fold of bills. She took out several euros and put the rest back. "I'm not exactly sure what the fare is, but this should do it."

Ugo stared at the money. The back of his neck tingled, and he looked up to meet Laurette's blue gaze. "Write your address for me," he said. "So my parents can pay you back."

"I'll do that." Laurette pointed out the window. "My son is here."

Ugo turned to look out past the lace curtains. A white Peugeot with red and blue markings had pulled up in front of the chalet. A man in the uniform of the Police Nationale climbed out and approached the front of the house with deliberate steps. "Really," Ugo said, looking up at Laurette and striving for a look of wounded innocence. "I'd much rather walk. I appreciate the money, though, and my parents will—"

She said, with the authority of someone used to being obeyed, "No need to walk in this cold. Hubert will drive you."

Ugo turned, thinking he would dash out the back door, but Laurette moved, just slightly, to block his way. Ugo spun the other direction and found that the policeman had let himself in and already stood in the opposite door of the kitchen.

Ugo made himself relax. He said, in very American English, "Gee. That was quick."

Laurette answered, "Yes, wasn't it?" and gave a hearty laugh.

Not until Ugo found himself locked in the backseat of the Peugeot did he realize she had spoken in English.

The holding cell was spotlessly clean, with a neatly made cot and shining toilet fixtures against the wall. It didn't get much use, Ugo suspected. Aspin-en-Lavedan probably had no need for a proper jail.

From its small barred window Ugo could see the Pic du Jer, which Hubert kindly pointed out to him when he led him in and locked the door behind him. "Wait till it gets dark," the policeman said. "You'll see the cross then, when it lights up at night. It will give you something to think about."

"What am I being arrested for?" Ugo asked.

"You're not being arrested. You're being held for your own protection."

"Thank you, but I don't need protection, monsieur."

Hubert raised his brows. "My mother tells me you're covered in bloody scars. Someone did a thorough job of beating you up."

"But they're—they're far away now. They brought me here, somehow, and dumped me."

"Well. You're safe in this place."

"But why keep me here all night? Don't you need a—a warrant, or something?"

"I have my mother's word that you shouldn't be allowed to run off."

"That's reason enough?"

Hubert laughed. "Oh, yes. In this *commune*, that's enough. Laurette has a nose for trouble, and with the tourists we get every year, it's most useful."

"Could I have a phone to call—to call my parents?"

"Tomorrow. You can call them from Pontalie. Which, by the way, I'm not able to find on a map." Hubert gave Ugo a narrow-eyed look. His eyes were the same pale blue as Laurette's, and like her, he was tall and rangy. His thick hair was a neutral brown, and one day it would no doubt be as white as his mother's. It felt odd to Ugo to be wearing this man's cast-off clothes.

Hubert said, "You know, *mon ami,* you don't look so young to me."

"I'm eighteen," Ugo said.

"So you told my mother. But with no proof, and no papers—"

"I told her what happened!"

"She says you told her a tale. She's not sure she believes it."

"But she—she must have. She gave me some of her own money." Ugo shook his head in frustration. He should have known the kindness didn't feel right.

"Yes, for the train. I'll keep it safe for you till morning, and then I'll put you on the train to Rennes." Hubert turned smartly about, a satisfied look on his face, and moved toward the door. As he opened it, he smiled back at Ugo. "Oh, and I'll go along with you. Just to make sure you arrive safely." His grin widened. "*Bonne nuit,* my young friend. Sleep well." The lock snicked shut behind him, and Ugo sagged against the nearest wall.

He had caught a look at a calendar over the desk when Hubert brought him in. It had been ten days since he left Octavia to see the *strega.* That meant twelve since her infusion in New York. And nine since he had taken the *strega*'s herb.

That explained awakening in this odd place. The wolf had been seeking its usual destination, no doubt, but had been distracted by something—the hunt, or someone with a gun—and the transformation had taken it by surprise.

Ugo stared blindly at the brilliant mountain beyond the window. She must have fed by now, somehow. She must. She had said she couldn't resort to the tooth anymore, but her thirst would drive her to it.

Please, Octavia, he thought. *No latter-day attacks of honor. Or distaste. Just do what you need to do.*

And he would do the same, if providence would send him a moon.

He went to the barred window and stood on tiptoe to look out. It was still broad daylight, with afternoon traffic buzzing along the road to Lourdes. He slapped the wall with his palm in frustration. The opening of *Don Giovanni* was getting close.

He threw himself on the cot and put his arm over his eyes. There was nothing to do but wait for darkness and hope that the lunar cycle was high. *Octavia*, he thought. *Hang on, Octavia. I'm coming, somehow. I'll be there as soon as I can.*

24

Ma che ti ho fatto, che vuoi lasciarmi?

But what have I done to you, that you want to leave me?

—Don Giovanni, Act Two, Scene One, *Don Giovanni*

Opening night was a week away. Rehearsals moved from the ellipse to the wide stage, with its vast banks of machinery and its
web of ropes and lifts for moving set pieces. Octavia usually
loved this part of the preparations. The first walk-through of the
set, with the empty theater echoing beyond the stage, filled her
with anticipation. The moment was approaching when the red
velvet seats would be filled with patrons beneath the sparkle of
the Bohemian crystal chandeliers. The seat screens would come
to life, offering the libretto in multiple languages. La Scala would
be transformed into a place of magic.

But this particular morning Octavia struggled to keep the
smile on her face, to chat cheerfully with her colleagues, to follow Giorgio as he led the members of both casts across the stage,
pointing out the entrances and exits, the obstacles in Donna
Anna's garden, the levels of the windows and the walkways. The
five-degree rake of the stage required a few small changes in
blocking. There was still painting to be done, but Giorgio was
pleased with the set, and Octavia agreed. It was a bit darker than

some *Giovanni* sets, but Giorgio meant to stress the tragic side of the opera rather than the comedic.

Octavia tried her first entrance through the door of Donna Anna's house. "It's a little narrow, Giorgio," she said. "I can't remember how wide the skirt of the first-act costume is."

Giorgio nodded. "I'll check that." An assistant, trailing at his side, scribbled a note.

Nick Barrett-Jones lounged against the proscenium, watching everyone as they roamed the set. Giorgio called to him, "Nick! Don't you want to try the rake?"

"No. It's fine," the baritone said, so abruptly several heads turned to look at him.

His haggard look startled Octavia out of her own preoccupation. Perhaps it was the flu he had suffered from that made him look thinner, his eyes more hollow. It was more than a case of flu, though. He had managed to learn his blocking at last, but the vigorous ego he had displayed at the beginning of the rehearsal period had been replaced by something grimmer. He was less jocular, less confident, but somehow the change made him seem even more self-absorbed. He had missed only one day of rehearsals, but he refused all invitations to socialize and spent his free time alone in his dressing room.

Octavia turned away from him. She had no energy to worry about Nick Barrett-Jones's problems. Her own weighed on her enough.

She had counted the days that morning before coming to the theater, and there was no doubt she had good reason to feel as she did, restive and anxious. She had lain awake most of the night before, racking her brain for something to do. There was only one answer she could think of.

She wandered backstage through the maze of equipment and found her way to her dressing room. She sat down on the little settee and then jumped up again to pace before the double mirror, to touch the keyboard of the little piano, to riffle through the finished costumes already hanging ready for the opening. She poured a glass of water from the bottle of Pellegrino the theater had ready for her, and drank it. It barely soothed her parched throat.

She rubbed her forehead, trying to think. The theater would be dark the night before the opening. She would have one day in which she could slip away, fly to the elders' compound, plead with Zdenka Milosch for help.

If she could last that long.

This was the moment she had dreaded. The idea of returning to the tooth filled her with loathing, and with a deep and terrible sadness. She meant not to give in. But the demands of her body had their own urgency. Her body cared nothing for her mind's reluctance.

Somehow, she maintained her composure through the long day of rehearsal. She sang *mezza voce*, remembered all of her staging, tried, bit by bit, to coax some subtlety from Nick in their scenes together. When they reached the last scene, she stood in the wings to watch as the Commendatore pulled Don Giovanni down below the stage in his fiery descent into hell. Only then, in his defiance, his refusal to admit wrongdoing, did Nick show some understanding of what the libretto meant.

Giorgio took pity on all of them after the exhausting day and announced they would receive their notes in the morning. With relief, Octavia turned toward her dressing room for her coat and scarf.

When she emerged, she found Massimo Luca's lean form lounging in the corridor. He wore a pair of beautifully made jeans that exaggerated the length of his legs, and his white shirt was open at the collar. The bruise on his jaw, which he had never explained, had healed. He straightened when he saw her and pushed back the perennially floppy lock of hair. "My second chance?" he said with a grin.

Octavia paused in the act of closing the door. An automatic refusal rose to her lips, but the dark porcelain texture of his neck beneath the white shirt, the steady beat of his pulse in the hollow of his throat, distracted her. She stumbled over her words. "Massimo, I—really, I can't. I'm—" She blinked and forced a little laugh. "I'm just so tired. All I want is a long bath and an early night."

"Come now, Octavia," he said. His voice rumbled in the narrow hallway. "You have to eat."

"In my hotel room," she said.

"No, no, not in your room. That's not restful!" He took her elbow in his muscular grip. "I promised you I would behave, and I will. But let me give you a good dinner. When you've eaten, I'll drive you to your hotel myself, and then you'll have your rest."

She wanted to say no, to pull away from him. But Brenda and Marie emerged from their own dressing rooms at that moment, pulling on their coats, turning away together. Brenda said over her shoulder, "Octavia, we're going to have dinner at a little place I know near the Galleria. Why not come with us?"

Massimo spoke before Octavia could gather her thoughts. "I'm afraid I've made arrangements for Octavia's evening. One of my family friends begged to meet her. You'll forgive us, won't you?"

Brenda waved a beringed hand. "Oh, of course, of course. You two have a nice time."

Marie Charles threw Octavia a look of manifest envy. Octavia said, "Marie—have a good dinner."

Brenda said, "Oh, we will. Iris makes a wonderful *antipasto*," as she steered Marie down the hallway away from them. Marie cast a glance over her shoulder at Massimo, disappointment in every line of her face.

When they were gone, Octavia blurted, "You should ask Marie to dinner."

Massimo's caramel eyes darkened. "Why should I do that?" he demanded.

Octavia's cheeks warmed at her own clumsiness. "I'm sorry," she said. "It's just—she's more . . ." Her voice trailed off. It had been a stupid thing to say, and she wished she could take it back.

She wished her throat didn't burn so. Massimo's nearness made her body tingle with awareness, and that frightened her.

"I told Brenda the truth," he said, guiding her down the hall. "My father's cousin has a wonderful old house near Sant'Ambrogio. She makes the best *ossobuco* in Milano, and she does, in fact, want to meet you. She wants to know when you're going to make a studio recording of *Rusalka*."

Octavia found her refusals fading away as she walked beside him toward the artists' entrance. He was so deliciously tall, and so assured. His hand was firm under her arm and then on her back as he guided her through the door. And he smelled tantalizing, a clean, almost lemony fragrance. Octavia felt her resolve weakening like candle wax softening beneath a flame. When they reached Via Filodrammatici, she tried again, gently pulling her arm free of his hand, busying herself tying her scarf around her throat. Headlights pierced the early darkness, sweeping across them, bringing a gleam from Massimo's eyes. The lights from Piazza della Scala shone upward on the big statue of Leonardo da Vinci, scowling down on passersby from beneath the gathered brim of his cap.

Octavia tried one more time. "Massimo, really—I'm not very hungry. And you know, this just isn't a good idea."

He stood in front of her, blocking her path, and looked down at her with his languid smile. "That's what a person says when they're tempted," he said. "Admit it. We had a great time the other night."

Chattering choristers flowed out of the artists' entrance in a busy stream, parting around Octavia and Massimo. Several nodded and bade them good night, and Octavia answered absently, all the while trying to articulate a reasonable objection to Massimo's invitation. She wasn't hungry, it was true. As always, when she began to thirst, food had little appeal. But she was very, very thirsty. And she dreaded being alone.

She lost the last of her composure when Massimo said, "What happened to your assistant? He never did come back, did he?"

Fatigue and confusion sent blinding tears to Octavia's eyes. She tried to step away from Massimo, but she stumbled, catching her heel on the uneven edge of a cobblestone. Massimo put out his hand to steady her and saw the glisten in her eyes. "Octavia, what is it? Are you worried about him?"

She didn't dare speak through the ache in her throat. Massimo gave an exasperated click of his tongue. In a gesture that brooked no refusal, he put his arm around her, startling her with the authority of it. She suspected he was not accustomed to being refused—anything. He led her down the street to where he had parked the Mercedes, and almost before she knew what was happening, she was belted into the passenger seat, her handbag on the floor at her feet, and the big old car was purring swiftly westward, toward the outer edge of the city center. She gave up. It had been settled for her.

She laid her head back against the cool leather and closed her eyes. Massimo clicked off the radio, and her lips curved a little in appreciation. After a long day of rehearsal, the last thing she wanted was to listen to music. Or to listen to anything, for that matter. Part of her would have liked to drive for hours with nothing but the hum of the fine old engine in her ears and the company of this intense young man beside her.

When the car stopped, all too soon, she opened her eyes. Massimo had parked behind a squat, unremarkable building. A faint glow showed through its curtained windows. Massimo opened her door and escorted her to a short set of cement steps that led down below the street level.

The bustle of traffic in the city center receded to a distant drone. Octavia paused before descending the stairs and gazed up at the towers of the Basilica di Sant'Ambrogio, their rectangular shapes outlined by twinkling stars. She knew Sant'Ambrogio. She had heard Mass there when she first came to Milan, and she remembered, with a rush of nostalgia, coming through the great portico with Vincenzo and crossing the atrium. Vincenzo had climbed the stairs to the women's gallery, and she had followed.

From that vantage point he had sung his part in a motet for two choirs. The other voices answered his across the great nave. She had crouched at his feet, so as not to be seen by anyone looking up, and had closed her eyes to listen to the men's and boys' voices blending with those of the *castrati*, saturating the arched interior of the church with glorious sound.

The narrow lanes of the neighborhood were dark and quiet now. As they went down the steps, a bell tolled from the *campanile*, and she shivered a little at the beauty of it. "It's peaceful here."

"Yes. Have you been inside the Basilica?"

Octavia shook her head, unable to explain.

The last time she had been in the church had been at the end of Teresa's career. She was trying to decide what to do, where to go. She had not dared go into the lovely old sanctuary, where the blessed water threatened to scald her and the very images of the saints rebuked her. She had wandered down into the crypt, instead, to sit on a cold marble bench and stare through the grille at the coffin of St. Ambrose, trying to imagine what it must be like to die. She thought of her mother, gone almost ninety years. She thought with pain and guilt of her father, who had died at a great age, but alone in Limone sul Garda. How had it been for them to face the darkness, the chasm from which no one returned? Had they been afraid, or joyous? Anxious, or relieved? She had seen the face of death so many times, but there was nothing in those still faces to tell her what the journey was like. All she read in the wide, sightless eyes of the dead was surprise.

Teresa had sat in St. Ambrose's crypt for a long time, until the bells above her head told her Mass was beginning. She had been one hundred six years old, and no longer dared show her face in Milan.

But Octavia could not share this memory with Massimo Luca. She couldn't share it with anyone except Ugo.

Massimo reached for the doorknob and turned it. When he opened the door, brilliant light poured over them, and the muted clink of china and glasses met their ears. Octavia sniffed in appreciation, and Massimo grinned. "As I told you," he said with satisfaction. "The best *ossubuco* in the city."

Massimo's cousin was an elegant elderly woman, and her home was both rich and comfortable. There were only two other guests. No one made a great fuss over Octavia, but they made her welcome with good conversation and a minimum of curious questions.

And Massimo was right about the food. Though Octavia's stomach rebelled at the sight of the generous *antipasto* and the *insalata Toscana*, the aperitif was a clear, sparkling *prosecco*, and it soothed her a bit. The *ossobuco* was a dish Teresa Saporiti would have recognized, prepared *in bianco*, as tomatoes had not been introduced in Milan until the nineteenth century. Despite her queasiness, Octavia managed to eat a good bit of it. A nice big Barolo helped. Its flavors of chocolate and tobacco and plum calmed the burning of her throat and placated her reluctant stomach. Massimo had poured her a third glass before she realized it. The hostess had prepared everything herself, so Octavia was grateful to find a way to do justice to the dinner.

As dessert was being served, Massimo's cell phone rang from his jacket pocket. Octavia turned to him, surprised that he would have the phone on during a social evening, and she caught the hard look that crossed his face. He looked infinitely older at that moment, his eyes darkening, his generous mouth pressed into a narrow line. He pulled out the phone, glanced at it, and shoved his chair back with an angry gesture.

The others at the table made an evident effort to ignore all of this. Someone asked Octavia a question about her performance in Paris, and her hostess broached the subject of her *Rusalka* recording. By the time she finished her answer, Massimo had returned. He muttered an apology as he sat down, and drained what was left in his wineglass in a single swallow. No one asked who had called, and he didn't offer the information.

The smooth, cool *panna cotta*, served in an antique sherbet dish, was the perfect ending for the meal. Octavia refused the proffered glass of port afterward, pleading the need to sing in the morning. Massimo's bout of temper seemed to have passed, and his hand was gentle when he handed her back into the Mercedes. As they drove back to Il Principe, she lowered the window a bit, to let the passing breeze draw Massimo's alluring scent from the car. She kept her eyes on the lights of the city as they drove. A full moon had risen, and it cast silver shadows on the public gardens. Massimo spoke from time to time, pointing something out, asking a neutral question. When they pulled into the circular drive of Il Principe, the doorman hurried to open the door.

Octavia turned to Massimo. "The dinner was wonderful," she said. "And so is your family. Thank you so much for taking me there."

"You're welcome." His eyes crinkled as he smiled, but he made no move to touch her. Part of her regretted that until, when she looked up at the line of his throat outlined by his white shirt, her teeth throbbed. She swallowed hard, denying the melting sensation in her breast, the warmth of her palm as he squeezed her hand and released it.

Moments later, she was safely inside the ornate gilt lobby of the hotel. She took the stairs to her room to work off the last of the Barolo. She promised herself, as she climbed, that when Ugo returned—if Ugo returned—and it was safe, she would see Massimo again. Then she would not be forced to hold back.

Octavia slept for a time, lulled by the soporific effect of the Barolo, but at midnight she startled awake. She had forgotten to pull the drapes, and moonlight flooded the bedroom. She lay for a moment, longing to sleep again, but her burning throat drove her to the bathroom for a glass of water.

She drank it and then refilled it to drink another. Her reflection in the mirror showed her hair in a hopeless tangle. Her eyes looked wide and hungry. She flicked off the bathroom light and went back into the bedroom, which was nearly as bright with moonlight as if the lights had been on. She went to the window to draw the curtains but instead stood, wringing the heavy fabric between her hands, staring out into the night. She followed the sparse line of traffic with her eyes, the headlights sweeping down Via Turati, past the new hotels and the old businesses. None of them had been there in Teresa's day.

Four years were to pass before Teresa saw Mozart again. The very day after *Don Giovanni* closed at the Nostitz, she started the long journey back to Italy. She wasn't without work for long. With Vincenzo's help, she won rôles in Venice, in *Arsace* and *Rinaldo*, and she returned to Milano the next year to reprise the rôle of *Donna Anna*, though not under Mozart's baton.

The director of La Scala called her to an extra orchestra rehearsal. As she sang her arias, he strolled about the house, listening from various vantage points. When she had sung "Or sai chi l'onore" and "Non mi dir," he walked down the aisle to stand beneath the stage. His eyes appraised her, running over her figure, narrowing as he looked at her face. "Your voice is not so white as it was, signorina."

Her temper flared, and she put indignant fists on her hips. She was no longer a novice desperate for approval. She had had a taste of success in Venice, and she had expected the same in Milano. She spoke with an asperity that made the conductor, in the pit, hide his smile. "I'm not so young as I was, signore."

"*È vero.*" The director spoke with a satisfied air, nodding as if he had known all along her voice would darken as she grew older. "Better."

Teresa spun in an irritated whirl of skirts and marched off the stage and back to her dressing room. It was blessedly empty, and she dropped onto a stool before the mirror. She raised the wick on the oil lamp for more light and sat for long moments looking at herself before she put a fingertip to her upper lip and lifted it.

Her eyeteeth had grown by a third, and their tips tapered to sharp points. They were slightly darker than the surrounding teeth, gleaming with a faint tinge of gold in the lamplight. She touched one with a fingernail, tapping it. It seemed harder to her than the others, and smoother.

She had seen a cur in the street one evening not long ago, snarling at a pack of boys who were tormenting it. Its teeth had looked like this: long, pointed, and strong. Teresa had chased the boys away, flinging curses after them through the dusk.

Her teeth were as utilitarian as any dog's. For two years, she had used them when the thirst came upon her. Beggars, thieves, drunkards, ruffians—and, although she deeply regretted it, a maid or two. With each came a fresh onslaught of memories. She thought of these memories as the blood price.

Teresa remembered mothers she had never seen and fathers who shouted or abused or embraced. She could anguish over every detail of the faces of faithless lovers, though she had never met them. Her heart ached at the treachery of sisters who knew how to cut with their words. She knew the long days and uncomfortable nights of arduous journeys she had never taken. She recalled wedding days and funerals of strangers. She knew the rending pain of giving birth, the delight of a beloved infant's face, the unthinkable grief of a child's death.

At first, she feared these swiftly accumulating memories would drive her mad. One dark night, newly come to Venice, she paced across the Ponte Vecchio, clutching her head with both hands as if she could squeeze the burdensome recollections out of her head. She stopped at the highest point of the arching bridge and stared down into the dark waters of the canal for an hour, wishing the swirling current could wash her mind clean.

But her ovations grew bigger and longer each night. She pondered every memory of Mozart's. The way he colored a phrase, how he shaped a cadence, the abundant inventiveness with which he spilled music onto a page in the form of notes and accidentals and rhythms, informed her own music making. She treasured images of Mozart's sister Nannerl at the harpsichord, or laughing with him over some jest. She revisited endless lessons with Leopold and felt Mozart's mixture of affection and frustration. She exulted in his first hearings of Bach and Allegri and Handel, feeling his own excitement, the thrill of discovery.

What she needed was a way to filter out the memories she didn't want or need, that were only debris to clutter the workings of her mind. And the way she found was discipline.

Teresa learned to close such memories off from the everyday flow of her thoughts. She created a cupboard in her mind, a cubbyhole. With an iron will, she shut unwanted memories into it and latched its door. The same steely resolve that had driven her to Milan in search of an audition served her well. The distractions in her mind cleared away, like the mists on the canals dissipating before the rising sun.

But Mozart's memories she kept in the open, as fresh to her as if each of them had happened only hours before.

To hide her teeth, she learned to sing with her upper lip pulled down, letting her jaw drop back to make space for resonance. It was this that had darkened her tone, and the effect pleased her audiences. They no longer referred to her as *la voce bianca*. They began, instead, to call her *La Saporiti*. Her public loved her, and she loved it no less in return.

She had just completed a run of *Figaro* in Milan when word came that Mozart was ill.

Teresa had followed Mozart through letters and reviews and reports from colleagues. She knew he had been back in Prague for the premiere of his opera *La Clemenza di Tito*, then had returned to Vienna with Constanze to open another new opera, *Die Zauberflöte*. It was rumored that he was at work on his masterpiece, a *Requiem*.

Vincenzo received a letter from one of his fellow *castrati*, a singer at the Viennese court. His friend wrote that everyone was worried about Mozart. No one had seen him in public since late November. Vincenzo told Teresa, thinking she would be interested because she had sung the premiere of *Giovanni* with Herr Mozart.

A terrible premonition seized Teresa. She had no more contracts until after the new year. After spending a day and a night pacing her room, worrying, she made her decision. Hurriedly, she packed her valises, gathered up the maid she had acquired in Venice, and departed for Vienna.

The trek was long and taxing, a succession of post chaises, carriages, once a wagon that reminded her of her very first journey and the kindly fishmonger for whom she had sung on the open road. Winter snows now blocked the mountain passes, and the roundabout roads slowed her progress so that she thought she would go mad before she reached her destination. Her maid complained bitterly of the conditions and the poor inns they stayed in, but Teresa would hear none of it. Compulsion drove her, a need to see him that was almost as urgent as her thirst. When she saw the spires and roofs of Vienna at last, she nearly wept with relief. It had taken her ten days to reach the city, and it was already the first of December.

She left her maid to sort out their rooms while she set out straightaway for die Rauhensteingasse, where Mozart and Constanze had their apartment. Vienna was already bright with Christmas colors. Pulling her fur stole snugly around her shoulders, she hurried past shop windows full of glistening pastries and tiered plates of chocolates, of children's toys and festive ornaments.

At first she thought she must have been given the wrong address. Rauhensteingasse was a dreary street, clogged with dirty snow and garbage. She found the number and stood beneath it, looking doubtfully up at the slanting walls and grimy windows. It seemed just the sort of place meant for black bunting and covered mirrors, a fitting house for sickness and death.

With a sinking heart, she raised the knocker and let it fall. It was a heavy cast-iron affair with a gryphon's head, and its echoing clang made it sound as if the house were already empty. Her heart plunged to her snow-stained calves' leather boots.

She waited for a long moment, listening for footsteps. Once more she raised the knocker, but before she could drop it, the latch clicked and the door opened a crack. Teresa expected a manservant, or at least a housemaid, but it was Constanze's face she saw, her eyes red, her usually plump cheeks drawn. She looked as if she had aged twenty years in four.

"*Ja?*" Constanze said in a faint voice.

"Frau Mozart," Teresa said. Her voice cracked, and she cleared her throat. "It's I. It's Teresa Saporiti."

"Saporiti . . . Do I know you?"

"Yes. We met in Prague, when I sang Donna Anna. I've come to see your husband."

The door wavered in Constanze's hand, as if she started to pull it open, but then thought better of it. "My husband is ill," she said. Her voice was a thread of misery.

"I know," Teresa said. "It's why I came."

Constanze shook her head. "He's too ill for visitors." The door began to close.

Teresa felt a rush of fury, dangerously like the need that came over her when she thirsted. She put a hand on the door and shoved. Constanze fell back with a little exclamation, stumbling a step or two. Teresa looked past her, up a broad set of steep stairs. A door was ajar at the top. She felt her lip begin to curl, and she hastily put her hand over it. She spoke through her spread fingers. "I have to see Herr Mozart. I may be able to help."

"How?" Constanze's head came only to Teresa's shoulder, but she stood in front of her, barring her way, puffing her breast like an angry sparrow defending its nest. "How can you help him when the physicians can't?"

Teresa's lip relaxed, and she dropped her hand. She held it out to Constanze, but the other woman refused to take it. "Frau Mozart," Teresa said gently. "I care as much for him as you do. I—I know a thing or two about his illness. Let me try."

"You're mad!" Constanze blazed. "You're one of his fancy women, aren't you? You were in love with him. And even now, you can't leave my husband alone!"

"It's not that," Teresa said tightly. She trembled from the effort of restraining herself. "And yes, I was. But everyone was in love with Wolfgang. You must know that." She tried to bring a persuasive smile to her face. She had not, after all, traveled all this way to be stopped at the very door of his house. "Please," she said. She fixed Constanze with her eyes as if she could force compliance through sheer need. "Let me see him for just a moment. As a friend only, I promise you. If he wants me to leave, I will. I give you my word."

In the end, Mozart's wife, fresh tears of despair brimming in her already-irritated eyes, stepped aside. She stretched out her arm to point up the stairs. "Five minutes," she said brokenly. "No more."

Teresa didn't answer but leaped up the stairs, taking them two at a time. She took one look back at Constanze, who stood passive and defeated in the entryway, gazing up the stairs at Teresa. Teresa gave her a nod before she slipped in through the open door of the sickroom and closed it quietly behind her.

Mozart lay on his side on his pillows. His eyes were closed. One of his fine small hands was outflung, resting on a sheaf of music paper. His hair had grown thin and straggled about his face. His features had grown sharp with illness, his nose jutting, his pale cheeks hollow. The rest of his body swelled strangely, mounding the quilt that lay over him. The hand Teresa could see was also swollen, the delicate finger bones hidden beneath puffy flesh.

As she approached, his eyes opened. "I've been poisoned," he said hoarsely.

"No, Wolfgang," she breathed. "Surely not. Who would poison you?"

His gaze wavered at first, his eyes wandering this way and that as if they were out of his control. He narrowed his eyelids, searching for her face. With obvious effort, his eyes focused and his gaze sharpened as he recognized her. "It was you!" he cried in a guttural tone. "You poisoned me!"

"No! Oh, no!" she said. "It was not I, Wolfgang."

"It was," he said. And with tears in his voice, "You bit me."

"No, no . . ." Teresa leaned across the bed. "No, you can't think that. It was she! It was Zdenka Milosch who poisoned us both!"

He drew a gurgling breath that filled her with terror, and his eyes rolled again. "Oh, God, I am so ill," he croaked. "Ill unto death, I think."

Teresa knelt beside the bed and took his hand between hers, lifting it from the sheet of paper beneath it. The score, she saw, was the *Requiem*. As she moved it aside, he bestirred himself. For a moment, his voice was perfectly clear, the light baritone she remembered. "It's for myself," he said. "My own *Requiem*."

"No, Wolfgang! Listen to me," she begged. "I was bitten by the Countess Milosch at the same time as you, and I'm not ill. I've never felt so well in my life!"

His eyes settled on her face again, and she sensed his faculties gathering, concentrating. The effort brought oily beads of sweat to his brow. "How many?" he rasped.

"How many what?"

A queer, bitter smile twisted his lips. "How many have you killed?"

This, Teresa knew, was the moment for which she had traveled all this way. She tightened her grip on his hand. "It doesn't matter," she said grimly. "And it doesn't matter how many you have taken, either. You've waited too long, haven't you, Wolfgang? And now your thirst is destroying you."

His hand turned in hers, seizing it, kneading it with frantic fingers. "I can't do it, Teresa. I can't do it anymore. Their memories . . . each and every one . . ."

"You have to shut them away," she said. Her voice scraped in her throat, dry with desperation. "Wolfgang, you must ignore them, set them aside."

"I can't," he moaned. "I can't. Their memories weigh me down. I can't think, I can't play, and when I try to compose I see scenes before my eyes, between my eyes and the score, and I can't stop them. They won't leave me alone. They're driving me mad!"

"No, no," she cried, her voice low and urgent. "You mustn't let them. You must—"

His eyes suddenly opened wide, their pupils dilated so they almost obscured the iris. They fixed on her face with an expression that filled her with horror. "Hell," he whispered. "You know that. I'm going straight to hell, and so are you."

She gripped his hand as if she could bend his thoughts to hers with the strength of her fingers. "No," she grated. "Not for a long, long time. Unless you die, Wolfgang."

At that his eyes rolled back in their sockets, and for one awful moment she thought he had died right before her. His features went rigid, his mouth open, his eyelids shut. She started to get up, to reach for him, but he took a rattling breath, and his swollen body heaved. His eyelids trembled, lifted, lowered again. "Go away," he said. He pulled his hand away from hers. His voice was barely audible. "Leave me alone."

His puffy fingers scrabbled over the half-finished bars of the *Requiem*. She watched them, pitying the swollen flesh. Beneath them she saw that the movement was the *Confutatis*. She looked up at Mozart's face, some comforting word on her lips, but she found that his gaze had fixed on a crucifix hanging above a dressing table. He whispered, "Teresa. Have you tried to go to church?"

"I've gone in," she admitted.

"The blessed water?"

She hesitated, and then admitted, very quietly, "It burns me."

"*Ja*. And me." Tears formed in his eyes and spilled over his sunken cheeks. "We're cursed," he croaked. "Damned forever."

"No! It can't be!"

His lips quivered, and his swollen body thrashed from side to side, crinkling the score on the coverlet. "Get Süssmayr," he pleaded. "Tell Constanze I need Süssmayr!"

"Who is Süssmayr?" Teresa said.

"My student. He'll write for me, my fingers are too swollen. I'm poisoned," he moaned again. "Poisoned. O God, to be damned forever, and not even for my own sins!"

Teresa tried to recapture his hand, tried to find words to persuade him, but he shook her off, rolling his head back and forth on his pillow. "Süssmayr! I need Süssmayr!" His voice rose and thinned, nearly a shriek.

The door opened, and Constanze came running. Teresa leaped to her feet to get out of the way as Mozart's wife bent over the bed. She had a damp compress in her hand, and her lips were pinched white. She laid the compress on Mozart's brow, crooning meaningless words in her light voice. Under her ministrations his spasms slowed, and he quavered something to his wife that Teresa couldn't hear.

Teresa wrung her hands together, searching for something she could do, something she could say. Downstairs the door knocker sounded, and sounded again. "Frau Mozart," she said in an undertone. "Shall I answer that?"

"Don't let anyone else in!" Constanze snapped, and then threw her head up. "Oh, unless it's the doctor."

"Süssmayr!" Mozart cried.

"No, no, Wolfgang," Constanze murmured, reversing the compress on her husband's forehead. "You can work on the score later. Not now."

Teresa backed to the door, and put her hand on the latch. Behind her Constanze murmured a stream of consoling words, but Mozart still scrabbled at the papers on the coverlet. He muttered the Latin words of the *Confutatis*, over and over:

"Confutatis maledictis, flammis acribus addictis."

And then the plaintive cry of the sinner for mercy:

"Voca me, voca me cum benedictus."

Teresa's heart thudded sickeningly in her breast as she hurried down to the door. Who would call her blessed, or Mozart? What if he was right, and they were both damned forever?

She gritted her teeth, collecting herself before she put her hand on the latch. If they were damned forever, there was all the more reason not to give in. Not to die.

Teresa spent a restless night in her rooms. The next morning, she presented herself once again in Rauhensteingasse. A stranger opened the door and stood glaring at her with a suspicious expression.

"I'm Teresa Saporiti," she said. "I've come to see Herr Mozart."

"No visitors," the man said flatly. He was a bony, stooped man with a face so dour, it was as if the deathwatch had already begun.

"Who are you?" she asked.

"Go away. Mozart is ill."

"I know that." Teresa put her palm on the door to stop him from closing it. "I have to see him. Tell Frau Mozart I'm here. *Bitte.*"

He looked her up and down, from her ermine-trimmed cape to her well-cut boots. His eyebrows rose. "Saporiti?"

"Yes. I've come all the way from Milano."

"A singer," he said.

"Yes," she said, made breathless by a sudden rush of hope. "I created the rôle of Donna Anna in—"

"*Don Giovanni*, yes, I know it well. Although I wasn't able to attend the premiere." He stepped back without warning, so that she stumbled into the foyer. "I am Süssmayr," he said, straightening his bent spine so he could bow to her. He added, with evident pride, "I am helping the *maestro* with his *Requiem.*"

"Herr Süssmayr," Teresa said. "I need a moment alone with Mozart. Just a moment! Could you persuade Constanze—"

"Oh, no, no, madame. She won't leave his side. The doctors—" He glanced up the narrow staircase, and then back at Teresa. He leaned closer, and she smelled stale tobacco on his breath and the sour tang of old perspiration on his clothes. "They say it won't be long," he whispered. "They say he has miliary fever."

"No!" Teresa snapped. She thrust past him and started for the stairs. "No, he doesn't. I need a few moments alone with him."

She ran up the stairs, not bothering to remove her cape. He came after her, but too slowly to catch up.

She tapped briefly on the bedroom door and went in without waiting for an answer.

The curtains were drawn, closing in the fetid air of the sickroom. Teresa longed to open the windows and let the cold December air blow through, but she didn't dare. Constanze sat on a little stool beside Mozart's bed, chafing his swollen wrists in her small hands. On the other side of the bed a woman in an apron stood holding the shoulders of a small boy. They both looked up as Teresa came in, but Constanze didn't take her eyes from Mozart's face. His eyes were closed, and his face, so sunken the day before, was now swollen nearly beyond recognition.

Teresa said softly, "Frau Mozart. Constanze."

Slowly, Constanze turned her face. For a moment it seemed she didn't recognize her, but then awareness flickered in her eyes. "You again," she said.

Teresa crossed the room, and knelt beside Constanze's stool. "Yes," she said quietly. "Me again. Teresa."

Constanze's lips trembled and her eyes brimmed. "He's dying," she said. The small boy whimpered, and the aproned woman shushed him. Constanze's eyes fixed on Teresa. "The doctors have given up," she said. "There was one here last night, but he said there was nothing he could do."

Teresa looked across the bed at the woman and boy. "Frau Mozart needs to rest," she told her. "Why don't you take her to her room to lie down for a while? I'll stay and watch."

"I want to be here if . . . when . . ." Constanze choked.

"Yes, yes, of course," Teresa said in as soothing a tone as she could manage. "If he gets worse, I'll fetch you."

Mozart didn't open his eyes as his wife left the room, followed by the woman and the little boy. Süssmayr hovered in the doorway like a hungry crow, but the aproned woman closed the door after she passed through, shutting him out on the landing. Teresa tossed her stole toward a chair. It missed, landing in a pile of silvery ermine on the floor. She let it lie and turned to gaze down at Mozart.

His head turned on the pillow even as his swollen hands reached blindly for the *Requiem* score. Teresa gathered up the pages, moving them out of his reach. She tidied the stack and laid it on the bedside table.

"Wolfgang." She touched his hand. "Wolfgang, open your eyes. Look at me."

His eyelids trembled, then opened slowly, painfully. Teresa nearly sobbed aloud at the hopelessness in his eyes, the slack resignation of his lips. She leaned over him, remembering how those lips had tasted, how she had longed for the touch of them. With a swift gesture, she tore open the neckline of her bodice, ripping the fine cotton lawn beyond repair. There was no time to trouble herself with the buttons

"Wolfgang!" she said urgently. She stretched her neck, tilting her chin to one side, offering him her throat.

He turned his head away. *"Nein, nein,"* he groaned. "No more. Not again."

"You must!" she said. "You can't hurt me, Wolfgang. It will get you through, until . . . until you're strong enough to . . ."

But his eyes closed again. She might have thought he was asleep except for the quivering of his lips, the clawing of his fingers on the coverlet as they searched for the *Requiem*.

"You can finish it," she said, straightening. "If you will only let me help you. Let me feed you. You can finish your *Requiem*."

He moaned, without opening his eyes, "Süss—"

"No! Mozart, look at me!" When he didn't respond, Teresa pulled back the long, lace-trimmed sleeve of her bodice. She turned her left wrist upward, exposing the delicate blue rivers of life running beneath her skin. She looked over her shoulder to be certain the door was still closed, and then, with a sharp breath to steel herself, she lifted her upper lip and drove her teeth into her own arm.

She bit deeply, fiercely, tearing skin and flesh in one gesture, opening the barrier to the radial artery where the blood flowed from heart to fingers. It hurt, but pain didn't matter. Nothing mattered at that moment but Mozart.

She felt her own blood hot on her lips as she lifted her head, but she wasted no time wiping it away. She pressed her bloodied wrist against Mozart's mouth, forcing his lips apart. She caught a brief glimpse of his teeth before her arm hid them. They were not so long as hers, nor so sharp. He had not used them enough, she thought.

"Drink!" she hissed. "Mozart, drink!"

At first it seemed he would not accept her offering. Her blood seeped down his chin and fell in vivid scarlet droplets onto the muslin of his nightshirt. A moment passed in which she hardly breathed. She pressed her wrist more tightly against his mouth, like a mother suckling a babe. She forced the sweet, hot taste of her blood onto his tongue.

Slowly at first, then eagerly, she felt the suction of his lips, the papery scrape of his tongue against her skin. A sensation akin to pleasure flowed over her, a sort of ecstatic shudder. Her knees weakened, and she sagged against the bed, struggling not to dislodge her wrist from his mouth.

As she fed him, she remembered her dream of years before, the peach that was no peach, but a fruit full of blood. She was that fruit for Mozart now, an offering, a sacrifice. She knelt beside him, her wrist at his lips, and willed him to take what he needed.

Only when she began to feel light-headed did she pull away. Gently, she broke the seal of his lips against her wrist. Tenderly, she wiped his mouth with a handkerchief from his bedside table. She bound her wrist with the same handkerchief, knotting it, pulling it tight with her teeth. Trembling now with weakness, she rearranged her clothes, pulling down her sleeve, pressing the flap of her torn bodice over her shoulder. She retrieved her stole from the floor and twisted it around her neck to hide her ruined dress.

Mozart's eyes were closed again, but his lips and hands were still. A faint color showed in his cheeks.

Surely, she thought, he would recover now. He would finish his *Requiem*. He would write more operas.

And he would remember that she had saved him.

Octavia turned from the window, rubbing her left wrist. The scars there had faded long ago, indeed almost immediately, as all her scars did. But the memory of Mozart's lips on her skin, the burr of his tongue as he suckled, was as fresh as if she had left his bedside only yesterday. She set it aside, gently, sorrowfully, to be considered another time.

As she did this, her thirst returned with a rage. Need drove all other thoughts, even memories, from her mind.

Hardly aware of what she was doing, she threw off her nightgown and pulled on a pair of jeans, a black sweater, a pair of soft-soled boots. When she left the suite, shrugging into a three-quarter-length wool coat, she turned away from the staircase that led to the lobby. She took the back stairs, slipping past the dark kitchens and out through a service exit, taking care not to be seen by the night guard in his lighted cubicle.

In moments she was striding through the public gardens across from the hotel. Her upper lip felt hot and swollen, and her teeth throbbed. Her body felt utterly alive, supremely focused on her goal, all long-denied, exquisitely familiar sensations. She was a huntress again, a predator, a creature of the night. She belonged to the darkness, grim and fierce beyond the civilizing lights of the city.

The moon had gone down, and the sculptures in the park made dim, amorphous shapes in the washed-out starlight. She encountered no one on the gravel paths as she cut across the park to Via Venezia.

She found her prey in an alley behind a travel agency, digging through a Dumpster. Her legs, in ragged jeans, wriggled out over the top of the big green container. As her grimy hightop sneakers settled onto the pavement, Octavia said in a throaty voice, *"Che successa, ragazza?"*

The girl gasped and whirled to face her. Octavia struck without further nicety.

It was not subtle, and it was not pleasurable. It was necessary, a bad meal for a hard hunger. She took only what she needed to slake her thirst, and then she broke away, leaving a panting, bleeding girl on the cobblestones. The girl cried after her as she strode away, "What did you do? What was that?"

Octavia didn't answer.

25

No, no, padrone! Vo' andar, vi dico.

No, no, master. I'm off, I tell you.

—Leporello, Act Two, Scene One, *Don Giovanni*

The moon rose early, silvering the snowy mountain slopes, shining through the window of Ugo's prison. Its delicate light fell upon his face, enticing him with the cool invitation of the music of the spheres. He sat up, facing the window, and began to unbutton his borrowed shirt.

Occasionally, the wolf retained bits of his clothing when it raced away. It was sometimes a useful trick. Once in a great while, Ugo was spared the inconvenience of scenes like the one at the house of the formidable Laurette. More often the clothes he found himself with were unwearable, inadequate scraps—a sock, or a shirt with no pants, or once, oddly, a handkerchief. Ugo cared no more about nakedness than the wolf did. Society was another matter.

He stood to remove the too-large trousers Laurette had given him. He took off the socks and underwear, too. He folded everything and piled it neatly on the bed before he went to stand in the shaft of moonlight. He gazed up at the white disc where it floated, full and brilliant, above the glowing silhouette of the mountain.

He tipped his head back and opened his eyes wide to let the

moonlight flood his corneas, fill his expanded pupils, pour into his retina, flow through the optic nerve into his brain. His neural pathways widened and twisted, processing moonlight. The moon fed the *lupo mannaro* the way sunlight fed the pines on the mountain slopes above Aspin-en-Lavedan. It was idiosyncratic, a strange kind of photosynthesis no scientist would ever study.

Ugo felt it first, as always, in his fingertips and his toes. With an electric tingle, his nails began to extend and harden. His metacarpal bones shortened and thickened. His thumbs retracted, pulling back and up, burrowing through the bones, then sprouting through his wrists as dew claws. Pain blazed along his spine as it thickened and bent. The follicles in his skin stung as the coat began to sprout. His skull began to elongate, pressing on his brain, reshaping and redistributing its mass. It pained him, not only in his body, but in his soul. He would, in a few moments, no longer be himself. He would lose all control, but it was not that so much he minded. It was that he would become that other, that alien he could never know.

An anxious growl began in his throat.

The wolf fell to all fours, muscle and bone and heart thrumming with animal energy. It paced the little cell, around and around, looking for an escape. Its tongue lolled and the hair along its shoulders bristled. Nothing about the cramped space made sense. Its nostrils pulsed, seeking something to orient it. Faintly, barely discernible under the smells of wood and steel and paint, came the distant scents of pine and soil. The wolf paced faster, wheeling this way and that, wanting out.

Ughetto, under the Countess's authority, submitted to a carriage ride of many days that wound north over twisting roads to Firenze, on to Bologna, over the mountains to Vienna, and finally to the outskirts of Prague. He wished he could have bid Cesare farewell, but he was allowed no time. Their departure from Rome took place only hours after his confrontation with Leonino at the concert.

The Countess was bad company on a journey. She sat for hours without speaking, not even watching the scenery. She stared steadily at the opposite wall of the carriage, her black eyes hardly blinking, until Ughetto had to look over his shoulder to see if there was something of interest there.

He gave up trying to engage her in conversation after the first day. In silence, he watched the changing of the landscape as they clattered north. The soft hills of Lazio gave way to the tantalizing farmlands of Emilia-Romagna, then melted into the steep mountains of Trentino-Alto Adige. These, in their turn, sloped down into the Austrian river valleys.

They stopped at inns where it was clear the Countess was known. Fresh horses were waiting each time, and rooms were made ready. Ughetto squirmed under the anxious regard of the staffs of these places. The maids were round-eyed and white-faced. The innkeepers trembled with eagerness to serve the Countess, and even more eagerly hurried her on her way.

One night, as they ate an excellent meal of freshly baked bread and *zuppa di agnello*, Ughetto said, "They're all afraid of you."

Her eyes came up to his with maddening deliberation. "And so should you be."

He didn't shrink from her gaze, or the implied threat. Already he had begun to think of escape, of fleeing the carriage at some stop, to take his chances in the countryside. He kept his face as still as hers as he said, "I thought you meant to help me, Countess."

"I do. And you will help me in return." A faint gleam escaped her black gaze. "It's all that protects you, my young friend."

"From what?"

She laid aside her spoon. She picked up a napkin and dabbed at her mouth. Then, slowly, elegantly, she lifted her upper lip.

Ughetto stared. Her teeth were a startling white against her olive skin, and they shone in the lamplight like polished marble. Her canines were as long as the first joint of his thumb, and sharper than the knife beneath his hand. It was no wonder she never smiled, and spoke no more than necessary. It must have taken her years to learn to manage such teeth, to keep her lip pulled down over them, to refrain from revealing them at inopportune moments.

Stunned, he realized his own mouth was open. He closed it with a small moist noise.

She folded her lips together again and gave her mirthless smile.

"What—what *are* you?" His voice rose a little, babyish, wounded.

She picked up her spoon. "I am what I am," she said. "Trust your eyes."

She looked away from him, down at her bowl, as if what he thought, what he deduced, were of no moment to her at all.

He whispered, *"Vampira."*

She only dipped her spoon into her soup and sipped it without making a sound.

The carriage stopped at last at a small stone house with a vine-hung wall behind it. The Countess stepped out as a huge man in the shirt and trousers of a working man emerged from the house. "My gardener," she said disinterestedly.

The big man, thick-featured and dull-eyed, hardly looked at Ughetto before he turned to help the driver unload the portmanteaus and trunks roped onto the back of the carriage. Zdenka Milosch walked into the little stone building, Ughetto following. She walked straight on through the modest dwelling, which had stone floors and scattered plain wooden furniture. She went out a back door, Ughetto a pace behind her. They emerged into a garden so overgrown it seemed no light could penetrate the thick shrubbery and unpruned trees.

Ughetto looked about at the grounds and wondered if the gardener ever did any work. He saw, as they trod the moss-covered stepping stones of a narrow path, that they were now inside the circle of the wall. Hanging vines and drooping tree branches hindered their progress, and they walked in near darkness, though it was midday. When they came out into the open, all at once, a great house sprawled before them. Ivy shrouded its walls and even grew over the windows. Chimney stacks dotted the immense roof in a random pattern. Everything was dark: gray stone, charcoal tiles, bricks gone black with age. Even the leaves of the ivy were the darkest green Ughetto had ever seen.

His eyes were used to the generous sun of Italy, and he struggled now, in this watery northern light, to make out details, to make sense of what he saw. He followed the Countess's narrow back up a set of stone stairs slippery with mold. They passed through a studded door of dark wood and into a foyer lit only by the dimmest of oil lamps.

Here she turned to him, her eyelids lifting briefly, then dropping, almost as if she were suddenly sleepy. "This is Kirska," she said.

Ughetto started. A short, plump woman had appeared as if out of nowhere and stood silently waiting at one side of the foyer. He nodded to her.

"Kirska will show you to your room," the Countess said. "I will see you at dinner."

She was gone without further comment. The whisper of her bombazine skirt was the only sound in the intensely silent house.

Ughetto followed Kirska as she climbed a broad staircase, then navigated a maze of dark corridors. Every door was closed. Ughetto could hear no conversation, no noise of cooking or cleaning, no sound of breeze-stirred curtains or fires crackling in hearths. The air in the house smelled oddly rank, as if its windows had not been opened in decades. The whole combined to give a sense of the suspension of time, a place in which neither air nor sound could move.

Ughetto wished with all his heart he had stayed in Rome.

"Is your room acceptable?" the Countess asked when the gloomy Kirska had retrieved Ughetto for dinner.

He sat opposite her in an enormous, shadowed parlor. An abundance of sofas in styles of bygone eras filled the space.

Heavy carved-wood chairs ranged around low tables or rested beneath what Ughetto assumed were meant to be candelabras for reading. None of them had been lighted. On the inlaid table between him and the Countess were three thick beeswax candles, flickering in heavy cut-glass candleholders. They were the only light in the room. A huge fireplace yawned behind the Countess, but no fire had been laid.

"The room is all right," Ughetto said. "I'd like to be able to open the window and air it out. It seems to be painted shut."

Zdenka Milosch nodded. "I'll speak to Kirska." She leaned back on the sofa and stared into the candle flames. Ughetto waited for her to say something else, but she seemed to have forgotten his presence.

A servant he hadn't seen before, a scurrying little man with a face like a wizened mouse, came in with a drinks tray and poured Ughetto something in a wide-mouthed goblet. Ughetto eyed it, but didn't pick it up.

After a pause, the Countess said, "It's only cognac, Ughetto. You can drink it if you like." By her tone, he could guess that she had no interest in whether he did or didn't.

"When are you going to explain to me why I'm here?"

She emitted the tiniest, shallowest sigh he had ever heard. "Patience."

"I've been patient for days, Countess Milosch."

She closed her eyes. He decided they must be waiting for something, or someone. He picked up the goblet and tasted the liquid in it. It was indeed cognac, better than any he had ever had before. He tossed it off in a swallow and reached for the decanter.

Just as his fingers closed on it, a door opened at the far end of the long room. He pulled his hand back and peered through the dimness. He heard shuffling footsteps, and then, coming out of the shadows like wild animals slipping from their forest cover, came three figures.

At first he was not sure they were people at all. One was a shapeless form in a hooded cloak of a type not seen in two hundred years. Another was draped in a dark robe tied at the neck, its hem trailing on the carpet. The third wore trousers and a jacket, with a cravat swathing his chin and neck. They moved slowly into the faint circle of light thrown by the candles, and there they stopped, staring at Ughetto.

He stared back. Their features were hard to discern in the faint light. But he could see that each had long, gleaming canines protruding from the mouth, extending over the lower lip, arching down to press into the chin.

Ughetto's belly crawled with horror. He stood up abruptly, knocking the table with his leg.

The Countess opened her eyes and turned to the three dark and terrible figures. "Ah," she said as if there were nothing unusual at all in this grim sight. "Ughetto. Meet my brethren. The elders."

Ughetto sniffed at the smell that came with these creatures, the unmistakable stench of decay. Instinctively, he understood that while Zdenka Milosch was far older than she appeared, these others were old beyond belief. That they walked, and breathed, was beyond his comprehension. It seemed impossible that they had once been human. He had no wish to greet them, certainly not to touch them. He didn't want to be in the same room with these ruins.

One of the ancients, the one in the hood, drew a rasping breath. With an inclination of the head so slight it was almost imperceptible, a voice rattled from beneath the dark fabric. "Too young."

The Countess, astonishingly, laughed. The harsh sound startled Ughetto, and he turned to look at her. Her lips were parted, and her own elongated teeth caught the candlelight with a brief glimmer.

"Anastasia," she said. "Compared to you, everyone is too young."

An angry hiss escaped the hood, and Ughetto flinched.

The Countess said, "Pay no attention, Ughetto. That is Anastasia, and despite her appearance, she is past hurting you, at least while I am here. The others are Eusebio"—she pointed, and the one in the jacket and trousers bowed slightly—"and Henri." The creature in the robe shifted his body in what might have been a nod of acknowledgment or could have been a spasm of pain.

Ughetto set his jaw, and gave his most elegant bow. *"Che piacere,"* he said, untruthfully.

"And now," the Countess said, rising from the sofa with the fluid movement of a girl, "we will go in to dinner. Afterward, we will explain to our new young friend what we need from him and what we will give him in return."

Ughetto, suppressing his aversion, offered the Countess his arm. Her lips curled in that tight, cold smile. She laid her thin, icy fingers on his sleeve and pointed to a door at one side of the parlor. Together they led the way out of the room.

The ancients followed. Ughetto felt them behind him, creatures of nightmare. He couldn't repress a shiver of revulsion. Beside him, he felt the Countess's hand quiver with a silent laugh.

26

Chi a una sola è fedele, verso l'altre è crudele . . .

If a man keeps faith with one, he is cruel to all the others . . .

—Don Giovanni, Act Two, Scene One, *Don Giovanni*

Domenico picked up the phone on the desk a dozen times, his finger poised above the keypad, but then set it down again. There were people he could call, in London, or in New York, to replace Benson and Marks. There was a plentiful supply of those willing to do anything at all to win a chance at near immortality. But since Ugo had escaped, it hardly seemed worthwhile. Ugo was the one and only link Domenico had. Until he had a new idea, or Ugo turned up, he didn't know what to do next.

He knew from the diary that there was a place, a great house somewhere where the elders lived. He imagined it as an elegant, quiet dwelling, a *villa* perhaps, or an old European castle, where the elders lived their long, long lives in seclusion, sending people like Ugo out to do their bidding. Of course they had to feed, but he thought they must have people brought to them, easy targets. Certainly the Countess Milosch, opera patroness, a member of the nobility, would not go out into the streets like a tramp. Nor would she allow anyone into La Società who would.

Benson and Marks hadn't had a chance of achieving entrance into La Società, even if that—that *creature*, that beast, hadn't torn them to shreds in the basement room.

Domenico shuddered, thinking of it. There had been blood everywhere, streaking the walls, running in dark rivulets across the cement floor. He had made it to the door with the wolf snapping and slashing behind him, and only barely made it out. Marks, hearing Benson screaming in agony, went rushing past him into the room and threw himself straight into the jaws of a violent death. The noise had been ghastly. Domenico had raced down the hallway to get away from the tormented howling, leaving every door open in his haste. He couldn't bring himself to go back to face the torn remains of Marks and Benson. He fled the area as swiftly as he could, abandoning the rented Fiat, leaving the carnage to be found by someone else.

They had been misinformed about Ugo. Their intelligence was, in fact, backward. Ugo's herb didn't trigger his transformation. It prevented it.

By the time he understood that, it was too late. Regrettable, especially for Benson and Marks. Naturally, such an end had been waiting for them in any case, one way or another. The diary made it clear that such as they would never be allowed to join the select few. Still, Domenico regretted the gory circumstances. The whole thing had been rather embarrassing, actually. And now he was back where he had begun.

Domenico turned away from the phone and went to the bathroom to shower and dress. He couldn't be late for the curtain.

Under the pleasant sting of hot water, he remembered his first sight of Zdenka Milosch at the opera, standing alone in the lobby of the Royal Opera House in Covent Garden. She looked like royalty herself: tall, thin, beautifully dressed in a silky black gown. Her haughty black gaze forestalled anyone who might think of approaching her.

There had been a rumor in the circles Domenico haunted, a story that one of the elders was in the city, had been seen at the opera. He had followed several women in those days, hoping for a clue as to which was the one. He had a feeling, when he spied the hawk-nosed Countess for the first time, that he had found her at last. And when he followed her out of the theater doors and into the street, he saw a slender young man, little more than a boy, really, open a car door for her, then slide into the backseat beside her.

Domenico had the license, and he had the name of the car service. It was easy to find the car and ridiculously simple to claim he had come in search of an item left behind by the Countess. It was a stroke of the purest luck that left a strangely bound book in his hands, forgotten—or dropped—on the leather seat.

What had not been easy was tracking her across London. A rash of missing maids and two or three unexplained bodies in the city made the final connection. Domenico's special gift—his real talent—was persistence. In divining that Zdenka Milosch was the one he sought, his persistence paid off. He soon learned that the slender boy he had seen was in actuality an enigmatic man named Ugo, a lover of opera, evidently a servant of the Countess. Domenico followed Ugo to try to reach the Countess, and in a second burst of happy fortune, was present when this strangely youthful man, standing in a shaft of moonlight in a London garden, transformed into a great gray wolf and bounded off into the darkness.

But Domenico was not surprised by good luck. What could have been luckier than to lay his hands on Zdenka Milosch's diary, and to find Mozart's name in it? Surely, he often thought, it was not so much luck as it was destiny that had led him to this point. How foolish it would be to waste the opportunity!

Domenico climbed out of the shower and rubbed himself dry. He admired his lean body in the bathroom mirror, his flat belly, his sculpted jaw. He didn't want to lose any of it. He wanted to stay just as he was, not too young, but not at all old. He would remain strong, healthy, capable. And if that meant others less persistent, less committed than he, had to pay a price, so be it. He could live with that.

Live nearly forever.

27

Finiscila, non soffro opposizioni!

Have done, I won't be argued with!

—Don Giovanni, Act Two, Scene One, *Don Giovanni*

The opera opened with a minimum of trouble. Octavia forced aside her worries over Ugo and immersed herself in her rôle. Brenda's Donna Elvira surprised her with its vigor and commitment. As usual, Masetto and Zerlina received enthusiastic ovations. Nick Barrett-Jones sang exactly as he had sung in every rehearsal, without nuance or depth of meaning, but without errors. Peter's performance, of course, was a delight. Octavia hugged him before the curtain calls and told him so. Their applause was satisfying, and the alternate cast, coming backstage from their seats in the house, was generous in its compliments.

Russell and Octavia rode together in a limousine to the Ristorante Romani for a private reception. In a back room, tables were laid with linen and silver. Candles in hurricane glasses flickered everywhere. Colorful dishes of grilled eggplant, *gamberoni*, and tiny rounds of artisan cheeses filled a sideboard. A waiter circled the room with a bottle of champagne and a tray of glasses.

Octavia, grateful for not being thirsty for the moment, accepted a glass of champagne, but held it without drinking. Russell stayed at her elbow, reliving moments of the performance.

"The 'Non mi dir' went particularly well, I thought," he said. He rubbed the stem of his glass with nervous fingers. "But perhaps we could speak to Nick about the first ensemble. I still would like the tempo to be flexible there."

"I was watching you," Octavia said, and smiled as Russell rolled his eyes.

"I know *you* were," he said, and then, as Nick approached them, he stopped.

"Great show," Nick said heartily.

"Yes, very good," Russell answered. "I hope it will go as well with the other cast."

"We all do," the baritone said, making an expansive gesture with his glass. "So what's your next engagement, Octavia?"

"After this run, I have a *Figaro* in Houston. The Countess."

"Oh, good, good."

"And you?" she asked politely.

He answered, with a little swelling of his chest, "I've just heard from my management. Another *Giovanni*, this one in Chicago."

Octavia said, "That's very short notice. Is someone ill?"

"He had terrible notices in Seattle. They cancelled his contract."

"Really!" Russell raised his eyebrows and asked for more details about the event. Octavia gave the conversation half her attention, letting her eyes stray idly around the room. When her gaze reached the doorway, she stiffened.

A woman in a long black lace dress stood there, surveying the room through tinted lenses. She was rather tall, narrow-shouldered, with a hawkish nose and a tight black chignon. She scanned the room steadily until her dark gaze alighted upon Octavia. She began to work her way through the room without hesitation.

Zdenka Milosch.

Octavia froze for a long moment. There was a door behind her that she was fairly certain led to the kitchen, but there was little point in using it. If the Countess Milosch meant to talk to her, such evasion would merely be postponing the inevitable. She sighed and set her glass down on a nearby table.

She murmured, "Russell, will you excuse me? I see an old friend." With a nod to Nick, she turned toward the door. Her jaw was clenched, and she deliberately loosened it as she wound her way through the crush. The Countess came forward, too. They met in the middle of the room.

Zdenka Milosch put her cold hand on Octavia's arm to steer her to an empty corner. When she was certain no one was watching them, Octavia shook her arm free. She was careful to keep her face impassive, but her voice was bitter. "What are you doing here? I thought we had an agreement."

"So did I," the Countess said. Her voice was like shards of ice. Octavia felt a chill on her arm where she had touched her. "You broke it."

"It was necessary." Octavia met the Countess's stony gaze with one just as hard.

"She was not worthy to be one of us."

"That street girl?" Octavia remembered the girl crying out, "What was that?" and a wave of nausea made her swallow. She tried to keep all feeling from her voice, emulating the Countess. "She may not survive in any case," she said.

"She survived," the Countess said, in an offhand tone. "For a while."

Octavia's heart lurched. She stared at Zdenka Milosch for a long, awful moment, trying to absorb her meaning. In a voice that shook with fury, she finally said, "You killed her."

With the faintest curl of her lip, the Countess answered, "It was necessary."

Octavia pulled back a step, as if she could no longer bear the proximity with Zdenka Milosch. The memories of the street girl filled her mind, nearly blinding her for a moment. There had been a little brother, who died of some illness, and an inconsolable mother. There was a grandmother, cooking in a small, dark kitchen, smiling across a bowl of *pasta*. There was a teacher who took advantage, under the guise of sympathy . . . a screaming argument with a father, a family fractured, a home lost. . . .

With a supreme effort, Octavia shoved these memories aside, walled them off. She glared at the Countess, her body vibrating with impotent fury. "I can't talk to you here," she said. "You shouldn't have come."

And as if he felt her distress, Massimo Luca appeared at her side. She managed to smile up at him, though she still trembled with anger.

If he noticed, he gave no sign. He bent to kiss her cheek. "You were fabulous," he said.

"You had a great ovation yourself," she answered. "And you earned it."

"*Grazie.*" He glanced at the Countess and nodded politely. "Did you enjoy the opera?"

She stared at him without answering, until Octavia said hurriedly, "This is my—the Countess Milosch, from Prague. Massimo Luca, our Masetto."

Massimo grinned at the Countess's indifferent silence and turned a dismissive shoulder to her. To Octavia, he said, "Not a fan, I gather. But I came to ask if I can drive you home."

"Yes," she said instantly.

"No," the Countess said at the same moment.

Massimo's brows rose, and Octavia touched his hand. "Massimo, a moment, please? I'll meet you . . . over there, where Russell is standing. Five minutes."

He turned his hand to caress her fingers. "*Va bene.* Five minutes."

When he was gone, Octavia said bluntly, "Ugo is missing."

The Countess's eyelids flickered. "Missing? How can he be missing?"

Octavia gave an exasperated sigh. It was useless, she supposed, to comment on the stupidity of the question. She said only, "He disappeared our first night in Milan." Anxiety welled anew in her throat, and she had to drop her eyes. She dared not show weakness in the presence of Zdenka Milosch. The network of La Società was complex, and Ugo was not their only resource.

Their creatures went armed with wicked little knives, and they knew how—and where—to use them.

"No word?" Zdenka said.

"None." Octavia regained control and lifted her head.

Zdenka's lips curled in the barest of smiles. "You can come home with me."

"No, I can't. I'm under contract, and I have another performance in three days."

The black eyes narrowed. "What do I care about that?"

Octavia felt her cheeks warm, and she seized the Countess's arm, relishing the faint wince at the strength of her fingers. She hissed, "Listen to me, Zdenka. You knew I was a singer when you began all this. I have a right to live the way I like, just as you and those walking corpses do at the compound!"

The Countess's upper lip lifted, slid up just enough to give Octavia a glimpse of her fearsome teeth. "You would have been dead two centuries ago if it weren't for the gift of the bite, Teresa! *My* bite!"

"But I'm not dead. And I am what you made me." Octavia dropped the Countess's arm and glanced across the room to where Massimo stood smiling down into the eager face of Marie Charles. "Go back to the compound," she said in a hard voice. "Go now. And don't come near me again."

"No more conversions, Octavia. This is our last warning."

"You would rather see me die?"

"If necessary." The Countess's lip released, and her face settled into its customary mask. "Surely, my dear, you don't expect me to have an attack of conscience at this late date?"

"No. I know your loyalties are reserved for the elders." Octavia couldn't keep the bitterness from her voice. The elders had offered her neither sympathy nor friendship. To them, she was only a vessel.

Zdenka Milosch appeared not to notice her tone, or not to care. She gathered her shawl around her, preparing to leave, and fixed Octavia with her hooded gaze. "We will not admit any more to our number, not without very good reason. The risk of exposure is too great."

"What do you expect me to do?" Octavia nearly snarled the words. She saw Massimo bend down to hear Marie say something and then toss back his errant lock of hair as he laughed.

"You know perfectly well what we expect," Zdenka said. She turned toward the door, adding over her shoulder, "If you must feed, kill."

Octavia forced a pleasant expression to her face as she turned back to the party, but her nerves vibrated with rage. The face of the little street girl danced before her, and her stomach turned. She had no illusions about the nature of the world. Predator and prey. Winners and losers. The conquerors and the vanquished. She had been naïve to think she could compromise, that she could take what she needed without paying the full price. It seemed, after all, that there was not enough blood in the world to go around.

She had once more to face the war that raged in her soul, if she still possessed such a thing. It was a great battle waged between the artist struggling to survive and the human being longing to be restored. To surrender would be to lose her music, to lose her deepest desire. But to continue was to give up on the last shreds of her humanity.

A waiter was passing, and she seized a fresh glass of champagne. She had almost drunk it all when she felt Massimo's warmth behind her, his hand slipping around her waist in a gesture of familiarity, of confidence. She turned to look up at him, her body still throbbing under the tide of emotion.

His eyes widened. "Octavia?"

She took a swift breath and drank off the rest of the wine. "Can we get out of here?" she asked in an undertone. "Have we stayed long enough to be polite?"

Massimo took the empty glass and set it on the buffet table. "Yes," he said, with a husky edge to his deep voice. "We'll just slip out. Where's your coat?"

"I don't have one."

He grinned, and his eyes kindled with a conspiratorial light. "Good. I know where the back door is."

The staff of Ristorante Romani looked up as they passed through the kitchen, but no one interrupted them. The old Mercedes was parked in a nearby alley, and in moments they were safely inside, with the heater warming, the motor purring as Massimo drove expertly through the cramped and twisting streets. Octavia knew Milan, but Massimo knew side streets and hidden lanes she had never discovered.

She forced herself to focus on his profile as he drove. It would do her no good to think about Zdenka Milosch anymore . . . or about the girl by the Dumpster. There was nothing she could do, nothing she could have done. She felt as she had in the beginning, when Teresa struggled against the thirst, slowly coming to understand what she had become.

And she remembered Mozart's refusal.

Teresa Saporiti went back to Rauhensteingasse the next day and found Mozart a little stronger. Constanze whispered to her, "What did you do? What did you give him?"

Teresa couldn't meet her eyes. "I talked to him," she said. "I told him how much we all care about him, how much we want to sing another opera."

Constanze seemed to think this was reasonable. But Mozart, though he was clearly better, his hands less swollen, his color stronger, would not speak to Teresa. He turned his head away on the pillow, and his curling hair hid his eyes. Constanze shrugged and shook her head. "I'm sorry, fräulein. He's not himself yet."

Teresa nodded and excused herself. As she walked back to her lodging, she told herself it would be all right, that he had taken enough for the moment. One more day wouldn't matter. She would go tomorrow, and again the next day, until he would listen, let her explain how important it was that he preserve himself, how great his gifts to the world could be.

That night the thirst came on her, sooner than it should have. She had given Mozart so much, and her body demanded its return. With an unbearable burning in her throat, she slipped out into the night and wandered the streets of Vienna, hunting.

She knew by then the sorts of taverns that were the natural habitat for her prey, and she found her way to one of these in the Kärntner Viertel, the southeast quarter. It was a ramshackle place, too rudimentary even to have a sign. Its uneven roof appeared to be made of scavenged tiles. It had three walls cobbled together with planks that didn't match, and the city ramparts formed the back wall. The single door hung crazily in its frame, emitting a rectangle of lurid yellow light. Patrons toppled in and out like rodents from a rat hole.

One presented himself to her like a gift, reeling out of the sulfurous glow of the tavern into the starlit night. He was a redfaced, big-bellied man reeking of beer and insensate with lust. The veins in his neck were swollen, and capillaries laced his fleshy nose. He seemed a man bursting with what she needed, and she barely restrained herself from sinking her teeth into him right there in the street. She managed to lead him to a shadowed place beneath a jutting support for the ramparts. He had time only to make a clumsy grab at her skirt before she fell on him.

When she was finished, she left him propped against the ramparts and strolled back to her lodging. Sated, she fell into a heavy, dreamless sleep, and woke with a start when the winter sun was already high in a pale blue sky. She leaped out of bed and hurried to wash and dress her hair. The maid, hearing her moving about, offered coffee, but Teresa refused. She wanted to see Mozart. She wanted to show him how well she felt, how strong she was. She wanted to persuade him that he should seize his opportunity, as she had. That although their path had not been of their own choosing, and though they had lost any hope of heaven, there was still life, and there was music.

She rehearsed all of this in her mind as she hurried once more to Rauhensteingasse. She had forgotten her hat, and the cold sunlight, reflecting from ice-glazed streets and snow-buried gardens, dazzled her eyes. She knocked on Mozart's door. Someone opened it, but at first she couldn't make out who it was. Half blinded, she stumbled forward.

A hard small hand stopped her.

Teresa said, "Excuse me. Frau Mozart?"

It was a woman who answered, but it was not Constanze. "Weber," she said sharply. "Frau Weber. You can't come in now. This is a death house."

"No!" Teresa blinked, trying to see the woman who stood in her way. "No, I—listen to me, please!"

The woman's features began to come clear as her eyes adjusted to the dimness of the foyer. She was very like Constanze, though her hair was gray and her figure square and solid. "I'm sorry, fräulein. I wouldn't have opened the door, but I thought you were the doctor." She stepped back into the shadows and began to close the door.

Teresa put out a hand to prevent her, saying swiftly, "Frau Weber. Are you Frau Mozart's mother? I'm a friend of the family. Please tell Frau Mozart—Constanze—please tell her I'm here."

"She is at her husband's bedside," Frau Weber said. Her voice dropped. "He's dying."

Teresa searched for something to say, anything that would make Frau Weber allow her to enter. As the door began to close again, she saw the older woman's eyes well with tears. In a soft voice, Teresa said, "May I just pay my respects, *gnädige Frau?*"

Frau Weber began to speak, but her voice caught in a sob, and she began to weep openly. Teresa instantly stepped forward. She pulled a handkerchief from her bag and pressed it into Frau

Weber's hands. Frau Weber buried her face in it, weeping, while Teresa closed the door on the brilliance outside.

Someone had drawn all the curtains in the house, as if a death had already occurred. A mirror Teresa could just see in one of the ground-floor rooms had been covered with a swathe of dark fabric. She stood waiting while Frau Weber collected herself. When she led the way up the stairs, Teresa followed at a respectful distance.

The door stood open to Mozart's darkened room. Constanze knelt at the bedside, her husband's swollen hand in hers. Several more people stood around the room in attitudes of sorrow, but Teresa barely saw them. She saw only Mozart.

His face was like the wax of an old candle, gray and oddly shiny. His eyes were closed, and his breath whistled in his throat. Teresa stopped in the doorway and stood gazing at him as a feeling of hopelessness rose in her breast, nearly choking her. Hardly knowing she did it, she breathed, "Oh, Wolfgang. Oh, no."

She felt, rather than saw, the attention of everyone in the room come to rest on her. Constanze got to her feet and came forward. "Signorina Saporiti. He's given up!" she blurted in a rushed whisper. "He says he's poisoned, he insists he's dying. He won't drink anything, he won't see a priest. . . . Not even last rites! Can't you do something?"

Teresa stared over Constanze's head at Mozart. His head lolled on the pillow, and the resurgence of color she had seen two days before was gone. He looked—the thought made her shudder— he looked like one of her victims, spent, drained of all life. She said hoarsely, "Constanze. Can I talk to him alone?"

And Mozart's wife, pitifully eager for any shred of hope, bustled about the bedroom, shooing everyone out, stopping at the door for one more longing look at her husband. She went out, closing the door behind her and leaving Teresa alone with Mozart.

She approached the bed gingerly and sat beside him. As Constanze had done, she took his distended hand in hers. "Wolfgang," she said, urgently. "Wolfgang, look at me."

His eyes didn't open, but his upper lip lifted, showing her his teeth.

"Yes, yes," she said softly. "If that's what you want. Anything you want! But look at me first, talk to me."

His eyelids fluttered and opened. His eyes, which she had known to be a mild brown, with a steady sparkle, were dark and angry. His voice was no more than a croak. "Poisoned."

"No," she said. "No, changed. It's not the same. It doesn't have to be like this."

"Damned," he said.

She had begun to roll back her sleeve, to offer him her wrist once again, but she stopped with her cuff half undone. In a firmer voice, she said, "Perhaps, Wolfgang. Perhaps we are damned. But it wasn't my choice, nor was it yours."

He coughed several times, with a hard, tearing sound. "Doesn't matter," he said, when he had caught his breath. "Choose now."

Teresa's own breath caught. "Choose now? What do you mean?"

But Mozart's eyes had closed again. Teresa squeezed his fingers and called his name, but he wouldn't open his eyes, though the lids jerked and trembled. She called his name again, and this time, with what must have been a terrible effort, he pulled his hand away from hers.

She sat on for long minutes, trying to think what to say, what to do. She felt as if he had struck her. "Choose now." What were they to choose? What could he mean? It had great import, that was clear. Because Mozart was prepared to die for it.

Teresa wandered the streets of Vienna that afternoon, hatless, her ermine stole wrapped tightly around her shoulders, the hem of her wool broadcloth dress bedraggled with melting snow. She stood opposite the Cathedral of St. Stephen, watching worshippers come and go. Its lacy Gothic façade and the richly colored glazed tiles of its steep roof soared above the city. Its massive south tower pointed to heaven, a heaven now denied to her.

Would Mozart win his way there, with his sacrifice? Was that what he meant when he said to "choose now"?

She turned away from the church she dared not enter and made her way slowly back to her lodging. Tomorrow, she told herself, tomorrow she would go back to the house in Rauhensteingasse, and she would ask him.

She slept badly that night. She dreamed of the night they had shared the tooth, she and Mozart, reliving the heat and the exhilaration and confusion. She dreamed of Mozart drinking from her wrist like a babe at its mother's breast. And she dreamed something else, something awful that brought her bolt upright in the darkness.

With her heart thudding in her chest, she staggered out of bed and went to the window. The night was nearly as bright as day, with moonlight reflecting off the banked snow in the empty streets and on the slanting rooftops. The floor beneath her feet was as icy as the street outside must be, and when she touched the ewer beside her bed, her fingers slid on a film of ice. The fireplace was dark, all embers dead.

She pulled the quilt from the bed and bundled it around herself, but still she shivered from the aftermath of her dream.

There had been a procession of people dressed in black. A mourning procession, it seemed to be, with veiled women and men in formal dress. Teresa had followed them, begging to know whose funeral it was, but no one would speak to her. When they went into St. Stephen's Cathedral, she tried to follow them up the steps, but someone—a woman in a long veil like a shroud—turned and pointed a finger directly at her face. Teresa put her hand to her mouth and found that her teeth had grown so long her lips could no longer cover them. When the procession had gone inside, she took her hand down and found that her teeth had pierced the skin of her palm, and blood ran down her wrist in dark, glistening rivulets. A strange music sounded from the cathedral, a melody built on the tritone. F–B, F–B, the calling of the seabirds above Lake Garda, the motif of her departure from home. Someone was singing—was that Vincenzo? It was the high, sweet tone of a *castrato*, and it pierced her heart with sadness.

Now, awake beside the window, she put her fingers up to touch her teeth and found that they were no longer than they had been the night before. She leaned into the window, her face burning with relief, though her body was so cold. Just as she pressed her forehead against the icy glass, the bells of St. Stephen's struck one o'clock.

Teresa shot bolt upright. One o'clock, December fifth. It meant something, something evil. She didn't know the reason, but the tolling of the bell made her heart quiver with dread.

She stayed by the window a long time, shaken by premonition.

Massimo's chest, Octavia found, was smooth, his belly flat and ridged with muscle. She knew already that his hands were strong, but his long fingers were as deft as a violinist's, precise on her zippers and buttons. He kissed her as if the night were endless and explored her body with those sensitive fingers, a feathery touch of her breast, a stroke of her buttock, a long sweep from her ankle to her thigh.

She had turned the lights off in her suite and left the curtains open. The only illumination came from the window. The night lights of Milan, white and red and amber, flickered over Massimo's long, lean body, glimmering on the hard muscles of his thighs, the silken flex of his biceps as he lifted himself above her.

It had been a long, long time for Octavia, and the craving in her body, the yearning ache in her loins and her belly, had an intensity that approached that of her thirst. She put everything aside—her worry for Ugo, her sorrow over the street girl, her loathing for Zdenka Milosch. She pulled the pins from her hair, and it swept across her face and her breast. Massimo pushed the strands aside so he could kiss her again, her lips, her cheek. She lifted her chin so he could kiss her neck, and she felt his lips at that pulsing fountain, that source of life she knew so well.

It was ecstasy to open herself, to expose herself to him. His skin was warm and firm, and hers came alive wherever he caressed her, yearning for more, craving a deeper touch. He kissed her breasts and her belly as her breath came faster. He touched her throat with his tongue. He kissed her deeply, sweetly, until she could hardly breathe at all.

She pressed hungrily against him, eager now, impatient. He pulled back so he could put one hand beneath the small of her back to lift her, move her into position below him. And at last, when she thought she could wait no more, the welcome thrust, the piercing that was like pain but was all bliss.

His movements were confident and strong, and she answered him with her own. His throat was at her cheek, near her lips, but she was not thirsty. He was in no danger. She gave herself to him, took him in return, moved with him, shuddered with him.

Afterward she cradled his head against her shoulder. His hair tickled her chin. She pushed it back and stroked his cheek with her fingertips, trying not to think of anything.

It was so good not to be alone. Even if it was just for a little while.

28

Non so s'io vado, o resto.

I don't know if I should go, or stay.

—Donna Elvira, Act Two, Scene One, *Don Giovanni*

Teresa stood outside the house in Rauhensteingasse, staring in horror at the black bunting draped over the front door and covering every window. Her ermine cape slipped from her shoulders to trail in the dirty snow of the street as she stood, frozen, staring at the undeniable signs of mourning. She knew what it meant, but somehow it seemed that if she didn't knock, if she didn't ask, it might not be true.

It was what her dream meant. It had been too much for him. The weight of memory had crushed his sensitive spirit. The thirst and its attendant violence had broken his tender heart. He was gone.

She trembled in the cold sunlight, her knees so weak she could barely stand. "Oh, no," she murmured to herself, again and again. "Oh, no, oh, no." She didn't realize tears were on her cheeks until the cold air began to chill them. Her face crumpled and her vision blurred as she wept painful, tearing sobs. The pain in her heart was so sharp she thought it must choke her.

Mozart gone. It didn't seem possible. The world would be intolerably empty without this brilliant man, with his fine small hands and his merry eyes . . . and his music! There would be no more operas, no quartets, no symphonies . . . no *Requiem*. The loss was too great to comprehend.

Teresa could not bear to hear confirmation. With a cry of anguish, she turned and fled from the sight of Mozart's death house.

The whole world soon knew that Mozart had died. For days Teresa huddled in her lodgings, refusing to go out, only eating or drinking if her maid brought things to her door. She couldn't face Constanze, and she didn't try. She didn't attend the funeral, nor was she invited. She was nothing to the Mozarts. She was less than nothing. She was just a singer who had been lucky enough to work with him once, and now, never again.

She tortured herself with thoughts of what she should have done to save him, arguments she should have made, words that might have changed his mind. In the daylight hours she tried to convince herself it was not her fault, but in the long, lonely hours of darkness she berated herself, fought herself, grieved and raged and suffered.

Then, a week after that darkest of days, the thirst came upon her.

For a whole day she wrestled with it. She drank water until she thought she would burst, then drank glass after glass of wine, trying to cool the fire in her throat, to damp the blazing need of her body. She kept seeing Mozart's swollen face, hearing his voice when he said, "Damned . . ."

Damned, of course, because people died. Killing was a sin, condemned by the church, by the law, by Christ Himself.

It was then she began to wonder, for the first time, if she could take what she needed but leave her victim alive. It could be as it was with Mozart! She had given him enough to get stronger, to begin his recovery, but she was not really harmed.

In the pale gray hours of dawn, Teresa ventured out into the streets of Vienna. She knew she looked haggard, her eyes reddened and her cheeks colorless. She staggered slightly, drunkenly, on the cobblestones, and a solitary man passing by gave her a wary look.

"*Sto bene,*" she said.

He shook his head at her, not understanding. She pulled herself upright. "I'm all right," she said in German. "Tired."

"Ah." He came closer to her. He had a slight frame, with a heavy paunch that protruded beneath his waistcoat. As he approached, her nostrils flared at the scents of old wine and recent sex that preceded him. He looked her over and gave a small nod at the quality of her clothes. He put out his arm, the elbow crooked. "May I walk you home, fräulein?"

Teresa hesitated. He looked like a respectable burgher, though he had evidently been out for a disreputable evening. It was a risk. Such a man was just the sort to attend theater and the opera, and he might recognize her in the daylight.

He giggled and pressed closer to her. She realized he was even more drunk than she was. "Come on, little fräulein. You can trust me."

"Little?" she said, laughing. "I'm taller than you are."

He giggled again. "*Ja, ja.* Then you can escort me." He slid his arm around her waist and leaned against her, his hot breath blowing against her cheek.

Teresa sobered instantly. "Yes. Thank you, *mein Herr.*" She pointed toward the wall that encircled the old city. Her upper lip had begun to throb in anticipation, and saliva filled her mouth. In a throaty voice, she said, "This way, sir."

He was more than cooperative, she found. He was also younger, and lustier, than she had first thought. By the time she could pull aside his collar to expose his throat, her own clothes were half off and the damp stones of the ramparts were scraping her bare thighs.

It didn't matter. She drank, quickly and deeply, but she stopped just when her thirst was slaked, and when the good burgher was still breathing, even still grasping at her with his soft, plump hands.

She wriggled away from him and stood rearranging her skirt, pulling the ermine cape around her shoulders.

At her feet, the burgher sighed, and his eyelids twitched for a few seconds before he lay still. Asleep. Not dead, but sleeping. She suspected he would think, in the morning, that he had found a second sexual partner.

Satisfied, she spun about and marched back toward her lodgings.

By midday she and her maid were on a coach, beginning their long journey back to Milan. She wrapped herself in her traveling cloak and hid behind the shield of a long silken veil wound around her neck. Through all the days of travel, she mourned for Mozart and wept her regret for what she had learned too late.

Vincenzo dal Prato encountered Teresa upon her return, backstage at La Scala. He embraced her and drew her to one side, stepping around the dozens of water buckets always laid ready in case of fire. "Where have you been?" he asked her in his high voice. "The *direttore* has sent to your rooms a dozen times!"

Teresa leaned on Vincenzo's ample shoulder. "It's so good to see you," she said, her voice catching in her throat. "You've heard the news, haven't you?"

"You mean Mozart," he said. "Yes, we've all heard. The *direttore* wants to stage a memorial concert. You'd better go see him straight away."

Teresa straightened, and took a deep breath. "Yes. What are we doing?"

"He heard there's a *Requiem*."

Teresa's eyes widened. "Vincenzo, it's not finished. He was working on it when he—when he—" Her throat closed, and she couldn't go on.

The *castrato* took her hand. "Teresa," he said. "I'm sorry. I know how much you admired him."

She closed her eyes and clung to her friend's hand with all her strength.

"He would want you to go on singing," Vincenzo murmured.

Teresa swallowed and opened her eyes. She didn't think that was true, but she couldn't tell Vincenzo that. She wished she could blurt it all out, how she had tried to save Mozart, how he had repudiated her, how utterly bereft she felt. She wished there were someone she could talk to, someone who could understand. But there was not. She didn't dare confide in Vincenzo. She couldn't have borne the horror in his eyes, the shock and distaste at what she had become. There was, in fact, no one she could confide in.

The only person she could have talked with had died hating her.

The bite had isolated Teresa Saporiti, surely and irrevocably. She had nothing to alleviate the desolate landscape of her life but her music.

She straightened, leaving the comfort of Vincenzo's shoulder, standing upon her own feet, her head high. "Of course," she said. She hardened her heart and composed her features. "Of course I will sing, Vincenzo."

She went out into the house to look for the director. The oil lamps were dark, and the house echoed with emptiness. Teresa stepped into the aisle, walking gingerly, waiting for her eyes to adjust to the darkness.

Someone spoke from the dimness. "Teresa."

It was Zdenka Milosch, standing in a row of seats. Teresa turned slowly to face her. The Countess's erect figure was swathed in her usual black bombazine. Jet beads on the bodice caught what little light there was, gleaming through the murk.

"Welcome home," the Countess said in her uninflected tone.

"Countess," Teresa answered. She heard that same cool, emotionless quality in her own voice. She wondered if, in times long gone, Zdenka Milosch had suffered the same loneliness she felt now.

"Mozart is dead," the Countess said.

"I was there."

"I know that, of course." The Countess sidled between the rows of seats and came into the aisle beside Teresa.

"How?"

Zdenka Milosch shrugged, a nearly invisible movement of her shoulder. With an air of infinite boredom, she said, "My dear, we have been building La Società since before your great-great-grandparents were born."

Teresa looked into the Countess's eyes. This woman alone, in all the world, could understand what she felt. But there was no possibility of sympathy in that hard, patrician face.

"I want to show you something," the Countess said. She turned on her heel and swept up the aisle without waiting to see if Teresa would follow.

Teresa, curious, not knowing what else to do, went with her. In the foyer, Zdenka Milosch stopped and faced her. She opened a small string bag of black velvet that hung at her waist. With her thin white fingers, she pulled out a small leatherbound book and held it out.

Teresa took it and let it fall open on her palm. The Countess exclaimed, "Careful! It's very old."

Teresa frowned at the urgency in her voice and put her other hand under the open book. The leather felt odd to her, thicker than the split calfskin she had expected, with a texture that sent a shiver through her fingers. She lifted it higher, into the light from the lamps of the foyer.

The pages were filled with lines in an old-fashioned hand, with elaborate capitals and little punctuation. Teresa peered at it more closely, then looked up at the Countess. "I don't read Latin," she said.

"You don't need to." Zdenka, with careful fingers, took the little book back and gently turned the pages. "I will read it to you."

"Why?" Teresa asked in a peremptory tone. "I'm busy. The *direttore*—"

Zdenka went on as if she had not spoken. "Here it is," she said. "Twenty-ninth October, seventeen eighty-seven. Prague."

Teresa caught her breath and put a hand to her lips. "Prague . . ."

Again the Countess ignored her interruption. "Wolfgang

Amadeus Mozart, composer, and Teresa Saporiti, singer." She stopped reading and gave Teresa a look that made her heart skip a beat. She said, "And now Mozart is gone. There is only you."

"What do you mean, only me? That whole book is full of—"

"Oh, yes," Zdenka said, with a dismissive wave of her hand. "Full of names, none of them of importance. Even yours is of no importance."

Teresa pursed her lips at the irony. "Then why are you showing it to me?"

The Countess's eyelids lowered and closed, slowly, like a snake's. "Mozart," she pronounced, slowly, as if she relished the taste of the syllables. For the first time her voice betrayed some feeling, a small unevenness of tone that spoke of emotion. "You shared the tooth with Mozart. His blood runs in your veins."

"There must be others!" Teresa cried. Her voice echoed in the empty foyer, her words coming back to mock her. "He fed. . . . He must have!"

Again the negligent shrug. "Like Mozart, they did not survive."

Teresa stared at her for a long moment, trying to understand. "You mean that I—only I—carry Mozart's memories?"

"His genius."

"No. Not his genius. I have his recollections, and his thoughts, and his feelings."

"What do you think genius is? *Cretina!*" The Countess spoke the insult as casually as if she were saying hello. "You, Teresa Saporiti, are very special to us. To La Società."

"What does La Società care about Mozart's blood?"

At this, Zdenka Milosch lifted her head and gazed over Teresa's at the sculptures of composers that dotted the foyer of La Scala. She drew a long, whistling breath through her nostrils and breathed it out, her eyelids drooping like a woman in ecstasy. "It's the music, Teresa. The music. There are so few pleasures left to us—food, wine, even sex pales after so long—but music endures. And

Mozart's music . . ." Her voice trailed off, and the faint glimmer of emotion in her eyes faded.

Teresa stared at her. "But some of my . . . some of the people I've . . ." She couldn't bring the word to her lips. She said at last, lamely, "It can't be true. I can't be the only one."

The Countess brought her eyes, hooded and blank now, back to Teresa's face. She didn't answer. She opened her string bag without looking at it, slid the diary into it, and pulled the strings tight. She said, "I look forward to the memorial concert." She turned and walked away, out through the doors of the theater, neither speaking a word of farewell nor glancing back.

Teresa stood where she was, alone. She would never, she decided, tell Zdenka Milosch how she had tried to save Mozart. She would never tell her anything again.

She turned and went in search of the *direttore*, to find out what she was to sing for the concert. Like La Società, what she had left to her was music. And she would not let Zdenka Milosch, or anyone, take it from her.

29

Crudele! Se sapeste quante lagrime e quanti sospir voi mi costaste!

Cruel one! If you only knew the tears and
sighs you have cost me!

—Donna Elvira, Act Two, Scene One, *Don Giovanni*

The wolf stretched, exulting in the flex of its spine, the fluid sensation in the bend of its ankles and hocks, the broad toughness of its paws. Moonlight flooded its reflective retinas, and it turned its narrow head to escape it. It blinked as it circled.

The air was stale, and far too hot for its double layer of fur. The smells were maddening to its keen olfactory sense, and the mechanical clicking and whirring seeping through the walls irritated its nerves. It paced back and forth, long claws clicking, the fleshy pads of its paws slipping on the hard surface. It snarled and slavered, wheeling around the cramped space as it sought a way out.

It rose on its hind legs to put its front paws on the windowsill, squinting against the brilliant moonlight. Its nostrils quivered, yearning toward the cooling scents of pine and fir that meant there was forest nearby. It whuffed against the glass, pushing with its nose, then dropped back to all fours to circle the room again. It snuffled at the jointure of floor and wall and scrabbled at the door with its claws, where air blew lightly through a narrow gap. Nothing offered as much promise as the thin glass.

The wolf went back to the window and pawed at it. The panel gave a little, like a thin sheet of ice on a mountain pond. The pad of the wolf's foot squeaked against the surface, first sliding, then finding traction. The wolf stepped its hind feet closer to the wall so it could thrust both front feet against the window. It growled and whined, eager to be free. It fell back to the floor, gathered itself, then made a great leap, its forelegs bending on impact so that its snout banged against the glass.

The glass cracked. The tantalizing smell of the mountains intensified as fresh air seeped through the break.

The wolf fell back. It turned to the pile of clothing left on the floor. Instinct prompted it to seize a random piece in its jaws, to carry that familiar scent. The scent that clung to that clothing meant something. The wolf could not have reasoned what that was, but it felt right to keep it.

With the fabric secure between its teeth, the wolf crouched low. With one great bound, springing on its powerful hindquarters, it threw the entire weight of its long body at the window.

The pane exploded in a splatter of glass. The wolf dropped to the floor once more, whining, licking its chops. Then, in a fluid movement, it jumped a third time. Its lean, muscled body flowed through the broken window like water. Shards of glass still clinging to the frame caught at its fur, digging into the flesh, scratching its feet as it sailed by.

It landed on hard, cold pavement. It paused to sniff the air, searching for the source of those inviting smells. A heartbeat later it was off, dashing down moonlit streets between darkened buildings, where confusing scents of garbage and gasoline and flowers nearly vanquished the fragrance it sought. It found an opening and veered through a space of lawn and shrubs toward the woods beyond. Exhilarated at its freedom, it raced up the steep mountainside, dodging stands of broom, slipping between slender trunks of pine and fir, flying through clearings.

It ran until it was tired, then trotted, climbing, searching for ways through the underbrush, cleansing its nose with the myriad smells of the forest. When it surprised a vole in a meadow, it dropped the cloth it carried in its jaws and fed. When the meal was finished, it picked up the fabric again and trotted on, ever upward, searching for the place where the trees would diminish and it would be safe to rest.

The wolf's experiences of the world came in fragments, separated sometimes by long insensate periods. Its memories were a flow of images, beginning with its first race through an orange grove, away from tormentors with blades that slashed and screaming voices that grated on its sensitive ears. There had been many such flights, some through urban jungles with acrid smells and ear-shattering noises, others through parks and gardens where cover was meager and prey was scarce.

There had been only one place where the wolf always felt safe, where the fragments of existence melded together into a consistent whole. There had been no need to flee in that place, no need to escape. There had been only periods of freedom within the vine-covered walls that smelled comfortably of old stone, and not of the poisonous fumes that filled the cities. The wolf was called to that place. Without need for explanation, its inner compass turned toward it, unerring and insistent.

The wolf reached the mountaintop and found a protected spot beneath a thick clump of broom where it could wait out the hours of daylight. The memory of that place of safety filled its narrow brain. It closed its eyes in the quiet of the sparse forest, calmed by the cool, clean air. When daylight faded, it would set out again with its ground-eating trot, feeding along the way, resting during the treacherous hours of light. The wolf had no concept of distance. It wasn't concerned with how far away the goal was, or how long it would take to reach it. It would simply keep moving, as long as it could, and as long as it needed to.

Ughetto learned the power of moonlight from Zdenka Milosch.

Three days after his arrival at her mansion, Zdenka rose from the dinner table and said, "Ughetto. Come with me."

He came to his feet slowly, apprehensively. His days here had been long and empty, but the feeling of dread that had settled over him when he first entered the doors of the Countess's house had not dissipated. He was grateful not to have to see the three ancients, Anastasia, Eusebio, and Henri, except at dinner. They hardly spoke, either to him or to each other. The rest of the staff, as dour as Kirska, as dull as the putative gardener, were no company at all. He had begun to wonder why he had been brought there.

He followed the Countess out of the dining room, through the vast shadowy parlor, and on to the front door. She opened it, and a flood of perfect moonlight filled the foyer, brighter by far than the dim oil lamps favored in this house. In the glow, Ughetto saw the Countess's lips curl. He had the distinct impression that she expected to enjoy herself.

"What is it?" he asked. His voice cracked a little, boyishly.

"It is," she said coolly, "a full moon."

"*Certo.* Why are you showing it to me?"

"Go out, Ughetto. Go out into the moonlight." She made a negligent motion with her long, thin hand, as if shooing a cat out of the house.

He was not at all reluctant to go out of the dank, dark house into the brightness. He stepped through the door and stood on the top step, gazing out into the overgrown shrubbery. Patches of moonlight shone on the cobbled walk and silvered the leaves of the big oaks, which lifted their branches into the moonlight as if asking a blessing.

Ughetto glanced back at the Countess in the shadow of the doorway. "Look up," she told him. "Look at the moon."

He lifted his head. The moon was nearly at its zenith. It was whiter than he expected it to be. Its silver disk was marked with faint shadows. It outshone the stars and illuminated the few clouds that puffed across the night sky.

Ughetto lowered his head again, looking into the Countess's eyes. "Why am I doing this?" he asked.

"Look up," she said again. "Open your eyes as wide as you can. Let the moonlight in."

He shrugged. It all seemed foolish to him. The Countess had no sense of humor that he could ascertain, but surely this was some sort of joke.

"Do as I say," she commanded.

He laughed a little, but he tipped up his chin. He opened his eyes wide and let the metallic light of the moon flood his pupils.

A memory suddenly flooded him. He seemed to smell the salt air of Trapani, to hear the voices of his sisters, to hear the slap of the water against the docks. They were waiting for the squid fishermen to come in, he and his *nonna* and his *mamma*, but something went wrong. He wasn't allowed to stay there in the friendly darkness, watching the lights on the bay where the jigs were set for the squid. His *nonna* hauled him away, back to the tavern, for some infraction he didn't understand.

Ughetto shook off the memory and brought himself back to the present. The moon above his head seemed to grow brighter, its glow increasing in intensity so that he had to half-shutter his eyes. Just as he did this, he felt that prickling sensation in his fingertips and his toes, the familiar pain raging along his backbone.

He spun to face the Countess. "No!" he rasped. His tongue and his teeth had already begun to change, to make words impossible. He tried anyway, snarling, "I don't want—I hate to—"

Her chilly smile was all he could see, all he could register, before his skull began to cramp and contract, and the transformation began in earnest.

When Ughetto came to himself, he was curled under a yew tree, its low-hanging branches grazing his head and his naked back. At his feet were the remains of what he thought must have been a rabbit, though there was little left of the creature except the rags of its hide and a single bloody paw. He wriggled out from beneath the yew and stood, brushing leaves and dirt and busy insects from his skin. He put his hand to his face and felt the stickiness of gore on his lips and chin. He looked back at the carcass and suddenly, violently, vomited into the thick mat of old leaves and moss.

When the agony of his stomach ceased, he scrubbed at his face with his fingers, then looked about to ascertain where he was.

He dreaded these awakenings. He never knew where he might be. He had come to himself in strange places, not always safe places. The worst had been waking, naked and exposed, in the unfinished church of San Ignazio in Rome. It had been very early in the morning. The workers had not yet arrived, but two Jesuit priests were strolling through the interior, pointing at half-built walls, talking animatedly about mosaics and tiles, about sculptures and trompe l'oeil ceilings.

On that morning in Rome, Ughetto blinked slowly into awareness, not yet aware of his lack of clothing or his location. The priests spotted him and pursued him into the tiny, treeless piazza, shouting. Only Ughetto's knowledge of the city's back alleys saved him from whatever punishment they had in mind.

But for Ughetto, the loss of control was worse even than waking up lost. Had he had a choice in the matter—had he not been the seventh son after six daughters, his fate sealed by a power beyond his comprehension—he would have banished the wolf forever. He would never have willingly suffered the brutish twisting and changing of his body. He loathed relinquishing his consciousness, forfeiting his identity to a creature he neither knew nor understood.

After Zdenka tricked him into transforming, he blundered about in the overgrown garden of the compound until he came upon the house by accident. When he realized where he was, still within the vine-covered walls of the Countess's property, he trembled with impotent fury.

She was watching for him. She sent Kirska out with a banyan of silk to wrap himself in and a pair of black leather slippers to protect his feet. Kirska showed no surprise at his nudity. She handed him the clothes, then turned, wordlessly, to lead the way back indoors. Ughetto would have preferred to run as far from the compound as he could, but he had no clothes, no money, and he spoke only a few words in the language of the country. He followed Kirska with resigned steps, tying the dressing gown about his middle as he walked up the moss-slick stairs and into the gloomy great parlor.

"Ah," the Countess said in her disinterested way. "You have returned to us."

"Did I have a choice?" Ughetto threw himself on the sofa opposite her, folding his arms and glaring at her.

Zdenka raised one black eyebrow. "You're angry."

"You forced me to . . . you forced the wolf to appear."

Her thin white hands lifted briefly, then subsided into the black bombazine of her lap. "It was something you needed to know, Ughetto, if we are to have an association."

"I still don't understand it."

She put her head against the scrolled back of the sofa, and her eyelids slowly closed as she spoke. "The moon, my young friend. You must understand the moon's power. It calls the tides. It rules the issue of blood and dabbles its hand in the processes of birth. It impels madness and fires lovers . . ." The corners of her narrow lips curled. "Which may be the same thing, after all."

"What does any of that have to do with me?"

"Nothing," she said. He was about to protest, but her eyelids lifted again, and her eyes, expressionless as black granite, fixed on him. "It has to do with the wolf, Ughetto."

"The moon brings out the wolf?"

"It can. That can be useful."

"Useful," Ughetto said bitterly. He unfolded his arms and rubbed his burning eyes. "If I avoid the moonlight, and avoid pain, can I suppress the wolf?"

"There's something else you can do." The Countess picked up a tiny bell from the table beside her and shook it. It clinked more than it rang, but it was enough for the wizened manservant to hear. He came with his tray. A twist of brown paper lay in the center of it. The servant presented his tray to the Countess, and she picked up the twist of paper.

When the servant had gone, she held out the paper to Ughetto. "What is this?"

"Take it." When he had taken it from her cold fingers, she said, "Open it."

Carefully, he untwisted the stiff paper. Inside were several stems of palmate leaves and dry purple flowers.

"*Aconitum lycoctonum,*" she said. "A poisonous herb."

"You expect me to poison the wolf?"

Her eyelids drifted closed again, and her voice faded to a whisper. "If you poison the wolf, you poison yourself, Ughetto. You should know that."

He held the paper in his palm, gazing down at it. "The wolf is not me."

"It's part of you. It's the way you're made."

"I know you don't care about this, Countess Milosch, but if I could banish the wolf, I would. If I could, I would kill it."

"That would be a shame."

"Not to me."

The Countess opened her eyes, and this time a faint, impatient light shone from them. Her hands twitched in her lap. "Don't be stupid, Ughetto. If you killed the wolf, you would die, too. There's a reason for its existence."

He shot to his feet, crumpling the herb in his hand. "A reason?" he cried. "A reason it should ruin my life, keep me running and hiding, make it impossible to have friends, to have work . . . to have my music?"

The Countess's hands relaxed. "I'm sorry about your music," she said. "You're right, of course. The wolf prevented your castration." She sighed. "But it will also protect you from other harm. And"—a careless flick of the fingers of one hand—"it will prevent you dying at some ridiculously young age."

"What are you telling me?" Ughetto's voice rose, shrill with fury. When she didn't answer immediately, he leaned forward, his slender body shaking, and shouted at her. "Tell me, you—you *anziana!* You bring me here, promising me some sort of bargain, and then you call out the wolf! What do you want from me? Are you telling me I have to suffer like this for eternity?"

Zdenka Milosch looked up at him with narrowed eyes. Her upper lip lifted, exposing the dull gleam of her long teeth, and she hissed, a sound so light he was not sure he heard it. The look on her face was that of something vicious, something utterly without empathy.

Ughetto froze, his complaint dying on his lips.

"Eternity?" she said, drawling the word, mocking him. "Hardly eternity, young fool."

Ughetto swallowed. More quietly, he said, "How long, then? How long will the wolf prevent me from dying?"

The Countess lowered her upper lip, and looked into the candle flames. "So long, Ughetto," she said, "that you will no longer object to death."

Ughetto sank back into his chair, his knees suddenly gone to water. *"O Dio,"* he breathed. He looked away from the Countess, staring blindly into the dimness of the cavernous room. *"Madre di Dio*. What am I to do?"

"Use the herb to hold back the wolf. Do a few tasks for me and my brethren, some small, some great. I will supply you with *aconitum lycoctonum*, or see that you know where to obtain it."

"Do you expect me to live here?" Ughetto made no effort to keep the distaste from his voice.

"No," she said. "I expect you to go out into the world and manage our interests. We have . . . needs."

Ughetto stared at her. With a dry mouth, he croaked, "You want me to bring your victims to you?"

Again her lip curled. "No, no, Ughetto. We have people to do that, Kirska and Tomas and others. What we want you to do is to offer hope to the foolish ones. You will look over those who want to become one of us. You will judge their worthiness. You will discipline some who violate their promises . . . or who talk too much."

"Why should I do these things? Surely I can find this—this herb—" He held out his palm with the crumpled leaves and flowers in it. "I can find this on my own."

"I assure you, Ughetto," Zdenka said, "that in time you will accept our ways. They are perfectly natural."

He spat, "Natural!"

"They are the ways of nature, the way of the world. Predator and prey, rulers and the ruled. You eat meat, don't you? In time, it will mean nothing to you to kill, as the wolf kills. You will find that everything, and everyone, is meat in the end."

"I don't believe it."

"No," she said, closing her eyes again and settling back against the sofa as if she meant to stay there all day. "No. But you will. You will."

30

Son per voi tutta foco!

I am aflame for you!

—Donna Elvira, Act Two, Scene One, *Don Giovanni*

Octavia moved through the days following Zdenka Milosch's appearance in a haze of misery. On alternate cast nights she obediently attended the opera, ready to rise from her seat and go to work should her colleague be indisposed. On her own performance nights she left her dressing room only to go onstage. When the theater was dark she paced her suite, longing for Ugo, loathing Zdenka Milosch, and remembering. Always remembering.

The specter of the street girl's shocked face—"What did you do? What *was* that?"—haunted her. At night, tossing in the wide bed at Il Principe, a parade of such faces marched through her mind, hundreds of them, escaped from her mental cubbyhole and refusing to go back inside. All of these, according to the Countess, dead. Convicted by the edict of La Società. Driven to their deaths by Teresa, by Hélène before Ugo came, and now, all unwilling, by Octavia.

After curtain calls one night, Peter took her arm. "Halfway through," he said.

Octavia looked at him in surprise. "Are we?"

"Yes," he said. "Didn't you know that?"

She shook her head. "I've lost track of the days."

"You need your assistant, Octavia. It's difficult to do this alone."

"I do, Peter. You're right. And tonight was . . . a little hard."

It had indeed been a difficult evening. Russell's beat had occasionally been erratic, but worse, her voice felt stiff, a little heavy, as if she hadn't slept. Her ovations had not been satisfying, and she knew the performance had not been her best. It had been hard to concentrate, and she had nearly missed two cues, something that had never happened in rehearsal. It hadn't helped that Nick got in a muddle with his blocking in the second act.

David came up on Peter's other side and leaned around him to say, "Octavia, when the run is through, Peter and I are going on a nice holiday in Tuscany. Wouldn't you like to join us? There's room in the *villa*—six bedrooms. You can bring your delightful Ugo!"

Octavia smiled, touched by the kindness. "Why, thank you, both of you. But I'm going directly to Houston from Milan."

"Oh, I don't think you told us. That's your first time with Houston, isn't it? What are you singing?" Peter asked.

Together, the three of them threaded their way through the maze of set pieces backstage. Octavia was aware of Massimo walking behind them. Massimo's performance tonight had been as strong as hers had been shaky. He and Marie had been charming in their duets, and Massimo's character had grown convincingly through the opera, from the gawkiness of a country boy to the dignity of an enraged husband. His voice grew richer and more confident with each performance. He was on the verge of great success, Octavia felt certain. A sudden longing seized her, and she wished she could turn to him, run to him, hide her face against his strong shoulder. It was a preposterous thought, of course. How Ugo would laugh at such weakness! And how shocked Massimo would be to know the truth about her.

These thoughts made her answer Peter a beat too late. "Oh, Houston. It's *Figaro*."

"The Countess," David said, a hand to his heart. "You must be divine in that rôle."

Octavia laughed. "Flatterer. I love singing the Countess, though."

"Why didn't Ugo come to Milan with you?" David asked. "Peter always envies you your wonderful assistant." He chuckled and put his arm across Peter's plump shoulders. "He has only me, and I forget things constantly!"

Peter smiled and patted his partner's hand as they watched Octavia, awaiting her answer.

"Ugo had . . . had business," Octavia said. "Out of the country. He's supposed to meet me at the end of the run."

"That's good," David said. "Maybe he'll be here for the last party."

"I hope so," Octavia said. She turned in at her dressing room. "Good night. Good show tonight, Peter. I'll see you both Thursday." She slipped inside and tried to shut the door, but found a strong brown hand between the door and the jamb.

Massimo pushed the door open gently and put his head inside the room. "Octavia. You've been avoiding me."

There was an edge to his voice. She looked up at him. The dark pancake makeup made his eyes vivid as candle flames. He needed no wig, and the usual lock of hair hung over his forehead. He looked delectable in Masetto's peasant coat and breeches. The knee pants and traditional white tights accentuated the long muscles of his calves.

Octavia sighed. "Massimo, I'm sorry. I hate theater gossip."

"That doesn't mean we can't speak to each other." He came in, bringing the rich scents of sweat and soap and melting makeup with him. He closed the door behind him. "They'll be saying we've had a falling-out."

The dresser called from the corridor, "Signorina?"

Octavia called, *"Momento, per favore."* To Massimo, she said, "I have to shower."

"So do I," he said. His usual smile was absent, and there was an air of tension about him. "Have a drink with me afterward."

The mention of a drink reminded her she needed water. She turned away from him to pour from the bottle of Pellegrino on her dressing table. She took a deep draught of it, and then another. She had turned off the lights around the mirror, and her eyes looked shadowed, her cheeks colorless. She turned her back on her image. "Massimo, I don't think . . ."

"We'll go somewhere private. My hotel. Or yours." When she hesitated, he said in a low tone, "I won't leave until you say yes." He smiled then, but there was something in it, some emotion she couldn't quite identify. He seemed older somehow. Harder.

She set her glass down. Her thoughts were sluggish, slowed by the fog in her mind. She gave her head a little shake, as if that might clear it. Massimo gave her a quizzical look, and she shrugged. "Go now," she said, striving for a light tone. "The dresser's waiting."

He bent and kissed her cheek. She closed her eyes at the sensation of his smooth lips against her skin. Remembered passion quickened her breath.

He whispered against her ear, "I'm waiting, too," and a thrill ran through her belly. "Meet me outside."

The words to refuse him simply would not rise to her lips, though she despaired at her weakness. He opened the door. The dresser sidled past him to come to Octavia and begin undoing the fastenings of her costume. As Octavia unpinned her wig and settled it on its stand, she tried to remonstrate with herself, but it seemed she had lost the argument before it began.

She peeled off her false eyelashes and laid them in their case, then stepped into the little shower. As she scrubbed pancake and powder from her face and neck, she promised herself she would have a drink with Massimo, nothing more. She would tell him something, anything, to put him off.

She made herself take her time about dressing, applying street makeup, brushing out her hair and tying it back, winding her long scarf around her neck. When she emerged from her dressing room, the corridor was empty. Massimo's door, with his name scripted beneath the little star, was closed. There was no sound behind it.

He was waiting for her at the artists' entrance, lounging in the glass-doored lobby, chatting with the guard behind the desk. He wore his usual jeans and white shirt and leather jacket. His hair was still damp from the shower. She joined him, feeling a twinge of compunction at the sweetness of simply walking at his side, going out into the cool bite of the breeze, strolling with him down the street to the waiting Mercedes.

Massimo held the car door for her, and she slid onto the leather seat with a dangerous sense of belonging. Octavia knew better than to form attachments to such things. But Massimo's profile against the city lights, the smell of his shaving lotion, the scent of old leather lulled her. It all seemed so normal. Other people had drinks together, went out to dinner, had love affairs. Ugo would have prevented this, by his very presence. But Ugo was not here.

And Massimo was.

He drove her to Il Principe in silence and let the doorman call for someone to park his car. They walked together into the bar. Without consulting her, Massimo ordered a sparkling *prosecco* and a plate of *antipasto*, which came in the form of black olives, tender baby artichokes, paper-thin slices of *prosciutto*. When he tipped his head back to gaze up at the Tiffany-style ceiling, his jaw muscles flexed as if he were controlling himself. When their order arrived, he nodded his thanks at the waiter and poured her a glass of wine.

Octavia said, frowning, "Massimo. Are you angry with me?"

He shook his head and drained half his glass in a single swallow.

"You're angry about something."

For a moment he was silent, as if he were gritting his teeth.

Then, pushing the *antipasto* plate aside, he leaned forward. "I'm sorry, Octavia. I thought if we—I thought I could distract my-self."

She put her head on one side, regarding him, waiting.

He made a rueful face. "I told you about my brother."

"Yes—your family's black sheep."

"He's in trouble."

Octavia's eyebrows rose. She picked up the bottle and poured more *prosecco* into his glass, and waited.

"You might remember the bruise I had. Made Russell ill."

"I remember," Octavia said carefully. She remembered how she had wanted to lick the blood from his cheek.

"The night before that rehearsal, I had to go and roust my brother out of a card game. It wasn't easy." He gave a sour chuckle. "He's bigger than I am. He socked me."

Octavia winced at the thought. "He was gambling?"

"Again." He sighed. "And it didn't do any good. He's gotten sideways with some pretty bad people, and my family expects me to do something about it."

"What can you do?"

He shrugged. "Nothing at all that I can see. But my mother—" His face tightened, and he averted his eyes. "He's her baby. It's hard being the oldest."

She put her hand over his. "Massimo, you must let it go."

"I know," he said. "I just wanted to enjoy this run. This chance."

"Is he jealous of you?"

Massimo said bitterly, "Of course. But what can I do about that?"

"I don't know, Massimo."

He brought her hand to his lips, and his eyes softened a bit. "I'm sorry. Didn't mean to talk about it, really." He reached for a slice of *prosciutto*. "Let's forget it. I'm sorry I told you."

"No," she said firmly. "Don't be sorry. I'm glad to know."

He smiled at her, a little sadly. "It's nice to be able to talk to someone." He chewed the *prosciutto* with a slice of bread and poured the last of the *prosecco* into her glass. "I envy *you*, Octavia. You don't have to answer to anyone, do you?"

It was her turn to shrug and avert her eyes. "Ugo, sometimes. But that's not always good, Massimo. It can be lonely."

He took her hand again and caressed the fingers with his thumb. In an intimate tone he said, "Not lonely tonight, though."

She smiled. "No. Not tonight."

He grinned, looking more like himself. "And now let's talk about something else—anything else! Nick forgot his blocking again tonight, didn't he?"

She laughed. "That was a mess! Nothing I could do because he was halfway across the stage from me."

He grinned. "Poor Richard! How did he manage?"

She began to tell him, pleased to hear the edge vanish from his voice, to see his eyes brighten. Other people in the bar looked at them from the corners of their eyes, as if trying to guess who they were. It felt to Octavia as if she and Massimo sat in a bubble of light. They were golden people at that moment, young, successful, fortunate. She was sorry when the barman began putting things away, getting ready to close. With reluctance, she said, "We should go."

"Wait," Massimo said. He went up to the bar and came back a moment later grinning, flourishing a bottle of uncorked Barbaresco in one hand, two wineglasses in the other. He nodded toward the bank of elevators.

Octavia hesitated only a moment before she followed Massimo into the elevator. She told herself that she would be gone soon in any case. This affair, if that's what it was, would be over. It was perfectly likely she might never see Massimo again.

She leaned against the elevator's parquet wall and looked at their reflections in the gold-flecked mirror opposite. Her eyes sparkled now, and her cheeks were pink with wine and laughter. Massimo looked tall and dark and delicious.

The Barbaresco was magnificent, a spicy, strong red. It was not until Massimo poured her second glass and began to slowly unwrap her long scarf from her throat that she felt the first intimations of real thirst come over her. She tried to pull back then, but his lips were already on her cheek, on her neck. His strong arm pulled her against him, inviting her, tempting her.

With his free hand, he touched her glass with his. "To you," he murmured. "My favorite soprano. *La divina*." Octavia drained half of her glass at a gulp, hoping to quell the sensation rising in her throat. She was burning now, not only with desire, but with the sudden, devastating onset of thirst. There was no time to wonder how she had not seen this coming, had not known.

He kissed her mouth, then set his glass down and took hers to set beside it. He drew her into the dark bedroom, one hand on her waist, the other wound gently in her hair. He coaxed her to lie down, then stretched his length beside her.

He pressed his mouth to hers, and her lips parted, not with volition, but helplessly, eagerly. Encouraged, Massimo kissed her more deeply, stroking her face, her breast, her back with his fingertips. His mouth tasted of wine, and her head spun with it.

"Clothes," he laughed, his mouth still on hers. He began to tear away his shirt, wriggle out of his jeans. He held her close with one arm and unbuttoned her blouse with his free hand.

Her blood rose in answer to his, a surge of heat, a flood of passion. Her skin came alive at every touch of his hands, his thighs, his smooth chest. Her eyelids were heavy with desire. Her lips swelled with hunger for the taste of him, for the feel of his body against hers, for the hard pressure of his mouth . . . and with thirst.

At the supreme moment, when the pleasure was almost too great to be borne, when his body arched above hers, he threw back his head. His throat hovered above her face. Just above the collarbone, the muscles stretched aside and revealed the beating pulse, the external jugular vein, where the blood ran tantalizingly, maddeningly close beneath the surface of silken skin. She heard the call of that hot tide and craved its source.

In her moment of abandon, her upper lip lifted and her mouth opened. It was involuntary. Instinctive, as always. She sank her teeth into and through the barrier of Massimo's skin.

He stiffened in shock, moaning something, but she held fast. She couldn't help herself. The taste of him, sweet and hot and salty, filled her mouth. She clung to him with her arms, her legs, her teeth. He fell back, and she rolled with him, her body covering his, her hair spilling across his face, across both of them, a golden veil behind which Octavia took from Massimo what she so desperately needed, and he, shivering in ecstasy and submission, gave it. Energy poured through her, thrilling in her arms and her legs and her breast. The murk she had been moving through lifted all at once.

With the return of clarity, her mind rebelled against the demands of her body. Panting, she withdrew. Still holding him close, she licked his skin where two scarlet drops welled, then licked it again. When no more drops appeared, she untangled herself from him, pulling back to look down at him, pushing her hair back so she could see his face.

Confusion shimmered in his eyes. He tried to speak to her, to say something, but it was no more than a mumble. A second later his eyelids fluttered closed.

Numb horror seized Octavia. Her blood, which had been so hot a moment before, ran suddenly cold. She jumped from the bed and stood looking down at Massimo, lying naked and vulnerable on the tumbled bedclothes. With shaking hands, she pulled the quilt up over him, tucking it under his shoulders as a mother might do, trailing her fingers across his cold cheek. He sighed at her touch and rolled to his right side. His thick mop of hair fell back, exposing the two umistakable wounds at the base of his neck.

Octavia covered her mouth with her hands. Her lips were sticky with his blood, and her body glistened with sweat. With a moan, she tore her eyes from Massimo's inert body and rushed to the bathroom.

She stood under the shower for a long time, letting the hot water sluice her. Every cell of her body seemed to vibrate with energy and strength. It was her mind that reeled, turning this way and that, looking for escape.

How would she ever forgive herself? She let the water sting her eyelids and soak her hair until it hung in lank strands across her shoulders. How would she explain—aside from the guilt and regret that consumed her—the changes that would come over Massimo? He would demand answers from her, as she had demanded them from Zdenka Milosch. She didn't know if she could face it.

But she must. The only other option was the one that Vivian Anderson had been forced to exercise. She hated to flee now, abandon her contract, ruin the years of work in building the life and career of Octavia Voss. Even worse, she could never bring herself to abandon Massimo Luca to the cruelty of Zdenka Milosch and La Società.

The thought of the Countess made Octavia's heart lurch with panic. She wrapped herself in a bathrobe and went back into the bedroom, determined to make a clean breast of it all, to tell him everything and accept the consequences.

But the bed was empty. Massimo was gone.

Opera in America suffered between the world wars, and with it, Hélène Singher's career. Audiences wanted the forgetful antics of speakeasies or vaudeville, not the challenging music of the opera. Nightclubs sprouted during the Great Depression, where those who could afford it went to drink and listen to big bands play hit tunes. To complicate things, Hélène Singher, who should have been growing older along with her colleagues, looked no older than in those difficult days of Caruso's *Carmen*.

Hélène suggested to Ugo that she return to Europe to begin a new career, but he told her that disaster was brewing there. An oddly malevolent figure had risen to power in Germany, where there were more opera houses even than in Italy.

"It wouldn't be possible now to make a big career without singing in Germany," he told her. "And the elders tell me this man's strength is increasing every day."

"Are they helping him? La Società?"

Ugo nodded, his face grim. "Many of their acolytes are members of his secret police. They say he's interested, too. Endless life is a hard prospect to resist."

"It's not truly endless."

"No." He was leaning against the window frame of their suite in the restored Palace Hotel, staring down into the busy streets of San Francisco. "No, but sometimes it seems like it."

"I will never understand," she said darkly, "why God would allow such things."

He turned his face to her without moving his body. "Hélène. Why torment yourself? It's not God who allows it."

She shook her head, tired of the old argument. "If we can't go to Europe, then where shall we go? I can't stay here."

"I know. Someone asked me just the other day to tell them again where you made your début—and when."

"What did you say?"

He gave her a narrow, distracted smile. "The usual. The obscure French town, then a contract in New York, and I'm always vague about the year. But they remember *Carmen*, because of the earthquake. And you don't look a day older than you did then." He straightened and turned his back on the street scene. He was quiet for a time before he asked, "What would you think about Melbourne?"

"Melbourne? Where Nellie Melba was from?"

"That's it. Australia."

"I thought there was no opera there. That she went to France because there was nothing in Melbourne."

"That was then." He crossed to the desk and pulled out a folded sheet of paper. As he unfolded it, it crackled, shedding bits of paper on the glass top of the desk. He smoothed it with his fingers before he handed it to her. "See? Melbourne has an opera house. There's talk of one in Sydney, too, and there are touring companies."

Hélène took the stiff paper in her hands, and scanned it. "Touring, Ugo? Do you think we can manage—that is, that *you* can manage—touring in such a wild place?"

He said, a little sourly, "According to our Zdenka, I can."

She made an unhappy gesture. "But do you want to? Maybe I should just stop singing for a while. A long while."

He came to her and sat down in the little armchair opposite her chaise. Gently, he took the flyer and laid it aside, then put his hands on hers. "It was twenty-five years between Teresa and Hélène. I can't imagine how you tolerated that, all alone, no colleagues, no work. . . . Do you want to be idle another twenty-five?"

She shook her head.

"And I don't want you to go through that again." He released her hands. "I think Hélène should develop some illness—rheumatoid arthritis, possibly, or senility."

"Senility! No, Ugo!"

He laughed. "All right, no senility. But something that requires her to retire." He touched her cheek with one finger. "A nice sea voyage sounds nice, doesn't it? And no one from America is singing in Australia these days, except for tours. They all go to Europe."

"I'll need a new name."

"I know. And a different accent."

She laughed. "I'm getting awfully good at accents!"

"Yes. It helps to have plenty of time."

Melbourne seemed a rough-and-ready place after the sophistication of San Francisco and New York. The Depression had hit the city hard. Its population had swelled in recent years with Greeks and Italians pouring in to fill the Victorian terrace houses. But nearly a third of the workforce had lost their jobs, and with them, their homes.

Ugo had no trouble finding a pretty apartment in the center of the city. It felt strange to take someone's home, someone who might now be standing in soup lines and begging for handouts, but it was lovely to have a place of their own. The mood in Melbourne was troubled, with politicians ranting on street corners and charities struggling to meet the demands on them. It was an odd time, in which the wealthy lived in comfort while the poor— whose numbers seemed to be growing every day—struggled just to eat.

Ugo and the new singer, Vivian Anderson, scoured the newspapers and collected playbills, searching for theater companies. On the ship from San Francisco they had developed the new persona. Vivian now had a history, a slender résumé, and conservatory credentials. Three months after her arrival in Australia, Ugo arranged her first audition at Her Majesty's Theatre on Exhibition Street, the theater where Nellie Melba had sung Violetta and Gilda and Mimi nearly thirty years before.

Vivian chose her dress carefully, a flared skirt with a fitted bodice and open collar. She brushed her hair back and tied it with a loose ribbon beneath a small dish hat. She was an expert now at auditioning, both at choosing her repertoire and at presenting herself well to an audience of no more than two or three. At Her Majesty's Theatre she sang arias of Susanna and Cherubino, selections suitable for a very young soprano. She offered the director a short list of credits, mostly conservatory productions and one or two musical theater parts in obscure Canadian cities. The director of the theater hired her on the spot.

With Ugo's help, Vivian had a much easier time building her career than had Hélène. Besides Her Majesty's Theatre, she sang recitals in Brisbane and Canberra and Sydney. She sang oratorios with regional orchestras and added several musical theater parts to her repertoire. She was asked several times to sing at St. Patrick's Cathedral in Melbourne, but somehow she and Ugo always found a conflict in her schedule, and her refusals seemed not to attract much notice.

They moved to a more spacious apartment, with a lovely veranda overlooking the Yarra River. Ugo bought a two-year-old 1937 LaSalle. Both of them wore better clothes, and on nights Vivian wasn't singing they drove out in the LaSalle to restaurants and nightclubs. They were delighted when the director of the theater decided to stage *Così fan tutte* as part of the city's festivities for Christmas 1939. He engaged Vivian to sing Fiordiligi, and he brought in a young conductor from Canberra who was just beginning his own career.

But halfway through the rehearsal period, the conductor broke his contract and enlisted in the military. Australia had declared war with Germany in September. The news from Europe was even worse than Ugo had predicted. The German houses were playing nothing but Wagner. Only the largest Italian companies were able to keep up their performances. Rumors abounded, and Jews and Gypsies were already fleeing Germany and Austria.

The cast of *Così* gathered on the stage of Her Majesty's Theatre to hear their director address the crisis. Ugo lounged in the front row of seats with the stage manager and the lighting designer, all of them waiting to hear what conductor would replace the one who had gone to be a soldier.

When the name was announced, the cast and crew applauded. The director went on speaking, detailing how they would manage rehearsals until the new conductor arrived from America, but Vivian heard none of it. She fled the stage the moment she could and found Ugo waiting for her just outside the stage door. The December day was hot and windy, with what looked to be a thunderstorm building in the north.

She said, "Ugo! What are we—" but he hushed her with a finger to his lips. He took her arm and led her around the corner to where the LaSalle was parked. Not until they were inside and driving toward their apartment did he speak.

"There's nothing for it," he said. "We'll just have to go."

"Oh, Ugo! All this work wasted!"

Keeping one hand on the big wheel of the automobile, he put

out his free hand to take hers. "There's no choice, Vivian. I'm sorry."

With sinking heart, she stared out the window of the car at the Yarra spilling alongside the roadway. "I like being Vivian," she said. She knew she sounded petulant, but she couldn't help it. "And I wanted to sing Fiordiligi."

"I know, *bella*," Ugo said gently. "I know you did."

"Now I have to begin again, start all over. How long? How long until I can sing again?"

He shook his head. "It will be a long time, I think."

They were just pulling up in front of their building when she cried, "The pictures!"

In the act of opening the door, he turned back. "Pictures?"

"In the lobby! The theater put up photographs of every cast member."

"Not in costume?"

"Ugo, we don't have costumes yet. It's a new production. The pictures are in street clothes—mine is a very nice little suit with that silly blue hat. He's bound to recognize me."

Ugo turned the door handle and climbed out of the car. "Let's go inside," he said. "We'll make a list of things we need to do."

They talked through the afternoon, while thunder shook the windows and the fierce Australian summer rain rattled on the roof.

The conductor coming to Her Majesty's Theatre was one Hélène knew. She had sung under his baton twice in San Francisco, when he had been a man of thirty-five or so. It had never occurred to either Vivian or Ugo that a man of seventy would take a ship across the Pacific in wartime to conduct Mozart in Melbourne, Australia. But evidently he would, and he was, and it meant the end of Vivian Anderson's brief and promising career.

"We'll wait," Ugo said at length. He stood beside the window, watching raindrops slide down the glass. And then, with a laugh, "Maybe his ship will sink."

Vivian poured herself a glass of water and came to stand beside him, looking down at the Yarra. It churned energetically between its banks, enlivened by the rainstorm. "A little harsh for all those passengers, don't you think?"

"Darling," Ugo said, "conscience at this late date?"

"I don't think we can put our hopes on a sunken ship, Ugo."

"No. And besides, why waste all that nice *sangue* on the fishes?"

"Ugo." She shook her head. "Not something to joke about."

"Just trying to make you smile," he said.

"How long do you want to wait?"

"The voyage should take a week. That will give us time to pack a few things, choose a place to go. Sell the car."

"Sell it? Why don't we drive it away?"

"*Carissima,*" Ugo said in a dry tone. He sighed and turned his back on the view to lean against the window frame. "License plates and so forth. Really, we can't take anything but our clothes and whatever cash we can round up."

"Oh, Ugo. All this lovely furniture—and the car? All of it?" She gestured at the grand piano they had recently acquired. Her *Così* score was open on the scrolled music stand.

"Yes. All. We'll just have to walk away." And at her expression of despair, he put his fingers under her chin. "I've done it before," he said. "And so have you."

"Only twice. Teresa went into retirement in respectable fashion. Hélène gave a proper announcement to the papers that she was going into a nursing home. This—this will have everyone talking!" She leaned forward to watch the water swirl below the veranda. The idea of starting over again, when her new career had just begun, made her feel unbearably weary. "Where will we go, Ugo? I can't go back to San Francisco."

"No. I think you're in for a long holiday."

Vivian straightened and walked to the piano. With reluctant fingers, she closed the score and laid it aside. "I don't like holidays. I like working."

Ugo said, "You'll have to carry on with rehearsals this week, just as if nothing's changed."

"I know."

"I'll slip in the night before we leave and lift those photographs."

"Take them all, so it's not obvious," she said.

"Of course." He walked to the carved armoire they used as a coat closet, taking out his overcoat and hat, a nice fedora he had bought in Sydney. He lifted his umbrella from the stand beside the door.

"Where are you going?" Vivian asked.

He put on the fedora, checking its tilt in the armoire's mirrored door. All softness had disappeared from his face when he turned to her. His eyes glinted darkly beneath the brim of the fedora. "Stocking up," he said briefly.

"Oh." She went back to the window, drawn to the constant movement of the water. She heard the door click shut behind him. She sighed, tracing the pattern of raindrops on the glass with an idle finger.

She had not used the tooth since before the earthquake. Ugo had set her free. She knew nothing of his network of suppliers. Occasionally she roused herself to ask, but he always refused to tell her. And it had been such a relief, after the long years of Teresa's life, and then Hélène's struggles, to surrender. To not have to go out into the streets and alleys—to be cared for instead, protected, even indulged—it was a gift she had never expected and could not have anticipated. Not since leaving Limone sul Garda, so many years before, had she experienced such tranquillity.

In the early days after the earthquake, she had asked Ugo why he should do this for her, what his gain could be.

He had smiled. "Even such as I can be lonely," he said. "And then—there is the music."

And now that she was in danger of being exposed, he turned his astounding abilities to the problem without complaint and without hesitation. Vivian pressed her hand against the window, feeling the condensation build beneath her palm. Not since Vincenzo had befriended her, a seventeen-year-old girl alone in Milan, had there been a person she could truly consider a friend. And Ugo, whose nature was as conflicted as hers, was even better than a friend. He was a companion, a brother, closer than she imagined a spouse could be, though he would have laughed to hear her say it. Every time he went out into the city in search of what he needed, she worried until he returned. Every time he administered her infusion, eliminating her own need to hunt in the streets, her gratitude was intense.

Teresa, and certainly Hélène, would have taken this setback with resignation. But when she became Vivian, she became someone different. She was more vulnerable, less resilient. She had grown soft. Her disappointment over the loss of Vivian's persona grieved her out of all proportion.

She turned from the window with a little exclamation of disgust at her own weakness and started for the bedroom to begin to pack her things. Ugo would think of someplace for them to go, and he would no doubt have contacts there as well. There was nothing for it, and no other choice. They would simply have to begin at the beginning.

The day before the replacement conductor for *Così fan tutte* arrived in Melbourne, the soprano Vivian Anderson vanished from the city. Her assistant, well known to her colleagues, disappeared with her. Police found all of their belongings in the large apartment they shared on the banks of the Yarra River. Their two-year-old LaSalle automobile was still parked behind the building. The police found no clues at all as to their whereabouts. The newspapers proclaimed the production of *Così fan tutte* to be cursed, losing first its conductor and then one of its stars. In a mysterious coincidence, a set of photographs of the entire cast of the opera had been stolen from a display in the theater lobby. The purpose of this theft no one could imagine.

For several days reporters hung about the theater and Vivian Anderson's apartment. They talked to everyone who had known the two missing persons. The maid only came in during the day. The assistant had paid cash for the LaSalle. The apartment owner cleaned it out, finding no papers, no address book, nothing to link the singer to relatives or business associates. No one had heard anything, no one suspected anything. The most popular theory was that, somehow, both had been drowned in the Yarra, their bodies washed out to sea. For a week, the papers talked of nothing else.

But the war was going badly, and Australian forces were being deployed. The story of the singer who disappeared was submerged by accounts of battles and munitions. There were rumors of a Japanese invasion, and talk of the Americans coming into the war. Soon another soprano was found to sing Fiordiligi, and the story of Vivian Anderson was forgotten.

But Vivian and Ugo knew that her colleagues at Her Majesty's Theatre would not forget.

Rôles were too hard to win for singers to simply walk away from them. She would not be able to show her face in Australia— or perhaps in any opera house anywhere—for a very long time.

31

Par che la sorte mi secondi.

It seems that fortune is on my side.

—Don Giovanni, Act One, Scene One, *Don Giovanni*

Domenico opened the English *Times,* which he had delivered with his breakfast each morning. He rarely bothered with much beyond the art pages. He had little interest in the current wars, or the state of American politics, or the wrangling of the United Nations. He flipped through to Arts & Entertainment and smoothed the pages beside his plate. He took a sip of coffee and ran his finger down the page, looking for something that would appeal to him.

He found it almost immediately.

The *Times* and several other papers had been following the current La Scala production with some energy, mostly because of the up-and-coming American soprano, Octavia Voss. Her reviews in New York and Paris had been raves, and now, even in Milan, she was being received with gushing enthusiasm. Domenico thought it was all over the top, a sort of hysteria, just because she was young and attractive. He read the articles anyway, though they made him grind his teeth in irritation.

But today's article . . . now, this was news.

"Italian basso Massimo Luca," the article ran, "has withdrawn from La Scala's production of *Don Giovanni,* starring American soprano Octavia Voss."

Must they work that woman's name into every article? And what was with Luca?

"The young bass could not be reached for comment, but a spokesman for the company said he had gone to a *pronto soccorso* after his last performance, and was hospitalized with exhaustion and possible anemia. His understudy, Pietro Ricci, will—"

Domenico laid the newspaper aside and picked up his coffee cup. Ignoring the plate of *prosciutto* and melon and croissants waiting for him, he found the television remote and clicked it on. He hoped to hear more news of what had happened to Massimo Luca, but he could make no sense out of the Italian newscaster. He flipped channels, looking for the BBC, but there was nothing but a subtitled comedy. He turned it off and went back to his breakfast tray.

This meant something. He knew it in his bones. He just had to figure out what it was.

He would eat and shower. And then he would find out what hospital Luca was in. He wanted to know.

32

Ah, dimmi un poco dove possiamo trovarlo.

Ah, just tell me where we can find him.

—Masetto, Act Two, Scene One, *Don Giovanni*

Octavia ordered a taxi the moment she heard the news, although she dreaded the look she must see in Massimo's eyes. She presented herself at the Ospedale Fatebenefratelli at the earliest possible visiting hour. She wore her trench coat slung hastily over jeans and a sweater, an Hermès scarf wound carelessly around her neck and her hair pulled back in a clip.

She was empty-handed, knowing flowers were hypocritical. It was her fault he was there. No gift or gesture could change that. He would have questions. She didn't know, as yet, how she would answer them, but she meant to try.

In the cab, she tormented herself with self-reproach. When she walked in through the main doors of the hospital and asked for his room, she could barely look into the eyes of the receptionist. She rode up in a sterile-looking elevator and walked down corridors marked with terrifying words: *Radiografia* and *Chirurgia* and *Oncologia*. They were words she had never had to confront. She had never been hospitalized in all of her long life.

She found Massimo's room in a quiet corner of the floor. It was dim and quiet inside. The door was half open, and only a curtain blocked the view of the bed. The smells of alcohol and disinfectant fought with the dull smell of floor wax in the corridor.

Octavia paused for a moment in the doorway, listening to the silence. It seemed Massimo was alone, a small blessing. If his family had been there, she would have had to turn and leave without a word.

Quietly, she slipped in through the door and closed it behind her with a small click. There was almost no light in the room now, and she waited for a moment for her eyes to adjust to the shadows. When she could see again, she put a hand on the curtain and gingerly pulled it aside. Its plastic rings rattled softly against their pole as she drew it closed again and turned to the bed.

He lay quietly, his eyes closed, his hair very dark against the bleached white of the thin hospital pillow. An IV tube ran from an elevated bottle into a needle taped to his hand, which lay limp and unmoving on a beige blanket. His chest barely moved. His legs were too long for the bed, and his bare feet stuck out beyond the blanket, his toes propped against the metal footboard. He looked unbearably young, and thin, and ill.

Octavia stepped close to the bed, and bent over him. "Massimo," she said softly. "Massimo, dear. It's I. It's Octavia."

Immediately, startlingly, his eyes opened. The caramel color darkened to milk chocolate in the bad light. The whites were bloodshot. He stared at her as if he had never seen her before.

She said, with a dry mouth, "Massimo. Do you know me?"

And in an eerie echo of the words of the now-dead street girl, he said hoarsely, "Octavia. What did you do? What was that?"

She hesitated, touching his hand with her fingers. His smooth skin was so cold it frightened her. The doctors would have infused him immediately, of course. Now it looked as if they were hydrating him. He would recover, but he looked so weak. She meant to tell him everything, as soon as she could, but . . . would the shock be too much, at this moment? Days would pass before he believed her, and even then, not until the thirst overtook him would he truly understand.

And now he had withdrawn from the production. It was in the news. Zdenka Milosch would know what had happened. La Società would know. Massimo was in danger.

Before these thoughts finished whirling through her mind, while Massimo's eyes were still fixed on hers with that shocked stare, the door to the room opened, its rubber seal hissing on the gray linoleum.

Octavia stiffened, and the back of her neck prickled. It was very soon for Zdenka to have sent someone, but the elders were nothing if not thorough. She turned, putting her back to Massimo, placing herself between him and the door. She would not allow it. She simply would not allow it, even if it meant her own death.

The curtain slid back, slowly. Octavia tensed in readiness.

When he came forward, relief made her knees go weak, and she sagged against Massimo's bed. "Nick! For God's sake, what are you doing here?"

Nick Barrett-Jones stopped where he was, one hand still on the curtain. His eyes narrowed as he recognized her. He held a spray of flowers, the kind available for purchase in hospital gift shops, in his other hand. "Octavia," he said sourly. "Do you think you're the only one concerned for our young colleague?"

And behind her, Octavia heard Massimo repeat, "What was that? What did you do?"

Nick's eyes blazed with a sudden, avid curiosity. "What did he say?"

Octavia turned quickly to bend over Massimo, to take his free hand, the one not tethered to the bottle of saline solution. She squeezed it, willing him not to speak again, not to let Nick hear that damning question. His eyes on hers lost their focus, and the lids fell, slowly, inexorably, until his eyes were closed. He slept again, his features softening, smoothing, looking unbearably vulnerable.

Octavia, with an aching heart, laid Massimo's hand gently on the blanket and stepped back. She spoke over her shoulder.

"He's sleeping, Nick. We'd better let him rest, don't you think?" She turned and reached for the ridiculous bouquet. "Why don't we find some water for these?"

She put her hand under Nick's elbow and steered him toward the door, much as she had steered him around the set when he forgot his blocking. She felt the resistance in his muscles, but her fingers were hard on his arm.

They reached the corridor just in time to see a little knot of people approaching. A nurse was with them, speaking quietly. When she saw Nick and Octavia, she frowned. *"Solo famiglia,"* she said sternly. She pointed to a sign on the door.

"Mi dispiace," Octavia murmured. Nick looked resentful, but he didn't argue as she handed his flowers to the nurse, then guided him down the long hallway toward the elevator.

In the lobby they found that other singers had arrived, with Giorgio and Russell. Russell gave a little nervous cry when he saw Octavia, and came to rest his trembling hand in hers. The tip of his nose was scarlet, as if he had been weeping. One of the artists' liaisons was there, bearing a mass of roses and a card already signed by members of both casts. Octavia saw her dinner hostess of several weeks earlier hurry through the lobby, a worried look on her face. The opera people stood about, murmuring together, wondering at how the young bass could have fallen so ill. There was talk about pickup rehearsals and understudies.

Octavia learned from someone who had spoken to a doctor that Massimo would be hospitalized for at least three days. The general assumption, it seemed, was that he had been hiding an illness. There were whispers of a curse on the production. Octavia could only hope that three days in a hospital room under constant supervision would keep Massimo safe for the time being. She drew Russell aside and said, "Russell, do you think I'll be needed for the pickup rehearsal? I have business out of town."

He shook his head. "It will be Marie, mostly."

"Thank you. I'll be back in two days," she said. "And I'll be calling to check on Massimo's progress."

After a word to Giorgio, she slipped out of a side door of the hospital and flagged a taxi. At Il Principe she threw a few clothes in an overnight case, with the minimum of toiletries she needed for a short trip. She let the front desk know she would be away for a couple of days, and they called the limousine to take her to Malpensa. The clerk offered to arrange her air tickets, but Octavia said she would do it at the airport. She didn't want to leave a trail. She didn't intend anyone to know where she was going.

Octavia took a window seat in the business-class compartment. Tense and unhappy, she stared out the window of the Czech Airlines flight at the distant earth spinning beneath the wing of the Airbus, and reflected on the strangeness of leaving Malpensa at six in the evening to arrive in Prague ninety minutes later.

Teresa's first trip to Prague, as a young singer traveling from Milan to join the Bondini theater company, had meant nearly two weeks spent in coaches and roadside inns.

For Hélène, it had been a journey of two days. She and Ugo had taken the train from Paris, with lengthy stops in Nancy and Munich. By the time they arrived at Hlavní Nádraží the station in Prague, Hélène felt as if the cinders from the locomotive had permeated her clothes and saturated her hair.

It was called the Franz Josef Station in 1907, a towering art nouveau complex, still under construction. The noise of the builders and the bustle of travelers grated on Hélène's nerves. She was tired and dirty and anxious. The scents of frying food from the vendors that crowded the station turned her stomach.

No one was on the platform to meet them.

Ugo merely shrugged at that. "When you see what it's like, you'll understand," he said.

Hélène had little choice but to follow him as he worked his

way through the crowd to a set of stairs leading down into a dim tunnel and on to the main hall on the ground level. The atmosphere in the hall was a bit more orderly. A line of hacks waited outside in the street. As Ugo negotiated with one of the drivers, Hélène looked to her left, where she remembered the Horse Gate set into the city walls. She didn't recognize the silhouettes of the buildings that had been erected in her long absence. A huge neo-Renaissance structure dominated the skyline, and she supposed there was nothing left of the Horse Market.

Ugo called her name, and she allowed herself to be handed into a hack, settled with a blanket around her legs. She pulled her traveling hat firmly onto her head.

Ugo asked, "Are you comfortable?"

She nodded but turned her face away, to watch the changed face of the city roll by.

She was not yet certain of Ugo, and not sure she trusted him, though they had traveled in company for more than a year now, since the day of the earthquake.

She had, in fact, tried to leave him in Golden Gate Park, to go back to the Palace Hotel for her things.

The park had become a place of madness. A makeshift hospital had been set up near one of the entrances, with the ill and dying who had been moved from the nearby Mechanics' Pavilion lying on pallets on the grass. Families were collapsed around heaps of their belongings, all they could carry. Already soldiers were organizing lines for food and water. Hélène averted her eyes from those huddled, weeping over their losses.

She made her way out through the Page Street Gate, hurrying down the hill toward Market Street. The streets were full of smoke, and ominous flames shot up before her, obscuring the eastern horizon. She couldn't think what else to do but press on, though she was jostled by running people, her ears assaulted by the clanging of fire bells and the shouts of men struggling to put out fires here and there. As she struggled down Market, the smoke thickened. The road was a mess of jumbled paving stones.

To her left she saw that only the framework was left of the dome of City Hall. On her right, the Post Office and the Mint were ablaze. The Emporium and the Flood Building had vanished as if they had never been built. Everywhere people struggled to get away from the business district, their eyes blank with shock, their faces smudged with soot and tears and blood.

It looked to Hélène, as she pressed on, that virtually everything south of Market had toppled, brick walls smashed, wooden buildings turned to splinters. Plaster dust clogged the air, and she pressed her sleeve to her mouth, trying to filter out the worst of it. She turned right on Second, her heart quailing in her breast, expecting to see that the Palace Hotel had suffered the fate of so many other buildings.

A spurt of hope filled her when she saw through the smoke that the flag still flew from the roof of the Palace. Jets of water played around it, the first sign of hope she had found. As she stood below, gazing up at this wonder, a man at her elbow said, "You should get away from here, miss. It's going to burn."

"But the water!" she said, pointing up at the bright streams arcing through billows of smoke from nearby fires.

As she stood looking up at the elegant façade of the hotel, the jets faltered and died. Moments afterward the fire, which had been growing inside the two-foot-thick walls, exploded through the roof. Hélène stood helplessly in the street, watching the fire blossom and burst through the many floors of the Palace Hotel. The last thing to burn, consumed by flames running up its supporting pole, was the American flag flying above the devastation.

Hélène stood where she was for long minutes, unable to think what to do next. Everything she owned had been in her room at the hotel—her money, her clothes, her scores. The little garnet brooch, Vincenzo dal Prato's gift, was the last remnant of Teresa Saporiti's life, and the only one she had dared to keep.

Hélène wept sooty tears and watched in stunned amazement as the hotel collapsed on itself, shooting clouds of ash into the already-fouled air of the city.

She was hardly aware when Ugo appeared silently beside her, took her arm, and led her gently away. She found herself on Market Street before she regained her composure. When she did, she pulled free of Ugo's grip. "I have to go to the opera house," she said. "Perhaps they'll pay me, at least for last night."

"No," Ugo said. "The building is gutted. They lost all the sets, all the costumes, and the manager is nowhere to be found."

She couldn't take it in. "How do you know that?"

"Hélène," he said. "We need to get out of the city. There won't be enough food or water. There won't be anyplace safe to sleep. We have to go."

It seemed to her the city was dying around her. People jammed the streets, hoping to gain passage on one of the ferries. Children, separated from their parents, wailed until kind strangers picked them up and held them. Charred and smashed bodies were stacked like firelogs at street corners, with an occasional weeping survivor lifting their heads, scanning their faces in dread. Hélène had seen a great deal of death, of course. But the magnitude of the losses in San Francisco was numbing even to her, who was already inured.

Though she didn't want to, she walked away with Ugo. His arm was around her back, and his steps were steady and purposeful. She went where he directed, feeling as if she had lost her own will. She was like one of those lost children, wandering aimlessly about, waiting for someone to choose a direction.

Ugo led her through the death and confusion to the Pacific Mail dock, where a paddle steamer was being loaded with patients and nurses from St. Mary's Hospital. Through some means of persuasion Hélène never understood, Ugo secured space on the *Medoc* for them, and within the hour they were steaming out into the safety of the bay, surrounded by one hundred seventy seriously ill patients and a handful of Sisters of Mercy in their black habits, their white coifs spattered with ash.

The decks were jammed with pallets. Some patients lay two to a bed. At one end of the steamer, the dead and dying had their

own area. At the other end, the Sisters of Mercy were busy tend-
ing to those were ill, but who might survive. Ugo left Hélène in a
sheltered corner and went to one of the nuns. She saw him bob
his head, make a gesture, say something. In a short time he was
carrying bedpans, spreading blankets, bringing bandages and
medicines to the sisters and the two doctors they had with them.

Hélène, ashamed of her lassitude, rose and went to offer her
own services, and she and Ugo worked side by side, in comple-
ment with the Sisters of Mercy, until the steamer reached Oakland. The sisters prayed ceaselessly, a comforting chant beneath
the slap of the paddle wheel and the groans of the ill and injured.
Hélène, with her hands full of noisome basins or fouled bandages, found herself praying with them, automatically reciting
the beautiful old verse, *Hail Mary, full of grace* . . . as if she were
still allowed to practice her faith.

When the steamer docked in Oakland in the early morning
hours, they said farewell and prepared to disembark. One of the
sisters reached out a hand to touch Hélène's forehead in blessing.
Hélène, realizing at the last minute what she was about to do,
jerked away. She feared that even the lightest touch of those
sanctified fingers might burn her skin. The nursing sister dropped
her hand. She said nothing, but only turned away, too weary even
to be offended.

Hélène was exhausted beyond imagining, and she thought
Ugo must be the same. Neither had slept for two nights. Hélène
couldn't think, couldn't plan, could barely put one foot in front of
the other.

Ugo, though, seemed to have deep resources of strength and
energy. He helped her off the *Medoc* and walked with her to the
Oakland train station. Though the station was crowded with
refugees, he arranged something, and before the day was out, the
two of them boarded a Southern Pacific train that would make
connections to New York. As it chugged out of Oakland, Hélène
collapsed onto a padded bench seat in a blissfully quiet compartment, listening to the soporific rhythm of the wheels against the

rails. She gazed across at Ugo, this slender, capable man who had suddenly become part of her life. She had not given him permission to travel with her, nor had he asked for it. But it was clear he meant to stay at her side.

They were six hours into their journey when he brought out the flat, tabbed packet of fabric he had first shown her in the Palm Court of the Garden Hotel, when they were surrounded by people in evening clothes and waiters with trays of drinks.

Irrelevantly, she wondered what had become of the woman in pink satin. Was she, like the Palm Court, the hotel itself, now reduced to ash, nothing left of her but charred bones? Or perhaps she was one of the lucky ones and had made her escape from San Francisco. The pink satin woman would have won passage through wealth and privilege. Hélène had escaped only because of Ugo.

He grinned at her, looking more like a naughty boy than an ageless creature of secrets. "I think you're ready for this," he said.

"Ready . . . for what?" she stammered.

He sat down beside her. He laid the packet on the little fold-out table and began to untie the linen tabs. He smoothed back the panels of cloth, and she transferrred her gaze from his face to the equipment. The steel needles glittered in the light from the window. And the vials of brownish glass, empty before, now held something dark.

"What is it?" she asked, touching one of the vials. It was cold, and beads of condensation sparkled on its surface.

"Come, Hélène," he said gently. "*Bella*. You must know."

The vials mocked her, reminding her of her need, and her shame. "Where did you get it?" she asked in a hushed tone.

"You don't need to know."

"But is it . . . is it . . ."

He touched her hand. "Yes, it is. *Sangue*. Now roll up your sleeve."

The process seemed strange to her, a bizarre echo of that which had kept her alive for more than a century. She folded back the full sleeve of her shirtwaist and watched with a kind of stunned fascination as Ugo bound her upper arm with a strip of black silk. He touched the vein on the inside of her elbow with one finger. It swelled invitingly under the pressure as he tightened the binding. At the bite of the needle, she shuddered and closed her eyes. Just so had she pierced so many veins, veins beyond counting. Her only consolation, and a faint one, was that she no longer brought her victims to the point of death. That, at least, she had learned.

And in so doing had attracted the attention of the elders, and of this strange man.

When the *sangue* began to flow into her vein, her eyes flew open. It was cold at first, but it warmed quickly as it wound its way into her body, and then it was hot, and sweet. She felt a dizzying rush of energy that took her breath away.

Ugo murmured, "Yes. I thought you would feel that."

"Did you know? Have you done this before?" she said faintly.

"No, *bella*. No." Gently, as though he had practiced it a hundred times, he withdrew the needle and pressed a bit of clean cloth to the site.

"Then how could you have thought . . ."

He was deftly repacking his things, coiling the tubing, rolling the strip of black silk. "I am," he said, with a self-deprecating lift of his shoulders, "a student of history. And the history of intravenous injections is a long one."

"You must tell me where you got it. Especially now, of all times."

He lifted his eyes from his task. They had gone hard, like coals, with no light reflected in them. "Don't ask me that," he said. His accent was suddenly that of an American, the vowels flattened, the consonants dull. "I've told you. You don't need to know."

"But, Ugo . . ."

"No. Don't." He tied the tabs of his packet with a sharp tug and put the whole into an inner pocket. He stood up, taking three steps to the window, where the desert scenery jolted past. When he looked at her again, his face had resumed its mild, faintly amused expression. "A gift," he said lightly. He flicked his fingers over the pocket. "My gift to you. *A caval donato non si guarda in bocca.*"

Hélène frowned, not liking the feeling of being dependent. But she felt so well—so strong and full of life—that she found it in herself to put her question away. She could press him another time, perhaps, if he were still here.

She lifted the bit of cotton from the tiny wound. A single drop of blood rose to the surface of her skin. She dabbed it away. There was no more, only a small red spot that began to fade even as she watched. In moments it was gone, leaving no evidence of what had just taken place.

She jumped to her feet, feeling too full of vitality to sit still. "Some of the other singers are on the train," she said. "I'm going to find them."

And he, with a limpid, white-toothed smile, said, "Have fun, *bella.*"

A year passed before she asked him again about the source of his supply. This time they were in the train station in Prague, and Ugo had a hand over the pocket where he kept what she now thought of as her packet. Fretfully, she said, "What's wrong? Is it there?"

"Of course. What's bothering you?"

"I don't know." She tried to brush scattered flecks of ash and soot from the short jacket of her traveling suit. "I don't want to see her. I don't like her."

He patted her arm. "I don't either. But we won't stay long."

"And what if I . . . what if I need . . ."

He touched his pocket again. "It's here, Hélène. I told you."

"But if you run out, what will I do?"

"I won't run out, silly girl." He put his hand on her back and began to steer her through the crowds. It had been a long time since she had heard the Czech language, and it made her feel even more out of place to be unable to catch more than a word or two of the hundreds shouted and called around her.

As they waited for a hack to be free, Hélène asked him. "I can see it doesn't last long, Ugo. Tell me where you get it."

He flashed her a look, and she remembered now how hard those limpid dark eyes could turn when he was angry. He said, in that same American accent she had heard on the train from Oakland, "I won't tell you. And I don't want the Countess entertaining the question."

Hélène felt a chill in her belly that crept up to her breast. "Ugo," she said breathlessly. "She doesn't know?"

His full lips pressed into a tight line. He shook his head.

"Then—what does she think? How does she think I—I manage?"

"She thinks you feed, of course. But that you kill." His flat vowels made her nerves jump. "Don't tell her, Hélène. She won't like it."

"Teresa." The Countess Milosch rose from her seat in a vast, dim parlor. "You've changed."

"It's Hélène." Hélène came forward into the vague circle of light cast by three thick beeswax candles in old cut-glass holders. She glanced briefly about her. Everything in the room was old. The furniture spoke of other centuries. The carpet beneath her feet had gone hard as the cobblestones outside, as if the years had dessicated it, petrified its fibers into a fossil of itself. Even the air seemed to have been breathed too often and too long.

"Hélène. Hmm. I suppose it's useful, to change your name." The Countess looked as Hélène remembered her, or more properly, as Teresa remembered her. Her sharp-featured face and sharp-boned shoulders looked as if they had been carved from stone.

"It's necessary," Hélène said. "If I want to have a career."

"You're having success in America, then." The Countess's voice held no real interest.

"In some places," Hélène answered.

Zdenka Milosch sat down again and let her head fall back against the sofa. "I don't like America," she said.

Ugo waved Hélène to a chair and took one himself. "Why don't you like America, Countess?" he asked. His tone was conversational, as if this bizarre place were a normal home, as if this were a social meeting.

"Colonials," she said sourly. "They're never civilized."

"It's been a hundred-odd years since America was a colony," Ugo said, smiling. "They might surprise you."

The Countess didn't bother to answer.

Hélène gazed at her with mounting resentment. "Why am I here, Countess? I don't like being given orders."

"Indeed." The Countess lifted her head and fixed Hélène with her unfriendly gaze. "My brethren wished to meet you," she said.

"The elders," Ugo said quietly. He leaned back and crossed his legs, adjusting the careful pleat of his elegant flannels. "Hélène has a contract in New York in six weeks," he said. "We can't stay long."

One of the Countess's narrow brows rose. "We?" she said, her voice no more than a thread of sound.

Ugo laughed. "I am now the assistant to Mademoiselle Hélène Singher, up-and-coming French soprano, who made a miraculous escape from the disaster in San Francisco. I like it." With an elegant gesture of his slim fingers, he said, "It keeps me off the streets, you know."

"We must not be giving you enough work," the Countess replied. Hélène blinked, surprised at the near humor of her remark.

Ugo shrugged. "I'm busy enough," he said. "Your interests will be seen to in all the cities Hélène will visit."

The Countess sat up a little straighter, in a rustle of bombazine. Her dress was fifty years out of date. Hélène wondered if she ever went out anymore. She fixed Hélène with her cold gaze. "Ugo has made it clear to you, I gather," she said. "What it is we require."

Hélène, her temper gathering, opened her mouth, but Ugo

forestalled her. "You haven't heard of any exceptions, have you, Countess?" he drawled. "It's been a year."

Again, Zdenka Milosch did not bother to reply. Her lips curled in her mirthless smile, never revealing her teeth. Hélène drew breath again, a retort rising to her lips, but Ugo found her foot with his and pressed down. Her gored skirt was cut in the new style, short enough to expose her soft-heeled boot. It appeared Ugo didn't care if he damaged the leather. His meaning was clear, and she subsided.

The servingman, a scrawny, dark little man, scuttled in with a tray and an assortment of bottles and glasses. He set it on the inlaid table and went out again. Ugo removed his foot from Hélène's boot and reached for one of the bottles. A slight rustle sounded from the far end of the long room and he stopped, his hand outstretched, looking into the shadows. Hélène followed his gaze.

Ugo had told her they were old. Ancient, he had said.

Even that word hardly served. They shuffled forward, one after the other, their clothes hanging about them in shapeless silhouettes that shifted vaguely as they moved. The woman—if woman she could still be called—peered out from beneath her hood. The men swayed from side to side as they coasted to a stop just beyond the circle of candlelight.

No, not ancient, Hélène thought. Atavistic. Primeval. Surely even their long, long memories could not contain the years that had passed for them.

One of them spoke in a thin voice. "Is this the one?"

The Countess stood, and pointed at Hélène. "It is she."

Hélène stared up at the three gloomy figures. When one of them—Anastasia, it must be—moved closer, a smell like that of rotting meat came with her, overpowering the scents of beeswax and dust. The creature leaned forward, into the light, and Hélène caught a glimpse of hooded eyes, a nose that drooped over wrinkled lips, and fearsomely long teeth.

Unconsciously, Hélène touched her own canines with her tongue, reassuring herself. They had retracted slightly, subtly, since Ugo's advent. They were still long, but they were nothing like Anastasia's. Anastasia's teeth were a marvel, a grotesquerie. They were fangs, tusks of yellowed ivory. They protruded, curved, depressed the papery skin of her chin. Hélène's stomach quivered with nausea at the idea of those teeth, of lips that could no longer close, of a face that must not be seen.

The Countess said, "Teresa. Stand up so the elders can see you."

And without protest, hypnotized by those terrible teeth, she obeyed. Anastasia's mouth stretched in a ghastly attempt at a smile. "Sssssing," she hissed.

Hélène said faintly, "What?"

Anastasia's face receded into the shadows of her hood, but she stood, hands folded, as if waiting. Hélène turned to the Countess. "What does she want?"

The Countess nodded to the three elders. "They want you to sing."

Ugo stood now, too, and Hélène felt his shoulder just touching hers. She gazed into the dark depths of Anastasia's hood, then peered into the shadows where the others, Eusebio and Henri, loomed like great wordless crows, staring back at her. One of them, she didn't know which, lifted a trembling hand and pointed at her.

"Is this," he said in a hoarse and horrible voice, "the vessel?" The *s* was distorted, as if his tongue could no longer reach his hard palate.

"Vessel?" Hélène said. "What does he mean?"

"Vessel," the Countess replied, with a hint of impatience. "Container. Receptacle."

"I know what a vessel is." Hélène felt Ugo's hand come up to encircle her waist. "What is this about?" she snapped. "I've come a long way, and I'm certainly not going to sing tonight. I'm tired and I need a bath." She gestured to the three ancients. "And I would venture a guess that I'm not the only one."

Anastasia hissed something, a warning sound, and Ugo's arm tightened around Hélène.

Zdenka Milosch said, "Have a care, Teresa. Anastasia may not be able to hurt you anymore, but she employs people who can. I am one."

Hélène's anger flared, and her lip lifted involuntarily.

The Countess's black eyes narrowed. She stiffened, seeming to grow taller and wider. With deliberation, she revealed her own impressive teeth, with a glimmer as of ivory knives in the dim light. "I don't think," she said clearly, "that you want to try me."

Hélène turned to Ugo. "I want to leave," she said. "Can we go?"

The Countess answered. "No. You can't." Her lips folded again, hiding her teeth, but her eyes still glittered dangerously. "However," she said, "you can wait to sing until tomorrow, when you're rested. I'll have Kirska show you to your room. And you may certainly have a bath."

The elders pulled back, out of the light. Hélène took a deep breath, leaning into Ugo's arm, trying not to think about the specter that Anastasia's face had become, nor to guess at the years reflected there.

The Countess rang a small bell that waited at her elbow, and the stolid, silent Kirska appeared. As Ugo and Hélène followed her upstairs, Hélène looked at her curiously, wondering what kind of creature she was. She seemed ageless, like the Countess . . . like herself. Kirska, the hulking gardener—Tomas, he was called—who had met them at the gatehouse. The other employees who lurked here and there in the dimness, like rats waiting for crumbs. Why would they stay here, serving in this dark place?

Kirska opened the doors to adjoining rooms, and without a word, bustled off down the corridor. Hélène hoped that meant a bath would be forthcoming. She stood in her doorway and scowled at Ugo in his.

He lifted his shoulders and gave a light laugh. "I tried to warn you what this would be like. Words don't suffice."

"Why should I sing for these . . . for them?" she demanded. "I owe them nothing."

"Actually," Ugo said, sobering, "you do."

"Why? Because they didn't kill me?"

He leaned against the doorjamb. Whitened lines pulled at his mouth. "Hélène. It's more than that."

"What, then?" she demanded. Fatigue and irritation made her querulous. Even as she spoke, she shook her head in frustration, knowing she sounded like a spoiled child.

But Ugo straightened and came to her, taking her arm, guiding her gently into her bedroom. "Sit down, *bella*," he said.

The bed was a four-poster affair with a carved wooden canopy and a coverlet of heavy brown wool. Hélène sat down on it, finding as soon as she took her weight off her feet that they ached. She bent and began to unlace her boots. She glanced up at Ugo. "Go on."

"You know, Hélène, what I am."

"Only what you've told me." Hélène straightened and worked at her left boot with her right foot. It fell to the bare floor with a light thud. She bent her knee to bring her left foot onto the bed and massaged it with her fingers, giving Ugo a narrow-eyed look. "I haven't seen it."

"I hope you never do." He went to the window and drew back the heavy drapes. Dust rose in little spirals from the folds. "And with the help of La Società, you never will."

He came back and stood before her, his slight body tense, his face intent. "They found me in the streets of Rome," he said. "Zdenka Milosch came for me. She taught me what it was, and how to control it."

"And so you do as she tells you."

"I need La Società. I need the network."

"Why, Ugo? There are herbalists everywhere, aren't there?"

"Not who carry what I need." He shook his head, a slight, graceful movement. "Please trust me. I need them, and so, if you want to continue as we have been, you also need them." He hesitated, his lips twisting. "Hélène, if you want to continue . . . you need them even more than I do."

She sat quietly then, one boot on and one off. Oppression weighed on her until she thought her shoulders must bend beneath it. The past year had been more peaceful, more serene, than any she had known since the bite. The thought of going back to the streets, driven by thirst, losing herself in need and urgency—it was a grievous prospect.

"Ugo," she said softly. "Could we not manage on our own?"

He stood looking down at her, his face as dark as her own heart. "I can't go back any more than you can. I know what it is to have no control. To lose myself. And—" His eyes left hers and drifted around the high-ceilinged bedroom. "I loathe it," he said, so low she almost didn't hear him. "I have loathed it from the very beginning."

Octavia had checked no luggage. She fidgeted impatiently as the passport control officer flipped through her much-used passport, and as soon as he let her through, she hurried into the terminal. She found an exchange and fidgeted more while the agent exchanged her euros for Czech crowns with their sepia portraits of emperors and saints. She stuffed the bills into her bag and followed the signs to the taxi stand. From her prodigious memory, she dredged up the name of the road where the elders' mansion was. She knew no number. There had been none in 1907.

She was fortunate to encounter an enterprising cab driver, who laughed over her predicament and listened to her explanations of how the place looked the last time she saw it, of the ivy-hung walls and the little stone gatehouse. The man's English was paltry, but his German was quite good, at least as good as Octavia's. His cab was passably new and had been outfitted by the state with a GPS device. After a drive of thirty minutes, with a mechanical feminine voice reciting instructions, they came to Mohács Road and began cruising down it.

The scenery had changed, of course. Wars and their subsequent political upheavals, a burgeoning population, and membership in the EU had brought a flourish of new construction. Other estates flanked the road, filling spaces Octavia remembered as orchards and fields. The cab's headlights picked out elaborate scrolled-iron gates and elegant landscaping. But the same gentle mountain still sloped up above the road, and the inviting sparkle of blue lakes showed here and there between the rooftops and the landscaped gardens. In the distance, the red roofs of Prague glowed through the gathering darkness.

The cab driver kept his speed down, chattering away to Octavia in German sprinkled with oddly anachronistic English phrases, perhaps picked up from someone who had learned English in another time. Octavia answered absently. They had been on the road for perhaps ten minutes when she cried, *"È qui!"*

She didn't realize until he looked at her oddly that she had spoken in Italian. He grinned as he pulled the cab to the side of the road. *"Signorina, parla italiano? Ho pensato che fosse americana."*

"Yes, I am American," she said. "But I've been working in Milan."

He nodded as if this were perfectly normal and went around to open her door for her. She climbed out with her purse and her little night case. She paid him in crowns, and he stood with the money in his hand, looking dubiously at the dark, overgrown grounds of the mansion, the shuttered windows of the gatehouse. He turned to her, his brow furrowed. *"Si sente al sicuro, signorina?"*

She gave him a rueful smile. "I know it looks awful," she said. "But I'm all right. I promise. *Molto gentile, signore.*"

With evident reluctance, he climbed back in his cab. As he drove away, she saw him looking at her in his rearview mirror as if expecting her to change her mind.

She waited until he was out of sight before she walked up the moss-covered cobblestone path to the gatehouse and knocked firmly, and loudly, on the door.

Hélène had soon found that baths at the elders' compound were taken in a small building behind the main house. Kirska led her through the maze of corridors and stairs, out a back door, and on to the bathhouse. A huge, battered tin tub steamed on a floor of flagstone. The workers who had just filled it slipped away the moment Hélène appeared. A fire burned in a small grate, and an oil lamp shed yellow light over wooden benches and a low table holding soap and towels.

As Hélène began to undo the fastenings of her short suit jacket, Kirska stepped forward as if to help her. Hélène said, "No," shrinking away from her touch.

Kirska gave a short nod, her mouth twisting. She pulled a painted screen forward and unfolded it so the tub was hidden from the door. Before she left, she raised her eyebrows as if to ask if there was anything else. Hélène shook her head.

The water was clean and hot. Hélène put a fresh cake of soap on the edge of the tub before she draped her suit and shirtwaist over the screen and folded her lingerie into a tidy pile. She unpinned her hair and stepped into the warm water. She sank beneath the surface with a sigh, letting the water lap at her chin. Her hair trailed in wet strands over her shoulders as she laid her head back against the edge of the tub. She closed her eyes, giving herself up to the warmth.

She thought she might have drowsed for a time. When a wave of cool air touched her wet shoulders, she opened her eyes. She hadn't heard the door, but she thought Kirska must have come back. She called out, "Kirska? I'm not done yet. I want to wash my . . ."

She stopped speaking. The smell that permeated the bathhouse was unmistakable. She sat up, catching her wet hair back with one hand. She snapped, "What are you doing here?"

There was no answer, but the smell intensified, and there was a rustle of fabric against the flagstones. Hélène thought of jumping out of the bath, but she would be wet and shivering. "What do you want?"

The creature, ancient and wavering, put a spotted hand on the edge of the screen, then shuffled forward to stand beside it. Her hood had fallen back, showing a thatch of thin white hair, raggedly chopped. Hélène stared up at her face, fully revealed now in the light of the oil lamp. She expected to feel the same horror she had experienced earlier in the day, but this time, what she felt was sorrow. And sympathy.

Anastasia struggled to speak past her teeth, emitting only an unintelligible sibilance.

Hélène said, "What? I can't understand you."

The ancient tried again, leaning forward a little, as if propinquity might help. Her skin was an indeterminate color, as if whatever melanin had been there once had leached away over the years. She peered from beneath her sagging eyelids and croaked, "Vesssssel."

At least, that was what Hélène thought she was trying to say. Her lower lip could not quite reach her upper teeth to form the initial consonant. Hélène let her hair drop back into the water, and she folded her arms around herself. Her exposed shoulders prickled with chill. "Vessel? Is that what you said?"

The ancient bobbed her head, once. "Ssssssing."

Hélène stared at her, oddly touched. "Yes. I will sing. But tomorrow, not tonight."

The ancient nodded again and started the laborious movement of turning. Hélène said, "Wait. Anastasia." The creature's head swiveled painfully toward her. "Why do you call me that? Vessel?"

Anastasia's mouth flexed horribly as she said, "Lasssst."

Then she was gone, leaving Hélène in her cooling bath, staring in confusion at the flames flickering in the grate.

There was a pianoforte at the opposite end of the parlor where Hélène had met the ancients for the first time. When the moment came, Hélène found that a generous fire had been laid in a yawning fireplace, and the end of the room that had been entirely in shadow now glowed with light. An assortment of furniture had been arranged in a semicircle around the pianoforte. Eusebio, Henri, and Anastasia were already there, each with their layers of clothing folded and draped around them.

Hélène expected the pianoforte to be dusty and out of tune, as neglected as the rest of the parlor. She opened the lid of the instrument and touched the keys. She struck a C chord, and then G, the dominant. Eyebrows lifted, she rolled the subdominant, F, with both hands now, and then again C.

Ugo, taking a chair nearby, chuckled. "I told you," he said in an undertone. "Music is their only remaining passion."

Hélène pulled out the stool and sat down. She had no score, but of course she needed none. She glanced up at Zdenka Milosch, who sat on an eighteenth-century French love seat, turned so that her half of it faced the pianoforte.

"I never really learned to play," Hélène warned her. "I know only the music that Mozart knew. And knowing it and being able to play it properly are sometimes not the same thing."

The Countess's voice vibrated with anticipation. "An accompanist is not possible."

"Of course." Hélène looked around the little circle of her audience, at the firelit parlor with its semblance of social nicety, of a *salon* concert about to begin. Candles had been lit in the wall sconces, and the bent little manservant had laid trays of glasses and decanters on scattered low tables. The ancients leaned forward, their faces shadowed by hood and hat and drifting gray hair, their bizarre teeth glimmering when a twig occasionally blazed up in the fireplace. The grotesquerie of the scene was intensified by its pretense of normality.

Hélène looked to Ugo. She saw in his parted lips, in the gleam of his dark eyes, that he, too, awaited her music with eagerness, though not so overt as that of the ancients. She knew he cared about music, about her singing, but this avaricious look startled her. Her eyes passed over the ancients once again. She half expected to see saliva dripping from their tusks, like dogs awaiting a tidbit dropped from the table.

She drew a deep breath, trying to banish the gorge that threatened to rise in her throat. She would give them what they craved. Then, perhaps, she could leave, she and Ugo.

Because she could play it, because she could remember the piano reductions, she gave them Mozart. She sang "Laudate Dominum" and "Abendempfindung." She sang "Exsultate, Jubilate," and she sang a fragment from the Great Mass in C minor. She sang the Countess's arias, and Pamina's.

They did not applaud, her bestial audience, but they breathed. It was evident, each time she played the final cadence, that their combined breaths came faster, whistling through fragile and failing larynxes, rattling in decrepit lungs. Zdenka Milosch patted her knee with a sound like that of bat wings in the trees. Ugo sat back in his chair, his chin on his fist, his eyes closed.

Hélène was done. She was tired. With a decisive movement, she closed the lid of the pianoforte and pushed her stool away from the keyboard.

One of the ancients, Henri, she thought, lifted his trembling head to fix her with a rheumy gaze. "Mozaa-aaa-rt," he stammered. "Blood."

Hélène's mouth dried as she stared at him, and her skin prickled.

Eusebio gave a shaking nod and repeated Henri's words, less intelligibly. "Blood . . . Mozaa-aaa-rt."

Anastasia made a terrible sound that Hélène feared was meant to be a laugh. Hélène looked to Ugo, then to the Countess, for explanation.

The Countess stood up and inclined her head as if she were bowing to one whose title exceeded her own in importance. "Yes," she said. "Yes. They know about you, Hélène. It was important for them to hear you. They know you shared the bite with Mozart."

"So did you," Hélène said.

Zdenka waved a negligent hand. "I have no musical ability. No voice, and no skill."

"But there must be others. Others I . . . that I . . ."

Zdenka's lip curled at Hélène's inability to speak the word. "That you, shall we say, infected?" Something flickered in her eyes, and her lips parted as if she would say something more, but she closed them again and shook her head. She said only, "No."

Something kept Hélène from asking again, some dread she couldn't face.

33

Lascia, lascia alla mia pena questo picciolo ristoro.

Allow my suffering at least this small relief.

—Donna Anna, Act Two, Scene Two, *Don Giovanni*

Ugo opened his eyes gingerly, squinting against the light. He flexed his toes and his fingers and painfully moved his ankles and his legs. He had no scars, no wounds he could sense, but his body was stiff with cold. He drew a ragged breath and rolled to his side before he struggled to sit up. He bent his knees and wrapped his arms around his legs, trying to warm himself while he looked around to discover where the wolf had carried him this time.

Until the current fiasco with Domenico, it had been a very long time since the wolf had emerged. Zdenka Milosch's bargain had been a good one.

She had taught him, those first months he spent behind the ivy-hung walls of her compound, just how wide the elders' network was. He learned for himself, when he went out to do her work, how eager the recruits were to do whatever was asked of them. They were convinced, each one of them, that the translation of their mortal state into that of the near immortals was a mere matter of obedience and dedication. They found each other, these hopefuls, and banded together in New York and Rome, London and Paris, Berlin and Riyadh. They gathered in taverns, in underground catacombs, in secret upper rooms where they attempted rituals they had heard of, chanted offices they found in arcane manuscripts, cut themselves, branded each other, anything they could think of to attract what they craved.

Their credulity caused Ughetto to feel pity at first. He resisted lining them up for La Società like calves for the butcher's knife. But decades of suffering the gullibility of fools eroded his sensitivity until the last of his empathy scarred over and disappeared.

The Countess took him out into the compound one day, leading him between clumps of yew and browning spruce yearning upward in search of sunlight. It was a huge garden, crowded with trees and shrubs. Ughetto recognized the heart-shaped leaves of linden trees, and the palm-shaped ones of oak. One of these had grown into the stone wall, pushing the stones aside to make room for its trunk. Its branches hung low on both sides, inviting squirrels to run in and out at will.

The Countess gave no sign that she cared about the state of the garden, except for a small space of earth that had been cleared of low branches and vines so that it was filled with sunshine. It looked out of place, a neatly tilled and weeded spot in the midst of a riot of unchecked vegetation. A double row of perennials thrust up into the sunshine, vigorous stems that came almost to Ughetto's waist and bore dark violet flowers. The Countess stopped and turned to be certain Ughetto was paying attention.

She put one slippered foot into the carefully raked soil and lifted one of the violet flowers with a fingertip. "This is *aconitum lycoctonum* still growing. I thought you should see it before it has been dried. Some call it northern wolfsbane." She stepped back, dusting her hands together. Ughetto bent to sniff at the blossom. "I've had it planted here specially for you, Ughetto."

He gazed into her expressionless face. "I have to come here for it?"

Her lips curled in her sparse smile. "No. I mean to help you, as you will help me." She turned away from the cultivated plot, back toward the house. "*Aconitum vulparia* has a different flower. Yellow, quite pretty. Less reliable in suppressing the wolf."

He walked on behind her, pondering the possibility that he might never have to transform again. They passed through the high-ceilinged kitchen with its pitted stone sinks and enormous pantry. The Countess pushed open the door of the pantry and pointed to bundles of herbs hanging from drying racks. Ughetto recognized basil and chives, thyme and oregano. On a separate dowel, away from the edible herbs, he saw sprigs of *aconitum lycoctonum*. The violet flowers had gone gray, and the leaves were curled and dry.

"Take some," she said. She went into the pantry, reached up and broke off a stem. "You will be able to test it at the next full moon." She turned to him and held out the herb on her palm.

Ughetto didn't take it. "How do you know this works?"

She blinked once, slowly. "You're hardly my first *lupo mannaro*, Ughetto."

"There are others?"

"There were."

"What happened to them?"

"Dead. Killed."

He took a half step back, reaching the support of the wall. "How?"

"The transformation is dangerous. Men hate wolves, and with good reason. Any self-respecting householder will kill one that gets close to his property."

Ughetto stared at her in wonderment. "So, if I'm not killed that way, then . . . how long will I live?"

Her gaze drifted away as if the conversation had become tedious. She shrugged her thin shoulders. "Who knows? None of the others lasted for long. But it may be you could live as long as we do, if you can keep yourself safe. All the more reason to learn to use the herb."

Ughetto learned little else from her. He tried asking her in different ways. He thought of catching her in a better mood, but such an event never came to pass in his presence. He tried tricking her into telling him more, asking oblique questions, even attempting to get Kirska to talk to him, but his efforts bore no fruit.

He had to discover on his own, through trial and error, how much of the wolfsbane to take, and how long it would last. Sometimes it made him sick, and he threw up what he had taken before it could work. Sometimes he didn't take enough, and the unimpeded light of the full moon proved it.

The catalog of places the wolf left him continued to expand. Once he ran out of his herb in the wilds of America's West and came back to himself on a high plateau where nothing moved but mountain sheep and a sharp, incessant wind. Another time the wolf left him, naked and confused, in Fort Tryon Park in New York. He woke beneath the stone wall surrounding the fort with soldiers marching guard above his head. When traveling by ship, he awoke one night deep in the hold, where cattle were chained in noisome rows. One was dead at his feet, its heart and half a rear haunch consumed by the wolf.

And now, abandoned once again in a winter forest, Ugo shivered in the cold. Across a shallow valley, snowy peaks speared a clear blue sky. Beneath his feet, the ground fell away in a gentle incline. The wolf had slept beneath a boulder, in a little nest of dirt and moss and alpine bracken. A bit of filthy cloth lay among the litter. Ugo shook it out and laughed when he saw what it was. He could use it, at least what remained of it. One leg of the borrowed trousers was missing, and the other was shredded to the knee, but he could at least cover his privates.

Shrugging, resigned, he pulled what was left of the garment up to his waist and started down the hill to see what might be at the bottom.

Early darkness was already falling, making it hard to see his way. Footsore, miserable with cold, he watched the lights of an unknown city spring to life through the evening gloom. The glitter of civilization promised warmth and shelter and food. All he had to do was find something, or steal something, to cover himself decently. Perhaps he could steal a little money while he was at it.

He pressed on, skidding down piney grades, treading gingerly where deadfall and bracken bit at his bare feet. He saw the lights of aircraft blinking overhead, descending to some airport. The planes were heavies, big jets, which meant the city twinkling through the darkness must be a significant one. A wide ribbon of darkness wound through its lights, a river cutting through the urban landscape. The headlights and taillights of cars, white and red and amber, crawled along several roadways that circled the city.

In fifteen more minutes, he was crouched above a busy highway. He recognized, now, the outlines of the city that sprawled at his feet. He was not in the wilds of some distant mountain range after all. The wolf had succeeded, at last, in bringing him home.

He saw the silhouette of Prague Castle and the spires of St. Vitus Cathedral, fully lit against the evening sky. It was the Vltava River that curved through the city, lights glimmering from the stone bridges that arched above the slow-moving water. He couldn't make out the tower for the Astronomical Clock, but he knew it was there, set into the Old Town wall.

Somewhere below this hill on which he crouched was the elders' compound. The home of La Società. The only place in the world where the wolf felt safe.

Ugo sighed and got to his feet. He would have been pleased never to enter the gatehouse of the Countess's dismal mansion ever again. But he was naked and alone, and he needed help to get back to Milan, and Octavia. Uncomfortable it might be, and oppressive, but on this night, it was the safest place for him, too.

Feeling his way in the dark, he scrambled down the slope to the road beneath. He climbed over the concrete barrier and struck the pose of a youth in trouble, in need of a ride. He put out his thumb and waited, shivering, for someone to take pity on him.

* * *

Octavia stood tall as the door to the gatehouse opened and the stooped, faded figure of the servingman peered up at her. He looked little different from the way he had a century before, slight and gray haired and somehow desiccated, as if there weren't enough flesh under his skin to fill it out. The vertical wrinkles in his lips lengthened as he folded his upper lip over his teeth. She let him gaze at her for several seconds before she said, in the tone of one who expects to be obeyed, "You know who I am. Take me to the Countess. It's urgent."

He didn't speak. In fact, she had never heard him speak. Perhaps he couldn't. Perhaps the Countess had seen to it that he couldn't.

He stepped aside so she could enter and closed the door behind her. He gave her a wide berth as he passed by to lead the way through the gatehouse, out the back door, and down the path toward the house.

Octavia had to duck hanging branches and step over roots pushing up from beneath the cracked and crumbling paving stones. The grounds were more jungle than garden, as if the hulking, dim-witted Tomas had given up completely.

When she came out of the wilderness of overgrown yew and bedraggled spruce, the house loomed before her. The ivy had evidently been allowed to grow without restraint, so that it smothered the foundation. The windows had all but disappeared beneath its persistent branches. Even the chimney was nearly swallowed by dark green leaves that seemed more to repel sunlight than to absorb it. It was a miracle that the place hadn't crumbled to dust beneath the onslaught of vegetation.

For a nasty moment, Octavia thought of turning on her heel and fleeing back to the road.

She resisted the urge and held her ground as the servingman opened the door of the house. She followed him into the dim interior. The moment her foot touched the floor, two servants working in the entryway faded into the shadows, like cockroaches scattering when a light comes on.

The servingman disappeared into the bowels of the house, and Octavia walked on alone into the parlor to await the Countess.

She didn't have long to wait. Zdenka Milosch appeared promptly, clicking into the cavernous room on a pair of stiletto heels. She wore a lightweight black sheath dress that had the look of Gaultier. Perhaps, Octavia thought, she had gone shopping when she was in Milan. Around her neck was a long string of pearls, and she had cut her hair into a bob that just reached her chin, accentuating the arch of her nose and the sharpness of her cheekbones. "Teresa," she said, without inflection.

There was a susurration in the shadows behind the Countess, and Octavia, with a quiver of nausea, saw that the ancients had also gathered. She sensed them more than she saw them, shadowy figures wavering in the background, bending slightly forward to peer at her.

She stiffened her neck and faced the Countess. "It's Octavia, of course," she said. "As you know very well."

"Oh, yes. The name slipped my mind. It's the surprise of seeing you here, I think." The Countess waved at one of the couches and settled herself into one opposite. "Why have you come? I've never had the impression that you enjoy our company."

Octavia remained on her feet. "Something's happened," she said. "I've come to explain."

The ancients moved forward a little, curiously, avid in their rusted way. One of them was leaning on a stick. He tapped it against the hard carpet as he shifted his weight, and it made a rubbery thud in the silence.

The Countess gave the slow blink that always made Octavia think of a snake deciding whether or not to strike. She said, "Yes. I know." She lifted one languid hand. "A member of La Società called this morning from Milan. It seems one of your colleagues received a strange injury." She let her hand drop, as if it were too much effort to hold it up. "But he didn't die, this young man. Everyone at the opera is relieved, of course." She blinked again.

"I'm not. He should have died, Octavia. I thought you understood that."

Octavia's heart clenched. It was all she could do not to press
her hand to her breast. "You didn't—tell me you didn't give the
order to—"

She broke off, realizing she no longer had the Countess's attention. The Countess's gaze slid to the doorway, though there
had been no sound, no announcement.

Octavia watched Zdenka Milosch stiffen and stare. Her upper
lip began to curl. She rose to her feet as smoothly as a serpent
uncoiling, and demanded, "How did you get in here?"

34

Ecco il fellone! Com'era qua?

There's the villain! How did he get here?

—Donna Anna, Don Ottavio,
Act Two, Scene Two, *Don Giovanni*

Domenico had spent the better part of a decade on his quest. He had grown adept at following rumors, hearsay, hints—and people. Compared to shadowing Zdenka Milosch, following Octavia Voss was laughably easy.

He buttoned his ceramic knife into his inner pocket, patting it to be certain it was secure. He followed her to Malpensa and watched as she bought a ticket for Prague. He acquired a ticket for the same Czech Airlines flight she took, sitting in the back of the plane with whiskered grandmothers and snot-nosed infants. He shadowed her as she changed money and wended her way through the terminal to the taxi stand. He noted the number of the cab that picked her up, and by the time it returned for another fare, he was ready.

Domenico hadn't bothered to change his money into crowns, and it cost him twenty euros to secure the cab he wanted. When the driver balked at revealing where he had dropped the blond American, Domenico showed him the neat, sharp blade.

"I love knives," he said conversationally. "I've made a study of them, actually. Hunting, filleting . . . and this sort, that you can carry everywhere without detection." The cabbie's eyes rolled toward him, but he drove on, pale and silent. He spoke almost no English, of course. But the message of the knife was universal.

As they turned into Mohács Road, the cabbie seemed to dredge up a few English words. "Mister. Knife, no. Please."

Domenico laughed and let the point press into the fabric of the man's cotton jacket. "Just drive. Don't talk." The cabbie pressed on the accelerator, and the cab careened around a curve. Domenico laughed again and pulled the blade back. It would be ridiculous to be in a crash now.

Everything was going beautifully. Finding the right cab, and an easily persuaded driver, seemed a good omen, further evidence that he was destined to succeed. Fulfillment was within his grasp.

He knew what was said about him. But soon, very soon now, they would no longer mock him behind his back. They would give him the respect he deserved, that he had earned. Thinking about it, thinking about the reward awaiting him, sped his heartbeat and filled him with fierce glee.

The driver swung the cab onto the shoulder of the road across from a dingy little stone building hung with vines. He said, without looking at Domenico, "Here."

Domenico eyed the small house with high stone walls extending from either side of it. "If you're thinking of dropping me in the wrong place, believe me, you'll regret it."

The cabbie, not understanding, shook his head.

"Damn it," Domenico said. "Why don't you bloody people learn English? You're happy enough to take our money. You could at least learn the language."

The cabbie only said, pointing a shaking finger across the road, "Here. Lady here."

Domenico lifted the knife and pressed it against the side of the man's neck. "Are you sure?" he said softly.

This, at least, the stupid man understood. He nodded and said again, "Yes, yes. Here."

The cabbie was trembling now. Domenico stroked his neck with the side of the blade, and a thin line of blood welled from his skin. The cabbie closed his eyes.

"Don't worry," Domenico said in a soothing tone. "You're very fortunate. I'm not actually going to kill you, although I wouldn't mind doing it. But I don't think La Società would appreciate a dead man in a cab outside their compound."

When he withdrew the knife the cabbie took a ragged breath and said something in Czech.

"Praying?" Domenico said. "Always a good idea." He put his hand on the door handle, and as it began to turn, the cabbie opened his eyes and looked at him. Domenico pointed to the identification card set into the dash. "Don't forget," he said. "If you've tricked me . . ."

The driver shook his head and said quickly, "Lady here. Here."

"Right. I certainly hope so."

Domenico climbed out of the cab and shut the door. The cabbie gunned the engine and shot away down the road in a spray of fine gravel.

Domenico straightened his jacket and dropped the knife into a pocket where it would be easy to grasp. He spared a few seconds to gather himself, to focus his mind on what was to come. It was not every day, after all, that a man achieved his destiny.

Ugo waited a half hour beside the road, hopping from foot to foot to try to stay warm. He began to think no one would pick up a half-naked youth, no matter how lost and vulnerable he managed to look.

When a Skoda hatchback pulled up beside him with a splatter of gravel, he was surprised to see a middle-aged, plump woman lean across the passenger seat to shove open the door.

Ugo bent to look inside the car. A wave of warmth swept out, scented by paint and paint thinner. The back of the hatchback was full of drop cloths and brushes and cans. The driver had dyed red hair and a generous, drooping bosom, half hidden by a pair of unlikely painter's coveralls. Her face was plump and pleasant.

"Thanks for stopping, madame," Ugo said in Czech. "Can you give me a ride? It's not far."

"I don't know, young man. You look like trouble to me," she said, laughing. She pointed a paint-stained finger at his bare chest. "But I can't see where you'd hide a weapon."

Ugo climbed into the Skoda and settled back against the vinyl seat. The warmth in the car enfolded him, and he heaved a grateful sigh. He rubbed at the goose bumps that stood out on his arms and chest. "Thank you so much, madame," he said. He let his voice go high, like that of a young boy, and deliberately softened his features before he turned his face to her. "I was camping, and I got lost."

She lifted one thick eyebrow. "Camping in January? Without a shirt?"

"I had a shirt," he said sadly. "And shoes, and a backpack with money in it. But I was washing in a creek, and when I tried to go back to my campsite, I couldn't find my tent."

"Silly thing to do," she said with asperity. "If you don't have experience."

"My mother said that. I guess she was right."

She nodded knowingly. Passing headlights illuminated the alarming red of her hair. "You should call your mother right away, young man. She'll be worried."

"I will. I have friends in Prague, in the New City. They'll let me use their telephone."

"Good. I'll drop you in the square, will that work?"

"That would be great." He gave her his best smile. "This is so nice of you."

"You're lucky I saw you," she said. "I don't usually pick up hitchhikers, but you looked pretty miserable." She drove on, tapping her fingers against the paint-stained steering wheel to the strains of some sort of ethnic folk music coming from the radio.

"I have a son of my own, and I wouldn't be too happy to see him stuck out here in the cold with no shirt." She glanced at his feet. "Good grief, and no shoes! What were you thinking?"

Ugo endeavored to blush, shrugging and making apologetic noises. As she chattered on about her son and his youthful foibles, Ugo watched the passing road signs. It had been a long time since he had been to the elders' compound. The landscape was considerably changed since his last visit. He wasn't sure of the way, but he suspected he was fairly close. The wolf's instinct for direction was better than his own.

After a drive of fifteen or twenty minutes, the painter pulled off at one of the city exits. She turned off the roundabout and stopped the car under the too-bright lights of a filling station. "I'm just going to get some petrol. Sit tight."

Ugo watched as she inserted a credit card into the pump, then went off toward the restroom, unbuttoning the straps of her coveralls as she did so. When she was inside, he opened the car door and slipped out. A man filling a Volvo stared open-mouthed at the sight of a shirtless, barefoot man. Ugo touched his forehead in a mock salute.

"A little cold to be half dressed, isn't it?" the man said.

Ugo grinned at him. "I'm freezing my ass off, actually," he said before he sprinted away into the darkness behind the filling station.

He regretted not thanking his benefactress properly, but there was nothing he could do about it. He had seen a sign in the roundabout, with an arrow pointing to Mohács Road. He hoped there wasn't more than one road with that name.

Regretting the lost warmth of the Skoda, he set out down the road, slapping his arms for warmth and trying to ignore the discomfort of his bare feet.

Octavia felt a sudden, overwhelming sense of disorientation. In the dim light of the entryway stood Nick Barrett-Jones, who should have been in Milan. On her right were three ancient, unspeakable creatures and Zdenka Milosch, pale as death. Her colleague's healthy skin and clear eyes looked utterly out of place. The only detail about his appearance that seemed to fit the scene was a generous splatter of blood across his white shirt.

The Countess hissed at Octavia, "Teresa! What have you done?"

"I've done nothing!" she retorted.

But a moment later, as Nick strode out of the light from the hall and through the dimness toward her, she realized she had. She had gone to Massimo's hospital room, and Nick had found her there. She grasped everything in an instant.

He had followed her from Milan. It defied logic, but it had to be true. And it meant that Nick Barrett-Jones knew what she was.

He stopped a few feet from her, just beyond the circle of candlelight. Now, shrouded in the habitual darkness of the elders' parlor, he became as baleful a figure as the others. His eyes gleamed through the shadows, focused in a way she had never seen, either in rehearsal or on the stage. He was breathing hard, as if from some exertion.

"You have it, don't you?" Zdenka Milosch said, her voice low, almost intimate in tone. "You took it."

Octavia instinctively shrank away from the cold fury emanating from the Countess. Her impression of a serpent was stronger than ever, and she knew the danger of those serpent's fangs.

Nick said, "I do. I did." He bowed, as elegantly as any Don Giovanni could, and added, "How good to see you again, Countess Milosch."

"You know each other?" Octavia demanded. "Nick, what are you doing here?"

"Have you brought my diary back?" the Countess said evenly.

"Oh, no," Nick said. "But when I have what I came for, I'll be happy to restore it to you."

There was a sound of feet slithering across the decrepit carpet, and one of the elders wheezed a word Octavia couldn't understand. The Countess said, "Yes, Anastasia. I know." She reached down to the little table beside the sofa and rang the bell.

Octavia said, "Nick, you fool! You've taken your life in your hands."

His laugh grated on her ears. "My life? What about yours, Octavia? Or should I say—" He bent forward, bringing just his chin and mouth into the light. He finished softly, "Should I say, Teresa?"

Octavia's knees turned to water, and she groped for a chair to support herself. She was ruined. He would tell them all, he would expose her. Her career—her life—would be destroyed. And Massimo—it would mean the end for Massimo, too, the innocent. A wave of hopelessness swept her so that her head spun. She had never longed for Ugo's clear mind and hard courage so much as she did at this moment.

As the Countess bent to ring the bell again, sharply, Octavia started around the sofa toward Nick. "You don't know what you've done, Nick. You don't understand—"

"He does, Teresa." The Countess moved faster, pacing around the opposite end of the sofa, threading through the scattered tables as if they were made of air. She was at Nick's side in seconds. "He understands perfectly." Her white claw of a hand seized his neck, and she pulled his head toward her. The ancients made whining noises, whimpering hungrily among themselves like dogs waiting to be fed.

In the same instant, the hulking gardener, Tomas, answered the bell, charging into the room with Kirska at his elbow. Octavia stopped where she was, one hand on the sofa back, the other pressed to her mouth.

As the Countess's lips parted to show her fearsome teeth, Octavia's stomach quivered in disgust. It didn't matter that she had done the same, countless times. It was still repugnant. She didn't want to watch, but she couldn't look away. She expected to hear Nick cry out, to protest, but he bent his neck forward, as if eager for the bite.

Octavia heard herself cry, "No, Nick!" she cried. "Don't do that!" At the same time, a part of her mind knew that it was just the answer, that the Countess could put an end to this now.

Anastasia whispered, "Hurry, hurry, hurry."

The candle flames wavered, flickering over the grotesque scene, turning every player into a phantasm, a monster. It was hard to discern the actual figures from the shadows they cast. Kirska produced a ewer, a long narrow-necked pitcher, holding it ready before her.

But Nick, with the same speed and agility he had shown with Don Giovanni's épée, stepped behind Zdenka Milosch. He flung his arm around her throat with such force that she choked on her gasp of surprise. He bent her head back, and her fangs snapped uselessly, grotesquely, at empty air. A knife, its four-inch blade already bloodstained, glittered in his free hand. Before Octavia could comprehend what was happening, he slashed the fabric of the Gaultier sheath, exposing the Countess's hip and leg. They were so white they appeared phosphorescent in the bad light.

The ancients froze. They pulled back into their shapeless clothes, wheezing with alarm. Anastasia's face hid behind her hood. Eusebio reeled backward, nearly dropping his stick, hanks of thin gray hair flying about his head. Henri tottered a step or two, lurching into Anastasia.

Kirska fell back, too, muttering some imprecation, gripping the pitcher in her hands. The gardener, with an incoherent roar, lunged at Nick, showing his large, curving teeth.

"Not you!" Nick shouted. "Get back, or I'll kill her!"

The Countess, her voice constricted by the pressure of Nick's arm, ordered, "Stop! Tomas! Wait!"

It did no good. It seemed that the gardener's long service had erased the last of what wits he had. He was trained to protect the elders. There was no subtlety, no comprehension in his dim brain. Consequences were beyond his powers of reasoning.

He leaped upon the two, Nick and Zdenka Milosch, and the knife flashed up and out. Octavia cried out.

Tomas crumpled to the floor. Kirska was beside him in a heartbeat, crouching in a spill of dark skirts. At first Octavia thought she had gone to help him. But she saw, as she sagged against the sofa, that Kirska held her pitcher to Tomas's throat, where the knife had pierced it. She pressed the curved lip against his skin to catch the flow of blood.

Octavia straightened and took two steps toward Nick and Zdenka Milosch with some thought of separating them. She was extending a hand, thinking to plead reason and restraint, when the Countess gave a terrible shriek.

Octavia froze. The cry seemed to go on and on, a scream that died away slowly, the pitch dropping, slowly descending. The sound lasted so long it seemed it was not breath that sustained it, but blood.

Octavia watched, amazed and repelled, as Zdenka Milosch's heart's blood, that blood that sustained the life of even a near immortal, pumped out through her severed femoral artery. Nick dropped the Countess as if she were a rag doll. He held the bloody knife before him in a fencing pose, and he showed his own even, short teeth in a grimace—or a snarl.

Kirska, quick as a flash, was beside her mistress. She bent, pushing aside the torn flaps of the Countess's dress. She pressed her narrow-necked pitcher against Zdenka's white thigh. Octavia heard the swishing of jets of blood collecting in the ewer.

The ancients muttered and moaned, huddling in the shadows.

Octavia, immobilized with shock, stared at Zdenka Milosch, dying on the floor. Nick stepped sideways to seize her at the same time that Tomas began to struggle to his feet. The wound in Tomas's throat was already closing, the flow of blood drying on his neck.

Nick seized Octavia with one arm and pulled her against him, her back to his chest, his breath hot and sour against her neck. The flat of his blade, sticky with Zdenka's blood, pressed against the inside of her thigh, that most fragile of places, her one vulnerability.

"I don't want to kill you," he gritted. "But you can see I know how to do it. I want the bite. I want Mozart's blood!"

35

Mi tradì quell' alma ingrata: infelice, O Dio! mi fa.

He deceived me without pity, and such misery,
O God, he caused me!

—Donna Elvira, Act Two, Scene Two, *Don Giovanni*

Ugo padded across the icy stepping stones that led to the stone gatehouse. He lifted his hand to knock on the door, but at the first touch of his knuckles, it swung inward and stopped halfway, blocked by something on the floor.

Ugo sidled in and stood looking down at the inert form of the old servingman, the little wizened fellow who had been part of the staff since Ughetto's first visit to Prague. He lay in an enormous pool of dark blood that had already seeped from the gaping wound on his inner thigh to flood the tiled floor. The grout lines had become threads of vermilion. His head had fallen back, and his mouth was open. His long canine teeth pointed skyward.

Ugo blew out a breath. He stepped over the corpse's splayed legs and hurried toward the back door. When he reached the garden, he didn't bother to take time to scrape the blood from his feet. He suspected there would soon be more.

He broke into a run, dashing beneath the hanging branches of the yew trees that crowded the path, dodging cobwebs, slipping on the mossy cobblestones. He had almost reached the house when he heard the unearthly scream. It racketed around the garden, rebounding off the stone wall, shattering the darkness. It hardly sounded human, its pitch so high, its duration so long, its timbre like that of a broken violin.

It jangled even Ugo's hardened nerves. As it wavered and began to drop, he burst into the house, striking the door hard with both palms. It banged against the wall just as the scream died away, then slammed itself shut.

Ugo was already in the parlor, staring at the body of Zdenka Milosch, the near immortal, who should have outlived him ten times or more.

The scene was wreathed in shadows, with only the feeble flicker of candle flame brightening one end of the long parlor. The ancients wavered and hissed like a trio of great unsteady crows. Kirska was kneeling beside the Countess's body, sobbing in a mindless monotone. She had a pottery pitcher in her hand. It tilted as she got to her feet, and a rivulet of blood spilled down its neck.

Tomas, the brutish gardener, staggered around Zdenka Milosch's crumpled form. His shirt was soaked with blood. His face was a mask of dumb rage, and he emitted a steady river of obscenities in Czech.

And just beyond him Ugo beheld the appalling sight of Domenico, one arm securely around Octavia's body, the opposite hand poised above her thigh. A bloodstained knife shone in his fist, and Domenico's eyes glittered. When he saw Ugo, he laughed.

"Now, you see!" he exclaimed. The knife moved lower, its point depressing the fabric of Octavia's jeans. "I didn't need you after all!"

Octavia spoke with stubborn dignity. "Ugo. At last. We've missed you."

Ugo held up both hands, palms out. "Domenico, let her go. You're here now. Isn't that what you wanted?"

Octavia said, "Domenico? Ugo, this is Nick! Nick Barrett-Jones, our—" She grunted as Domenico squeezed her tighter, wringing her ribs as he might a wet towel. She finished in a constricted voice, "This is our *Don!*"

"You laughed at me, didn't you, Octavia?" Domenico said. His deep voice echoed against the high ceiling, and the ancients cooed and swayed at the sound of it. "You think I didn't know? That you, and Russell—and that young fool Massimo—"

"Let her go," Ugo said in a conversational tone. "If it's the bite you want, we have Tomas here, or Kirska. They can help you."

Nick gave a short bark of laughter. "Oh, no, my friend! There's only one bite I want, and she's going to give it to me."

Ugo took a tentative step forward. Nick pressed the knife deeper into Octavia's thigh, and through the gloom, Ugo feared he saw blood well beneath it, a dark stain on the blue denim.

"Stop right there," Nick said. "We'll just be leaving now. Octavia and I, together. You're going to stay back and let us pass."

Octavia held her body still. Her eyes were fixed on Ugo's. Her face was tense, her lips bloodless. Domenico—Nick—knew what he was doing. She must know that if things went badly, he could kill her.

Ugo said, "Anastasia. Eusebio, Henri. If he kills her . . . it's all gone, you know that. Mozart's blood. Gone."

One of the ancients gave a rattling gasp, as if it drew breath into a cage of naked bones. Another muttered something unintelligible. The three of them began to move, parting from each other as they circled the scattered furniture. Their garments flapped like raven wings.

Tomas and Kirska froze where they were. Tomas muttered an endless stream of curses, without seeming to pause for breath.

Domenico swiveled, keeping Octavia in front of him, and began to back toward the door. Octavia's hair had come undone and spilled over one shoulder. In her sweater and jeans, she looked like a teenager playing some strange game.

Ugo said, "You can't get past me, you know. I'm hardly going to move out of your way."

Domenico—Nick—lifted his knife to point it at Ugo. He said

grimly, "You're not immortal, are you, my friend? Move. I knifed that bloody giant over there, and I won't hesitate to do the same to you."

The blood soaking her jeans alarmed Octavia. It was hot at first, but cooled quickly as the denim soaked it up. Nick's arm was hard as iron. She could hardly breathe for the pressure on her ribs.

In the midst of the shock and alarm, she felt a wave of relief at seeing Ugo. Though he was half naked, barefoot, and missing one leg of his trousers, he was still Ugo. He was alive, and she meant to keep him so. Ugo was more vulnerable than she. The threat to him was all too real. And it was her fault.

"Stand aside, Ugo," Octavia gasped through the constriction of Nick's arm. "He won't hurt me. He wants—"

Nick's arm tightened. "Shut up."

Ugo said, "I know what he wants."

The ancients crept closer, faltering, weaving, murmuring unintelligible words. She thought she heard Anastasia saying, "Mozart, Mozart," but she couldn't be certain.

Octavia felt her toes catch in the stickiness of the Countess's lifeblood. Nick hadn't hesitated to use his knife on her, and Octavia, through her shock, had no doubt he would use it on Ugo.

Kirska kept up her continuous, toneless mourning, standing with her back bowed, the pitcher held before her like the chalice it had become.

One of the ancients managed to grind out one comprehensible word. "Ughetto!"

"I know, Anastasia," Ugo said. He raised his arms as if to demonstrate what a worthy target he was. His bare chest made an easy target, a pale rectangle in the dimness. "Stab me if you have to," he said to Nick.

Nick gave a triumphant laugh as he dragged Octavia with him. "Last warning," he said. "Don't think I won't do it." He brandished the knife.

At least it was no longer poised over Octavia's thigh. She wrestled with Nick's arm, but she couldn't budge it. It was the fencing, she supposed, that had developed his muscles. He grated in her ear, "Stop that, bitch. I'll kill you both if I have to."

He lifted her nearly off her feet as he dragged her toward the door.

Ugo braced his hands on the door frame. He no longer looked like a half-naked waif. His face was fierce and hard, his eyes mere slits.

Nick said again, "Move, goddammit!"

And Ugo, slowly, shook his head.

Octavia pleaded, "Ugo! Be careful!"

Nick raised the knife, and she felt his muscles tense as he prepared to strike.

Free of the threat of the knife for the moment, she gathered herself and poured all her energy into one great effort. Just as Nick struck at Ugo, she kicked with both feet and writhed in his grip with all her strength.

At the same moment, Tomas lunged toward them, grunting.

Ugo's hands had come up to seize Nick's arm, and Octavia thought he could surely succeed in blocking the knife. Ugo looked slight, but she knew the strength of his hands and arms.

Just as she had the thought, Tomas collided with Nick. Octavia heard Ugo's gasp of pain even as she found herself slammed against the wall, mashed there by Tomas's bulk pressing Nick against her. He gave a great "Oof!" as Tomas's momentum knocked the air from his lungs.

Octavia slid down the wall, borne to the floor beneath the tangle created by Tomas and Nick. They fell, all three of them, in a pile. Octavia frantically pushed at the legs and arms restraining her, hardly knowing if she was right side up or upside down. Nick, breathless, had gone limp. He was heavier that way, but after struggling for a few seconds, she managed to wriggle out from beneath him. Tomas was just getting to his feet as she scrambled to hers and turned instantly to Ugo.

Tomas's tackle had changed the trajectory of Nick's knife. Ugo should have easily deflected it, seized Nick's arm, protected himself.

Instead, she saw to her horror that the knife had found its home in Ugo's chest after all. As she watched, he pulled the blade free. Blood poured out of the wound just below his collarbone. He fell back against the door frame, pressing his fingers over it. She was at his side in a stride, holding him, helping him as he sagged to the floor.

She ripped her scarf from her neck and pressed it against Ugo's chest as hard as she could. In seconds it was soaked through. "Kirska!" she commanded. "Bring me something to stanch the bleeding—a towel, a cloth—something!"

She heard Kirska's feet as the housekeeper hurried the length of the parlor toward the dining room. Behind her, she heard Nick's breath come back in a noisy, inward rush. Then all sound faded away from her as she watched, stunned, as Ugo began to disappear.

His fine features distorted. His hands twisted, hardened, distended. His back bent until it was horizontal, and his knees, exposed by the torn trousers, seemed to turn inside out, the angle of the joint reversing until it was no longer recognizable.

Octavia dropped her blood-soaked scarf. She said, "Ugo!" faintly, but it was pointless. Ugo was gone.

In his place the wolf bared its teeth and gave a great snarling roar. Still kneeling, she spun to watch as the wolf, a river of silver and gray, flowed past her in a long bound to leap at Nick Barrett-Jones.

It seemed strange to her now, watching the great sleek creature, that she had never seen it before. Its ferocity was noble, undiluted by complicated emotions. Its body, its sharp claws, its white teeth, were beautiful beyond words, purely animal, unfettered by scruple or principle.

The ancients shrank back, and their mutterings ceased. Kirska, returning with a kitchen towel in her hands, stopped where she was. Tomas, confused, turned in a circle, and then, with a plaintive whine, turned the other way.

Nick scrabbled on the floor for the knife Ugo had dropped. He barely retrieved it in time, seizing it with its point upward, before the wolf was upon him.

The three candles guttered in their cut-glass holders, their flames burning low. Octavia groped for the wall and leaned on it as she struggled to her feet. She could barely make out what was happening. The wolf growled and snapped, and Nick gave a shout of pain. It seemed to her the wolf drew back to find his target, surely Nick's throat, but this gave Nick his opening. The knife caught what little light was left in the room, a single dim gleam.

This time the cry was from the wolf, a chilling whine. Though Octavia could see it was trying to press its attack, its limbs crumpled beneath it. It fell to one side. Footsteps thudded on the hard carpet and then clattered on the parquet of the entryway. Someone's breathing tore in his chest, ragged and shallow. The door opened and closed with a bang, leaving silence behind. Octavia knew that Nick was gone, but she gave him no thought.

She was already beside the fallen wolf. It lay on its side, panting, whimpering in its throat. The whites of its eyes showed, rolling as she approached. Its lip pulled back, showing its long, sharp teeth, and it snapped at the air near her hand as she knelt beside it.

She jerked her hand back, but she didn't move away. After several moments, she extended a wary hand to touch the coarse silver-gray fur. She felt the spasm of its muscles as it tried again to snap at her, its head twisting, then falling back, as if it hadn't the strength to resist.

"*No, no,*" she murmured. "*Buono, povero. Son io. Buono.*"

Someone—it may have been Kirska, but she didn't turn her head to see—lighted one of the oil lamps. In the flare of light, Octavia tried to discover where the wolf was injured. Its eye rolled, trying to follow her movements as she probed for the wound. Hardly able to breathe herself, she ran her hands over its chest and body, threaded her fingers through its double coat of coarse fur, touched its flanks as delicately as she could. The wolf's body quivered beneath her touch. Its forepaws twitched once or twice, helplessly, and she crooned again, *"Quieta, quieta."*

She found the injury on the wolf's hindquarter, just above the hock. She said, over her shoulder, "Kirska. Another light." When a second lamp was burning, she took the kitchen towel from Kirska's hands. She wound it snugly, but not too tightly, around the wolf's leg, tucking in the ends. "Water," she said then, and Kirska, though she moaned constantly under her breath like a demented child, hurried off and returned with a bowl of water.

Octavia dipped her fingers into it and let water drip from her fingertips onto the wolf's muzzle. To her delight, its lips opened, and she fed it a palmful, and then another. Its lips, whiskered as they were, were soft beneath the rough hairs. She heard it swallow. One hand on its chest told her its breathing had steadied. Though the towel was soon red with its blood, it seemed to Octavia the flow was already slowing. The other wound, in its chest, had ceased to bleed, but its fur was sticky with dried blood. When the wolf would drink no more, she used the rest of the water to wash its chest, then to gently dab at the slashed hind leg.

After the frenetic movement of the crisis, the hours of the winter night seemed to pass with glacial slowness as Octavia knelt beside the wolf. The ancients crept away with Kirska's pitcher of blood, squabbling incoherently among themselves. Tomas came to lift Zdenka's limp body. Her white fingers dragged on the floor as he carried her away.

Octavia ignored them all. She moved only when her legs cramped. She stroked the wolf's fur, tracing the lines of its magnificent body with her fingertips, feeling the swell of its muscles, the fineness of its bones, the arch of its skull, and the fullness of its chest. As dawn began to glimmer around the edges of the heavy drapes, she realized she had been humming for some time, old songs she had learned in her childhood. In that tentative morning light, she saw that the wolf's ears followed her voice, swiveling this way and that as the melodies rose and fell. Its breathing had steadied and deepened. Its paws lay still now against the blood-stained carpet.

Octavia lay down on the floor, one hand on the wolf's chest, the other pillowing her head. She closed her eyes, lulled by the rhythmic movement of the wolf's breathing. At length, as day-light grew beyond the elders' compound, she slept.

Ugo woke slowly, aware of pain in his right thigh and in his chest. There was a hard, scratchy surface under his left cheek. He opened his eyes, not willing to move until he knew where he was.

In his line of sight, illumined by filtered daylight, were chair legs, the bottom edge of a brown velvet sofa, and a glimpse of a closed door. Gradually, as he assessed his condition, he realized there was a hand on his bare ribs. Someone was sleeping behind him, the hand lax against his skin.

He was naked, of course. Cautiously, he wriggled out from beneath the hand, wincing as a fresh lance of pain shot up from his thigh into his belly. He turned, crouching, to see to whom the hand belonged.

Her eyes opened just as he looked down at her. She lifted her head. Her cheek was creased where her fist had supported it.

"Octavia," he said softly. "Damn."

She sat up, stiffly, and put a hand to her neck as if it had grown stiff. "You're naked," she said first, and then, "And you're hurt, Ugo. We need to bandage that."

"What are we doing on the floor?" he asked. He peered around at the dim parlor. No one else was in the room, but the old, dry carpet was splotched with blood. Too much, he knew, for all of it to be his.

"Don't you remember?"

"I never remember," he said, hearing the dull resignation in his voice. "I remember Domenico, and his knife." He touched his chest. "It feels like he speared me."

"He's good with a knife," she said and started to get to her feet.

"The wolf should have killed him."

"He got away, I'm afraid." She came to her knees and put out her hand to him. "Come on. Surely Kirska has something we can treat you with. Alcohol. Mercurochrome. Something."

She helped him up. He tried not to gasp, but he found that it was not only the wound in his chest that hurt. His upper thigh felt like it was on fire. "He got lucky. He should be dead."

Her eyes flashed at him, but she said nothing.

They hobbled slowly toward the door. It opened before they reached it, and Kirska came in. Her eyes and lips were swollen, distorting her dark face. She had been waiting, Ugo thought. The Countess must have—

Then he remembered. Zdenka Milosch was dead.

Ugo whistled through his teeth. "He tortured me," he said. "In Milan."

"Who? You mean Nick?"

"He wanted to know where to find the elders."

Her hands were gentle as she helped him up the stairs behind Kirska, but her voice and her eyes were like flint. "He knows about me."

"He's hardly going to talk about you to anyone. Who would believe him?"

"We'll have to deal with him sooner or later."

"It will have to be later, I'm afraid." Ugo grunted as they reached the top of the stairs and turned in at the door Kirska held open for them. As he lay down, with a sigh of relief at taking the pressure off his leg, he said, "Finish the run, *bella*. We'll think what to do afterward."

When she left him alone, he closed his eyes, expecting to fall directly into sleep. But something strange had happened, and as it surfaced, swimming to the top of his drowsy mind, he was suddenly awake again, pondering this great difference.

After all these years of oblivion as the wolf, he remembered something.

It was music. The tunes were as old as he, half buried in genetic memory, with childish words and simple melodies. But they had been in her voice. And they had calmed the wolf as surely as her gentle hands had calmed him only a short time before. She could have been in terrible danger, but the wolf had not fought her. The wolf recognized her voice.

Which meant that the wolf and Ugo were, in truth, one.

36

Per cagion vostra io fui quasi accoppato.

On your account I was nearly murdered.

—Leporello, Act Two, Scene Three, *Don Giovanni*

The closing performance of La Scala's *Don Giovanni* was a gala, with a patrons' reception in the gallery before the opera. When Octavia reached the theater, elaborately gowned women were being handed out of limousines and taxicabs in Via Manzoni by men in tuxedos and white opera scarves. Her driver circled the block and stopped in Via Filodrammatici, where the other members of the cast were arriving. She got out of the car, fixing a smile on her face to hide the dread that made her nerves jump.

At the artists' entrance, she met Russell, who exclaimed at seeing her and embraced her gratefully. "Oh, my dear, I was so worried you wouldn't be here."

"Russell, surely not! You couldn't have thought I wouldn't be back in time."

He laughed, but he was pale and hollow-eyed, and the hand holding hers trembled with nerves. An uneven flush stained his thin cheeks.

"I told everyone," she said. She squeezed his hand between both of hers. "I told Giorgio I had business out of town, and that I would be back in two days."

He said, "It's just—you know, this awful thing with Massimo, and then Nick disappearing."

Octavia raised her eyebrows, feigning surprise. "Nick disappeared? What happened?"

Russell still clung to her hand. "It's so strange, Octavia. He hasn't said a word."

She caught a breath. "He—you mean—he's here now?"

"Yes, thank God. He showed up half an hour ago."

It was Octavia's turn to tremble. She had hoped Nick would cancel, let his understudy go on. She had hoped to postpone this confrontation.

Russell looked at her strangely. "Octavia? What's wrong?"

She pulled her hand back, and put it in the pocket of her trench coat. Avoiding his eyes, she said, "Nothing, Russell, really. Nothing. It's cold out here. And I was hurrying."

"Well," he said with a tremulous smile. "I'm so glad you made it."

It had been a close thing. She and Ugo had had difficulty finding a car to take them to the airport. As soon as the car services heard the address of the mansion, it seemed all their cars were suddenly engaged. Kirska was no help, Tomas even less so. The ancients had vanished into the depths of the house, and they would have been useless in any case. Octavia finally succeeded in securing a cab by giving an address two houses away from the elders' compound. Ugo, in clothes borrowed from a musty closet, stood with Octavia on the side of the road, waiting for the taxi. When the cabbie arrived, he peered doubtfully at Ugo, and Octavia feared he would turn them down after all. Ugo's clothes were a mishmash of periods, a shirt from the turn of the previous century, a pair of fifty-year-old dungarees rolled up at least twelve inches, and loafers that looked as if they had belonged to a woman with big feet. There had been no socks to be found in the dressers and bureaus they had ransacked.

Octavia shrugged, as if to imply she had no control over what her companion wore. The cabbie pursed his lips, but let them climb in.

Octavia had found nothing suitable to change into and had settled for turning her bloodstained sweater inside out. It chafed her as they wound their way through the airport. It was a great relief to settle into their seats for the short flight. Ugo adopted a vacant stare, as if he were slow. This seemed to help with the flight attendants and the security people. Octavia towed him along after her as she might a recalcitrant child. They didn't speak of anything that had happened, or anything that was to come. That would have to wait until they were alone.

In Milan, all difficulties disappeared. Il Principe sent a limousine, and the driver pretended not to notice the strangeness of Ugo's clothes. Octavia kept an arm around him, as if he were ill. The doorman called the elevator for them, asked in a quiet voice if Octavia needed any assistance, then wished her a very good day. In the suite, they ordered dinner, and both bathed while they were waiting for it.

The waiter who brought the dinner trolley wanted to serve them, but Octavia assured him she could manage. They sat down together to the first good meal either had had in two days. Octavia knew there were challenges still ahead, but at least her anxiety over Ugo was relieved, and she was ravenous. They devoured a platter of *bucatini amatriciana* and a great bowl of *insalata mista*, along with a bottle of *Chianti riserva* and two big bottles of Pellegrino.

As they pushed the trolley out into the corridor, Octavia said, "Ugo. What will happen to Anastasia and the others, with the Countess gone?"

He closed the door and turned the lock. "You don't have to worry about that. Someone from La Società will succeed her."

"But who would be capable of—"

"Let it go, Octavia." He gave an enormous yawn as he turned toward his bedroom. "Let's just stay away from Prague for a good long time while they sort themselves out."

"I plan to stay away forever." And as she opened her bedroom door, she said, "I can't quite believe she's gone. I didn't like her, but it doesn't seem possible she's no longer there."

He paused in his doorway. "You all think you're indestructible. I've seen that before. And now you know it's not true." He lifted one finger, and gave her a tired smile. "Let that be a lesson to you, Octavia. Be careful."

"I will. But I'll be thirsty again just the same."

He gave her a mock scowl. "You should have taken more while you had the chance."

She knew he was teasing her, but it made her think of Massimo, and how weak he had been when last she saw him. Her face burned with shame and regret.

And now, as she turned to the *sala trucco* for makeup, she had to worry about meeting Nick, and worse, working with him. She tried to calm her breathing as the artist applied pancake and rouge and eyelashes. She went back into her dressing room and vocalized beside the Schulze Pollmann until the dresser arrived. She wasn't surprised at all to find that the costume had gotten loose. She had to stand still for several minutes as the dresser pinned the bodice and tightened the stomacher's laces to fit.

Octavia submitted next to the pinch of the wig as it was settled into place. She still needed to sing a bit more, to work through her *passaggio*. She told herself she must concentrate on the opera. She could think later about the elders, the Countess's death . . . and about the wolf.

In time, she would talk to Ugo about the wolf. She wanted to tell him how beautiful the creature was, how strong and fierce. She wanted to tell him it had responded to her voice.

She would also have to try to speak to Massimo. She had to explain, to teach him what he needed to learn. She would be a kinder teacher than Zdenka Milosch, but he might not want to listen. It was possible he would refuse ever to see her again, and she wouldn't blame him. He might feel about her just as she had felt about the Countess.

But all of that would come later. After the performance.

At the call for places, the cast gathered onstage, awaiting the beginning of the overture. They heard Giorgio announce that Massimo Luca would not appear in tonight's performance. He named Massimo's replacement, and there was a spatter of polite applause as he stepped back behind the curtain and came around the proscenium to give them all an encouraging, if somewhat anxious, nod.

When Nick appeared in the Don's costume, he fixed Octavia with a gaze at once predatory and triumphant.

The orchestra played the first bars of the overture, and she turned her back on him. Any nervousness always fell away when she heard the familiar D minor chords. The singers faced the curtain, waiting and ready. Octavia took a deep breath, closed her eyes for a moment, then put on Donna Anna as completely as she had put on her costume. The complications and distractions of the outside world fell away, and she became her rôle.

It was not so difficult, after all, to sing with Nick Barrett-Jones. The circumstances gave her energy. It felt right and natural to rage at Don Giovanni for violating Donna Anna. She shook her fist in his face as she sang *Non sperar, se non m'uccidi!* Give up hope, if you don't murder me!

His hands were hard on her arms as he thrust her away, and his voice thundered in her ears. *Taci, e trema al mio furore!* Quiet, and tremble before my fury!

Nick's rage was real, too. Octavia feared for Lukas when the Commendatore and the Don locked their blades. Giorgio wanted cold disdain from the Don, but Nick blazed with anger. From the shelter of Donna Anna's house, Octavia held her breath as Nick struck at Lukas, and poor Lukas tottered away from him, blinking in surprise. With his next blow, Nick's épée struck Lukas's sword so hard it flew from his hand. Only the bell guard, catching on one of the stage shrubs, stopped it from sliding into the orchestra pit.

Moments later, the Commendatore lay safely dead at the Don's feet. From her vantage point, Octavia was relieved to see Lukas's chest rise and fall with his breath, though he lay perfectly still, his silver hair spread upon the boards of the stage, his hands flung wide.

The rest of the act went forward without incident. Nick seemed to settle down a bit and sang well enough, though his blocking was unpredictable as always. The other singers compensated as best they could. Massimo's replacement hadn't Massimo's richness of tone, nor the same insouciant charm as the young *paesan*, but the duet was fine. Octavia was glad, for Marie's sake. The finale, with its buoyant dancing, layered ensembles, and ultimate confrontation, went well. The great chestnut vault of the ceiling filled to bursting with sound, and the audience sprang to its feet the moment the final C major chord sounded.

Octavia slipped through a giddy knot of choristers. Marie and her new Masetto were congratulating each other, and David stood waiting for Peter with a towel slung over his shoulder. Octavia went on to her dressing room, where Ugo had a cup of pineapple juice ready for her, and a sliced apple on a little plate. She settled onto the chaise with her feet up, careful not to crease the costume or disturb her wig.

She sipped the juice. "I thought Nick really might kill Lukas."

Ugo sat down in the straight chair and leaned back with his elbows on the vanity. "Giorgio was waiting for Nick when he came offstage. He looked like murder!"

"You saw the sword?"

"*Carissima.* Everyone in the theater saw the sword. The second violins nearly stampeded, and Russell turned so pale I thought he'd fall off the podium."

"Ugo," Octavia said, laughing in spite of herself. "It wasn't that bad, surely."

"Giorgio's just lucky Nick didn't run him through, as well."

"I'm glad this production is almost over," she said, and sighed. "*Figaro* has to be easier."

"It will be easier with no Nick Barrett-Jones," Ugo said. "But we'll have to deal with him. I don't like this situation."

She made no response. She didn't want to think about it now, with the second act still to come. When the knock sounded on her door, calling her to places, she rose, pulled Donna Anna's hooded mourning cloak over her costume, and made her way to the wings for her second-act entrance.

She startled at a sharp grip on her elbow. She pulled her hood back enough to see Nick glowering down at her. "Don't leave after the curtain calls," Nick hissed in her ear. "I warn you."

She jerked her arm away from him. "Don't touch me again," she snapped. "And forget this nonsense about warning me. It's I who warn *you*, you pompous fool! You should realize you're lucky to be alive!"

She had to stop speaking then. The other singers pressed past them, finding their places. Giorgio stood behind the stage manager's console at stage right, and she felt his worried glance at her and Nick.

She rubbed her palms together to calm herself and stepped aside to allow Brenda to get by, to take her place at the window of the inn. Nick and Richard went out onto the stage, taking their places in the street below Donna Elvira's window. Octavia watched from behind the proscenium, and Giorgio came to stand beside her, his eyes narrowed and his lips compressed. Tension emanated from him like body heat.

The G major chords sounded from the pit. Don Giovanni and Leporello set about deceiving Donna Elvira. Richard sounded marvelous, his bright bass deliciously flexible for such a big voice. Nick's voice, to Octavia's ear, seemed rough edged, and no wonder. Fuming at your colleagues was no way to prepare. She gave a small, private hiss of disdain at his shout of *"Pazzo!"* that veered off pitch.

She had forgotten Giorgio was close beside her. He glanced at her. "What's wrong with him?" he whispered.

She shook her head and widened her eyes as if she had no idea. She could hardly tell Giorgio that Nick's fury at his thwarted ambition was ruining his performance.

Everything settled down as Brenda, her plain, plump face transformed by pancake and rouge into that of a beautiful woman made tragic by sorrow, began her "Ah, taci, ingiusto core." Octavia couldn't see Russell from where she stood, but she sensed his relief. Brenda's dark soprano rolled out into the house, her tempo secure, her pitch as precise as Nick's was erratic.

The act proceeded smoothly after that, through the deception of Donna Elvira and the other characters, on to the cemetery where the Commendatore's statue came alive, spoke to Giovanni, and demanded an invitation to dinner.

Octavia's long "Non mi dir," sung to Peter in the fourth scene, drove everything else from her mind. She had the sense that she floated above the stage, above the orchestra, above the audience. She felt the spin of her voice beneath the vault as she sang *Forse un giorno, il cielo ancora sentirà pietà di me.* Perhaps one day heaven will once more take pity on me. Only in that moment, when all parts of her worked together to create art and magic, did such mercy seem possible.

She was sorry when she reached the final sixteenth-notes, *Pietà,* and then the resolution, *di me.* As she left the stage, her head high, her skirts sweeping the floor behind her, she savored the moment, appreciating its transitory nature, grateful only that her long years of work resulted in at least this one shining, fragile bubble of glory.

And then, the *Allegro* of the finale. Don Giovanni strode about the stage, commanding his festivities to begin. The chorus clustered around tables set with stage food and drink. Donna Elvira, rejected for a final time, left the stage, then rushed back through the door, screaming. And Lukas, back from his long rest since the first scene, marched in as the Commendatore's ghost, the marble statue from the cemetery.

Now it didn't matter so much that Nick's voice was rougher, more strained. As the Commendatore demanded his repentance, and Giovanni refused, the lights darkened. Cunningly devised flames began to burn from beneath the stage as the ghost condemned Giovanni to eternal damnation. Nearly shrieking his last lines above the steadier notes of the chorus and Leporello, Giovanni was drawn down into the pit, the flames and smoke engulfing him. Nick, a defiant fist still raised, disappeared below the stage on the descending platform.

The final ensemble thundered across the stage, full-voiced and triumphant as the opera concluded with its declaration that all evildoers must repent, or suffer Don Giovanni's fate.

The curtain fell on the D major cadence. The music ceased. The cast and chorus, laughing and talking, fell back to make room for curtain calls to begin. Octavia hugged Peter and said, "Thank you so much. This was a joy." He pecked her on the cheek and took her hand as they stepped behind the choristers, who would have the first bow.

Nick ascended from the lower level. Octavia saw him approaching, to await his turn to step before the great red curtain. She gathered up Donna Anna's voluminous skirts in preparation for her own bow.

When he seized her, she didn't understand at first what was happening. He threw his arm around her, lifting her nearly off her feet. She tried to twist away, gasping, *"Dio! Che successa?"*

He growled in her ear, "I warned you," and then, *"Teresa!"*

He dragged her backward through the crush of choristers just leaving the stage after their bow. They stared in amazement at the scene of two of their principals tangled together, leaving the stage during curtain calls.

Octavia felt the fastenings of her stomacher tear. The hem of the gown tangled around her ankles. "Nick!" she said. "Our curtain calls! Giorgio will be—"

"Fuck him," Nick said in a voice so harsh she hardly recognized it.

Octavia used all of her considerable strength to fight him. She kicked backward, aiming for his kneecap, but she was hampered by the heavy layers of her costume. She squirmed and elbowed him, catching him a sharp blow on what she thought was his chin, and another that made him groan as her elbow buried itself in his solar plexus. Still he held on, hauling her into the darkness at the side of the stage. Among the clutter of set pieces, she wrenched his hands from around her waist and spun away from him. Both of them grunted with effort, like animals in a battle to the death.

Nick swore, "Bitch! I'll kill you if I have to!"

She was already three strides away, hurrying back to the stage, hoping to salvage the curtain calls. She tripped over her skirts, and he was on her again. His grasping hands caught her head. The wig tore off, taking hanks of her hair as the bobby pins were yanked out and the wig cap came off. Tears of pain sprang to her eyes, and she, too, cursed.

He had his arm around her neck now, and the other hand striving to cover her mouth. She raked his arm with her fingernails. He yelped, and she twisted free once again. She began to run, but he was close behind her. She dodged left, but he preceded her, guessing where she wanted to go. She pivoted on her heel, turning right. There was a lift there for the technicians who worked in the stage tower. Someone was there, a man in paint-stained coveralls who gaped at her as she leaped into the gray metal elevator and hit the top button.

Nick caught up with her, though, sliding through the doors just as they closed. She flattened herself against the far wall, one hand out, the other bracing herself. "Don't touch me," she snarled at him. "If I don't succeed in killing you, Ugo will!"

He was panting, but grinning at her. Makeup streamed from his sweating cheeks and dripped onto the white silk of the Don's ascot. His heavily penciled eyebrows were smudged across his forehead, making him look as if he had indeed been burning in hell with the Commendatore. The ribbon tying his hair into a queue had come loose, and his dark hair stood out in spikes from his skull. "You know what I want," he said, puffing. "Just give it to me, and all of this will be over."

"You've ruined the closing of the opera," she said. "Poor Russell! And Giorgio!"

"I sang my part," he said. "They can't complain."

"Curtain calls," she snapped.

He snorted. "What the hell difference do bows make? They got their show."

Octavia made a disgusted noise. "You're a cretin. It's no wonder your performances are so stiff. You understand nothing."

He laughed, but she saw the flicker of doubt in his face and she realized that he already knew how weak his music was, how unsympathetic his acting. No wonder he wanted the bite. He wanted what she had. He wanted Mozart's memories.

But she had no intention of giving them to him. Not Nick Barrett-Jones.

The lift stopped, and the doors crept open. Octavia braced herself, then made a dash for them as soon as she dared, thumping the bottom button as she passed it. Someone would surely follow them. It would help if the lift were already at the bottom.

Nick was quick behind her as she cast about outside the lift, looking for someplace to run. Catwalks stretched to her left and her right in the cavernous space. Everywhere hung the great ropes that operated the sets. Octavia knew this area because she had toured it once, admiring the choice of natural ropes over steel cables, which made too much noise. Beneath the catwalks was the convex arch of the ceiling vault. Its chestnut wood had also been chosen for the acoustics.

She turned full around, identifying the catwalk she wanted. It led toward the winch housing, the framework protecting the machinery that lifted the great chandelier through the ceiling for cleaning. She picked up her skirts and walked toward it as fast as she dared.

He followed, but he didn't press her. He didn't want her to fall, she supposed. It would do him no good if she were to pitch from the catwalk to tumble down into the rafters.

She hurried on past the winch housing. There was a stairway at the far end of the catwalk that led down into the *loggione*. If she could reach it before he caught her, she could slip into the attic above the galleries. She had been there before, but she doubted Nick had. She could lock the door behind her and walk at her leisure back to the other end.

She nearly had her foot on the stair leading off the catwalk when he caught her.

He had pulled off his ascot this time, and he slipped it over her head like a noose, pulling it tight enough that she had to grab it with her fingers to keep from choking. He was breathing hard, noisily. His voice was tight and low. "Back up."

She tried to resist, but at each twist of her body, he tightened the scarf. She felt him shift his grip behind her head, and then one of his hands came around in front of her face to show her the knife he held. She supposed it was the same knife. She had already seen that he knew how—and where—to use it. She dared not fight any more.

He didn't speak again. He loosened the scarf a little, so she could breathe. He pulled her back a few steps, and then thrust her to one side. She stumbled as the floor disappeared from beneath her feet, and then her toes touched the first tread of a steep iron stairway. He prodded her hip with the knife, and the blade's nearness sent a shock through her nerves.

She descended the stairs and found herself in a long, dim space with a wooden floor and a low ceiling. She glanced around.

"Jews," Nick grated, seeing her look.

"What?"

He released her, and she faced him. "Jews," he said again. "World War Two. They hid them here, from the Nazis."

"Here? Are you sure?" She glanced around again, feigning surprise. In truth, she was searching for a way out, or for something to defend herself with.

He was not an intelligent man, but a cunning one. He gave a low bark of laughter. "You can't get away," he said. "There's no other way out." He took a step closer, twitching the knife in his fingers. "You know what I want, Octavia."

She brought her eyes back to him. She stood very still, watching him come, and she began to tremble with rage. There was no sound but her own harsh breathing and the soft brush of his shoes against the wood. They were far too high for the hubbub beneath them to reach. "People die of the bite, Nick," she said.

"I won't," he said. He loosened the collar of his shirt, pulling it open so his neck was exposed, then fisted the knife in his right hand, so the blade pointed downward. "And you won't take too much from me, because if you do . . ." He sliced the air with the blade.

"There are other consequences." She forced herself to speak matter-of-factly, her eyes holding his. Her body began to pulse, her throat to burn, saliva to fill her mouth. She had not been thirsty, but now she was. And she was angry.

He was healthy. Ripe.

And so very, very stupid.

He reached for her with his left hand and pulled her to him. Her eyes were inches from his, and the heat from his body burned against her breast and belly. He lifted her skirt away from her thigh and rested the flat of his little blade against her skin. His lips were slack, as if with lust, and his eyes were bloodshot, the pupils expanding in the darkness.

"Do it," he whispered, and then again, urgently, "Do it!"

Fury and loathing and thirst welled in her like a fountain, like a geyser, the pressure building in her belly and her lungs and her brain. She was facing the stairway down which he had forced her, and she saw that someone was there, bending down to see into the space, but she no longer cared.

Nick Barrett-Jones bent his head to the right, offering her his throat.

And Octavia—Teresa, Hélène, Vivian—bared her sharp teeth and buried them in his yielding flesh.

His grip on her tightened, and his blade pressed into her. She drank, and drank again, then again. He moaned and pushed the knife against her thigh. A heartbeat later, one strong pulse of heart's blood, his grip began to falter. The blade lifted, wavering over her leg.

She drank more.

He groaned, ecstatic and frightened. The blade slid away, and her skirt fell back over her leg. His arm lost its grip on her, but now she had her own arms around him, one at his waist, the other circling his neck. The knife clattered to the floorboards.

He shuddered from head to foot.

Octavia ignored the sound of footsteps on the wooden stairs. Now she bore all of Nick's weight in her arms as his legs gave way. Spasms shook his body, and she lowered him to the floor, her mouth fastened deeply to his throat, where his lifeblood fed her, energized her, assuaged her fury and her need.

"Octavia! Stop," someone said softly.

Octavia was beyond thought, beyond hearing. There was nothing in the world at that moment but the source, and she could not bear to leave it.

"Octavia!" Whoever it was dared to put a hand on her, dared to tug her free of her prey. The body collapsed to the floor in a nerveless heap.

Outraged, she whirled, teeth dripping, mouth open to strike again.

He sprang back, out of her reach, and put up his hands. "Octavia! *Bella! Son io!*"

She stopped where she was, her fingers curled like claws, her lip still retracted. His voice cut through the red fog of her fury like cold steel. Slowly, she lowered her hands. A moment later she palmed her lip down over her teeth, and when she withdrew it she found it dark with blood. Her costume was spattered, the ruffles at the bodice ruined.

At her feet, Nick Barrett-Jones sprawled, unconscious, but audibly breathing.

The fog before her eyes cleared slowly, and Octavia came back to herself. She looked down at Nick's white face, his bleeding throat. She remembered where she was, and who she was. "Ugo," she said. "What have I done?"

As calmly as if Nick's inert body were no more than an inconvenient bit of trash, Ugo bent and pulled him up by his armpits. "Gave him what he wanted, didn't you?" he said lightly. "I didn't think you would." He moved backward, dragging Nick toward the metal stairway.

"Where are you going?"

"Darling, we don't want him to die here. Too obvious."

She bent to lift Nick's feet. He struggled weakly and kicked out of her hands. "I don't think he's going to die," she said. "But he would have, if you hadn't come along."

Ugo made a face. "You make it sound as if I just happened to be strolling a catwalk at the very top of Teatro alla Scala and stumbled across a seventy-year-old hidey-hole by accident."

Nick groaned and rolled his head against Ugo's chest.

"Turn him," Octavia said. "He's too heavy to get up this stairway. He can probably climb it if we help him."

Nick's hands were useless, limp. They quivered occasionally as they tried to manipulate them. His feet, however, retained a bit of strength. In the end, Ugo went up ahead and leaned down to pull Nick up by his arms while Octavia set each of his feet on a tread, one at a time, and pushed from beneath until they got him up through the opening. He slumped on the floor while Octavia and Ugo caught their breath.

"What now?" Octavia panted.

For answer, Ugo pointed to the door leading to the attic. "Let's get him up there until things have quieted down. Then we can leave him in his dressing room. Someone will find him tomorrow."

"He should probably go to the hospital," she said glumly. "As poor Massimo did."

Ugo bent over Nick again and began to pull him upright. "We'll address the issue of Massimo later," he said. "For now, let's get

Nick away before some of the crew follow us to see what we're doing."

Octavia braced her shoulder under Nick's left arm, and Ugo took the right. "Ugo," she said, as they began their slow progress, "what happened with the curtain calls?"

"They brought the curtain down," he said, with a grin. "Right after the Leporello and Donna Elvira bows. What else could they do? Their *primo uomo* and their *prima donna* had disappeared."

"But what did the audience think?"

"They probably think you're both burning in hell with the Commendatore." He glanced at her, past Nick's drooping head. "We'll need to explain this, Octavia. To Russell, at least."

"I know." She sighed. "Well, we can start with the truth. Nick attacked me."

"Russell collapsed, Octavia. They called a doctor."

"Oh, no. Poor Russell! He was already on edge."

Nick stumbled, and Octavia readjusted his weight on her shoulder. "You were right, Ugo. I didn't mean to give him what he wanted . . . but he threatened me again with that knife, and I lost my temper."

Ugo raised his eyebrows and gestured with his chin toward Nick's bleeding throat. "You did a bang-up job of defending yourself. *Brava*."

"But now," she said, as they reached the door to the attic, "we're in more trouble than ever. What is La Società going to say about this one?"

Ugo braced Nick's nerveless form against his hip and reached for the door. "Don't worry about the society, Octavia. I have it under control."

37

Convien chinare il ciglio al volere del ciel.

The best thing we can do is submit to the will of heaven.

—Don Ottavio, Act Two, Scene Four, *Don Giovanni*

Octavia took a moment in her dressing room to wash any trace of blood from her lips and chin. Her dresser was waiting for her when she came out, and cried out at the bloodstains on the lace of the costume, but Octavia hushed her. "I'm all right," she told her. "A nosebleed." She hurried to Russell's dressing room and knocked on the door.

A woman she didn't know answered the door. *"Dottoressa?"*

"Sì, sì," the woman answered. She took in Octavia's costume at a glance, then opened the door wide. "Come in," she said. "He's going to be all right. A nervous collapse."

Octavia slipped in the door, and the doctor closed it behind her. Russell was sitting in a chair with his head resting on a pillow. There was a nurse beside him, urging him to drink something she had in a glass. His face was paper-white, and his lips were tinged with blue.

"Russell," Octavia said softly. "Oh, dear. I'm so sorry about everything."

He looked up at her and reached out his hand for hers. "Good

Lord!" he said. "Good Lord, I thought someone had abducted you!"

She gave a light laugh and took his hand in both of hers, crouching beside his chair. "It's a long story, Russell, and I'll tell you all about it. But now, you need to rest. Do what the doctor tells you."

"But, Octavia . . ."

She stood, and touched his cold forehead with her hand. "Don't worry about anything, Russell. It's over now."

He let his head fall back again, and his eyes closed. "I'm going to miss the party," he said in a thready voice. "I just don't feel well enough."

"Of course. What you need is several days of peace and quiet." Octavia raised her eyebrows in the doctor's direction. *"Va bene?"*

"Sì, esatto, signorina," the doctor answered. She already had her coat on and was snapping her medical bag closed. "Rest, good food. He will be fine."

On an impulse, Octavia bent and kissed Russell's cheek. His eyes fluttered open for a moment, and he gave her a tremulous smile. "I feel such a fool," he said. His eyes fell to the bloodstained lace at her neck, and what little color was left in his face bleached away. "Octavia! You're hurt!"

"No," she said, with a firm pat on his shoulder. "No, I'm not, dear. I'm not hurt in the least."

When she came out into the corridor, Octavia found herself surrounded by her colleagues. They were in various stages of undress, some still with their makeup on. She stammered the explanation she and Ugo had concocted, choosing her words carefully.

"I knew he was no good!" Brenda McIntyre announced to one and all, circling Octavia's shoulders with what was meant to be a comforting arm.

Marie Charles, wide-eyed at this latest disaster, breathed, *"Oh, ma pauvre!"*

Peter, with David at his elbow, uttered a number of British public-school curses.

Someone found Giorgio, and he came trotting down the hallway to join the growing crowd around Octavia. *"Che successa?"* he demanded.

She repeated her story. Her eyes stung at the kindness in the other singers' faces. "It was Nick, I'm afraid," she said. "He was so angry. He—he struck me. I had a ghastly nosebleed, Giorgio, and I didn't dare go onstage for the curtain calls." She made a vague gesture at the stains on her bodice. Everyone nodded, murmuring over the obvious evidence.

"Where is the bastard?" This was Lukas, in an absurd red silk dressing gown, his face still white with the Commendatore's ghostly makeup.

Richard said, "What on earth did you argue about?"

Octavia dropped her eyes. "He said I ruined the 'Non sperar.' That I upstaged him."

Richard gave a shout of laughter. "He's one to talk about upstaging!" There were more nods and general agreement that Nick Barrett-Jones was difficult to work with, although no one had suspected he could lose control in such a way.

At last Giorgio asked, "Where is he, Octavia?"

She turned to him, spreading her hands. "Giorgio, I'm sorry. I don't know. When he saw that—that I was bleeding—" She put her hand to her head, as if she had only just realized her wig was gone. "Oh, Lord, where is it? He pulled it right off my head."

"He ran off, didn't he?" Peter said. "The filthy coward!"

Giorgio sputtered, "He will never again sing at La Scala!"

At that moment Ugo sidled through the little crowd to put a protective arm around Octavia's shoulders. "Excuse us, everyone, won't you? She's had such a shock. She just wanted you all to know that she would never have missed her curtain calls, not for anything."

He led her away amid assurances from everyone present. Brenda called after her, "You'll come to the closing party, though?"

Octavia said, over her shoulder, "I don't know, Brenda. I think I need some time to—collect myself, I suppose."

Ugo said, "I'll take care of her. I'm sure she'll be fine. She'll see you there."

Once the dresser had taken the soiled costume away with her, and the dressing room door was safely closed, Octavia reached into the shower and turned on the taps. Her body sang with energy and warmth, and she yearned to be moving. She wished she didn't have to stand around at a cocktail party. She would rather have gone walking, prowling the streets of the city. She slipped out of her lingerie and dropped it on the floor. "Where did you leave him?"

Ugo was at the closet, laying out a dress and shoes for her. "In the attic," he said shortly. "I'll see you off to the reception, then I'll go back for him. I'll take him to his hotel, I think."

"He's still in costume," Octavia said, testing the water with her hand.

Ugo laughed. "I'll have it sent back to the theater. *Non ti preoccupare!*"

She climbed into the little shower, and said, over the rush of the water, "They believed me, didn't they?"

"*Ma certo, bella.* You told them the truth."

"So far as it went."

"*Esatto.*"

Octavia took her time with her makeup. She smoothed on a pale foundation and chose a bright red lipstick that made her skin look even paler. Ugo had brought a long sheath in dark blue silk. She stepped into it and gave herself a satisfied glance in the mirror.

Ugo chuckled. "Feeling better, I gather."

She smiled. "Yes. But I'm trying to look as if I've had a shock."

He narrowed his eyes, assessing her. "Muss your hair just a little. It's too smooth."

"Shall I put it up?"

"No, I like it like that, hanging loose down your back."

Obediently, she ran her fingers through it and shook her head to let it fall naturally. She put on the Ferragamo pumps, and Ugo held her coat for her. "Ready?" he said.

"Yes. More than." They went out into the corridor, empty now. As they emerged from the artists' entrance into Via Filo-drammatici, she said, "You'll be careful, won't you? He may be stronger than you think."

"He'll do as he's told," Ugo said. "I've had all I'm going to take from Domenico."

"You're not going to—"

He shook his head, and led her toward the waiting limousine. "I'm not going to kill him."

"But La Società will want him out of the way."

"I've got this, Octavia. Put it out of your mind."

The limousine driver got out and opened the back door. Octavia said quietly, "Ugo. Do you know who will take over La Società? Who will be in charge?"

"Oh," he answered, with a casual wave of his hand. "Someone will step in." He held her arm as she got into the car, then closed the door. As the car pulled away, she watched him turn and go back into the theater with a brisk step.

The *privè* of Ristorante Romani was already crowded when Octavia arrived. Candlelight glowed on its dark wood and bor-deaux leather furnishings, and side tables steamed with some of the best *antipasto* and seafood in Milan. A waiter ushered her in, and as he opened the door for her, a burst of applause broke out. Octavia stopped in the doorway, one hand to her throat.

Peter came to meet her, smiling. "Your curtain call at last, Oc-tavia," he said.

She smiled at everyone, and accepted the glass of champagne someone pressed into her hand. She felt the curious gazes of those who had not been backstage, who had not yet heard the story. Peter and David escorted her to the corner they had staked out amid the crush of people. David went off to fill plates for them while Octavia began to receive compliments and questions from a steady flow of opera patrons.

She was cautious about explaining the aborted bows. "It seems Nick isn't feeling well," she said, over and over. "Not well enough to come to the party." This she said without a flicker of her eyelids. It was true, of course. Perfectly true.

A reporter from *Il Corriere della Sera* came up and introduced himself, but Giorgio interrupted him just as he started to ask about the bizarre events of the evening, and carried him off to introduce him to Brenda. David returned with a platter filled with olives and *bruschetta* and tiny rolls of *prosciutto* stuffed with melon. Octavia accepted a napkin and took some *prosciutto*. "Thank you, David," she said fervently. "Suddenly I'm starving."

"Of course you are," he said, his round face creasing with his smile. "You look like you've lost ten pounds. Such a ghastly run," he added, shaking his head. "First Massimo ends up in the hospital—"

"Hospital," Peter put in with a laugh. "You Americans and your extra articles! He ended up in *hospital*."

David flapped one hand. "Whatever. The poor boy looked so awful, didn't he? And now Nick flips out! You'd think you were all doing *Macbeth*."

Octavia gave a delicate shiver. "Don't say that! I'm going right on to *Figaro*, and I don't want any superstitious thoughts!"

Peter, crunching on a piece of *bruschetta* rich with olive oil, suddenly choked, and pointed. David and Octavia turned to see what had caught his attention. Octavia hastily set her glass on the nearest table and wiped her fingers with her napkin. Conversation around them quieted as everyone stared at the doorway.

"Massimo," Octavia whispered.

Across the room, for a crystal moment, Massimo Luca's eyes found hers, and held them. He looked pale, and he was leaner than before, which made him seem even taller in his usual leather jacket and slim jeans. His hair was a bit long, as if he hadn't had a chance to get a haircut, and it made him look boyish and vulnerable. She forgot to breathe, just for that moment. Time seemed to stop as they gazed at each other above the heads of the crowd.

Then, in a rush, people began to say his name, to push toward him. He was surrounded, having his hand pressed, his cheek kissed by Marie and by Brenda, Giorgio and Richard and Lukas each taking their turn to go to him. David and Peter, too, sidled through the crowd to welcome him.

Throughout it all, Octavia stayed where she was. Her stomach contracted with a mix of dread and pleasure.

A woman at her elbow said, "That's the bass, isn't it? The one who fell ill during the opera and missed the final performance?"

And the man with her said, "Massimo Luca. They say he has a serious case of anemia."

Octavia had not meant to stay long at this reception. It had been important to put in an appearance, of course, after the mess of the curtain calls, but she had intended to get back to Il Principe at the first opportunity.

But now she couldn't leave. Not until she found a moment alone with Massimo.

She turned and picked up her champagne glass again. She could feel his eyes on her back, those sweet caramel eyes. She moved farther into the corner. A waiter refilled her glass, and she leaned against the wall, sipping it, waiting.

The older patrons began to depart, shaking Giorgio's hand, nodding to the singers, embracing each other as they said their good-byes. The cast began to leave, too—first Lukas, with his elegant silver-haired wife on his arm; then Brenda and Marie and Richard. Peter came back to Octavia to ask if she wanted to share a cab with him and David.

"No, thank you, Peter," she said. "I'm going to stay a bit longer and chat with Giorgio."

"Good luck in Houston."

She smiled and pressed her cheek to his. "It was lovely working with you again. I look forward to the next time."

The room emptied soon after, leaving only the stage manager and Giorgio, who had their heads together, and Massimo Luca, with three girls clustered around him. The waiters began to clear the tables, offering the guests one last drink, then carrying the dishes out. Octavia stayed where she was until she was sure Massimo knew she was still there before she went to say good-bye to Giorgio. Without glancing at Massimo, she left the *privè* and asked for her coat. As the restaurateur was helping her on with it and offering to call a taxi, Massimo came striding out into the entryway.

"*No, grazie,*" Octavia murmured to her host. She stood in the doorway, pulling up her collar against the cold, smoothing the cashmere around her throat.

She knew he was beside her by the warmth of his long body. Without speaking, she stepped out into Via Zebedia and began to walk.

He fell into step beside her. She lifted her head to let the chill night breeze riffle her hair. Via Zebedia was dark, but when they came out into Corso Italia, the lights of restaurants and hotel lobbies seemed to glare. Massimo took her elbow with a firm hand and turned her to the left. In Piazza Missori, the ruins of San Giovanni in Conca stood alone, its colored bricks an odd and lonely splash of color amidst the tall, many-windowed office buildings around it. It glimmered in the center of the piazza, lights outlining its curving, broken wall. Shrubbery softened the blind arches of the ruined apse. Its single mullioned window gave onto busy Via Albricci on the other side.

San Giovanni in Conca dated from the fourth century. It had been destroyed and rebuilt over the years, consecrated and deconsecrated, given to the nuns of the Carmelite order, then taken away from them. Teresa had visited the church of San Giovanni in Conca at a time when it was the private chapel of one of Milan's noble families, when she could still participate in the Mass. Whenever she passed it, she felt a twinge of loss, not only because it had been torn apart again, but because of that other, great loss that never ceased to trouble her.

Massimo disdained the bench that ran around the inner side of the old wall. He steered Octavia around to the back, where a little iron fence blocked the stone steps leading down to what was left of the crypt beneath Piazza Missori.

Octavia could have resisted him. Perhaps he was so angry with her that he meant to do her harm. Perhaps he meant to take from her what she had taken from him, and leave her bleeding and weak in the dark. She didn't care. She submitted to his intent, following where he led. She would accept—she was even eager to accept—whatever he had in store for her.

As he helped her over the iron fence and down the cold, rough stairs to the crypt door, a sort of eagerness came over her. She was ready to have it over, whatever it might be. And despite everything, she was glad to be with him, glad to feel the strength of his hand, the height of him next to her. She felt as alive as she had ever felt, skin and bone and blood. She felt as if she were poised on the brink of something, and whatever it was to be, she welcomed it.

The crypt was closed and locked, open to the public only a few days a week. In the doorway, below the reach of the headlights of passing cars, Massimo turned to her. His eyes were like coals in the darkness. They burned like coal, too, a spark of fury she recognized. Just so had she glared at Zdenka Milosch, those long years before.

Octavia said, "I'm sorry." The Countess had never said those words to her. Indeed, Octavia felt certain Zdenka Milosch had never felt regret about anything.

"Sorry?" he said. His deep voice resounded from the bricks, filling her ears with its richness. It seemed the cars passing over their heads should be able to hear it.

"I didn't mean to do it, Massimo."

He made a dismissive gesture with one fine, large hand. It hurt her to see it. She felt as if it were she being dismissed.

If he were as appalled as she had been, then he must hate her as she had hated Zdenka Milosch. He must wish he had never met her, never held her in his arms.

He said in a level tone, "Can it be undone?"

She shook her head, slowly, sadly. "No."

His voice dropped to a rumble. "All those people . . ."

"I know. I know."

He folded his arms and leaned against the thick door. He lifted his chin, and a glimmer of reflected light fell across the clean line of his jaw. "I haven't been thirsty yet."

"You're already having memories," she said.

Any hope she might have harbored for him—for the two of them together—slipped away like water poured out, leaving her empty, without expectations.

His eyes searched hers. "I have your memories. And Mozart's," he said. "Leopold, and Constanze . . . Prague . . . England . . ."

"Yes."

"It's astounding."

"Mozart couldn't bear it." She hesitated, almost afraid to ask the next question. She spoke softly. "And you? Can you tolerate it?"

He took a long time answering. She saw in his face the same conflict she had lived with for such a long, long time. "It's terrible, Octavia. And it's magnificent. To know what he meant, to know what he intended . . ."

"Yes."

"But at what a price!"

"I no longer resort to the tooth."

He gave a bitter, chest-deep laugh. "Except for me."

She turned her head away to hide the pain that must show in her face. "Yes, Massimo. Except for you." She didn't want to mention the Milanese street girl, though he must remember that, too. The memory of those wide eyes and stricken face was too grievous, and she shut it away as swiftly as she could.

"But, Octavia, someone provides what Ugo gives you. Is there a great difference?"

She stared blindly at the locked door of the crypt, the long-empty tomb. The treasures it had once held had been moved to a museum. "I was so glad," she said slowly, choosing her words with care, "when Ugo presented another way. I have asked where he finds his—his supply. He won't tell me."

"I know that."

A small noise escaped her throat that may have been a laugh or a sob. "Of course you do. I didn't think. It was different for me. It was some time before I experienced the memories."

"The moment I was out of the hospital," he said.

The little door before her blurred, and she realized with a start that there were tears in her eyes. It was guilt over Massimo, so young and fine and promising. And it was the rending sense of loss over what might have been.

She swung around to face him, her arms crossed protectively over her chest. "You have to block the memories, close them away," she said. "They'll destroy you if you don't."

He closed his eyes for a moment, tipping his head to one side. "I know how you do it," he said. "It's as if there's a room, or a lot of rooms, where you store them."

"That's it. That's good."

He opened his eyes, and looked into hers. "Why couldn't *he* do that?"

"Who?"

"Mozart."

"Oh, Massimo." Her eyes stung again at the picture of Mozart on his deathbed. "I did everything I could, but he wouldn't—"

"I *know*," he said impatiently. "I know all of that. What I don't know is why."

She lifted her shoulders in a despairing shrug. Her eyes brimmed and overflowed. Tears dripped down her cheeks, and she made no attempt to hide them. "I have never known. I think it takes a certain—a certain hardness. To do what you have to do, and to control the memories. Mozart was so highly strung, and so sensitive. But Zdenka Milosch was as hard as iron." She swallowed and swiped the wetness from her face with the heels of her hands. "She never cared," she said. "Not about either of us. She only cared about the music. It was all that was left to her, and to the elders."

"Are they going to try to kill me?" he asked.

The question startled her. "She's dead! Countess Milosch is dead."

"Is she? What happened?"

"Nick killed her. At the elders' compound."

"But the elders still live."

"They do. And Tomas and Kirska and the others."

"Someone will take her place. There's too much at stake."

His voice had softened a bit, and a little flame of hope flickered in her breast. She put out her hand to him. "Massimo, come with me. Follow us, Ugo and me. He'll protect you."

He drew back from her hand. He shook his head, and his lips curled slightly, a shadow of the sweet smile she remembered. "I have my own career to think of," he said. "Just as you do."

She dropped her hand, and the feeble spark of hope guttered and died. She said bleakly, "You must hate me. I hated Zdenka Milosch, once I knew."

"I thought," he said with a grimace, "that I was in love with you."

"And now that you know what I am, you're revolted," she said.

"I don't know yet what I feel," he said.

"No. I suppose you don't. It takes time." She straightened her scarf and looked away from him, up to the street where the passing headlights gleamed on the windows of the office building opposite the piazza. "There are compensations, you know."

"Singing."

"Yes. That above all."

He took a step toward her, his shadow swaying above her in the gloom. He bent his head a little to look into her face. "I can handle the memories," he said. His voice had gone hard again, with a deep steely note. "But I don't know if I can do what you do, Octavia. I don't know if I can do what you did to me."

She released a long breath, feeling as weary as if she were one of the ancients. She turned her face up to his, letting him see the naked sorrow in her eyes. "You will, Massimo. My dear. When you're thirsty enough, you will."

38

Più non sperate di ritrovarlo, più non cercate: lontano andó.

You'll never see him again; don't bother to look: he's far away.

—Leporello, Act Two, Scene Five, *Don Giovanni*

Ughetto left the elders' compound in the autumn, when the harvest of *aconitum lycoctonum* was in and drying in bundles in the pantry behind the kitchen. He took enough of the herb with him to last for a long time. He didn't tell anyone he was going, nor did he ask permission. From a small stash of money the elders kept in the kitchen, he lifted money for coach and boat fare. He slipped over the garden wall one moonless night and struck out on foot. He was, at last, going home.

The journey was long, and it was nearly a month before he reached Napoli. There he haunted the docks until he found a boat headed for Trapani. He stood on the deck all day as the boat bobbed its way across the peaceful Tyrrhenian Sea, and he peered ahead for his first glimpse of the harbor. He was the first off the boat when it tied up to the dock. Carrying a small cloth bag with his few possessions in it, with his herb in a pouch around his neck, he strode quickly up the road that led to his mother's tavern.

Eight years had not changed Trapani nearly so much as it had changed Ughetto. He saw faces he recognized, but no one recognized him. The same fishmongers plied the wharves who had once given him fish heads for his *mamma*'s soup pot. The same fruit sellers who used to hand out slices of lemon to thirsty children playing in the square still hawked their wares from beneath striped awnings or broad umbrellas. He passed them all with the most cursory glance. He was impatient now. He hardly looked at the vista of blue sea beyond the white beach. He didn't slow his steps to savor the salt tang in the air. The sun he had longed for shone generously on his head, but he barely noticed it.

When he reached the tavern, he stopped in the street and gazed at it for long moments. It was smaller and darker than he remembered. It had no real door, only a piece of canvas pulled across the entryway. He had forgotten that the main room gave directly onto the street. The canvas was pulled aside now, tied with a length of rope. He could see the same scarred tables inside, where sailors sat drinking and gambling, the same oil lamps that had always hung from the walls, the same bits of discarded fishing equipment propped here and there. The familiar smells of fish and beer and smoke wafted out through the open door and wrapped him in a fog of nostalgia. He felt as if he were eight years old again, as if his sisters might come tumbling out to drag him down to the beach, or to tease and torment him until he cried.

He took a step closer. Someone was moving between the empty tables, a thick-figured woman in a dark dress and an apron. A scarf covered her hair, and she carried a wooden tray on her hip. He didn't know if it was his *nonna* or his *mamma*. And he didn't know what he would say to either of them.

Ughetto drew a breath that puffed out his chest and lifted his chin. He put his shoulders back, hefted his bag, and went inside.

The woman in the scarf turned when he entered. At first she thought he was a customer, and an automatic smile began to cross her face. Then, as he stopped just inside the doorway, her smile vanished. She stared at him, her eyes wide, her mouth a little open.

Not his mother, but one of his sisters. Ughetto said, "Nuncia. Don't you know your brother?"

His sister gasped. She dropped her tray on the dirt floor, whirled, and ran back toward the kitchen, calling, "Mamma! Mamma!"

Ughetto dropped his bag near the door and waited, listening to the sudden tumult from the kitchen. There was a clatter, as if something had fallen. Voices raised, calling names, shouting orders. A few moments later, Nuncia came back into the tavern, with three of her sisters in tow. When they saw Ughetto, they stared as wordlessly as Nuncia had.

He gazed back at them. They had grown older, of course, but he still knew which of them was which. Nuncia was the plumpest. One had grown tall, another had retained something of her childish prettiness. One limped, as if she had suffered an injury.

And behind them came Ughetto's *mamma*. Like Nuncia, she wore a scarf on her head. She had grown stout and gray-haired. She stood in the passageway between the kitchen and the main room of the tavern, her plump jowls trembling. She looked as if she had seen a ghost.

She said, in a hoarse tone, "They wanted their money back. I didn't have it."

He shrugged.

"Ughetto," Nuncia said. "Are you a . . . a *musico?*" All the girls watched him, awaiting his answer.

His *mamma* took a step forward. "They said you ran away."

"They sent me away, Mamma."

"Because you can't sing?"

"I can sing. That is, I *could* sing." Ughetto stepped forward, where the light from the small window could fall on his face.

"What happened?" Nuncia asked. "Mamma said you were going to be a famous singer."

Ughetto ignored the question. "Tell me, Mamma. What did you do with the money? The money you took when you sold your son?"

His *mamma* dropped her eyes and stared at the floor. "We paid for Maria's wedding, and for Caterina's."

"For two weddings," Ughetto said, slowly and thoughtfully, "you sold my future."

Mamma said, "I have six daughters. What was I supposed to do?"

Nuncia crossed the floor to Ughetto and searched his face with her eyes. "You've gotten so handsome, Ughetto."

He smiled at her. "It's good to see you," he said softly.

She put her hands on his shoulders and kissed his cheeks, one and then the other. A moment later, his other sisters did the same. The youngest put her arms around him and hugged him tightly. *"Mi dispiace,"* she whispered.

"Not your fault, Anna," he said. "I know that." He looked around at his sisters, at the empty tavern. "Where's Nonna?"

Nuncia said, "She died the same year you left."

And Anna whispered, "Of a broken heart."

Mamma looked at him, above the heads of her daughters, and he read the fear in her eyes. She had not sold him to pay for weddings. She—and no doubt his *nonna*, too—had known what he was. That night on the docks, when the moon glimmered on the moving waters of the bay, hung between them.

"If you're not a singer, Ughetto," his *mamma* said in a shaky voice, "what do you do?"

"I have work," he said. "For a countess."

Nuncia said, "A countess! Is she very rich?"

He dug into his pocket. "Rich enough. I've brought you a bit of money."

Anna took the little purse he handed her and carried it to her mother. Mamma opened it, counting the coins with her eyes before she looked up at Ughetto again. She said only, with infinite sadness, *"Grazie."*

"Prego."

She looked as if she might say something else, but then caught her lip between her teeth and was silent.

Ughetto shook his head. He would not tell her, even if she pressed him. He had wanted to know if she understood, and it was clear to him she did. Perhaps she had hoped castration would cancel out the circumstances of his birth. He would not ask. He didn't want to know if it wasn't true.

Ughetto stayed in Trapani for three days. Nuncia cooked him enormous meals. Anna walked with him along the beach, asking him questions about the *scuola,* about Roma, about his life. He swam in the warm waters of the bay and slept long hours in the two rooms the family occupied above the tavern. His mother hardly spoke to him, and she looked wary whenever he came near her.

Ughetto found his *nonna*'s grave in the cemetery on its hill above the village. Her gravestone was a rudimentary monument, with only her name, the date of her death, and a rather crude crucifix carved into it. Ughetto sat down beside it in the untended grass. He stayed there a long time, talking to her as if she could hear him, telling her he wished he could have seen her one more time. He told her everything else, too, about the *scuola,* about his dashed hopes, and about the elders of La Società. "I don't know what will happen now, Nonna," he said. He stroked the soft grass growing on the mound of earth that covered her resting place. "But I'm sure you wouldn't like it."

He found a ship sailing to Rome from the Trapani harbor, and bought passage. He walked slowly back to the tavern, wanting to remember everything just the way it was at that moment.

His sisters gathered to bid him farewell. Maria came, with a fat baby on her hip. Caterina already had two toddlers clinging to her skirts. Nuncia and Anna and the rest hugged him, and Anna cried.

He wiped away her tears. "Just be happy, little Anna, will you?"

She buried her face against his chest. "I miss you, Ughetto! I want you to stay!"

Gently, he loosened her hold on him, and held her at arm's length. "It's Ugo now, Anna. And I can't stay, I really can't."

"But why not?" She lifted her tear-streaked face and gazed at him. Her eyes swam with real tears, shed just for him. He had to set his jaw to keep from giving in to his own loneliness and sorrow. Who would ever weep for him again? Certainly not Zdenka Milosch, or the ancients who haunted her mansion. His was going to be a lonely life. A long, lonely life.

When he could control his voice, he said, "I have work to do in Roma, and in Firenze and Milano, even Parigi."

Nuncia said, "You should be proud of your brother, Anna. He must be very important in the world."

Anna wiped her eyes with the hem of her apron and sniffled. The other sisters stepped back as their mother came forward.

"Ughetto," she began.

"Ugo now, Mamma," Nuncia said.

Her mother nodded. She looked older than she had just three days before, with dark circles under her eyes. Her lips were pale.

He said, *"Arrivederci, Mamma."*

She shook her head. *"Addio, mio figlio."* And in a low tone, meant only for his ears, she said, "Don't come back, Ugo."

He met her eyes with his own, and the last tender spot in his soul seemed to harden, to scab over, to begin to scar. "No," he said. "I won't."

She stepped back as he bent and picked up his bag. Anna came forward with a packet in her hands. "Bread," she said. "Some olives and a bit of dried fish."

"Grazie," he said. He kissed her cheek. He looked into his sisters' faces, each in turn.

Anna turned away, throwing her apron over her face, sobbing behind the folds of cotton. One of the toddlers began to wail along with her.

Nuncia and Caterina and the others followed him out into the road and stood waving as he descended to the docks. He looked back, imprinting the memory of his home, the dark, dank little tavern perched above the town, his six older sisters arrayed before it. Six of them, and he the seventh child, the only son. Their existence had doomed him to the life of the *lupo mannaro*, though they would never know it.

At the last moment his mother came outside to stand behind her daughters. She shaded her eyes with her hand, watching her only son leave home for the last time.

At the bottom of the hill, Ugo lifted his arm in a last salute. The girls waved, but his mother kept her arms folded over her long apron.

Ugo turned away and set off to catch his boat.

39

Forse un giorno il cielo ancora sentirà pietà di me.

Perhaps one day heaven will yet take pity on me.

—Donna Anna, Act Two, Scene Four, *Don Giovanni*

Teresa Saporiti traveled to Munich in 1805, to sing with Vincenzo dal Prato in his farewell performance. The production was a Mozart opera, *Idomeneo*. She had learned the rôle of Ilia for the first time. Vincenzo had created the rôle of Idamante.

He met her coach and walked with her to her hotel. He carried her valise in one hand and kept the other draped around her shoulders, chatting cheerfully. "*Gran Dio,* Teresa," he said in his fluting voice. "You don't look a day older than the day I found you at the bottom of the stairs in San Satiro."

She gave him the close-lipped smile she had cultivated, and let her cheek brush his arm. "Flatterer," she said.

"It's true, my dear," he said in avuncular fashion. He squeezed her shoulders with his long arm. "You're still the *piatto saporito!* Everyone marvels at it."

"It's because I come from Limone," she said. "Everyone lives so long there."

"Lucky," he said. He gave a great sigh. "And here I am, at the end of my career already. It seems I made my début only yesterday."

"Yesterday!" she laughed. "You were sixteen years old, Vincenzo."

"Yes. Sixteen. And now I'm nearly fifty."

"But that's wonderful, Vincenzo. You're still singing." They reached the hotel, and a doorman in livery held the door for them to pass inside.

As they crossed the lobby to the desk, Vincenzo said, with a deep sadness that made his voice tremble, "My voice is going, Teresa. I'm not the singer I was."

She cast him a worried glance, but there was no time to press him. The clerk was handing her a key, asking for a signature, ringing for a bellman. Vincenzo kissed her cheek and told her he would return to take her to dinner.

As he left, people watched his gangly figure curiously and murmured to each other. Teresa watched him, too, making the bellman wait for her. Vincenzo stood out among ordinary people. His great height, his odd proportions, his lined, beardless face gave evidence to what he was, a *castrato*, a *musico*. He had no wife, no children. Music was all his life. What would be left to him, when he could no longer sing?

As they began the *Idomeneo* rehearsals, she realized Vincenzo was right. His voice had grown thin at the top, and his *coloratura* was forced. His sustained tones had a tendency to waver, and his *cadenzas* were less elaborate than they had been. She stood in the wings, listening to him go through Idamante's first aria, and her heart ached.

Vincenzo's day was reaching its end, and she, too, would have to retire soon. It would be necessary. Soon even Vincenzo, her dear friend, her mentor, would not be allowed to see her. She would be in hiding until all those who remembered her were gone.

She watched him strike a pose as he brought his aria to its close. He stepped stiffly to the lip of the stage to listen to some word from the conductor. His hair was graying, and his belly drooped. Vincenzo was getting old.

A thought struck her like a bolt of lightning, a thought that made her cheeks burn and her heart pound. She had to turn away from the stage, to go to her dressing room where she could be alone to consider it.

She sat before the dressing table with its jars of powder and rouge, and stared at herself in the cloudy glass. What would he say, if she offered? What would he think?

She rested her head in her hands, trying to think. Sorrow and affection for Vincenzo battled with her instinct to protect her secret. What if he was revolted and denounced her to the world? What if he said yes, but then couldn't handle the memories? She couldn't bear to see someone else she loved crumble under the burden, as Mozart had done.

Outside her dressing room, cast and crew came and went. The noise of set pieces being dragged about came down the narrow hallway. Still Teresa sat, agonizing over her choice. If only, she thought, she could pray. But she had lost her right to that grace.

Vincenzo, released from the orchestra rehearsal, came to knock on her dressing room door. He took her by the hand and drew her out to meet the singers he had worked with in Munich for more than two decades. They complimented Teresa, assuring her they had heard of her work, had looked forward to singing with her. The men eyed her with admiration, the women with barely disguised envy. The conductor of the production said bluntly, "You're much younger than I expected. You've been singing twenty years, have you not?"

Vincenzo laughed. "It's her village, Maestro. They all live forever in that place!"

Idomeneo went forward. When the opera opened, Teresa's notices overflowed with effusive praise and helped to hide the fact that Vincenzo's were at best tepid, at worst cruel. Before the run was over the opera director offered Teresa a contract for the following season. She told him she would think about it.

And still, through it all, she pondered.

It was the last performance that settled the question.

Vincenzo struggled with his arias that night. His legendary long breath was no longer dependable, and his trills were ragged. Teresa, listening from the wings, made her decision.

The tooth would not help Vincenzo. He might die of it. He might come to loathe her, as Mozart had done. But even if he welcomed the bite and its consequences, it was too late. His voice was already gone. He would retire, and perhaps he would teach. He could no longer sing.

He seemed at peace with the end of his career. Teresa thought she would have grieved, resisted, tried anything to restore her voice, but Vincenzo, it seemed, was tired.

He came to see her off on the coach to Milano. He embraced her, kissed her cheek. He teased her a little about this and that, and she knew he was postponing their final good-bye. Perhaps he sensed that they would not see each other again.

As he handed her into the coach, he pressed a velvet-wrapped gift into her hands. She said, "Oh! Vincenzo, what is it?"

"Nothing much. A bauble. To remember me by."

She reached through the door of the coach to embrace him one more time. "As if I could ever forget! Vincenzo, thank you. Thank you for—for everything."

He kissed her again and closed the door of the coach. He gave a jaunty wave, then turned to walk away down the street, a tall, ungainly figure with an overly long torso and short bandy legs.

Another passenger in the coach said, with disdain, "Capon."

Teresa turned on him, fury in her eyes, a warning throb in her upper lip. "Don't say that again, signore," she said. "Don't you dare say that again, or—"

The passenger laughed. "Or what, little lady? What can you do to me?"

Teresa subsided onto the seat, holding Vincenzo's gift in her lap. She put a hand over her mouth to soothe the swelling of her lip. From behind her fingers she said, "You would be surprised, sir, to know what I can do. But you are fortunate today. I'm not in the mood."

He laughed again, scornfully, and turned to speak to his companion.

Teresa unrolled the bit of velvet encasing her gift and took out a lovely brooch, garnets set in gold. She touched it with her fingers, then held it as she gazed out the window to watch the plain brick buildings of Munich spin by. She passed all of that first long day of travel reliving her first meeting with Vincenzo and trying to say good-bye to him in her heart.

40

Da qual tremore insolito sento assalir gli spiriti!
Donde escono quei vortici di fuoco pien d'orror?

What terror never felt before assails my spirits!
Whence arise these whirling flames full of horror?

—Don Giovanni, Act Two, Scene Five, *Don Giovanni*

The flight to Heathrow and then on to Houston was an evening departure. Ugo rose early, packed his things, and let himself out of the suite as quietly as he could. It would do Octavia good to have a long lie-in. She hadn't returned to Il Principe until the small hours, and then so distressed he doubted she had slept at all.

Ugo stood in the mirrored elevator as it carried him down to the lobby, thinking about Domenico. About Nick Barrett-Jones, who had won his prize after all.

He had looked like utter death when Ugo retrieved him from the attic to transfer him to the hotel. It had been no easy feat to get him to his room without alerting the hotel management, who had been tormented by the theater people, by Giorgio, by the press. He managed it by depositing an outrageous number of euros in the eager palm of a maid, who let them onto the service elevator. She eyed Nick's alarming pallor with curiosity, but the euros in her pocket forestalled curious questions. They rode up in the plain metal elevator, Nick leaning limply against the wall. When the doors opened, Ugo surveyed the corridor before they stepped out.

Nick's wound was already closing, the bite invigorating his immune system even though it had caused such grievous damage. His legs trembled, and Ugo had to support him with a shoulder under his armpit lest he fall flat on his face in the hallway. He had said nothing so far. He made no sound other than the whistle of his breath as he struggled to walk.

Ugo, however, chattered at him in cheerful fashion as they made their slow progress. "We meet under much more pleasant circumstances now, don't you think, Domenico? Certainly I feel much better, though you look a little the worse for wear. I suspect your two companions in that nasty basement room have abandoned you. Benson, wasn't it? And Marks, I believe. Yes, I suppose they've left your service. Permanently, no doubt. I did warn them, of course, but men like that never listen."

Nick didn't answer. Ugo tutted. "I've seen it so many times," he said. "And you will, too, I suppose." They reached Nick's room, and Ugo fished out the key he had persuaded the maid to find for him. He unlocked the door, and they went in.

"My," he said lightly. "Bit untidy, aren't you."

The room had been cleaned, and the bed made, but stacks of the *Times* lay on most surfaces, and clothes were tossed here and there. It seemed the maid had tried to straighten things, but had given up halfway through. A suitcase lay open on one of the big beds, and a few things had been dropped into it, unfolded, as if Nick had been unsure whether to pack or not.

"Where do you go from Milan?" Ugo asked conversationally as he helped Nick to lie down on the other bed.

Nick said, his voice no more than a thread, "London."

Ugo tutted again. "I don't think you feel well enough to fly, *mio amico*. You're looking very poorly. Very poorly indeed."

Nick lay back on the pillows with a groan. He clutched his

head with shaking hands and pawed his eyes and cheeks with nerveless fingers.

Ugo bent over him. "Are you in pain? Would you like some aspirin? A drink?"

Nick dropped his hands and stared at Ugo. "Are you going to kill me now?"

Ugo straightened and smiled down at him. "Why, no. As it happens, I have other plans for you."

Nick seemed not to hear this. His eyes glazed again, and he rolled his head against his pillow. He pushed his fingers through his tangled hair and tugged on the ends so hard it made Ugo wince in sympathy. "God, my head," he moaned. "I can't . . . the bloody voices . . ."

"Hmm," Ugo said. "Hearing voices, Domenico? That can't be good."

Nick groaned again, and his eyes closed tight, as if the light hurt them. "So many," he muttered. "Everyone she ever knew . . . the people she killed . . ."

"Oh, come now," Ugo said. "She didn't kill all that many, you know. She let most of them live. As she did you, my friend. She has always been very delicate with the tooth."

"Mozart . . ."

"Yes, Mozart. You have his memories now. Do you like them?"

Nick twisted against the pillows. "Bloody hell! My head . . ."

"She has a technique," Ugo said conversationally, "that helps her with all of those memories. I don't know if I can explain it to you, but I could try. If you like."

Nick opened his eyes again with obvious effort. "Wh—what technique?"

Ugo gave an elaborate shrug. "I'm not her kind, as you know," he said. "But I believe she creates a sort of wall—a partition, if you will. A room where she closes off the memories she doesn't want."

"How?"

Ugo shrugged again. "Not a clue," he said.

Nick was quiet for several minutes. He lay still, though his eyes rolled once or twice, as if he were seasick. "I thought," he croaked, after a time, "that this would be easy."

"Oh, did you? I'm quite certain I mentioned . . ."

"Didn't believe you."

"No," Ugo said easily. He pulled a chair close to the bed, its high back facing the bed. He straddled it and rested his chin on his folded arms. "No, you didn't believe me. But now you know. It's a rare man—person—who can bear the weight of all those memories."

"She must—" Nick's voice faltered, and he drew a ragged breath. His eyes closed again. "Octavia must be tough."

"You have no idea," Ugo said. And then again, fervently, "You have no fucking idea, Domenico. She's as tough as they come."

With only hours to go before their flight, he took himself back to the *strega*'s shop. It was open this time, and he let himself into its shadowed, cramped space.

The old woman came out at the sound of the door and gazed darkly at him across the counter. There was no welcome in her seamed face, but he had expected none. She said, "You've run out already?"

"No," he said. He shrugged, and spread his empty hands. "It was stolen, signora."

"All?"

He nodded. "All. Do you have more?"

"*Sì.*" She turned toward the back room, and he followed her bent back, loosening the belt on his Burberry trench coat as he walked. The *strega* closed the curtain once they were inside. She hobbled across the little room and bent to pull a twist of newspaper from a low cupboard. She laid it on a counter littered with the dust and leaves of other plants, then folded back the newspaper to reveal a dozen stems of *aconitum lycoctonum*.

Ugo touched it with two fingers. The stem and flowers bent

under the pressure, and sprang back into shape when he let go. "This is very fresh."

"I cut it this morning," she said, peering at him from beneath her wrinkled lids.

Ugo's eyes widened, and he inclined his head respectfully. "I didn't know, signora, that you grew it yourself."

She pursed her lips and began to rewrap the herb. "I thought you might be back. I planted some." She tied the package with a length of string and pushed it toward him. "Not easy to get the seeds."

He pulled out his wallet and counted out a generous stack of euros. "How did you know?"

She folded her arms and lifted her whiskered chin as she stared at him. "Is it safe to tell you what I know . . . Signor Ugo?"

He raised his eyebrows. "You call me by name now."

She folded the euros in half, and although he barely noticed her hands move, the money disappeared somewhere in the folds of her shapeless black dress. "They come to me sometimes," she said. "They tell me things. They are fools, but they pay me well for potions and simples, things they think will help them find La Società." Her voice dropped a little as she spoke the name, and Ugo saw the little shiver that ran through her.

"Signora," he said quietly. "It's dangerous to know that name."

Her black eyes flashed, once, and then she dropped them. "I know. But I am a *strega*, and what I know, I know."

"Tell me," he said softly.

She folded her hands on the counter. The knuckles were swollen, the nails grimy. "I will tell you," she said. "And then you will go away, and not come here again. If they see you, they will never leave me in peace."

"The one who saw me," he said evenly, "will not bother you again."

Her eyes lifted to his again, and he saw the wisdom in them, and the fear. "The one who cheated you."

"*Esatto.*"

"Is he dead?"

"No." And at her little intake of breath, he smiled. "No, signora, but he will not be returning to Milano."

She nodded, and her face relaxed a little. She breathed out, sending a little gust of garlic and coffee to blend with the aroma of drying herbs and grasses. "They say that the leader of La Società is dead. And they say that the new leader . . ."

Ugo's back stiffened, and his lips compressed. The *strega*, seeing the change in him, stopped speaking. She lifted her hands and stepped back from the counter.

Ugo picked up his package and tucked it into the inner pocket of his Burberry. He belted it again and put his hands in the pockets. Very gently, as if in sympathy, he said, "It would be best for you to forget my name, signora."

"*Sì*, signore," she muttered. She wrapped her arms around herself. "It is forgotten."

"And if you see them again, these fools—tell them they, too, had best forget."

"*Sì, sì.*" She stared at the floor, as if not seeing him could make him disappear. She said, "*Addio.*"

"*Addio*," he answered. He had always thought it an ironic word to use with someone such as himself. But it was what they had. "I will see myself out."

She didn't look up. He pushed through the curtain and left the shop, shutting the door carefully behind him. He heard the lock turn before he had reached the corner. He strode away toward Il Principe, glad of the chance to walk off his fury. He would find them, silence them, if he could. But there was no time, and there was no space in his little refrigerated case for what he would take from them. Other fools had already filled it, happily making their offerings on the altar of hope.

Octavia frowned over his account of his meeting with Nick. "What should we do?" she asked. "Do you think he's going to recover?"

"Yes," Ugo said. "But it's taken care of, Octavia."

She played with the ends of her scarf, pacing the room. "Ugo, you don't know what he's like. He's so utterly self-centered. He'll talk, if he thinks it will save him."

"He will have no chance for that, Octavia. Trust me." He picked up his case and opened the door of the suite. "Let's go. The limo's waiting."

She gave him a searching glance as she walked past him into the corridor. He gave her a sweet white smile. "Hurry, *bella*," he said lightly. "We don't want to miss the flight. They won't hold a 777, not even for Octavia Voss."

As the plane rose from Malpensa and banked to the east, Octavia gazed down at the lights of Milan beneath her. The flight pattern took them directly over the city. She picked out the lights of the Duomo, sparkling up at her through the darkness. She wouldn't be able to find La Scala. The theater was dark now, beginning preparations for the next production.

Octavia always felt a wrench when she left Italy, a feeling that her heart and her mind flew in different directions. It was sharper this time. She closed her eyes, surprised at the poignant feeling of regret that trembled in her solar plexus. He was down there, somewhere.

His next engagement was in Bologna, not a long drive. She saw his clear profile in her mind, his fine hands on the wheel of the old Mercedes as he sped down the *autostrada*. He might already be thinking of his next rôle, perhaps humming the melodies as he drove.

She wished she could hear his Méphistophélès. It was a long and demanding rôle. His height and the lyric strength of his voice should fit the part, but the sinister quality of Gounod's devil was so different from the artless innocence of the peasant Masetto. It required a different vocal approach. She wondered if he had the experience to make the transition.

And if he could bring himself to feed, so that he would be strong enough.

"Octavia?" It was Ugo's voice.

She opened her eyes to find the flight attendant in the aisle, a tray of champagne in her hands. Ugo already had one. Octavia shook her head. "No, thank you."

"Do you feel all right?" Ugo asked as the flight attendant moved on to the next row in the first class cabin. "Do you want something else to drink?"

"I'm fine," Octavia said. "I'll have something with dinner."

"What are you thinking about?"

"Oh, nothing, really, Ugo. Just daydreaming."

She couldn't tell Ugo she was yearning for Massimo Luca. They had not spoken his name since the closing of the opera, but she knew what Ugo would say: "Forget him. Whatever he decides to do, however he manages, is not your business. He's either strong enough, or he's not."

But Ugo hadn't experienced Massimo's embrace. He had no idea of his charm, or the sweetness of his company. She sighed, remembering. She felt lonely, even with Ugo beside her. She felt forlorn, like a lost child.

Ugo lifted his glass to her. "Here's to *Figaro*," he said.

She drew a little breath, knowing she was being foolish. She smiled at him. "*Figaro,* yes. But I know you hate Houston."

He wriggled his eyebrows, and grinned at her. "Houston will be all right, with the charming Russell there."

"Oh, Ugo! You leave Russell alone."

He laughed. "I'm not going to hurt him, *carissima*. Just play with him a bit."

She touched the button to make her seat recline and stretched her legs as far as they would go. "Poor Russell," she said. "I don't ever want to see him so upset again."

"He was worried about you."

"I know. He's really very sweet."

"And sort of cute, don't you think? I mean, in a washed-out, nervous way." Ugo drained his champagne glass and gave it back to the flight attendant, who was passing out warm towels in preparation for the meal service. "And do tell me, Octavia. I can never figure it out. Just what color *is* Russell's hair?"

"Ugo. Stop."

"Oh, very well. *Bene.* I'll leave Russell alone. Just for you." He gave her a wicked look. "But he would love to conduct you in *Carmen.* We spoke of it at dinner, you know."

Octavia tossed her towel at him.

41

Lascia, O caro, un anno ancora allo sfogo del mio cor.

Dearest, wait another year, until my heart has healed.

—Donna Anna, Act Two, Scene Five, *Don Giovanni*

The streets glistened with the last of a cold February rain that had fallen during the opera. Massimo Luca had been walking for hours. He had watched the bars and cafés of the University Quarter empty of people, pull their shutters, extinguish their lights. He walked to the piazza where the two towers looked over *la rossa*, the red city of Bologna, then on, through the long portico with its hundreds of arches, all the way to the hilltop basilica, the Santuario della Madonna di San Luca. The basilica was closed, of course, and he knew better than to go in, even had it been open. He knew what would happen if he tried.

He walked back beneath the arches toward the Piazza di Porta Saragozza and pressed on along the cobbled medieval streets. As he walked, he compared her memories with what he saw now. The Teatro Comunale had changed a great deal since Teresa Saporiti had sung there. Even the auditorium's original bell shape, oddly appealing and intimate, had been altered to the more common horseshoe configuration. But these ancient streets, the Renaissance fountains, the squares like Piazza Nettuno and Piazza Maggiore, had changed little. And by the time a cold, late dawn began to lighten the eastern sky, Massimo had nearly seen it all.

He should have been exhausted. He had sung a long rôle, after an intense rehearsal period. He had basked in ovation after ovation, a triumph. And then, makeup and costume removed, street clothes resumed, he had begun his long walk. He felt as if he could walk for days. He doubted anything could tire him.

At last, because he didn't want to be seen abroad in the city as the sun rose, he found his way back to the Hotel Novecento, and his comfortable double room. It had none of the oppressive elegance of Il Principe, but it was simple and inviting, and offered an expansive view of the center of the city.

He ignored the elevator, taking the stairs two at a time to his third-floor room. He had showered at the theater, but he showered again, for the soothing feel of hot water. When he was done, he wrapped a towel around his waist and went to stand in the window and watch the city awake. Delivery vans and early workers passed below him, ordinary people with ordinary and predictable lives.

Short lives.

Massimo suddenly turned his back on them and pulled the drapes to shut out the view. He didn't want to think about those innocent people. They had no idea how vulnerable they were, how easily harmed.

It had been ridiculously easy, supremely simple. He had driven from Milan to Bologna before the first rehearsal. He had looked forward to the drive, but had felt thirsty and edgy all day. He kept bottled water in the Mercedes, but it didn't soothe the burning of his throat. He could hardly bear the confinement of the car. He pulled off the *autostrada* and parked in front of an Autogrill, hoping coffee might help. He bought an *espresso* and stood at the bar to drink it. It was early, a bright winter morning, and few people were about. The bar was nearly empty, and traffic was light.

He went back out into the parking lot, still feeling restless. His nerves jumped at every sound, every movement. He needed something, indeed he craved it, but he could not yet admit to himself what it was.

There was a man standing in the parking lot, a man with thinning hair and bad teeth. He was yelling at a youth struggling to start the motor of a Vespa. Massimo passed him on his way to the Mercedes. It seemed the youth was the man's son, guilty of some infraction or other. The longer it took him to start the Vespa, the more abuse he had to absorb. Massimo had his keys in his hand, looking over his shoulder, when the Vespa's little motor finally sputtered and caught and the youth zipped away, with his father shouting invectives after him.

When the boy was out of sight, the man bent his head, out of the wind. He cupped his hand over the flame of a lighter. When he lifted his head, with the cigarette between his teeth, he wore a satisfied smile, as if he had accomplished something.

Massimo dropped his keys back into his pocket and moved away from the car.

Thinking of it now, in this clean hotel room in Bologna, he could barely remember leaping on the man, pulling him around to the back of the Autogrill, where a few tables rested beneath collapsed umbrellas. Did he stop to see if anyone was watching? Did he look behind him, or ahead of him, or take any kind of care? He wasn't sure. The scene was a hot blur of movement, of need, of the gratifying taste of blood flooding his mouth.

What he knew for certain was that he hadn't planned it. He hadn't selected his victim in any conscious way. He wasn't punishing a bad father, or winning vengeance for an abused son. He could make no such claim to virtue. He had been thirsty, driven by a new and irresistible instinct. And he had taken what he needed, drunk to satiety, then left the man slumped over one of the picnic tables.

He unlocked the Mercedes, slipped behind the wheel, and drove out into traffic. He didn't look in the rearview mirror. Once in Bologna, he didn't check the papers. He didn't listen to the news to try to find out what had become of a man left unconscious—perhaps dying—behind the Autogrill.

When he reached his hotel, he went straight to his room and stood beneath a hot, stinging shower for a long, long time. He thought of Octavia, and that last night at Il Principe. He understood now. He recognized the unthinking need that had caused her to lose control. His experience had been just like that. It felt as if some animal part of his nature sprang forth in the moment to claim its own territory.

When he turned off the shower and climbed out, he brushed his teeth as thoroughly as he could and stood for some moments looking at them. He suspected they had changed in some way. He couldn't see a difference, but he couldn't shake an uneasy feeling of self-consciousness about them. He thought they must surely be longer, sharper than they had been. He would keep his lip down when he sang, he supposed, hiding them.

He felt stronger, that night, than he had ever felt in his life.

Now he dropped his damp towel in the corner of the bathroom and folded his long body beneath the bedcovers. He lay on his back, staring at the ceiling, and examined his memories.

The man's memories were thick and unpleasant, tinged by drunkenness and a sort of reflexive cruelty. There was an unhappy wife, several resentful children, an unappreciative boss. Massimo tossed these memories away as unworthy of retention. Octavia had spoken of rooms, cupboards. Massimo's image was different. He found that he could discard them, as effortlessly as if dropping trash from one of the two towers of Bologna.

But Octavia's memories—those were precious. He remembered Teresa's father, and the rudeness of a wealthy couple toward a penniless girl traveling from Limone to Milano. He remembered the kindness of the *castrato*, Vincenzo dal Prato, and the painful first audition at La Scala. He remembered the tribulations of the first production of *Don Giovanni* in Prague.

He remembered Mozart. The sparkling eyes, the cheery smile, the sensitive, deft fingers. The way music poured from him, orderly, inventive, diamond-bright, heart-full. Massimo understood, now, the way a phrase could be shaped, a cadence made graceful. Rhythm meant more than meter, more than tempo. Harmonies were like colors on a painter's palette, nuanced and emotional. Melody was the crown of it all, the jewel that made the creation sparkle.

Just so had Teresa Saporiti transformed from a good singer to a great one. It was not merely a matter of voice, but of understanding. And Massimo had received the same gift, and the same curse. Greatness was at his fingertips.

He didn't know, yet, if he was willing to accept its cost. He was beginning to feel thirsty again, that burning in his throat, the craving in his belly. He could, he supposed, ignore it. He would not die as Mozart did, the flame of his spirit suffocated by the weight of memory. But surely that thirst that had overwhelmed him at the Autogrill would burn him from within if he denied it. And he could never sing with such a thirst. Never.

Sleep surprised him, lying there on the bed in the Novecento. When he woke the light had changed, the early winter evening closing in. He had slept the better part of the day.

He rose and pulled on a pair of jeans, a fresh white shirt. He drank a glass of water, and then another, but they did nothing to assuage the dryness in his throat. He went to the window again, and looked down into the street.

Teresa, Hélène, Vivian, Octavia . . . she had made magnificent music, given great performances. She had bowed before thousands, sung in houses across Europe and America and Australia. He had longed for just such a career since he was an eleven-year-old choirboy. And he wanted it now.

Across the road, a well-dressed couple strolled down the sidewalk. The man wore an unbuttoned sports coat, and the woman was in high heels and fur. They paused outside a restaurant to read the menu posted in the window.

As Massimo watched, a woman in a shapeless raincoat bumped into the man. She made gestures of apology, brushing at his coat, shaking her head of wiry gray hair. The couple were laughing as she backed away from them, still apologizing.

She had picked the man's pocket. The couple went inside the restaurant, and the pickpocket disappeared down an alley, her raincoat billowing around her.

Massimo turned from the window to seize his leather jacket from the chair where he had flung it. He hurried out of the room and down the stairs. He was not sure if he had made the decision or his body had, but it came to the same thing, in the end.

Last night, in the Teatro Comunale, he had sung the best performance of his life. He wanted to do it again.

More than anything in the world, he wanted to do it again.

42

Questo è il fin di chi fa mal!
E de' perfidi la morte alla vita è sempre ugual.

This is the ending for those who are evil.
And evildoers always die the death they deserve.

—*Tutti*, Finale, *Don Giovanni*

Nick sang "Metà di voi qua vadano," from *Giovanni*, and "Se vuol ballare" from *Figaro*. He sang "Ombra mai fù," of Handel, because Mozart had known it well. He sang Papageno, and Mozart's concert aria "Io ti lascio." His fingers struggled with the notes on the piano, but he knew he had never sung better. The music had depths of meaning he had never guessed at, could never have understood before. His voice felt strong and full, and he played with dynamics in ways that would never have occurred to him. The high ceiling, the dim recesses of the vast parlor echoed with his sound, lavish and beautiful.

When he lifted his hands from the keyboard, he knew that he had just given the greatest performance of his life. But there was no applause, no flowers, no spotlight.

His only ovation was more of their bloody hissing, like hooded snakes wavering around him. These ghastly creatures seemed barely to cling to life, and then only so that he—their prisoner, their victim—could sing to them.

Every night. Endlessly.

He wished with all his soul—if he still had one—that he had never heard of La Società, or the elders. He longed to roll back time and return Zdenka Milosch's diary without ever opening it. He wished he had never heard that bitch Octavia Voss sing, with her pure tone and her dazzling musicianship. And he wished, above all, that he had never come to this grim mansion, where ancient creatures haunted the hallways and mute servants sprang to fulfill their slightest wish.

Those last days in Milan had been a nightmare in their own way, until he learned, as she had done, to dam the flood of memories, to pluck what he wanted from the stream and ignore the rest. He had only just achieved it, found some rest from the cacophony of voices in his head, when Ugo had shown up again, slim, dapper, and cruel.

For muscle Ugo had brought Tomas, brutish, mindless, silent. Nick had no choice but to go where he was told. And it seemed, now, that he would never leave.

If he so much as wanted to step outside this near mausoleum, he found Tomas in his path. When he slept, his door was locked from outside. When he ate, Kirska, with a wickedly sharp kitchen knife in her hand, watched him with eyes full of hate for what he had done.

And every night, these elders, these ancients, demanded the same thing. They gathered in the parlor, and they hissed at him, "Ssssing, sssing," and "Mozarrrrrt," until he thought he would go mad.

He sang until he was hoarse and played until his fingers ached. They were insatiable. If he tried to rise from the piano bench before they were ready to let him go, Tomas loomed above him, and the memory of his stabbing glittered in his eyes. If he tried to refuse, for even one night, Kirska brandished her kitchen knife and curled her lip to show her long, sharp canines.

Their patience was endless, and their cruelty absolute. He

could not leave. It was a living death, here in this great dark place where no light of day penetrated, where no one could find him.

Nick Barrett-Jones had won what he wanted. He possessed Mozart's blood. And he wished he could give it back.

AUTHOR'S NOTE

The names of the first cast of *Don Giovanni* are the real ones. I've taken some liberties with the details of Teresa Saporiti's life, but some fascinating facts accrue to this first Donna Anna: She lived to be 106, and she made her debut at La Scala at a very young age. Historical sources disagree about her exact position in the Bondini company. It's true that the people of Limone sul Garda have a genetic disposition to very long lives. I can't prove that Teresa Saporiti was born there, but it is a useful coincidence.

Vincenzo dal Prato was indeed a *castrato* who created the rôle of Idamante in Mozart's *Idomeneo*. Mozart didn't care much for his work, but he had great success in Munich. The only extant recording of a *castrato* singing is that of Alessandro Moreschi. He was already old when the recording was made, but it gives us a hint of how a *musico* might have sounded.

Caruso did, of course, sing *Carmen* in San Francisco the night before the great earthquake. The Micaëla, however, was a soprano named Bessie Abbott, from the Metropolitan Opera Company; for a number of reasons, it suited the story better to employ the fictional singer Hélène Singher in that rôle. The great Olive Fremstad sang Carmen, to rave reviews, and she was probably not so unpleasant as she has been painted in these pages. I hope she will forgive me, as one mezzo-soprano to another, for using her as a source of conflict.

The details of Mozart's death have been mostly lost, but from a letter from Constanze Mozart's sister, Sophie Haibl, we know that no priest attended Mozart on his deathbed.

The history of intravenous injections stretches back to 1642, and they were used by Christopher Wren and the physicist Robert Boyle, prompted by new information about the circulation of the blood. In 1853, the French surgeon C. Pravaz invented a small syringe, the piston of which could be driven by a screw. It was calibrated to measure an exact dosage, and a sharp needle with a pointed trocar was used to pierce the vein.